The Magnolia Ball-dash-Two

The Magnolia Ball-dash-Two

The Continuation

Volume II of THE MAGNOLIA Series

Rebecca Tebbs Nunn

THE MAGNOLIA BALL-DASH-TWO
THE CONTINUATION

iUniverse books may be ordered through booksellers or by contacting:

iUniverse
1663 Liberty Drive
Bloomington, IN 47403
www.iuniverse.com
844-349-9409

ISBN: 978-0-5953-3650-0 (sc)
ISBN: 978-0-5957-8452-3 (e)

Print information available on the last page.

iUniverse rev. date: 05/13/2022

Dedicated to the memory of my parents Stuart Thornton and Laura Cox Tebbs, who would be so proud.

Contents

Foreword ix

Chapter 1 Tennessee Meets Bonita 1

Chapter 2 "R & R" at the Peabody 8

Chapter 3 Luncheon with Lydia Henley 15

Chapter 4 Bonita Arrives in Spencer 19

Chapter 5 Rhetta Robin Shaw Ricks 25

Chapter 6 Bonita Takes Tea with Rhetta 36

Chapter 7 Lunch at Henley Plantation 39

Chapter 8 Precious Woodson 44

Chapter 9 Harcourt Ball 55

Chapter 10 Candy Martin 58

Chapter 11 Darling Huxtable 64

Chapter 12 Isaac Kahn 68

Chapter 13 Bonita's Social Secretary—Raven 72

Chapter 14 Desiree Compton 81

Chapter 15 Ridge and Kd Dodd 90

Chapter 16 Bonita, the Countess and Desiree Lunch 93

Chapter 17 Party Time in Spencer 107

Chapter 18 Precious and Isaac 117

Chapter 19 The Boy and His Uncle 121

Chapter 20 Meanwhile Back in Spencer 131

Chapter 21 The Luau 142

Chapter 22 Trace Leaves and Precious' Guests Arrive 146

Chapter 23 The Meeting 154

Chapter 24 Bonita's Proposal 161

Chapter 25 Trace Shocks Rhetta 171

Chapter 26 Separate Plans Set in Motion 176
Chapter 27 Isaac, Raven and Ridge 180
Chapter 28 The Costlowe Boys in Spencer 185
Chapter 29 Darling's on the Road 187
Chapter 30 Isaac Retains Harcourt 195
Chapter 31 Hell's Apopping in Spencer 200
Chapter 32 Southern Social Functions—Funerals! 209
Chapter 33 Plans for the Ball Proceed 224
Chapter 34 Phone Calls, Deaths and Salon Plans 231
Chapter 35 The Ricks' Trip and Desiree's Sunday Salon 247
Chapter 36 Trace Chases the Money 265
Chapter 37 Kiddie Porn Up and Running 268
Chapter 38 The Committee Meets 274
Chapter 39 Rhetta's at It Again! 280
Chapter 40 Intrigue in Tennessee 283
Chapter 41 Discoveries for Ridge and Rhetta 301
Chapter 42 Tea for Two: Feds and Debs 309
Chapter 43 Bad Times for Spencer 323
Chapter 44 The Feds Move in 329
Chapter 45 Ball—Yes or No? 333
Chapter 46 The Rehearsal and the Chase 338
Chapter 47 The Ball at Last 344
Epilogue 375
Afterword 377

Foreword

In the military, the second generation of a weapon or a plane was designated "–2" (dash 2), so a second generation Skyhawk airplane would be called a Skyhawk–2. The Magnolia Ball-dash-Two is a continuation of The Magnolia Ball, my first novel, and since Bonita is planning another debutante ball of the same name, it is given the "–2" designation. Additionally, dash-2 has special significance for me as my husband and I named our first-born son "Dash" since he was the second-generation replica of his father and was therefore a Spike–2.

Acknowledgements

A great big, Dixie hug and kiss to my editor, Nancy Nilsson, playwright, director, Southern lady and friend, who weeded out the mistakes and demanded reworks and rewrites. Thanks to David Hogan, one of my "surrogate sons" for his help and guidance about computers, Internet Access Companies, servers, hacking, IP numbers and everything else about the subject of which I had no knowledge, but needed to know in order to write this manuscript. A colossal heap of gratitude to my second "surrogate son," Bert Tuohy, who formatted the manuscript for publication; held my hand through the process, and kept me from crying. He's a genius! Thank you, William Kopcsak, attorney extraordinaire, for keeping me to the facts about arrests, reading of rights, bonds, bail, federal jurisdiction, and attorney-client privilege. Thanks to the late Paul Aubrey, a USMC squadron mate of my husband's and a fellow pilot in Viet Nam, for reminding us thirty-seven years ago of the "dash-2" designation. Eternal gratitude goes to my husband Spike for his patience, his suggestions, his assistance when I couldn't get my word processor to do what I wanted and needed it to do, and most of all for his enduring love.

1

Tennessee Meets Bonita

Once Alphonso cleared the town of Montiac, he headed toward I-95 South and Tennessee. Bonita, who ordinarily sat rigidly upright in the back seat of the maroon Rolls Royce, allowed her head to loll against the plush leather headrest. She was tired. The past six years had taken their toll on her.

Her mind wandered aimlessly for a few minutes and then she drifted back to her child hood in the rural Texas two-room shack where she had existed with her shiftless Mexican parents and her dozen siblings. Bonita's memories of that period in her life were painful. Worse than the poverty had been the squalor and the heat. The only time she could be alone was when she went to the outhouse. Even then, one or more of her younger brothers or sisters was apt to come bursting through the rickety door.

"How many miles we goin' today, Alphonso?" Hannah asked.

"We's goin' all the way to Nashville, I reckon. Look at that map. 'Bout five-hundred-miles or so."

Hannah turned and looked at Bonita, "You all right, sugar?"

"Mm-hmm," Bonita answered as she stirred from her reverie. A slight smile appeared on her face as she recalled the movie director she had encountered on her way back home from town when she was fifteen. Taken by her beauty, for Bonita had definitely been a looker, Marvin Hamblin had rushed her to Hollywood where he promised to make her a star. She recalled the lavish apartment where she lived, the massages, the makeovers, the acting lessons, the delicious food, the fancy clothes, and all the attention she had received. Marvin had even changed her name from Maria to Bonita.

Alas, Bonita had lacked that certain something that stars must radiate from the silver screen. The camera had not been kind to her and Mr. Hamblin had given her money for a flight back to Texas—and Hell. Bonita was not about to return to either. She took the airfare and checked into the Beverly Wiltshire, where she dressed in one of the gowns Mr. Hamblin had given her, and went to dinner in the posh hotel dining room. There she met Enrique Dubre, a pimp for ladies of the night who catered to an upper class clientele. Before the evening was over, Mr. Dubre and Bonita had struck a deal.

Bonita resided for the next thirty years in one of the cottages at the Beverly Wiltshire where she was a highly paid *lady of the evening* commanding fees of one-thousand-dollars per hour. Her business relationship with Dubre was ideal. She never gave him any trouble and he took care of her, paid her well, and provided her with the most interesting clients.

During all of Bonita's tenure with Dubre she ate well, something she had not been able to do before coming to California. As the years passed, she began to add the pounds and at middle age, gravity was beginning to win. Bonita was quite plump and Dubre began to worry about her continuing ability to attract clients.

About the time Dubre was considering letting Bonita go, one of her wealthier clients, Joshua Roberts, founder and owner of the internationally known Roberts' Publishing Empire, fell in love with her and asked her to marry him. Bonita left California and Enrique Dubre for a penthouse suite on Park Avenue in New York City and lived happily with Roberts for a few short months until he suffered a massive stroke.

"I brought some of my ham biscuits. You want one, Miss Bonita?" Hannah said as she passed the basket to the back seat.

"Why, thank you, Hannah—what a lovely idea," Bonita said as she took the biscuit and returned to her daydreaming. Semi-recovered, Joshua, Bonita's husband, told her he planned to retire and wanted to move to Dorchester County in South Carolina where he had spent many happy vacations as a young boy. Bonita agreed and within months, she and Joshua had relocated. Bonita settled into her new manor house, met all the right people and entertained lavishly. She also let it be known through hints here and there and a little name-dropping that she had at one time been a movie actress.

Eventually, Bonita happily recalled, taking a second ham biscuit Hannah offered, she was invited to emcee the Magnolia Ball, the longest running continuously held debutante ball in the South, which took place each year in Montiac, the county seat of Dorchester County, South Carolina. Soon, Bonita had enthroned herself as the chair of the Magnolia Ball Committee, the group that not only selected the young ladies to be presented, but also planned each and every detail of the ball. Bonita had become an important and powerful personage in Dorchester County and she wielded her authority with impunity.

"Did you bring anything to drink, Hannah? Them salty Virginia ham biscuits is makin' me thirsty," Alphonso complained.

"I did," said Hannah as she opened the cooler by her feet.

"I hopes you brought lemonade."

"I did, I did. I brought lemonade. Jest lemme get it poured into a cup."

"Oh, good! Lemonade. May I have some too, Hannah?" Bonita asked as she straightened her posture a little and recollected how she had denied invitations to young ladies whom she deemed not suitable, or those whose parents had annoyed her, or those whom she didn't care for purely on a whim. She had even determined that a member of the committee, Trudy Waltham, who had lied about her background, one very similar to Bonita's own, should be removed from the committee. Further, she denied Trudy's daughter an invitation to be presented, which tragically had led to the young girl's suicide.

Bonita's reverie continued until she was forced to deal with the memory of her downfall. Once again, her body slumped as the events of December 28, 1991, swept over her. Celestine Piersall, granddaughter of the first Magnolia queen, had been called to the microphone to speak at the ball. She brought her two-foot doll, Anthony, whom she regarded as her son, with her and began to speak for Anthony in that high-pitched whine of hers. *Anthony* had spilled out Bonita's life story and had ruined her right there in front of everyone who was anyone in Dorchester County.

Bonita couldn't recall the remainder of the evening, as she had fainted toward the end of Anthony's saga, but she read about the rest of the fiasco in the local newspaper, as had everyone else.

A drug deal had gone down the same night as the ball. Several husbands of committee members were involved in it as were some of the fathers of the young ladies being presented. After Bonita was carried off the stage, another committee member had stepped to the fore to introduce the young ladies.

At that moment, the authorities began their arrests and the Magnolia Ball turned into chaos. It was terminated-never to be held again.

"Look there! Look at that pick-up. Miss Bonita, look at all them chillen in the back of that truck. That driver hits the brake, them kids are all gonna fall out and break their little necks. Whatcha doin', Alphonso?"

"I's wavin' to'em, that's all."

"You sho' loves kids, don't you?"

"I shore do, Hannah. I always wished I had me some. Ain't you ever wished you had you some kids, Miss Bonita?"

"Well, I don't know, Alphonso. I never really thought about it one way or the other."

"I wishes I had me some too, Alphonso, but then Miss Bonita's my baby."

Bonita smiled, "Oh, Hannah."

"Well you is."

"Yes, I guess I am. You've always taken good care of me."

"How long you been with Miss Bonita, Hannah?"

"Ever since she was a movie star in Hollywood, that's how long."

"How come you was to give that up, Miss Bonita? Wasn't it excitin'?"

"Yes, I suppose it was, Alphonso, but the camera is very cruel—a few lines on the face and unless one is already a major star, there are younger girls available and a film career is over."

Hannah rolled her eyes, but she didn't say a word.

Once conversation ceased, Bonita painfully returned to her memories. She had rarely gone out of her mansion for the following year. She became a recluse since she knew she would be treated as a pariah in Dorchester County. Finally, she had made the decision to leave. She had told no one where she was going and had warned her servants to do the same. Her estate was put on the market and she packed her belongings. She, Hannah, and Alphonso were moving to Spencer, Tennessee.

Bonita sat very still for a few moments after reliving the horrors of the past year. Then, with almost super human resolve, she pulled herself together and reached for the maps and information she had received from the Spencer Chamber of Commerce. Because Bonita was leaving Dorchester County under a cloud, she had used Joshua's New York office to get the information from Spencer. She had no plans to tell anyone in her new location about her years in South Carolina or the Magnolia Ball debacle.

Although Bonita was silent, Alphonso and Hannah chattered away. Hannah said how much she was going to miss her friend Izonia, Celestine's and Jonathan's maid. Bonita interjected, "Does your friend Izonia talk to that stupid doll Anthony too?"

"Well she say she don't, but I think Miss Celestine's 'bout convinced her Anthony's real. I 'spects she talk to him some."

Bonita had certainly not confided in either Hannah or Alphonso what had transpired at the Magnolia Ball or about Celestine's standing at the microphone and in her high, whiny voice exposing Bonita and her past through Anthony. Both servants could read however, and since the scandal of both the ball and the Dorchester County drug deal had covered the front pages of practically every newspaper in the South, Bonita was relatively sure they were aware of her hatred for both Celestine and Anthony.

"I never want to hear Anthony's or the Piersalls' names mentioned in my presence again. Do you understand?" Bonita asked.

"Yessum," they responded in unison.

Hannah knew she'd have to be very careful because she planned to keep in touch with her friend, Izonia. She would have to remember not to mention anything to Miz Bonita she might hear about the goings-on in Dorchester County.

"Alphonso, you know we have to turn off this highway and head west before long, don't you?" said Bonita.

"Yessum. Don't you worry. I'll git you to Nashville 'fore dark."

"Not only before dark. I want to be there before five o'clock. I've booked us rooms at the Peabody. I want to get there in time to freshen up and I plan to be downstairs by five, libation in hand, to watch the ducks parade single-file from the elevator to the fishpond in the center of the lobby for their evening meal."

Hannah laughed and said, "Ducks! Lawd help us. What you talkin' 'bout, Miss Bonita?"

"The ducks at the Peabody Hotel are legendary, Hannah. At precisely five o'clock each evening, a bellman takes an elevator to the roof and collects the Peabody's pet ducks. When it opens on the main floor, the bellman escorts the ducks in single-file, to the fishpond in the lobby's center. The ducks hop in, swim around, and eat *dinner.* Once they're finished, the bellman calls to them. They hop out of the pond and again, in single-file, follow him onto the elevator where they are taken back to the roof until the following evening.

"Who cleans up them wet duck prints all over that lobby floor? Glad it ain't my job," Hannah said laughing.

"Why anybody want to watch a bunch of ducks eat is what I can't understand," said Alphonso.

"It's quite a show and people come from all over to see the ducks. I'm sure it would be all right if the two of you want to come see also."

"That's all right, Miss Bonita. I think once I's in my room, I's gonna rest 'til it's time for your bath," sighed Hannah.

Hannah realized that nothing that had happened to Miss Bonita in Dorchester County had changed her. If everyone who was anyone went to watch ducks eat at the Peabody and shit all over the pond and the lobby floor, that's where her mistress was going to be at five o'clock. They might be moving to a new place, but the only changes for her were going to be a set of different rooms to clean, a different view from her tiny room's window, and a different bunch of snobs to cook for, kowtow to, and to watch. Looking at them and seeing all the silly things they did was a big part of the fun. Hannah never ceased to be amazed at the get-ups, the jewels, and the downright plain phoniness of the people Bonita always picked as her closest friends. The only real person Bonita was friendly with in Montiac had been Miss Celestine and even she was a little strange talking to Anthony all the time, but at least she had been nice. Hannah closed her eyes and tried to imagine Spencer, Tennessee.

Bonita removed her Mont Blanc pen from her alligator purse and proceeded to make notes. In addition to the information she had requested from the Spencer Chamber of Commerce, she had also, again through Joshua's New York office, subscribed to the local Spencer newspaper, the *Spencer Spectator.* Included in each issue were *Social Notes* and Bonita had faithfully recorded those names recurring each week and had already decided some of the people she wanted to meet as soon as she was settled.

The name topping Bonita's list and the first person she planned to entertain was the daughter of Tennessee's immediate past governor, Rhetta Robin Ricks. According to the *Spectator,* it appeared that Mrs. Ricks was the premiere socialite in Spencer. Her name had headed the society section in each paper Bonita read. Mrs. Ricks held garden parties, was listed as the chair of several important committees and, best of all, had two daughters sixteen and seventeen. Bonita definitely wanted to interest the aristocrats of Spencer in a debutante ball—with her at its head, of course.

At present, the young ladies from old money and prestigious families of Spencer who came out were invited to debut in Nashville. A few of those who were not invited to debut in Nashville held their own simple little coming-out parties at either their homes or their parents' clubs, but there was no full-fledged ball there. Of course, the nouveau riche and classless paid money, and went to that dreadful Agnes Montclair's ball in Knoxville each year. Ms. Montclair had been in the faux debutante business for eons. She scoped out families who had money, but not necessarily any gentility or class, and invited their daughters to make their debuts in Knoxville using various museums and public buildings for her *galas.*

Several parties were held during her *seasons* and Ms. Montclair's palms were greased for each event. She had studied her craft carefully and always managed to get the girls coverage in the Knoxville paper. She hired professional photographers and had albums put together with pictures of each deb's *presentation.* The fee for the books was astronomical, but the pseudo-genteel parents were quite willing to part with their money and Agnes Montclair made sure the photographer gave her a cut of the money he charged for each book. Montclair's debutante business had prospered so that she advertised in the better periodicals including *Town and Country* and parents from all over the United States, whose daughters were not invited by any selection committee, placed calls to her and made arrangements for their offspring to *debut* in Knoxville, Tennessee. As if making one's debut at a commercial function were authentic; it was also a well-known fact that those who *debuted* under the wing and tutelage of Agnes Montclair were not eligible for the Junior League.

Bonita continued her list making. She would look up Darling Huxtable, the wife of one of the attorney's in Spencer, whose name also appeared with frequency in the social pages. The mayor of Spencer and his wife made her list as did Candy Martin, a spinster who lived on a large estate with her elderly mother. They were Philadelphia Main Line. One of the Senators from Tennessee and his wife were natives of Spencer and often spent weekends at the Senator's family home there. Bonita added their names as well. And she definitely wanted to befriend the lawyer/bachelor Harcourt Ball, who still lived on his family's huge estate with his widowed mother. Another power she anticipated knowing was Desiree Compton, although she was never mentioned as attending functions. She appeared to hold Sunday *salons*, mimicking European gatherings where the resident doyenne—*Desiree*—held court while she and her guests discussed literature and the arts, at her lakefront mansion. Desiree's added bonus was that her daughter was a countess.

Bonita capped her pen and laid her head back against the leather upholstery in the plush Rolls Royce. She intended to stay at the Peabody for several days. The past several years in South Carolina had been entirely too stressful on her. She practically never went out after the debacle at the ball since she didn't wish to face all those insipid, in-bred faces in bucolic Montiac. After so many years of ruling Dorchester County society, she and the ball had been disgraced.

After rising above her unfortunate background, which she always chose to forget, to have it all snatched away from her because of some friend of Celestine's who remembered her from years ago as one of Enrique Dubre's *escorts* at the Beverly Wiltshire. A well-deserved rest where she could be seen and didn't have to worry about prying eyes and gossip behind her back was just what she needed.

After a respite at the Peabody, when she felt refreshed and sufficiently relaxed, she and her servants would continue their trip of a mere one hundred and fifty miles to the little town of Spencer where she had booked a suite in the town's only hotel, The Volunteer. Once ensconced there, she would call Realtors and have them come to her. She would look over what was available on the market and then would have them drive her to look at the properties she had selected. When she had settled on her new home, she would pay cash with a wire transfer from Joshua's company. She had already had all of her money transferred to New York. She wanted nothing to tie her to South Carolina. Bonita had even thought ahead and had even arranged for New York license plates on the Rolls. No hints of scandal were going to mar her plans for the future and *The Debutante Ball* she had planned for Spencer, Tennessee.

2

"R & R" at the Peabody

Several hours later, Alphonso skillfully pulled the maroon Rolls to a smooth stop under the Porte cochere of Nashville's famous Peabody Hotel. The bell captain hurried out the massive front doors, as the doorman opened Bonita's door, to personally escort Mrs. Roberts into the lobby where the executive manager awaited her arrival. Bonita was in her glory again. Outside, a valet took the wheel of the Rolls from Alphonso and bellmen scurried to transport Bonita's luggage and that of her servants.

"Welcome to the Peabody, Mrs. Roberts," said Mr. Wigginton, the Peabody's manager, as he swept into a deep bow almost to Bonita's feet.

"It's my pleasure to be here, sir. I've read so much about your lavish hotel and am certainly looking forward to a pleasant stay with you."

"I think you'll find everything to your liking, Mrs. Roberts. We've put you in the Executive Suite. Champagne and a tray of our finest hors d'oeuvres are waiting for you and we've assigned Jaline as your personal maid while you're with us."

"Jaline won't be necessary. My maid Hannah is traveling with me."

"We thought perhaps you wished to give your servants a little rest too, Mrs. Roberts."

"How thoughtful of you. Jaline will be fine, but I prefer my personal maid Hannah for my bath," smiled Bonita.

She also informed Mr. Wigginton that Alphonso would be coming to her suite on occasion. "He mixes my favorite martini," Bonita explained. She tittered to herself as to what Mr. Wigginton would think if he knew the real reason Alphonso would be coming to her room.

"I understand. I will personally escort you to your suite. You have a private elevator," Mr. Wigginton replied.

"That will be fine. I wish to freshen up and return for the ducks' parade."

"You have plenty of time. They'll be down promptly at five o'clock. I shall make sure you have a comfortable chair next to the pond."

"Thank you," Bonita answered regally as Wigginton preceded her to the private elevator and the Executive suite. It consisted of a large living area complete with a wet bar and a grand piano, a sumptuously appointed bedroom with a king-size bed, antique armoire, dresser, and velvet chaise, a lavish bath, a formal dining area, and a small kitchenette. Both the living and the sleeping areas opened onto a wraparound balcony overlooking Nashville. Bonita was pleased. She thanked Mr. Wigginton and showed him to the door, however she offered him no gratuity as one does not wish to insult one of his position. However, if a bellman had shown Bonita to her suite, she would not have tipped him either. She left such trivial and mundane tasks to Alphonso.

Within seconds of Wigginton's departure, there was soft tap at the door. Bonita opened it to admit Jaline, a middle-aged, black Tennessee native, who immediately took Bonita's coat, asked if she would care for a drink, and scurried to the door to open it for Bonita's luggage being delivered by the bell captain. Jaline followed him to unpack and hang Bonita's finery. When the bell captain returned to the living area, he asked Bonita if there would be anything else. Bonita asked him to open a bottle of champagne and when he had filled her flute, she instructed him to seek out Alphonso who "would take care of him."

Jaline asked Bonita what she wished to wear that evening so she could lay out her clothes. After doing so, she asked Bonita if she were ready to bathe and Bonita told her that would be all for now. She informed Jaline her personal maid Hannah would be arriving momentarily to draw her bath. She thanked Jaline and told her she was free to leave.

As Jaline exited, Hannah entered and closed the door behind her. Glancing around, she said, "Law, Miss Bonita, this is some fine room. What's that piano in here for? You gonna have a private concert? You oughta see what they got me in. I ain't stayed in nothin' that fine since we was in LA."

"Hannah, you are never to mention LA."

"I don't, Miss Bonita. But I thought it was all right for me to say it to you. After all, we was both there together. I ain't never told no one else about it."

"Well, make sure you don't forget. Now, draw my bath. It's twenty past four. I don't want to miss the ducks."

"Yessum," said Hannah as she headed for the bathroom shaking her head. "Ducks! Law's a mercy! I don't know what's so intrestin' 'bout watching no ducks in a hotel lobby." *It's just another example of my old friend Queenie's favorite saying. 'Hen shit and lemonade.'*

She was back in less than a minute and said to Bonita, "I turned on the water, but I's gonna have to press your dress. That maid laid it out, but it needs pressin'. I guess you's gonna have to tell her she can skedaddle. She's worthless."

"All right, Hannah. I will. Now, go check on my water," Bonita answered.

She was amused. Hannah was jealous of anyone else taking care of her. Bonita loved Hannah and she knew her love was not unrequited.

Bonita crossed to the phone and dialed Mr. Wigginton. "Mr. Wigginton, thank you so much for putting Jaline at my disposal. She is wonderful and very capable, however Hannah has been with me for years and rather than have her nose out of joint, I think it would be better to assign Jaline to someone else. Of course, I will pay for her services for my entire stay. Thank you." Bonita replaced the receiver in its cradle. She called out in the direction of the bathroom, "It's done, Hannah. Jaline is history."

Hannah called back, "Good. You can't be going downstairs for no duck parade in a wrinkled dress. What was she thinking? I'll get plenty of rest while we're here. I don't have to do no cookin' or cleanin', just take care of you. Nothin' to that. Now, while you's at the duck parade, I's gonna go through this here closet and get the rest of them things pressed up. Come on in here now, child, your bath's ready and jest the way you likes it."

Bonita raised her bulk from the antique wing chair and crossed to the bath where Hannah began removing her clothing for her.

After her bath, Bonita reapplied her iridescent blue eye shadow and touched up her lipstick before applying several layers of powder to her heavily foundationed face. Hannah fluffed her bleached hair for her and made sure it would be as firmly in place as a soldier's helmet with a generous amount of extra hold hairspray. Bonita enveloped herself in a cloud of her favorite Opium perfume and Hannah helped her into the haute couture lavender and purple-striped *tent* she was wearing in an attempt to hide her three hundred plus pounds for the evening. She assisted Bonita in getting into her lavender sequined pumps and pressed the purple beaded Versace evening bag into Bonita's hand as she announced that she looked positively gorgeous. Bonita beamed. Hannah moved to the suite's elevator as her mistress entered. Hannah then leaned in and pressed the lobby button for her.

"Now you have yo'self a real good time, Miss Bonita," and then added with a laugh, "And be sure not to step in no duck doo with them fancy shoes on."

Bonita turned and gave Hannah a peck on the cheek. "Thank you, Hannah. You're such a dear and you do make me laugh. I'll be sure not to step in any duck doo," and with that, the elevator door slid shut and Bonita descended to the lobby of the Peabody Hotel for drinks and duck watching.

Duck doo—that Hannah is something. Maybe I should tell her that while doo is cute, shit by any other name smells as bad!

Bonita swept through the elevator door a la a morbidly obese Loretta Young. Mr. Wigginton immediately came from behind the front desk to her side and escorted her to an easy chair prominently placed adjacent to the pond. Within seconds, a bartender appeared in the style of the Greeks' deus ex machina with a martini, which he told her Alphonso had prepared only moments before. Bonita smiled and regally accepted the proffered libation. She slowly turned her head from side to side as if she were a queen acknowledging her loyal subjects.

As other guests began to gather in the vicinity of the pond, a bellman accompanied by the pet ducks marching in single-file exited the main elevator. The ducks headed directly for the pond where they hopped in one by one each waiting its turn and promptly began to swim around and quack. At least, the females quacked. Male ducks do not quack, but rather make a squawking sound. Duck aficionados know this to be a fact and they are also aware that only male ducks have the curly-cue in their tails.

Various guests milled around and some spoke to Bonita. She acknowledged them with a nod of her head and continued to enjoy herself and her high-visibility position immensely. One of the ladies in the group dragged an ottoman over next to Bonita and as she sat, said, "Well, isn't this something? I've heard about these ducks forever, but this is my first visit to the Peabody. Have you seen them perform before?"

"No, I haven't, but they are quite beguiling, aren't they?" said Bonita.

"I think they're simply precious. I'm Lydia Henley and who might you be?"

"My name is Bonita Roberts."

"Well, what you doing here, honey? Where you from?"

"New York. I arrived today on my way to Spencer where I intend to take up residence."

"Spencer. Oh, you'll love it. It's such a quaint little town. Have you found a place yet? You must get one of those big, old houses on the lake. Anybody that's anybody lives on the lake and you certainly look like you're anybody."

"Why, thank you. Do you live in Spencer?"

"No, I live in the next town, dreary old Weston. My husband is a tobacco farmer. He inherited the place and insists that we live there forever."

Bonita's computer mind kicked into gear. She recalled reading about a number of the socially prominent from Spencer attending a charity function in Weston at the Henley Plantation.

"I've been receiving the *Spectator* for several weeks. I seem to recall something about a charity function held in Weston recently," Bonita said.

"Oh, yes, the ball for the American Lung Association. Don't you think that's just adorable? A tobacco farmer hosting an event for the Lung Association? But, we have to do all that propaganda stuff to stay in business. You know, smoking is so passé these days. You don't by any chance smoke, do you?" asked Lydia.

"No."

"And you don't approve of it either, I imagine," Lydia queried.

"It doesn't bother me one way or the other. I think the whole second-hand smoke theory is ridiculous. I have a friend in New York who is an oncologist and he told me that the second-hand smoke reports were poppy-cock because all the tests were done without proper controls or blind testing."

"He's absolutely right. You know, darlin', for years tobacco and cotton were the mainstay of the South. Our whole economy was built on them. Now, we still sell our leaves to Phillip Morris, but most of the cigarettes they make are sold in foreign countries. I confess, I do smoke, and I love going abroad. Everyone everywhere smokes. Here, most of the time, I feel like a pariah. But enough about one of my pet peeves. After you're settled in Spencer, you'll have to come over to dreary, old Weston and visit us at our little tobacco patch," Lydia said with a smile.

"Why, thank you, Lydia. I'd be delighted. Why don't I write down your phone number and as soon as I'm moved in, I'll give you a call. I'd love to have you visit me also."

"That would be real nice, sweetie. Be sure to get yourself one of those big houses on the lake now."

"I shall endeavor to do that," Bonita said emphatically.

"Oh, there's Randolph," Lydia said as she rose and waved in her husband's direction. "He wants to go eat now. I hate getting old. We went to Florida last winter and Randolph dragged me to every Early Bird Special in the state. He always wants to eat early. I don't even feel like my lunch has settled before he's talking about going to dinner."

Waving again, she called, "Randolph, I'm over here."

Randolph crossed to her and Lydia made introductions. Randolph invited Bonita to join them for dinner in the dining room. She thanked him profusely, but said she had eaten a late lunch, with a wink at Lydia, and preferred to wait awhile. She asked how long they were staying and invited the two of them to join her for lunch as her guests the following day. Lydia quickly agreed, but

Randolph said he had to be out of the hotel the next day to attend a business meeting.

"I'm so sorry, Mr. Henley, but that means we two gals can have a hen party luncheon. Right, Lydia?"

"That sounds darling, Bonita. I'll meet you right here tomorrow at—"

"Let's eat at one o'clock. Is that all right with you?"

"Perfect. Bye now," Lydia called as Randolph took her arm and led her toward the Peabody dining room.

As the ducks filed back to the elevator, Mr. Wigginton approached Bonita and said, "I see you've already met another of our guests."

"I have and she seems quite charming."

"Oh, yes, Mr. and Mrs. Henley are both charming. They are also benefactors to many of Tennessee's charities. They're here because Mr. Henley is setting up yet another trust fund to provide scholarships for needy students to enable them to attend the University of Tennessee."

"How very nice of him. They must have quite a successful tobacco farm," Bonita cooed.

"Tobacco farm? Henley Plantation rivals the Texas King Ranch in size. It's the largest tobacco plantation in the entire South."

"I see," Bonita responded with a smile. She was quite pleased with herself.

I may have been down, but I am definitely not out. I haven't lost my touch to attract the wealthy and those to the manor born. Mrs. Henley will probably be quite useful to me in my plan to become the matriarch of local society in Spencer and its environs.

"Shall I escort you in to dine, Mrs. Roberts?" Mr. Wigginton said, as he offered his arm.

"Thank you, no. I believe I'll return to my suite and freshen up a bit before dining."

"Very well. Shall I escort you up?"

"That won't be necessary. You've been quite helpful, Mr. Wigginton. I'll be down in an hour or so," said Bonita as she hoisted herself from the chair and waltzed to her private elevator.

As she rode up, she thought again of Lydia Henley. She was quite friendly and certainly didn't put on any airs, but Bonita's antenna had picked up that she was wearing a designer dress by Vera Wang, clutched an eighteen-hundred-dollar purse in her hand and wore enough diamonds and emeralds to make a rather sizeable dent in the national debt. No slouch himself, Randolph had sported an Ives St. Laurent tuxedo that was obviously custom made. Bonita entered the salon of her suite and dialed Hannah's room.

"Hello, Miss Bonita. You wanna change now? I'll be right there."

Bonita removed her shoes and sat on the sofa. Shortly Hannah arrived. Bonita didn't have to rise since she had arranged for Hannah to have a key to the private elevator.

"Well, did you see them ducks? Did you have a good time, honey?" Hannah asked.

"I saw the ducks. I did not step in any duck doo. I enjoyed myself immensely and I met quite an interesting couple from the town south of Spencer. They own the largest tobacco plantation in the South. Lydia Henley will be lunching with me tomorrow at one," Bonita responded.

"That's my child. She don't miss a trick and she don't waste no time meetin' the right folks. What you gonna wear tonight, Sugar?"

"What do you suggest, Hannah?"

Hannah loved it when Bonita asked her advice about clothing.

"I thinks you should wear that stunnin' black evenin' suit. You know. The Ballentine."

"Balenciaga, Hannah."

"Uh-huh. Want me to get it ready?"

"Yes, I think that's a splendid recommendation."

Hannah beamed and hurried to the bedroom's spacious closet for Bonita's evening ensemble.

Forty-five minutes later, Bonita reappeared in the lobby wearing the flowing Balenciaga evening suit. An "heirloom" onyx bejeweled comb adorned her bleached curls and she wore onyx and diamond chandelier earrings. She thought she looked quite spectacular.

After being seated in the dining room, Bonita glanced around at her fellow diners nodding to one or two here and there. She ordered her usual fare of surf and turf and Perrier Jouet champagne. Dinner was excellent and Bonita was quite sated both physically and emotionally as she made ready to return to her suite. She thought she had definitely made the right decision to move, and Tennessee was definitely her kind of place.

3

Luncheon with Lydia Henley

The following afternoon, Bonita went to the dining room at a quarter to one and was seated waiting for her luncheon guest Lydia. Although Bonita had made a reservation the evening before, she wanted to make sure the table was a suitable one. Bonita had specifically requested the smoking section since Lydia had made a point of her addiction to cigarettes the evening prior. She found the table to be adequate and one well placed for seeing and being seen. She ordered a bottle of 1964 Dom Perignon to be poured as soon as Lydia arrived.

Bonita, covered from head to foot in crimson for the occasion, glanced around at the other diners. She peeked at her Patek Phillipe jeweled watch just as Lydia entered the dining room in a smashing chocolate brown Chanel suit complemented by lizard pumps and purse.

"Hello, Bonita," she trilled as she approached. "Oh, fantastic! I see you got us a smoking table. You are too kind. Are you sure cigarette smoke doesn't bother you? Everyone and their sister have suddenly become allergic to cigarette smoke," Lydia purred as she gave Bonita an air kiss and sat in the banquette opposite her.

"It doesn't bother me at all, dear. My, you look lovely. What a beautiful Chanel."

"This old thing? Thank you. It's old as the hills," Lydia replied through a veil of smoke as she exhaled.

"Chanels never age. They grow more stylish with each passing year."

"They do, don't they?"

The sommelier arrived and poured a soupcon of Dom Perignon into Bonita's glass. She daintily took a sip and nodded approvingly.

The wine steward poured a flute for Lydia and asked if they cared to order now or later.

"Later, I think," responded Bonita.

"Dom Perignon. My favorite. How did you know?" Lydia asked.

"We have something in common. It's my favorite too. I hope you don't mind if we wait a bit to order. I thought we could enjoy our champagne and get to know each other a little."

"That's a wonderful idea. I have hours. Randolph will be in his business meeting all afternoon."

"Is he selling tobacco?" Bonita asked coyly.

Laughing, Lydia said, "On my goodness, no. He's giving away money. Randolph loves to give away money. He's establishing a scholarship grant for poor, but worthy, students to attend UT, his alma mater."

"How very generous!"

"Yes, he's a wonderful person. He's always been good to me. I've known Randolph all my life," Lydia answered.

"Since you were children then?"

"Since I can remember. We played together when we were little. He took me to my first dance, gave me my first kiss, deflowered me, and we married the day after he graduated from UT," Lydia said as she extinguished her first cigarette and immediately lit another.

Bonita realized when Lydia said she smoked, she really meant it. She didn't smoke, she was a veritable chimney.

"You said that Randolph lived on the plantation all his life. Did you live on a neighboring plantation?"

"No, I lived at Henley Plantation. That's the name of the tobacco farm. And before you start thinking that Randolph and I are cousins or something, which some think is so common in the South-you know, marriage between family members like they think is rampant in West Virginia, we are not related.

"My father was a tenant farmer who went to work for Randolph's father before I was born. Old Mr. Henley liked my father so much that he kept him on the plantation permanently. He even built him a tiny house there. I was born on Henley Plantation and I literally knew Randolph from the first day I can remember," Lydia explained. "I was not to the manor born, but once I married Randolph, my past disappeared, although I was fortunate because Randolph's father paid for my college education, so I had a few years away from the old home place."

Bonita was astounded this woman who was obviously wealthy and seemed so well bred would simply spill the fact that her father was a tenant farmer to a relative stranger. Bonita certainly didn't care to share any of her secrets with anyone, strangers or those whom she had known for years.

Despite her background, Lydia was quite charming and even though Bonita would never have confided such a confidence as Lydia did, she found Mrs. Henley to be quite refreshing and unaffected.

"Now, let's talk about you, Bonita," Lydia said between puffs on her brown More cigarette.

"I'm moving to Spencer from New York. My husband Joshua Roberts was in the publishing business. He passed away last year."

"Oh, my, Roberts' Publishing. Everyone's heard of them. Did you live on Park Avenue?' Lydia inquired, seemingly quite impressed.

"Yes, we had an apartment there, but I'm so looking forward to being away from the city. I long for the quiet of the country after all the hustle and bustle of living in New York City, or the Big Apple, or Gotham, or whatever one chooses to call it."

"You simply must purchase one of those huge old homes on the *lake* in Spencer. Actually, there really isn't a lake in Spencer, there's a spillway from the Fall Creek Falls, but everyone refers to it as *the lake.* In fact, I believe I heard at my woman's club meeting last month that one of the *lake* estates is for sale. Along the shore of the spillway is the only place to live in Spencer, but usually the houses become available only when someone passes away, but I think it was the Briggs' home that I heard was for sale. The Briggs are elderly and their children are going to move them to Knoxville to an assisted living facility. None of the children live in Tennessee, so they're planning to sell the mansion. It's a gorgeous home. Three story brick with columns, huge public rooms, a ballroom on the third floor, servants' quarters attached to the main house, stables, a swimming pool, tennis courts, a Jacuzzi, and it was very recently renovated. That is, within the last ten years," Lydia reported as if she were the selling agent for the property.

"It sounds perfect. I love to entertain. The idea of a ballroom particularly piques my interest," Bonita said with a sigh.

"After we've eaten, I'll call Hilda Bowen. She handles all the large estates in Van Buren County. Spencer's in Van Buren County, you know. We're in the neighboring county, although we're only four miles from the Spencer line. In fact, the tobacco farm is on the county line. The Briggs' estate is the place for you to buy. Of course, you may want to change the name."

"What's it called now?" Bonita inquired.

"Brigadoon," Lydia said with a giggle.

"Yes, I believe I might be interested in changing that," Bonita tittered.

The women chattered on and then ordered poached salmon and lettuce wedges smothered in diced tomatoes, crumbled blue cheese, and blue cheese dressing. They accompanied those selections with cold asparagus and lemon sauce on the side followed by mango sorbet for dessert. They continued their luncheon until almost three o'clock over mocha latte and numerous cigarettes for Lydia while Bonita questioned her about the social happenings in and around Spencer. By the time they said goodbye, Bonita knew she had made the right choices in those she planned to meet in her new hometown.

4

Bonita Arrives in Spencer

Bonita spent three days at the Peabody before alerting Alphonso and Hannah they were leaving the following day for Spencer where they would be staying at The Volunteer. Once there, she would be meeting Hilda Bowen to look at the Briggs' estate and would more than likely purchase it. She also told Alphonso she would expect him in her suite that evening.

Alphonso, in addition to driving Bonita in the maroon Rolls and occasionally serving as a butler/handy man, was paid an enormous salary to service Bonita sexually. As a former prostitute, her favorite client had been a black man whose hardware she had greatly admired. After living in Dorchester County for a short time, following Joshua's stroke, Bonita had made a proposal to Alphonso that he had accepted. He had kept his mouth shut and he and Bonita had some very randy times in her boudoir. Bonita loved the arrangement.

Alphonso was a thoughtful, considerate, and untiring lover and Bonita could have him at her pleasure. When she was finished with him, she reverted to the role of mistress and dismissed him. Alphonso never complained because of the enormous salary he received. Hannah did not think much of the arrangement, but she knew better than to voice her opinions to Bonita. She had tried to stop Bonita from making the proposal to Alphonso, but Bonita always did as she pleased, so Hannah had never mentioned it again.

The next morning, the Roberts entourage checked out of the Peabody and headed south for Spencer. The Volunteer, the best hotel Spencer had to offer, was not up to the Peabody's standards, but Bonita had booked a suite and her rooms, while not opulent, were certainly comfortable. The dining room was neither as posh nor the chef as imaginative as at the Peabody, so Bonita took her evening meal in her suite. She retired early to rest before meeting the Real Estate Broker at ten o'clock the following morning.

Hannah zipped Bonita's dress as the bedside phone rang. Hannah answered and informed Bonita that Ms. Bowen was waiting for her in the lobby. Bonita hurriedly reached for her purse, blew Hannah a kiss, and departed.

"Hello, Mrs. Roberts. I'm Hilda Bowen," the attractive blonde said as she extended her hand to Bonita.

"My pleasure, Ms. Bowen. I understand you have a lovely lakefront estate to show me."

"I certainly do. Brigadoon has been in the Briggs' family since it was built in 1854. It was one of the few *lakefront* homes to survive that War of Northern Aggression because the home was so lovely. One of the lesser Yankee generals took it over as his personal residence for the duration of the sieges in our fair state. I think you'll find it absolutely charming, although it is quite large. Do you have a big family?"

"No. I'm alone. I have a handy man and a maid. My husband passed away last year," Bonita said as she brushed an entirely imaginary tear from her eye.

"I'm so sorry. Well, the home is quite spacious as are the grounds."

"I prefer a great deal of space and I plan to entertain quite frequently, so I'm definitely interested in something with a lot of room. Also, my new-found friend Lydia Henley tells me that I must have a home on the lake."

"Isn't Mrs. Henley lovely? She called to make your appointment and said she had advised you to buy on the lake. It's fortuitous that there's anything available and such a lovely home at that. Usually, someone has to die before one of the estates comes on the market," Hilda gushed.

"So I understand. It must be Kismet, as they say," Bonita laughed. Hilda nodded as she escorted Bonita to the chauffeur-driven limousine. She transported all of her important in grand style to see a property.

Bonita was immediately taken with Brigadoon. A gray stone wall enclosed the entire property with the exception of the lakefront into which was inserted a wrought iron gate at the driveway's entrance complete with a gatekeeper's cottage. Eight Doric columns supported the brick mansion's portico. The center hall could easily accommodate a grand piano and a stringed quartet simultaneously. The public rooms were well appointed and tastefully decorated, but Bonita made a mental note of several changes she would make when she became mistress of the manor. The third floor ballroom with elevator to it from the lower floors especially intrigued her and she envisioned the many soirees she would host in it. The kitchen was industrial size and equipped, but that interested her little since she didn't even know how to boil water. She glanced over it and felt Hannah would be appreciative. Behind the four-car garage, there were more than adequate servants' quarters with a sitting room for Hannah and Alphonso when they relaxed. Bonita asked Hilda the price.

"Three and one half million, but I think we could probably negotiate."

"That won't be necessary, Hilda. I love the property. I simply must have this house. I'll pay the asking price. I would like to go to settlement as soon as possible. I understand the Briggs have moved to an assisted living facility. I'm sure they'd like full price since their expenses there are probably quite high. I'll be happy to pay." Bonita said magnanimously.

Hilda couldn't believe her ears, but then Hilda didn't always have clients with as much money at their disposal as Bonita. She was Joshua's sole heir since he and his first wife had no children. Bonita was not merely wealthy, she was disgustingly and obscenely rich. And her motto was "Nouveau riche is better than no riche at all." The operative word was *riche.*

And so, Bonita became a resident of the fair State of Tennessee where certain iron clad rules prevailed. Spectator pumps are not worn before derby-day—*that's the Kentucky Derby*. White shoes are never worn prior to Memorial Day or after Labor Day. All velvet gowns and dresses, with the exception of red, are packed away after Christmas, however red velvet may be worn to a Valentine's Day dance or ball, after which it too is packed away until the following season. Pastel clothing is *in* during the spring and summer months and linen, which wrinkles so elegantly, is the uniform of the day from April until October while bold, primary colors usually adorn the Southern lady's home.

Every native born lady residing in the South has at the minimum two deviled egg dishes and sometimes as many as a dozen. The two national drinks are Coca-Cola, pronounced *Co-cola*, and sweet tea. Many a Southerner has been heard to make the statement, "And on the eighth day, God created sweet tea." Dolly Parton puts it another way, "Sweet tea is the house wine of the South." Mint juleps are sipped in the evening always from sterling silver or pewter Jefferson cups, which are removed from the freezer shortly before serving the libation.

It doesn't matter what sex or race a Southern lady retired with in the evening, one will never see her smoke a cigarette on the street the following day. It simply is not done. Etiquette is extremely important in the South and Southern belles never conduct themselves in a wanton manner. The mating call of the Southern belle is "I'm so drunk," and Southern ladies do not participate in group-sex. Why? All those thank-you-notes.

The Southern matriarchy has its own language too. One doesn't *take* or *drive* another to the store or to the doctor's office, one *carries* him or her there.

Nice is what one says if she doesn't particularly like something or someone. *Darling* is pretty good, but the ultimate compliment of the Southern lady is *precious*." And one can say the most vicious thing she wants about another as long as she adds the phrase "Bless her little heart." The "e" and the "r" on words such as sweater, mother, father, or daughter is pronounced *ah*," which is responsible for what many Yankees refer to as a Southern accent.

Teas are hosted frequently as are luncheons, bridge desserts and balls. Socializing is the South's national pastime. Gossip is whispered amidst giggles and expressions of amazement and those ladies who possess philandering husbands, more often than not, look the other way. Security, after all, is a highly coveted commodity, plus Southern ladies are aware of man's libido and his propensity to spread his seed hither and yon even to those darker complected gals who still today work along side migrant Mexicans in the cotton and tobacco fields.

Even the lower middle-class Southern lady employs household help. Gardening, a ladylike past time, is performed only while wearing gloves and usually a large straw hat to protect fair skin. The Southern lady's skin is legendary because of the constant heat that brings out its natural oils.

In the kitchen, the Southern lady is most often attired in a dress a la June Cleaver or Harriet Nelson, complete with a lace apron. She can fry chicken that will melt in one's mouth, make corn-meal dumplings that are as close to heaven as anyone could wish to get in this lifetime and chocolate cake and lemon meringue pie (only genuine if made with Eagle brand condensed milk) that can bring a grown man to his knees.

Bonita was in the heartland of the South. She moved into her new home on February 5th, renamed the estate "Villagio," from her "Spanish" heritage, no doubt. Bonita had repeatedly referred to her noble Spanish background while in South Carolina, neglecting that her background was Mexican from Texas rather than Spain. She immediately hired contractors to build a large reflecting pond in front of the house adorned with ornate fountains and to begin renovation of her mansion.

Three days after Bonita took possession of the estate, Mr. Briggs passed away at the assisted living facility in Knoxville. Bonita, magnanimously, politically correct, and wishing to win favor with the locals, called the Briggs' children and offered their home place Brigadoon for the reception after their father's funeral services. Fortunately, the contractors had not yet disposed of the Brigadoon sign that had graced the front gate, so Bonita had them remove the *Villagio* hammered gold letters and put the original sign back up for the day.

Bonita's nose for society had not failed her. The Briggs had lived in Spencer all their lives and had been social icons. Mr. Briggs had been a faithful contributor to major charities and to all art-related activities in the county. The wealthy and well connected all appeared at Bonita's doorstep for the reception.

Appropriately garbed in black from head to toe Bonita was the quintessential hostess, dabbing her eyes occasionally with her black Irish linen handkerchief trimmed in Belgian lace. She commiserated with the mourners and showed them to the open bar and the bounteously spread dining room table. Bonita had insisted on providing all of the food and beverages for the reception.

On her massive antique mahogany dining room table, she offered traditional Southern fare of fried chicken, deviled eggs, homemade biscuits, sliced country ham, sweet and sour potato salad, corn pudding, sliced tomatoes, macaroni and cheese, crudités and dip and finger sandwiches. Coconut and chocolate cakes and lemon meringue pies graced the dessert table.

In that one afternoon, Bonita met nearly everyone she had previously placed on her list of *People She Planned to Meet in Spencer.* It would be only a matter of time before she was invited to the homes of the most socially prominent in the area.

Several of the socially elite asked for Bonita's recipes, which were actually Hannah's, however Bonita was happy to comply with the requests.

HANNAH'S SOUTHERN CORN PUDDING

2 eggs
2/3 cup milk
1 t salt
2 cans drained shoe peg corn
2 T flour
¾ cup sugar

Mix in round two-quart Pyrex dish above ingredients and stir well. Place dots of butter on top of pudding. Place dish in pan half-filled with hot water and bake at 350 degrees on lowest shelf in oven until silver knife inserted comes out clean (approximately one hour.) Corn pudding is best served cold or at room temperature. There are those who prefer it warm, but they are usually from above the Mason-Dixon Line.

SWEET AND SOUR POTATO SALAD

Peel and cube five pounds of potatoes and bring to boil until tender.

Mix in pan on top of stove 1/3 cup apple cider vinegar, 1 egg, ¾ cup sugar, 1/3 cup water, 4 sliced green onions, 2 T pickle relish, 2 T flour until mixture is thick. Remove from heat. Add 3 T mustard. Stir. Drain potatoes. Rinse with cold water. Let cool about fifteen minutes. Pour sauce over potatoes and lightly mix together. Transfer to crystal serving bowl and sprinkle with paprika.

5

Rhetta Robin Shaw Ricks

Rhetta Robin Ricks, the socialite Bonita read about in the Spectator and one Bonita wrongfully assumed was a leader in society there, was for all intents and purposes the laughing stock of the county. Rhetta Robin was the only child of Thaddeus and Elvira Shaw and both of them spoiled her rotten from the moment she entered the world. The child was not blessed with good looks and as she sprouted past the terrible twos, she grew not only tall, but also spindly and awkward. Her mouth was much too large for her face and she possessed an inordinately deep voice for a female. Her unruly hair often looked like a rat had sucked on it.

Thaddeus and Elvira sent the ugly ducking to Miss Proctor's Day School for Young Ladies in Nashville, the halls of academe for the young darlings of the well to do in that fair city. Rhetta Robin was extremely unpopular and was not included in any of the little cliques in which the second-graders traveled. She longed to become friends with Melissa Parnee, the most popular second-grader at Miss Proctor's. Not only was Melissa beautiful with long, blonde, curly hair and big, blue eyes, but her father was the top agent for the William Morris Agency in New York City so Melissa knew many celebrities and movie stars. Some of them dined with her parents and they allowed Melissa to sit at the table with them. Melissa's father came home every weekend from New York, but his wife and lovely daughter lived in Nashville since Mrs. Parnee was a native of Tennessee and had tried *living up north* and simply couldn't tolerate it.

At recess at Miss Proctor's on April 2, 1950, all of the young ladies swarming around Melissa were in a titter. It seemed that Melissa's birthday party was to be held on April twentieth at her parents' estate. In addition to homemade coconut cake and hand-churned ice cream, a roster of stars would be in attendance. Kukla, Fran, and Ollie were to be on hand to entertain the young guests along with Shari Lewis and her puppets, but the most fantastic of all was that

Buffalo Bob was to be there along with Clarabell, Howdy Doody, Mr. Bluster, Flubadub, and Princess Summer Fall Winter Spring.

As Rhetta Robin lingered as close to the group as possible, she could scarcely believe what she was hearing. Melissa told her friends that her mother's social secretary would be mailing the invitations in the next few days and that she was inviting practically everyone in the class.

That evening at dinner, Rhetta Robin regaled her parents with her friend Melissa's plans for her eighth birthday party. She informed them the invitations would be going out in the next few days and she begged for a new dress for the *birthday party to end all birthday parties.*

Thaddeus smiled at his pride and joy and said, "Well, of course, you must have a new frock. Mother will take you shopping after school tomorrow."

Elvira chimed in, "At the same time, we can shop for a gift for Melissa. What would you like to get for her, Rhetta Robin?"

"I don't know, Mother. She has everything. Whatever it is, it has to be something very special and something very expensive."

"I see you are a girl after your mother's own heart, Rhetta Robin," Thaddeus said with a beatific smile at his daughter.

Rhetta Robin got her new dress the next afternoon. It was plaid taffeta with a bouffant skirt that did absolutely nothing for the child. It accentuated her spindly arms and legs, but Rhetta Robin was convinced she looked beautiful in it. Her mother purchased matching hair ribbons to tie in her undisciplined mousy brown hair and Mary Jane shoes and white socks trimmed with lace for her oversized feet.

They selected a sterling silver mirror, brush, and comb set for the birthday girl from Atley's Boutique, the only place the wealthy purchased birthday surprises, with the de rigueur pineapple motif of the store emblazoned in gold on the gift-wrapped package.

Several days passed. As Rhetta Robin entered her classroom on the following Friday, she saw some of the girls holding and admiring silver invitations.

"I love your invitations, Melissa. I can't wait to come to your party," exclaimed one of the children.

"I'm getting a new dress, Melissa. What are you going to wear?" asked another.

"I'm wearing a plaid taffeta. My mother and I bought it yesterday. I even got plaid hair ribbons to match," Melissa answered.

It didn't occur to Rhetta Robin that she hadn't received an invitation. The only thing she heard was that Melissa was going to be wearing the same dress her mother had bought for her.

"Where did you get your dress, Melissa?" asked Rhetta Robin.

"At Motson's Young Ladies' Dresses," Melissa answered. "Why?"

"I was just wondering. I have a dress that sounds a lot like that and I was planning to wear it to your party, but now I won't," Rhetta Robin said with a smile.

All of the other girls burst into fits of giggles.

"What's so funny?" asked Rhetta Robin.

"Oh, nothing," one of them replied.

At lunch that day, one of the second-graders, Beverly Preston, who on occasion was civil to Rhetta Robin, sat next to her.

"Rhetta Robin, why did you say you were planning to wear the same dress to Melissa's party she's going to wear?" Beverly asked her.

"Because my mother and I bought that same dress last week at Motson's for me to wear to Melissa's party," she explained.

"But you're not invited," Beverly said.

"Yes, I am. I heard Melissa say she was inviting practically everyone in her class."

"Practically everyone, but not everyone. She's not inviting you," Beverly said patiently.

"How do you know?"

"She told me," and with that, Beverly picked up her lunch tray and headed for Melissa's table.

Rhetta Robin couldn't believe she wasn't getting an invitation to Melissa's party. She was devastated! She so wanted to see Kukla, Fran, and Ollie, but Buffalo Bob and his gang were one of her reasons for living. Each evening at precisely 5:30, she was in front of the TV set to watch the antics of the red-headed puppet and his friends.

When she arrived home at the end of the school day, she asked her mother if the invitation to Melissa's party came in the mail that day.

"No, dear, there was nothing for you today. Have the other children received their invitations?"

"Not yet. I just thought it might come today. It should be here in the next few days," Rhetta Robin lied.

"Well, I'm sure it will be," her mother responded.

"Mother, there's a problem. Today, when I was sitting next to Melissa at lunch, she told me about her dress for the party. It's the very same dress we bought. We'll have to exchange it, won't we?"

"We certainly will. Melissa should have the first choice. After all, it's her party. She's such a lovely girl. I'm glad the two of you are such good friends.

We'll go straight away and exchange the dress, but I know how disappointed you must be. You look so pretty in that plaid."

The next morning before school began, the girls were again discussing the party and some were again perusing their invitations. At lunchtime, the young ladies filed into the cafeteria. Rhetta Robin went to her teacher and asked to be excused to use the rest room. She hurried back to the classroom and reached into the cubby under Linda Federline's desk and snatched Linda's party invitation. She quickly concealed it in her reading book and returned to lunch.

At home that afternoon, she proudly showed the purloined invitation to her parents and told how Melissa had brought them to school and handed them out to her special friends.

"It's a lovely invitation, Rhetta Robin. Where's the envelope?" her mother asked.

"Oh, I left it at school."

"Was it silver like the invitation?"

"Yes, ma'am."

"So the party is this Saturday at two o'clock?" asked Thaddeus.

"Yes, sir. I can't wait."

On Saturday, dressed in her new dress of pale blue organza and matching hair ribbon and the Mary Jane shoes with the lace-trimmed socks, Rhetta Robin rang the doorbell of Melissa's home and was admitted by the maid as her parents looked on from their car. They told Rhetta Robin they would call for her at five o'clock.

The maid showed Rhetta Robin to the back of the house and opened the sliding glass doors for her to enter the back yard where Kukla, Fran, and Ollie were greeting the young guests at pool side. Rhetta Robin walked over to Melissa and handed her the beautifully wrapped gift and said, "Happy Birthday, Melissa. Thank you so much for inviting me."

"But, but, but—I didn't invite you!" said Melissa.

"I received your invitation," Rhetta Robin said insistently.

"I don't know how," Melissa answered.

At that moment, Mrs. Parnee came over and took the gift from Melissa to add to others neatly stacked on a nearby table.

"What a lovely gift and from Atley's too. Introduce me to your little friend, Melissa," said her mother.

"Mother, this Rhetta Robin Ricks and I did not invite her and she is not my friend."

"Melissa. Please. I'm sure Rhetta Robin wouldn't be here if she hadn't received an invitation."

Rhetta Robin said, "I certainly wouldn't. You have a lovely home, Mrs. Parnee. I'm so glad I was *invited*," and Rhetta Robin walked over to where Beverly was standing.

"What are you doing here, Rhetta Robin?" Beverly asked her.

"The same thing you are, Beverly. I'm here for Melissa's birthday party."

"But you weren't invited."

"Would I come if I weren't?" asked Rhetta Robin.

And so, at seven years of age, Rhetta Robin had begun the pattern that would govern all her days. She wanted to attend every party. She would attend every party. And whether she received an invitation or not was merely something to which she paid no attention. In fact, she went to practically every birthday party given by any of her classmates during her entire stay at Miss Proctor's School. She always finagled a new dress out of her parents and she always took a gift from Atley's Boutique complete with the pineapple motif sticker.

Each year when her birthday rolled around and her mother suggested a party, Rhetta Robin sweetly replied that she preferred that the three of them go out to dinner. So, not only did she crash everyone else's affairs, she didn't bother to reciprocate since she knew in her heart of hearts that no one would come if she had a party and then her parents might realize she had attended all those parties without one single invitation to any.

As an adult, Rhetta (she had dropped the Robin while at boarding school during her teen years) was still not particularly attractive, but she was quite gregarious. In other words, she was loud and outspoken. All that aside, she was convinced she was the most socially prominent individual residing in Spencer, Van Buren County, and the State of Tennessee.

Rhetta had relished being the daughter of the Governor and living in the mansion in Nashville. The parties, the balls, the teas and her political and social clout had all been the pinnacle of her dreams. Now that daddy was no longer governor, Rhetta continued to trade on his reputation. Upon entering a room, Rhetta always marched right in with her hand extended and sought out the most important personages at the particular function—other than herself, of course. She strode over to them and regardless of whether that person was engaged in conversation with another or not, Rhetta threw out her hand and in her Southern drawl loudly proclaimed, "Hi, I'm Rhetta Robin Ricks. My daddy is the past Governor of Tennessee."

She even called her dad *Gov* when addressing him in public.

Rhetta and her handsome husband, referred to by many Spencerians as *Mr. Rhetta Robin Ricks*, had married her solely for her name, her prestigious family, and her money. Trace Ricks was from the wrong side of the tracks. Born into a poor family, he cut grass, trimmed hedges, did grocery shopping for elderly ladies and swept their porches and sidewalks beginning when he was eight years of age. At age fourteen, he applied for and received a work permit and took a position as a bag boy in a local Nashville supermarket.

A most intelligent young man, Trace earned top grades at Nashville Public High even though he was often working two or three jobs after school during the week. He had no social life as he spent almost every hour outside of school at one or another of his jobs. Although athletic, he didn't go out for sports because he needed to work to help support his family. When Trace won a scholarship to the University of Tennessee, provided for aspiring medical students by Randolph Henley, he had never been on a date.

He spent his freshman year attending classes, studying in the library and working in the dining hall to earn spending money. In college as in high school, he did not socialize.

On the second day of his sophomore year, the good-looking young man was headed for the library when he heard someone call to him. He turned and there stood a rather thin, homely girl. Trace waited and Rhetta crossed to him and asked if he were going to the library. When Trace nodded, Rhetta asked if he could help her find some books she needed for research.

"I just can't seem to get the hang of that Dewey Decimal System," Rhetta said with a smile.

"Sure. I'll show you. It's easy," Trace answered.

Now Rhetta was no dummy and she certainly knew how to use a library, but she saw something, or in this case, *someone* she wanted. Rhetta was accustomed to getting her way. She pursued the handsome Trace with all the tenacity of a squirrel determined to find a way into a well-protected fortified bird feeder.

Rhetta invited Trace out several times a week. At first, he refused, but as he got to know her better, he admitted that he didn't have the money to go out. She assured him this was not a problem as she had a more than generous allowance and she would be happy to pay for his company. Trace was reluctant, but Rhetta was insistent and after a few times, Trace seemed to forget that he was bordering on being a kept man. Rhetta bought him gifts too. She got him the latest in sport jackets, a school sweater, ties, shirts, and even a suit.

Rhetta wanted to own Trace Ricks. She was drawn to him the first time she saw him. Not a ravishing beauty herself, Rhetta loved being on and being seen on the arm of the attractive med student. She reveled in the attention and respect her relationship with Trace garnered her from her dorm and classmates. Because of his good looks and the fact that he was in medical school and would someday be making megabucks, Rhetta overlooked Trace's heritage, or lack of it, and the fact that he was studying on a scholarship.

The generous allowance Rhetta referred to was probably from her mother's coffers since the governor's family had the name, but her mother's family had the cash. Rhetta had no compunction whatever in paying for all of her dates with Trace. Trace, on the other hand, was quite taken with who Rhetta was, the daughter of the current Governor of the State. He delighted and amazed his sharecropper parents with his tales of dating the Governor's daughter.

Prior to Rhetta's junior year, she pleaded and begged with her doting parents to allow her to have an apartment off campus. Within a few weeks of Trace's senior year, Rhetta convinced him that he would save a great deal of money by not living on campus and moving into the apartment with her where she would take care of all his bills. Trace complied.

Rhetta was a product of the period when young ladies attended college for one purpose only and that was to obtain an MRS degree. She planned to marry as soon as she graduated. In fact, if she could have had her way, she would have changed from her graduation cap and gown into her wedding dress and pulled off both ceremonies on the same day.

Trace's grades continued to be top-notch and in April of his senior year, he was accepted at UT's medical school. The couple continued to live together during Rhetta's senior year while Trace started medical school. Rhetta's grades were "B's" and higher therefore she was eligible for graduate school and convinced the Governor and the First Lady that she wished to further her education. Rhetta kept the apartment and she and Trace lived there during his second year of medical school.

Rhetta constantly nagged Trace about getting married. He had one more year in med school and wanted to wait until he finished that to marry. Rhetta, unhappily, took a position for a year teaching young ladies at Nashville's Finishing School. Later, she would regale anyone within earshot about how she had put Trace through his last year of medical school. The truth was that Trace was still on his scholarship and Rhetta didn't contribute one peso towards his education expenses. Oh, she still paid for the apartment, where they continued to cohabitate and their dinners at posh restaurants. She used a portion of her salary to purchase what she considered suitable attire for Trace to wear to their many social engagements.

Once Trace completed his third year of study, he learned he would be doing his internship and residency at Nashville General Hospital. Rhetta decided the time had come for the wedding. As she had learned early in the relationship to tweak the ring she had placed in Trace's nose, when she gave him an ultimatum, he agreed almost immediately.

Rhetta called her parents to tell them the glad tidings and she and her mother began to plan the ultimate Southern wedding. The Shaws, although they wished Trace had come from worthier stock, were quite smitten with the handsome young doctor with whom their daughter was besotted. The wedding was to take place at the Governor's mansion, (*where else, for heaven's sake?*) on June 30.

Rhetta and Trace's nuptials were the Tennessee wedding of the century. All of the newspapers in Tennessee of any consequence covered the event. The Johnson girls' weddings in the Rose Garden during LBJ's tenure in The White House did not compare to all the preparations for Rhetta's marriage ceremony.

Each invitation was nestled on a bed of white feathers within a gold beribboned silver box placed in a mailing carton. Rhetta was feted at twenty showers including lingerie, kitchen, around-the-clock, garden, bar and cocktail. She and Trace were guests of honor at outdoor barbecues, cocktail parties, a pontoon cruise on the lake in Spencer, elegant dinner parties and a full-fledged ball at the mansion prior to their wedding day.

On June thirtieth, precisely at noon (the time Elvira said royalty always married), Rhetta descended the curved mahogany staircase on her father's arm into the colossal mirrored parlor of the mansion. The groom was delivered to the nuptial site in a horse-drawn coach pulled by six snow-white stallions—one of Rhetta's many wedding gifts to her new husband-to-be. One hundred white doves were released at the moment the minister declared the couple husband and wife. White rose petals were strewn over the entire grounds surrounding the mansion. Fourteen bridesmaids were in attendance gowned in dresses ranging from the palest lavender to the darkest purple, the color of royalty.

At the reception held on the mansion's lawn, food stations groaned with huge quantities of food under a mammoth tent. Hundreds of lobsters, a whole pig, a side of beef, and a pasta station with chef in attendance were only a portion of the food provided. There was also a dessert station, a grilling station for shrimp and lamb, also with a chef, a salad station, a caviar and smoked salmon station and four bars, all of which testified to the fact that this was a fete honoring the most important of personages.

Favors consisted of crystal miniatures of the mansion specially designed by Lalique in France. A white limousine with sunroof and a hot tub whisked the two away to the airport. A private jet, lent to the couple for the occasion by one of Governor's Shaw's wealthy supporters, flew them to Little Palm Key in the

Florida Keys for their honeymoon in a twelve-hundred-dollar a day rustic cottage. Trace's parents hardly closed their mouths throughout the entire affair as they watched the proceedings slack-jawed. Their *almost a doctor* son had definitely hit the big time.

Once Trace finished his internship and residency, he established what became almost immediately a thriving practice. He made a great deal of money and he definitely needed it to pay all the expenses of equipping his medical office and to keep up with Rhetta's spending habits. Trace found it difficult to deny Rhetta anything, for he dreaded her acid tongue if he failed her in any way. He also found that if he attempted to put his foot down and say no to his wife, things got very ugly. Trace began to dabble heavily in the stock market to make more money to support Rhetta's lifestyle.

Rhetta and Trace were soon the parents of a baby girl. Rhetta was deeply distressed to learn the child had a learning disability when she was three years old. A learning disability was not acceptable in Rhetta's desire for a perfect life. She carted the child hither and yon to specialists. When Corinne was six, Rhetta bore a second daughter. She named her River. As far as Rhetta was concerned, the entire world revolved around her second beautiful daughter who was perfect in every way.

Rhetta went from being daddy's spoiled little girl to being Trace's spoiled wife. She never concerned herself with money and spent freely not only on herself, but also on her homes and on her second daughter River. Corinne was well dressed too and Rhetta spent mountains of money trotting her to specialists all over the world in an attempt to get the child's dyslexia and her learning ability *fixed.*

In addition to his regular practice, Trace was the doctor for both a retirement community and an assisted living facility in Nashville. The elderly folk, especially the ladies, loved and trusted him completely. Occasionally, one or two of the ladies asked the doctor's advice about their stock portfolios and Trace freely advised them on their investments, always cautioning them that he was not a licensed financial planner. Still, they persisted in asking his advice, and sometimes even gave him money to invest for them.

While Trace spent most of his time in Nashville where he and Rhetta inhabited a mansion she had insisted upon buying, Rhetta loved to come to Spencer and her summer home to *play with her little lake friends.* Her purpose in life was to socialize and when in residence in Spencer, she busied herself by paying early morning calls to all of her *little lake friends* as she referred to the residents of Spencer. The purpose of her early morning visits was to check out any invitations her *friends* might have received.

Usually, these invitations were mounted on their refrigerator doors with magnets. Rhetta always found a way to get into the kitchen. If there were no invitations posted on the fridge, she did not hesitate to peruse whatever might be on one's desk or, for that matter, in its drawers.

She must have had a photogenic memory, for she never took notes, but Rhetta memorized all parties forthcoming. If she had not received an invitation to a particular function, she would usually call the hostess announcing she was in town and inviting the hostess to some vague affair she may be having in the distant future, but never did. If that didn't work and the hostess did not proffer Rhetta an invitation to the upcoming function, sometimes she would out and out ask about the hostess' forthcoming affair and request an invitation. If none of the above gleaned her one, she would simply show up uninvited.

She crashed elegant seated dinner parties, always properly attired, by ringing the doorbell and declaring she and Trace "were just in the neighborhood and decided to drop by." She would appear at larger parties and smaller intimate gatherings to which she had not been included and declare that her invitation had only arrived that morning and that she simply had not had time to respond.

Rhetta faithfully read the society pages in both the local newspaper and in the Knoxville and Nashville papers. When she read of the daughter of a prominent family's engagement, she immediately sent a little gift to the girl—from Atley's of course adorned with the pineapple. She did the same if she read about a socially prominent family's daughter making her bow to society. That way, Rhetta batted almost a thousand on receiving an invitation to the wedding or debut.

The other little quirk that singled Rhetta out was on those rare occasions when she legitimately received an invitation to a party, she invariably invited houseguests to coincide with the time of the party and then would call the hostess to ask if she could bring them. And then other times, she *forgot* to call and merely arrived with them in tow. This cut down considerably on Rhetta's expenses in entertaining her invitees.

Once in a great, great while, Rhetta and Trace hosted a lawn party and it was always beautifully executed with bounteous food and more than sufficient liquid libations. However, her guest list was usually quite small. If anyone whose party she had previously attended, invited or not, asked her about her gala and was perhaps even bold enough to ask why they weren't included, Rhetta's standard answer was, "Well, my goodness, you know you were invited, honey. I sent you an invitation. I mailed it myself from Nashville. You know it must have been on that mail truck that burned between Nashville and Spencer. Did you read about that, sweetie?" Of course, no mail truck had burned.

Rhetta also entertained at small, intimate dinner parties for no more than four guests at a time at her *cottage* as she referred to the large lake home in Spencer. She had inherited it from her maternal grandparents and it was in excess of five-thousand-square feet. Her home in Nashville was much grander. She always played down the mansion in little Spencer. Rhetta served very simple, but good, fare at those intimate little parties and although her maid traveled with her to Spencer, Rhetta did all the cooking for her dinner parties so she said.

The Ricks' daughter Corinne, who suffered from a learning disability, was quite athletic and Rhetta made sure she took sailing lessons on the lake in the summers through the local yacht club, attended the little cotillions at the Spencer Country Club, and went to a pool at one of the clubs practically every day. Most often, the seventeen-year-old was accompanied to these activities by Rhetta's maid because often, sailing and the cotillions were held simultaneously with Rhetta's numerous social obligations, real or imagined.

The second Ricks' daughter, River, was the absolute apple of Rhetta's eye. Beautiful, tall, and shapely with almost ebony hair and luminescent blue eyes River was everything Rhetta could ever wish for in a daughter. She was the heir apparent and her mother attended almost any activity in which the lovely fifteen-old participated. Rhetta had gargantuan plans for her second offspring.

Bonita was not privy to Rhetta's history, her wrangling of invitations, her outright crashing of intimate parties or any of her other idiosyncrasies. She looked forward to taking tea with Rhetta, whose name was constantly in the social notes of the *Spencer Spectator,* at the Rick's lakeside home "RickShaw."

Rhetta prided herself on the naming of her cottage since her maiden name was Shaw. Many often wondered why Rhetta didn't introduce herself as Rhetta Shaw Ricks, but decided it didn't have the alliterative value of Rhetta Robin Ricks. And also, she probably didn't need to use the Shaw name because the very next words out of her mouth after introducing herself were always, "My daddy is the past Governor of the State of Tennessee." Everyone in Tennessee and especially in Spencer knew about Governor Shaw whether they wanted to or not.

6

Bonita Takes Tea with Rhetta

While Rhetta was prepared to entertain Bonita, Bonita had no inkling of Rhetta's history and her dropping in to functions as though she had been invited. Early in the morning, Rhetta had gone to her computer and pulled up information about Joshua Roberts and his publishing company. Rhetta did her homework before entertaining so she could carry on a lively conversation and bring out information about her guests. This usually lasted about five minutes before Rhetta launched in on talking about her favorite subject—herself.

She was quite taken with Bonita's astounding wealth and wanted to be sure to cultivate her friendship. Rhetta certainly didn't want to miss any of the balls, dinners, or cocktail parties that she was sure were soon to be held at Brigadoon. Villagio, she reminded herself. She must remember not to refer to Bonita's recently acquired estate as Brigadoon, but Rhetta thought it was definitely a class act when Bonita rehung the *Brigadoon* sign for Mr. Briggs' funeral reception. Attention to detail was so important in the society world.

The tea sandwiches were laid out and the sterling silver tea set was in readiness. Rhetta had decided to serve Bonita in her oversized Florida room overlooking the lake. Leading to the lake from the sunlit room were Rhetta's gardens on which she prided herself. The gazebo she had convinced Trace was a must, completed the month prior, was also visible. The maid had been instructed to play classical music on the compact disc carousel. Rhetta glanced at her diamond-encrusted wristwatch and took one last glance in the French Empire mirror in her foyer as the door chimes sounded. She had earlier instructed Hannah that she wished to answer the door herself when Mrs. Roberts arrived.

"Mrs. Roberts, how lovely to see you. I'm so happy you were able to come today."

"Oh, please don't call me Mrs. Roberts. That makes me feel so elderly. It's Bonita, dear."

"Then come in, Bonita Dear," Rhetta purred.

Bonita tittered. "My, what a lovely home you have," she remarked, as she entered the octagonal foyer of Rhetta's *cottage.*

"Just our little summer and weekend cottage, but we're comfortable here. You must come to our real home in Nashville sometime."

"I'd love to. I stayed at the Peabody recently. Nashville is such a lovely city."

"Yes, it is. Don't you just love the Peabody? Most of the social functions in Nashville are held there because the country clubs can't accommodate all the guests at the charity balls. Why don't we go out on the sun porch for tea? It's such a gorgeous day," Rhetta cooed as she preceded Bonita to the Florida room.

"My, Rhetta, your gardens are exquisite and what a delightful gazebo."

"This is my favorite view from the house. I love to garden. I can't get enough of getting my hands and fingernails in the dirt. Trace is always cautioning me to wear gloves, but I like the feel of the earth. It's a Southern thing, I guess. You remember Scarlet and her love for the land? But then, you aren't from the South, are you?"

Taking a seat to which Rhetta gestured and once again repressing the fact that she was originally from a two-room shack in South Texas, Bonita replied, "No, I'm not. Well, not from *The South* anyway. I am from the south of Spain however," Bonita said with a chuckle.

Rhetta smiled at Bonita's little joke. As Rhetta poured and passed tea sandwiches, she questioned Bonita in great detail as to how she came to this country, where she had lived previously, how she met Joshua Roberts, what brought her to Spencer, etc., ad nauseum. Bonita skillfully lied from the very first question throughout the friendly interrogation. Montiac, Dorchester County, the Magnolia Ball, or Bonita's years in South Carolina never found their way into the conversation.

During the course of their visit, Bonita mentioned to Rhetta that she had an idea that she thought some of the better families of Spencer would find appealing. She went on to say that when she was ready to present it, she hoped Rhetta would be available to attend a little meeting she had planned as she felt Rhetta would not only be interested, but could also be very instrumental in helping her.

Rhetta assured Bonita she was available though she had not a clue as to the nature of Bonita's idea. She spontaneously made the decision to do or say whatever was necessary to become a part of Bonita's inner circle. If she were invited to any and everything at Bonita Roberts' home, Rhetta was sure eventually she would be on everyone's invitation list. With her money, Bonita would surely rise to the top of Spencer society as surely as cream rises to the top of fresh milk. Rhetta determined she was going along for the ride—*invited* or not!

7

Lunch at Henley Plantation

Bonita was quite pleased when Lydia Henley called to invite her to lunch at the Henley Tobacco Plantation. She had so enjoyed Lydia at the Peabody and now that she was a little more familiar with the area, she knew Lydia was a must on her *list of people to know.* Lydia, too, looked forward to seeing Bonita again. Bonita was different and amused Lydia, for even though Lydia had many friends and acquaintances, she considered most of the people who lived nearby rather provincial.

Lydia had already confided her past to Bonita. She had always found it quite disarming to tell anyone straight out that she was a tenant farmer's daughter and had known Randolph since they were children and that by marrying him, she had hit the big time. Most of the people with whom Lydia and Randolph associated were quick to point out any and all illustrious events in their pasts, both real and imagined. They placed great stress on their heritage assuring any listening ear that they were truly members of the aristocracy, and their money was so old it was practically crumbling in the various vaults.

Lydia had long ago determined that she was not going to fabricate a past. Almost everyone in Van Buren County had known her since she was a toddler anyway, but she did enjoy spontaneously springing her story on strangers and newcomers. Some were visibly aghast. Others were amused and some, like Bonita, took Lydia's confession right in stride. Lydia had long ago learned that those who accepted her past the most readily usually had something in their own closets with which they were not too pleased. She wondered what secrets Bonita clung to her massive bosom.

During the Henleys' travels around the world without the encumbrance of children, Lydia had become enamored of life-size dolls she had encountered in various foreign countries. At first, she had purchased a few here and there, but soon her passing fancy had become almost an obsession. Lydia had over two hundred exquisite, handmade life-size dolls in her plantation mansion. They were not enclosed in glass cases, but were incorporated into the lifestyle of Lydia's home. Some were seated on settees in the grand parlor. Others were peering out the palladium windows in the dining room. Two sat in dining room chairs against the wall in the formal dining room. There was another on the piano bench in the music room—fingers poised over the keyboard in the playing position. Dolls were lounging on the window seat in the bay window of the breakfast nook. There were dolls in rockers in various bedrooms.

Most amusing of all was a life-size toddler seated on an antique potty-chair in the powder room on the main level. Clad in summer play clothes, a group of dolls were seated on the screened porch overlooking the gardens engrossed in a game of jacks. During the Christmas season, Lydia had three special dolls dressed for the occasion and arranged so it appeared they were trimming the tree.

Lydia's collection was worth many thousands of dollars and she delighted in finding new and different places and activities in which to place her darlings, which she and Randolph laughingly called their *children.*

The doorbell rang on the appointed day of Bonita's call. Lydia's butler showed Bonita to the parlor. Her eyes practically bulged out of her head when she spied Lydia seated on a settee between a two-foot lifelike male doll and a pigtailed female doll of equal proportions.

"Hello, Bonita. I'm so glad you could join me for lunch today," Lydia said with a smile as she rose to greet her guest.

"Thank you for having me, Lydia."

"Please have a seat. I thought we'd have a light libation in here before going into the dining room. You can sit over there next to Trina," Lydia said, indicating a doll on a love seat adjacent to the settee, as she retrieved a cigarette from her sterling slaver and lit up. Bonita sat.

Determined not to make the same mistake she had made in Dorchester County with Celestine Piersall by not speaking to Anthony, the doll Celestine Piersall referred to as *her son,* Bonita immediately turned to the doll and said, "Well, hello, Trina. That's a lovely dress you're wearing today."

Lydia chuckled and said, "I see you're a doll aficionado too."

"Oh, yes, I love dolls."

"You must. You even talk to them," Lydia said, still chuckling.

"You don't?"

"Hardly ever. I simply collect them and place them here and there, although Randolph and I do call them our *children,* but we rarely converse with them. You see, they can't answer back."

Bonita smiled with relief that she wasn't going to have another Anthony with which to contend. She was most uncomfortable though with several pairs of glass eyes seeming to stare at her from various points around the room.

Lydia started right in with chit-chat asking whom Bonita had met thus far, what parties she had attended, if she were involved with any of the local charities yet, how the renovations were coming at Villagio, and what church Bonita was attending. After several flutes of champagne, the ladies retired to the dining room where Bonita was accosted with more dolls.

Shortly after lunch, she excused herself to use the powder room and did a double take when she sat on the stool and glanced up to see a life-size doll in exactly the same position as she on the potty-chair opposite her. "What is this thing these Southerners have with dolls?" she mused sotto voce.

After lunch, Bonita asked for a tour of the antebellum mansion and Lydia was more than happy to comply. Bonita was completely confounded when she was confronted by dolls, all named, in each and every room, in the upstairs foyer, hallways, and in all the bathrooms on the second floor. Lydia even showed her the maid and butler's rooms that were equipped with dolls of color. There were dolls in the kitchen-one perched on the counter and another on a small footstool seemingly reaching for a foodstuff on a shelf.

Bonita was beyond belief when she met those playing jacks on the screened porch and then was introduced to yet another in the potting shed digging in a potted plant. Most of the dolls merely sat, but Lydia also had some that were mechanized. When she activated the switches, some danced while others sang in voices highly reminiscent of the one Celestine affected when she spoke for Anthony. Another hammered. One moved like a robot. It was like being in a giant toy store at night when all of the inhabitants seemed to come to life.

Bonita was glad when her visit was over. She couldn't imagine anyone living amidst all of those dolls day in and day out. She liked Lydia quite a lot, but she decided there must be something amiss in her life for her to surround herself with all those dreadful dolls. She further determined that she would enjoy Lydia's company at Villagio as much as possible and would limit visits to Henley Plantation except for very large and very important social functions.

She caught herself on the way home in the rear of the Rolls thinking how much Anthony would like to meet all of Lydia's *children*. When she realized what she was thinking, she shook herself. "What is the matter with me? I'm becoming as loony as Celestine and Lydia."

"What'd you say, Miss Bonita?" asked Alphonso.

"Oh, nothing, Alphonso. I was merely talking to myself. Do you remember Mrs. Piersall's doll?"

"Yes'm, I shore do. That Anthony was one cute l'il fellow. Izonia introduced me to him. After you's been around him awhile, you starts to believe he's a real l'il boy, don'tcha?"

"No, I didn't. Celestine talks for him."

"Yes'm. Izonia do too sometimes."

"Oh?"

"Yes'm. The day I met Anthony Miss Celestine'd gone out. Izonia told me what Anthony was thinkin' and talked for him."

"That's the most ridiculous thing I ever heard," Bonita huffed.

"Why you thinkin' 'bout Anthony anyway?"

"Because Mrs. Henley has dolls all over her house."

"Do she talk to them?"

"She says she doesn't and she didn't talk for any of them, but she must have two hundred of them and everyone of them has a name. She has them everywhere. There's even one on a potty-chair in the powder room, for heaven's sake."

"Rich folks is really different, ain't they, Miss Bonita? 'Course you is one, so I guess you wouldn't know."

"If rich folks are different, Alphonso, I'm glad I don't have any of their idiosyncrasies."

"What's idiotsyn—?"

"An idiosyncrasy. It's something strange and off the beaten path, Alphonso."

"Oh," was all Alphonso said, but he smiled to himself. He didn't reckon Miss Bonita thought her sexual relationship with her chauffeur/handy man was strange and off the beaten path. But he surely wasn't going to mention anything about that to her. She paid him handsomely for his sexual services and he really didn't mind even though she looked like a beached whale. He simply shut his eyes and thought about what he was going to do with all the money she was paying him.

It wasn't like he hadn't been to bed with a white woman before, although the other white woman had been young and beautiful. He had been a young buck and in love with her. Alphonso allowed himself to drift into a reverie of his beloved Billie Sue Barto for only a few minutes. Then he quickly turned it off. He knew thinking about her would only cause him to feel depressed. She was the daughter of Mr. Barto on whose estate he had worked when he was eighteen. He and Billie Sue had planned to run away together, but after a particularly passionate night of lovemaking, he never saw her again. She had been shipped of to school or so he was told.

Alphonso pined for her night and day, but he couldn't ask his employer about her. The following winter, Mr. Barto let Alphonso go with no explanation. After that, Alphonso completely lost track of her. It was only a short time later when he found work in the neighboring county of Dorchester. Whenever he could, he checked to see if Billie Sue had returned to her home, but as far as he was able to learn she never did. He had no idea what had become of her. Alphonso had loved her every day since he last saw her.

8

Precious Woodson

When one refers to the *wah* in the South, one is referring to the Civil War, known to Southerners to this day *as The War of Northern Aggression*. World Wars I and II, the Korean War, and the Viet Nam War are most often referred to in Dixie as *conflicts* and pale in comparison to the devastation of the South that took place between 1861 and 1865. Prior to that time, the South was a paradise of plantations, mansions, beautiful women in hoop skirts, mammies, servants, parties, teas, and luncheons—at least, that is what Southerners would have everyone believe.

And quite a few Southerners managed to hold on to some of it even after their fields were burned and salted, their mansions destroyed, their slaves freed, and their way of life desecrated. That money in the South today is referred to as *old money*. Amazingly, many old Southern families are still eking out an existence on money passed down to them generations ago.

These scions of old Southern families are those gentlemen in the South who attend the proper boarding schools, never referred to as *prep*, the right university, preferably the University of Virginia, known simply as *The University*, or the University of North Carolina. They then go on to law school, pass the bar, but do not practice. They dabble in the market, serve on prestigious boards, play golf, and attend charity balls with the proper young ladies whom they marry immediately after passing the bar.

The new couples move into one of the family manors left to them by their proper ancestors. These Southern heirs have one axiom hammered into their heads from the time they move from the breast to the cup and that is, "Don't touch the principal!" While it would be preferable for the patriarchs of modern day to add to the principal, that is not expected, but what is imperative is that they are to live on the interest the *old money* generates, so the cycle can be repeated again and again.

Unfortunately, in some cases, the nest egg is not always equal to either inflation or the lifestyles to which some of these gents have become accustomed. Thus principal is sacrificed to the point that in some instances the term "genteel poverty" has become rather ordinary.

Those who live in this situation may indeed still inhabit the family manor but have no visible means of support. Yet they hold proudly to their family name and heritage and continue to serve on boards, play golf, and attend those charity balls. How do they manage that? They sell their jewelry and the heirlooms from the manor house. And where do they go to cautiously sell these precious items? They go to Precious Woodson, a member of one of the old moneyed Southern families herself, a most discreet businesswoman and a representative of Sotheby, Park, Bernet.

Precious had long ago squandered what was left of her family fortune, but she still had bills to pay and appearances had to be kept up. She had a degree in interior design, but she certainly couldn't place herself in someone's employ, yet she had to do something to make ends meet. She packed several heirlooms in her Vuitton luggage and flew to New York and placed them with Sotheby's. Sotheby's, in turn, featured Precious' artifacts in their spring catalogue and Precious made a shitload of money.

Sotheby's was so impressed with the cache Precious provided they spoke to her about obtaining more items for them to auction. Precious realized there must be others in her state and she became a representative for the prestigious old auction house and the soul of silence. She never divulged to anyone where she obtained the gorgeous pieces she procured for Sotheby's, but she made a great deal of money and those who were in dire straits called on her frequently.

With her earnings, Precious had been able to repair her tumbling mansion, refurbish it, buy back some of her heirlooms and become quite a wealthy woman. She was renowned for her annual Christmas party and her lovely home was featured each year on the "Unique Houses of Spencer" tour. She had called on her decorating skills to make the house one of the true showplaces of the South.

In her day, Precious had been quite a looker. For decades, she was granted the title of "The Most Beautiful Young Lady to Debut in Nashville." As the years passed, Precious was escorted by numerous, handsome, eligible men and broke a fair share of hearts, but she never married. She kept herself immaculately and with the newfound money from her assisting others less fortunate than she, she was always perfectly coiffed, manicured, pedicured, and massaged. Precious was still sought after by divorced men and widowers and was very much a part of the social scene; however, her propensity was not for those few eligible men available to a woman of her age. Precious had always been drawn to much younger men, even those below the legal age to vote.

Her liaisons with younger men had been plentiful. She had fornicated with the young man who delivered her weekly groceries. Unfortunately, his family had now sent him away to school. She twice weekly took delight in her pool boy and occasionally if she were really steamed up, would even sleep with the young black boy who cut her grass each week. The gardener, alas, was in his thirties and therefore of no use to her. Precious also delighted in looking at pictures of young boys and had an extensive library of pornographic tapes. She spent several hours a day at her computer checking out Internet sites that featured pornography. She was the recipient of several plain-wrapped brown packages in her mailbox on an almost daily basis.

No one in Spencer would have expected this fading beauty with the Clairol enhanced auburn hair, the emerald-green eyes, the well-toned body, and the twice-lifted face to ever have an unsavory thought much less to engage in sex with young boys. But Precious did so and she did so with gusto!

Lila, Precious' maid, suspected her mistress' leanings, but she had served Miss Precious since both the elder Woodsons and Lila's parents, their servants, has passed away. She was not about to divulge anything that went on at The Woods, Precious' inherited family estate. Lila was well compensated and Precious was very good to her—generous to a fault—and therefore Lila remained mute. Anyway, she only had suspicions. She really didn't know anything.

Why I reckon Miss Precious and them young boys could be doing any number of things up yonder in her bedroom was the thought Lila always brought to mind when Precious was entertaining.

Appearances are extremely important in the Southern climes and it rarely matters what one does, but rather what others perceive one does that makes a difference. So Precious had it made. She'd figured out a way to stave off the wolves at her door. She was managing to hold gravity at bay. She was highly thought of in society and she was screwing her brains out on a frequent basis with young, hard bodies that she dearly loved. And she didn't mind in the least paying for that privilege when it became necessary. Precious called to mind Dolly Levi's famous quote, "Money's not worth a thing unless it's spread all over the place causing young things to grow."

Several weeks after Bonita's arrival in Spencer, Precious opened her mail and was elated at some of the offerings she had recently ordered. One of the pornographic magazines had an article about how to make real money. Precious was quite comfortable and didn't pay any attention to that one. She opened the magazine and began to scan the pictures of the young men. There were quite a few she hadn't seen before. Carefully, she replaced the magazine in the brown wrapper and put it in her desk drawer under lock and key. She would amuse herself with it tonight after she retired. Today she planned to call on her new neighbor Bonita Roberts.

Precious had heard a great deal about her and missed meeting her when Mr. Briggs died because she had been in New York conducting business. She had called Bonita the day before to arrange her call and she had asked Lila to make her simple and famous Key Lime Pie to take to Villagio as a welcoming gift.

LILA'S QUICK AND SIMPLE KEY LIME PIE

One graham cracker or chocolate crust—can be bought ready-made
One can Eagle brand condensed milk
½ cup limejuice—either from fresh limes or plastic one
2 egg yolks

Mix juice and egg yolks in condensed milk. Pour into pie shell. Make meringue from two egg whites and top pie. Bake at 350 degrees for ten minutes. Optional: Whipped cream maybe substituted for meringue. Frost pie after it cools. The especially lazy can use Kool Whip. Delicious!

Precious gathered her purse and the pie. She checked her eel skin wallet to make sure she had her cards, the social ones, not business, and called to Lila that she was leaving. Once in the garage, she opened the door to her white Jaguar, got in, and drove the less than two miles to Bonita's front gate.

Many of Precious' society friends had filled her in on Bonita and although Precious wasn't particularly looking forward to meeting her, one did what one must and Bonita had quickly made herself desirable among Spencer's socially elite. She had definitely acted properly when she had allowed the Briggs' family to return to their home place for Mr. Briggs' funeral reception even though Bonita was the new owner. Precious heard that Bonita had also insisted on paying for everything except, for those Epicurean offerings brought by the mourners. According to all Precious had heard, Bonita was obscenely wealthy and didn't mind throwing money around or flaunting it—something not usually done in the South.

Money, or lack of it, was never to be spoken of in genteel circles and one never asked how much an item cost or how much anyone made. Any reference to money was considered extremely common (*the Southerners' opposite of precious and considerably worse than tacky*) and nouveau riche. Apparently,

Bonita had more than enough money to rise above all of this because at the moment she was the darling of the social set and Precious had heard that she was talking about originating a debutante ball in Spencer. That was the most ridiculous thing Precious had ever heard. Why everyone who was anyone was invited to debut in Nashville, as she had been. Why in the world would anyone wish to debut in Spencer at where—possibly, the Volunteer Hotel—when they could come out in Nashville at the Peabody?

If today, while Precious was making her call on Bonita, her hostess broached that subject, Precious would repeat those exact words. She turned between the brick pillars topped with massive stone lions into what had been Brigadoon, but was now Villagio.

Precious was determined not to allow Bonita and her gazillions impress her.

Bonita, herself, answered the door when Precious rang. What a vision she was! Attired from head to foot in flaming red, Bonita looked to Precious like a gargantuan fire hydrant.

Cheap looking, that's what she is with that platinum hair and that iridescent blue eye shadow smeared all over her eyelids plus she must weigh over three-hundred pounds, Precious thought as she smiled at her hostess. Bonita welcomed Precious effusively and showed her into the main drawing room. Precious glanced around, but she had decided before coming not to make any complimentary comments about any of Bonita's furnishings or objects d'art.

In only a few seconds, Precious' trained eye took in more original works of art than were on display in the entire Spencer Art Museum. The twelve-foot high walls were covered in Renoirs, Picassos, Monets, and Gaugains. Two magnificent Remington sculptures graced each end table of the luxurious sofa which was covered in moiré silk that Precious guesstimated went for about four-hundred-dollars a yard. On a table adjacent to the fireplace were enough Faberge eggs to pay off Russia's national debt. Precious settled for, "My, what a lovely room!"

When Precious had called Bonita and asked to pay her a call, Bonita, ever the social butterfly, had immediately placed a call to Lydia Henley and found that Precious had a predilection for fine port wine and that she smoked Vanity Fair cigarettes. Bonita had dispatched Alphonso to purchase both.

After Precious was seated on a Louis XV chair, Hannah appeared with a sterling silver tray bearing several brands of the best and most expensive ports. Precious selected Sanderman, after which Bonita rose and crossed to her with a sterling silver cigarette salver filled with pastel-colored Vanity Fair cigarettes.

Taking one, Precious said, "Thank you, Bonita. I see we prefer the same brand."

"Oh, I don't smoke," Bonita said pleasantly.

"Then I shan't either," Precious said in a rather disappointed tone.

"Of course you shall. It doesn't bother me in the least and I always have cigarettes on hand for my guests. Please. Go right ahead."

Precious was delighted. Maybe Bonita wasn't so bad after all. She did at least know that one of the unwritten rules of Southern hospitality is to make one's guests as comfortable as possible. As Precious lit her cigarette from Bonita's proffered antique silver cigarette lighter, she wondered what treasures the rest of the giant mansion held.

This room alone has set her back several million dollars, Precious calculated.

The women chatted. Precious asked Bonita what had brought her to Spencer. Bonita asked Precious what it was like to have lived in Spencer all her life. They mentioned people they knew in common. Bonita asked Precious questions about some of those on her list that she had yet to meet. All in all, the two ladies enjoyed quite a pleasant visit. As Precious was preparing to leave, she simply couldn't resist and asked Bonita if she might have a tour of the house.

"I've been here to Briga-, I mean Villagio, many times, but it was long ago. I can see from the drawing room that you've renovated. I'd love to see the remainder of the mansion."

"Of course. Follow me."

And Bonita took Precious through the entire house including the ballroom where she had installed six Tiffany chandeliers. Each room they visited contained more valuables than the one before.

As they headed back to the main stairway and the entrance foyer, Bonita said coyly, "I understand you studied interior design. I'm sure my home goes against your grain as my tastes are so eclectic. Joshua and I traveled all over the world and there were so many items I couldn't resist. I just love having all of my things around me, so I put them all on display. I hope my style doesn't offend you. I'm sure some would find it tacky and inappropriate."

"Absolutely not!" Precious answered too hastily.

She had seen more fantastic possessions in Bonita's house than were often on display at one of Sotheby's auctions when she made her semi-annual trips to New York. She couldn't help herself. The cache was too impressive. She gave in.

"I love your displays. You have some unbelievable pieces here, Bonita. Why, I'd be afraid to ever leave home with all of this artwork and the beautiful furniture you have here."

"Well, I seldom travel anymore, but if I do, Hannah and Alphonso are here. They keep an eye on everything. But everything here is only material, isn't it? I wouldn't be able to purchase the same paintings, but I'm sure if the check were large enough, I'd be able to replace any of the artwork with another by the same master. I've never really been concerned about the cost of things. I purchase what I like, but I've always tried to keep in mind that they're only things and things are not what matters in life. Good friends and health—those are the important things. Don't you agree, Precious?"

"Naturally, but there are things I'd hate to give up."

"Of course, but that wouldn't really change our lifestyle, would it?" asked Bonita.

"You know, you're right, Bonita," Precious agreed, but that's not what she was thinking. She bet Bonita had never been unable to pay her bills, a condition in which she had found herself several years ago, before she had to sell some of her heirlooms. Oh, Precious was financially stable now, but she couldn't fathom having the amount of money that Bonita must possess.

"This has been lovely. I'm so happy to finally meet you, Bonita, and I look forward to seeing you again soon. You must come to The Woods and pay me a call," Precious said as she was leaving.

"I shall be calling on you very soon, Precious. I have a little plan for Spencer and I think you might be interested in serving on the committee for my project."

"I would be delighted to hear your plan," Precious responded.

What is wrong with my mouth? I know what her plan is—the debutante ball—and I think it's total nonsense. But she's asking me to serve on the committee. I'll just go along with this idea of hers for a while to see exactly what she has in mind.

Precious waved as she got into her car, "Bye, Bonita."

Bonita closed the door and smiled.

"She's in," Bonita said aloud to herself.

Precious was extremely careful in her selection of young men. After all, she was a paragon of society and had to be above and beyond reproach. She also made sure that she paid all of her young partners well enough to insure their secrecy.

For her business dealings with Sotheby and all of the many heirlooms and treasures of which she had to keep track, Precious had entered into the computer world. Her data was stored on her hard drive plus she did all of her bookkeeping on a computer spreadsheet. She was a member of American Online and often amused herself by surfing the net. On occasion, she logged on to pornography web sites, but she never ordered anything because she didn't want to reveal her credit card number on the Internet. She wasn't convinced it was secure. Mainly, she didn't want anyone to learn her identity and to realize she was visiting those web sites.

As Precious' computer skills matured, she became more adept at sniffing out specific web sites and selecting them. She found there were many subcategories of pornography and one, her particular favorite, was filled with titillating pictures of young boys. Some of them even had their own chat rooms. Precious resisted going to any of those for months for the very same reason she refused to use her credit card over the net.

One boy fascinated her so completely that she eventually gave in and entered his chat room to talk to him. They chatted for several months until at last, Precious could stand it no longer and arranged a meeting with him. As luck would have it, the young man resided in New York and Precious conveniently had a forthcoming trip to Sotheby's planned.

Two weeks after setting up the meeting, Precious checked into the Mayflower Hotel on Central Park West and phoned her contact at Sotheby's to confirm their meeting was the following morning. Then she nervously dialed the boy's number. He answered on the second ring. Precious suggested he come to her suite, but he told her it would be better if she came to him. He gave her the address and told her he was available right then.

The usual cautious Precious, without a thought for her safety or how someone as young as this boy could afford his own place, touched up her make-up. She spritzed on a few drops of perfume, called the front desk to alert them to have a cab waiting for her, grabbed her mink jacket, and took off for the Lower East Side.

When she arrived at her destination and saw that it was a tenement house, she was not deterred. She emerged from the taxi, paid the driver, walked to the front of the building, and rang the buzzer for apartment 3-C. The boy's voice immediately asked who was there. Precious identified herself and the buzzer sounded to release the door allowing her to enter the nasty building. As there did not seem to be an elevator, Precious climbed three flights of stairs amid garbage, human excrement, half-naked children playing on the steps, and a few derelicts on the second floor landing. She idly wondered how they had gotten in through the so-call security entrance.

At 3-C, she knocked and the boy opened the door. The apartment was not nearly as bad as the part of the building she had already seen. Although it was furnished in early attic and late Salvation Army, it was clean and tidy. The boy, on the other hand, was absolutely gorgeous and much taller than she had expected.

Wasting no time, he moved in close to her and said in a husky voice, "Hello, Precious. I'm so glad to finally meet you."

Although he was a mere fifteen years of age, Precious could tell that he was anything but naïve. He obviously had entertained previously. The guy had his own chat room on a pornographic Internet site—it only made sense to Precious that she was not his first encounter.

He offered her a drink. When she declined, he said, "Then I guess you'd like to get started."

Precious was taken aback by this remark. She didn't mind paying for the attention of young boys, but she preferred a little romance. She didn't want this to seem like a straight business deal.

"Well, I thought we could sit and talk for a few moments if that's all right?" Precious responded.

"Sure. Have a seat," he said gesturing toward the sofa.

Precious sat and asked, "How long have you lived here?"

"All my life."

"Oh, then you live here with your parents?" Precious asked anxiously as she looked around.

"I live with my uncle. My parents are dead. My uncle's at work."

"Do you go to school?"

"Sometimes, but not when I have a job," he answered.

Precious felt very uncomfortable. She was a job.

Precious reached in her purse for a cigarette and her monogrammed sterling silver lighter, "Do you mind if I smoke?"

"Nope. It's your dime." He slid an ashtray across the table to her.

As Precious lit the cigarette, she sat quietly for almost a minute and then asked, "How long have you been in this line of work?"

"Lady, do you want to do the deed or do you want to play twenty questions?"

This young man didn't seem as sensitive as the one she had chatted with over the past few months on her computer. Then he had seemed interested in her and had made small talk with her.

"I simply wanted to know. I suppose you have many partners and I'm certainly not interested in picking up any sexually transmitted diseases."

"Not to worry. I always use a condom. It's not like this is your first time either, so I have to protect myself too, you know."

A part of Precious' mind was screaming at her to pick up her purse and leave right away, but he was so delicious. In addition to his height, he was slender with brown eyes, dark hair, olive skin and she could tell he didn't have ghastly hair all over his body the way many older men did.

"We haven't discussed terms yet," Precious pointed out.

"Five-hundred dollars for half hour." He glanced at his watch. "Seven minutes of which is up."

"My, you must be very good. That's quite expensive."

"I am very good and I don't give no discount rates."

"I don't recall asking for a discount," said Precious petulantly.

"Do you want to get started or not? I have another job in fifty minutes."

Precious felt cheap and dirty. She knew she should leave.

Why did I ever enter that chat room? What am I doing here? This place is so seedy. What I'm doing is seedier. Why do I have this predilection for young boys?

Precious asked herself all the right questions and came up with all the wrong answers. She extinguished her cigarette, rose from the sofa, removed her coat, folded it and laid it on the sofa arm, opened her purse, counted out five one-hundred dollar bills and handed them to the boy. He counted them, walked over to a small table, put the money in a drawer, crossed back to Precious, took her coat, threw it on a chair, and began to remove his shirt.

"Aren't we going into the bedroom?" Precious asked.

"There ain't no bedroom, lady, this is an efficiency."

"Oh. Do you sleep on the sofa at night?"

"Yep," he answered as he removed his trousers and his briefs.

He stood in front of Precious looking every inch like a Greek god. She forgot all her reservations. She said, "Should I remove my clothes or will you do that?"

"Whichever you prefer, ma'am," he said with the slightest hint of a smile.

"You."

He moved to her and slowly began to remove her clothing. He steered her gently to the sofa where he guided both of them into a sitting position. He kissed her face and neck. He touched her in all the right places and he screwed her like she'd never been screwed before. In fact, Precious was the recipient of a double-header in her five-hundred-dollar half hour in which she had squandered twelve minutes with idle chitchat.

As they dressed simultaneously, Precious asked when she could see him again. He went to the small table where he had deposited the money and flipped open an appointment book. "I'm available tomorrow at three o'clock."

Precious promised she would be there.

In addition to his advanced sexual prowess at such a young age, the boy was a computer whiz. He knew a great deal about Precious. He knew she was an agent for Sotheby's, and she lived in Spencer, Tennessee. She had a large home on the lake there, and she was financially well fixed and she was from an old Southern family.

And, of course, he knew she liked young boys and was more than willing to pay for their attentions. He was aware she had many contacts and probably knew a bunch of old Southern broads who would be willing to pay for his line of work. The boy knew too he was definitely going to use Precious for more than a few five-hundred-dollar, half-hour rolls in the hay.

All he needed was the perfect scheme of exactly how to do that. His uncle was his business partner. The boy would discuss his latest find with him that night so they could parlay Precious into their plan to move into the big-time within the pornography world.

9

Harcourt Ball

Harcourt Ball, the senior partner of Ball, Bassin and Bowers, was sixty-two years old and was considered by many widows, both natural and grass, (divorcees are referred to as *grass*-widows in the South) in Spencer to be the town's most eligible bachelor. He lived in a lakeside estate with his mother Marietta who was eighty-two.

People, upon first meeting the two often thought they were husband and wife. Marietta willingly went under the plastic surgeon's knife in Nashville on a frequent basis and looked quite youthful for her age. Marietta was the perfect companion for her son. She was aware of his weaknesses, his likes and dislikes, and she was totally forgiving. She waited on him hand and foot. In exchange for his mother's attentions, Harcourt was more than generous with the amount of money he deposited in her account each month. It was an ideal arrangement for both.

The ladies who fawned over Harcourt and those who inevitably invited him to dinner parties to meet one of the newly single friends were all wasting their time. While Harcourt was certainly handsome enough and charming to the nth degree, he was not interested in the ladies at all. He had discovered at boarding school at the ripe old age of fourteen that he preferred those of his own sex. Introduced to homosexual love by a senior when he was a freshman, Harcourt was completely besotted and when his senior lover graduated, Harcourt became the predator of other boys at his school to the point where he was asked to leave.

Marietta was a widow, by the time she arrived in her chauffeur-driven limousine to collect her son and his belongings, but she didn't have the chauffeur drive Harcourt home. They drove two hundred miles to another boarding school where Marietta had made arrangements for her wayward son to matriculate. Marietta did not chastise Harcourt on the trip to his new school, but rather suggested gently that he not be so forceful in his attentions to other boys. Harcourt heeded his mother's advice and managed to stay at the new boarding school through graduation having been accepted to Harvard in April of his senior year there.

He continued his homosexual lifestyle in college, but was much more circumspect in his actions and did nothing to cause the administration to cast their eyes his way during his undergraduate years or during his years at Harvard Law. Once Harcourt graduated law school and passed the Tennessee bar, he returned to Spencer, moved into Ball's Manor with his mother and proceeded to set up his law practice.

For months, his newly installed telephone in his newly constructed law offices did not ring unless his mother called to ask how things were going. Harcourt dabbled with the idea of going down to the bail bond office and "hanging out" to drum up business. Thoughts of ambulance chasing entered his mind. Just as he was about to take some action to get any kind of case, Lady Luck bestowed a giant case upon him for the form of Mr. Winston Collier.

Mr. Collier was the local undertaker in Spencer. He was a quiet, unassuming man and the very soul of decorum. Mr. Collier appeared at Harcourt's office without an appointment and asked him to serve as his attorney.

"What's the nature of the case, Mr. Collier?" Harcourt asked.

"The IRS," answered Mr. Collier.

"Are you being audited?"

"No. The audit is over. I've been charged with fraud," lamented Mr. Collier.

"Fraud is extremely difficult to prove, Mr. Collier, especially the intent," Harcourt said with a smile.

"I heard you were good with numbers when you were in school."

"Some might say that. I specialized in tax law at Harvard. I think I may be able to help you, Mr. Collier."

Harcourt took the case. It seemed Mr. Collier faced charges of failure to pay the IRS over a million dollars in taxes on money he had earned in his undertaking business. Harcourt won the case and within months, he had to take on two more attorneys to handle all the business coming his way. By the time Harcourt was thirty-five, he had made several millions and he hadn't made a trip to the bail bondsmen's office nor had he chased a single ambulance.

Harcourt put his wealth to good use. He renovated and refurbished Ball's Manor that had fallen on hard times since his father's early death. He hired servants to help Marietta run the place, purchased expensive vehicles for both of them, gave Marietta a sizeable allowance each month, and took frequent jaunts to Nashville, New Orleans, Mobile, and other Southern cities that were homes to public baths. At those, he met various sexual partners for weekend frolics, but never became attached to any one individual.

Harcourt didn't enter into homosexual liaisons in Spencer or the surrounding area. There were some who thought Harcourt might be gay, but there was certainly no proof. No one in Spencer had ever seen him in the company of another man and he had never made a move on any man men in Spencer. If he had, none of them had spoken of it.

Harcourt was a great patron of the arts and sat on numerous committees. He was always at every charity ball or benefit with Marietta on his arm. Naturally, he was someone Bonita was interested in meeting and pursuing to set her Spencer debutante ball in motion. Bonita figured the best way to get to Harcourt was through Marietta and so she invited the attorney's mother to tea.

Mrs. Ball, like Precious, was duly impressed with Bonita's trappings, but was much more effusive in her praise than Precious had been. While she found Bonita a little cheap looking with the platinum hair and the blue eye shadow, Marietta warmed to Bonita's conversations about art, the great masters, and her travels around the globe. Bonita appeared to Marietta to be very worldly, educated, and refined. She was definitely someone Marietta hoped to get to know better and someone whom Marietta felt would add a great deal to the Spencer community. She readily agreed to be placed on Bonita's list for the grand plan to be presented to a select few in the near future.

10

Candy Martin

Candy Martin, another *must* on Bonita's list, resided on a spit of land at the upper end of the lake in a big, old, rambling house with her ancient mother. Mrs. Enid Martin, Candy's mother, was born with an entire set of silver flatware in her mouth if the phrase "born with a silver spoon in one's mouth" signifies wealth. Mrs. Martin's father had been the principal owner of Pennsylvania Steel and Iron Works. Enid was the only daughter of her wealthy, socially and politically connected Philadelphia Main Line parents. She had attended the best schools on the East Coast, debuted in Philadelphia where she had been selected "Debutante of the Year," and had married Dudley Martin, heir to the Mars candy fortune, thus the reason for her only offspring's name—Candy.

From the time she could walk, Candy had been a tomboy much more content to climb trees and play cowboys and Indians than to wear frilly dresses, Mary Jane patent leather shoes, and ribbons in her hair. She was always getting into mischief and was constantly dirty from head to toe. Enid was not delighted with her child, but figured Candy would outgrow her boyish ways as she approached her teenage years. Such was not the case. Candy was not interested in dating when she approached young womanhood, not that she had any suitors. Her interests were in horseback riding—Western style—not the approved riding style for young ladies of her station. She was much more excited about roping a calf and running her quarter horse around barrels set up in a paddock than about riding to the hounds, although she possessed the required regalia and once or twice a year joined the hunt to please her mother.

Candy refused to be sent away to an all girl boarding school and attended the local high school where she excelled in basketball, softball, and track. After she received her diploma, she insisted on attending the University of Pennsylvania. When invited to make her debut at the Benjamin Franklin Hotel in Philadelphia, she declined. Her parents were horrified, but no amount of talking to her or threats could change Candy's mind. She completed her four years at the university where she majored in physical education. Once she had received her degree, she returned home to the Main Line mansion and took a position teaching physical education at an elementary school in the inner city.

Enid discontinued including her daughter in the social functions she held in her home. She rarely mentioned her daughter to her friends and then only when she was asked a direct question concerning Candy. She ceased attempting to introduce Candy to suitable young men. In fact, Enid went out of her way to avoid her daughter as often as possible. This lifestyle continued for thirty years. During that time, Candy's father passed away, Enid began showing signs of anility, senility's female counterpart, and Candy retired from teaching.

In addition to horseback riding and sports, Candy also loved to sail and to fish. She decided seemingly "out of the blue" to move to Spencer, Tennessee, where there was a beautifully stocked lake. She made her decision known to Enid.

"This is our home, Candy. The Martins have always lived in Philadelphia. I don't want to move to Tennessee," Enid whined.

"I'm moving, Mother. You can come with me or you can stay here," Candy responded.

"Then I'm staying here," Enid pouted.

"Suit yourself," Candy said as she left the drawing room.

Within a month, Candy traveled to Spencer, bought an old home badly in need of repair on a point of land on the lake and hired contractors to make it sound. She returned to Philadelphia and advised Enid she would be moving within six months.

A few weeks after, Enid fell as she was descending the winding staircase into the main foyer. She broke her hip. Now, Enid had no choice but to go with Candy as she needed almost constant care. Candy listed the Main Line mansion and it sold within three weeks.

Once the lake house was completed, Candy hired an ambulance and had Enid driven to Spencer. They had lived there for some fourteen years. Candy was now sixty-five and Enid was ninety-one and still going strong after recovering from her fracture.

Enid could barely see, but she insisted on continuing to drive her pristine 1949 Cadillac into town on an almost daily basis. Whenever Candy mentioned to her mother that she should no longer be driving and that the chauffeur was available, Enid flew out of the house in a rage and took off in her vintage car. The inhabitants of Spencer were quite accustomed to seeing the old lady in her sneakers, housedress, and bonnet cruising slowly around the two-lane roads of the village.

Enid was quite attached to a see-through plastic tote bag. She took it everywhere she went. On her driving forays, she frequented certain stores. One of the stores she always patronized was the Spencer Drug Store and the other was Matilda's, an upscale dress shop on the main thoroughfare of the small town.

The owners and employees of both businesses dreaded Miss Enid's visits which were all too frequent. She had to be watched every minute. Several years prior, Miss Enid had shoplifted items from both stores. The proprietors, not wishing to cause a scandal or to offend Enid's daughter, an excellent customer, had refrained from calling the police and had called Candy.

Candy had immediately gone to both stores and paid for Miss Enid's *purchases* Candy and the storeowners now had an understanding. Miss Enid would appear and *shop* while an employee followed along behind her and made note of the items she *bought*. Candy would be called and she would come in and settle the bill.

Candy had attempted to speak with her mother about this problem, but since Miss Enid now had a few screws loose, she couldn't seem to grasp what Candy was upset about. So she continued to shoplift and Candy continued to pay.

Candy, meanwhile, was quite socially involved in Spencer. She was a den mother for the local Girl Scout Troop, heavily involved in the SPCA adopting many abandoned pets herself, and hosting fantastic parties throughout the year.

While Candy's once elegant mother now resembled a bag lady in her daily get-ups, Candy dressed exclusively in men's suits, Oxford shoes, and, more often than not, a man's fedora. It was hinted all over Spencer that she was one of those lesbians, but she hadn't made any overtures to any women, ladies, or little girls to anyone's knowledge. The Girl Scouts loved her and none of them had ever reported any untoward actions on Candy's part to their parents.

Each year, Candy held a New Year's Eve party, a large garden party in the spring, and a pool party in the summer, interspersed with smaller gatherings during the year. All the socially elite turned out for her fetes because Candy always included interesting guests. She made sure she had about ten houseguests in attendance when she threw a party.

She was a cousin of the late Sharon Mortimer of Philadelphia who was married to the pretender to the throne of Russia, Prince Alexander. Usually one or two of them were in attendance. Princess Alexandria, Princess Sharon's daughter and Candy's first cousin once removed—*it's a Southern thing*—attended one of her New Year's galas.

Gore Vidal was a personal friend of hers and delighted everyone with a reading from one of his books at her pool party the previous summer before executing a perfect belly flop off the high dive. Often she had a Roosevelt, a Dupont and sometimes a Kennedy in residence when she entertained. The locals fortunate enough to be included on Candy's invitation list did not dare miss one of her affairs.

Candy spared no expense at her parties. She owned a portable champagne fountain always strategically placed in whatever location her party might be taking place. Dom Perignon flowed endlessly from it until the last guest had either left or passed out. She generally served mounds of seafood, various breads, crudités, assorted dips, imported cheeses, caviar, smoked salmon and escargot.

Naturally, a full bar containing every spirit imaginable was also provided with tuxedoed bartenders and waiters in attendance. In Candy's opinion, money was to be spent. She had no heirs and other than her bequeaths to the Girl Scouts of America and the SPCA, what was she going to do with all that green?

Candy invited Bonita, the newest lake resident, to her "Spring Fling" and Bonita was in awe since Maria Shriver and Arnold Schwartzenegger were there. Bonita regaled them with her movie career of eons ago. Senator Strom Thurmond and his much younger wife had put in a brief appearance also and dottering though he was, Bonita had rushed right over and introduced herself to the elder statesman. The Senator died the following week.

This party was no exception and Candy's buffet was lavish as always. Each year, a small table was placed next to the larger buffet one where Candy placed a sheaf of her recipes available to her guests for their taking. Some of this year's delicacies included were:

CANDY'S EASY AND DELICIOUS SAUSAGE DIP

For one serving of approximately eight people, fry one pound of sausage and crumble it into small pieces. Mix with eight ounces softened cream cheese (non-fat may be used) and add one can of drained Rotel chilies and tomatoes. Mix together and bake at 350 degrees until bubbly. (May also be serving without baking.) Accompany with French bread. Absolutely delicious!

ASPARAGUS ROLLS

One loaf of white bread—crusts removed
One loaf of whole wheat bread—crusts removed
Two eight-ounce packages cream cheese—softened
Garlic powder
Two large cans asparagus spears

Spread cream cheese on slice of bread and sprinkle with garlic powder. Place on asparagus tip at edge and roll bread up. Cut into slices. Refrigerate until ready to serve.

HAM ROLL-UPS

One can hearts of palm or one bunch scallions
One eight-ounce package cream cheese
One package sliced ham

Spread cheese on ham slice and place on heart of palm or one scallion at edge. Roll and slice in three-quarter-inch slices. Stand upright to serve.

OYSTER DELIGHTS

Place raw oyster in clean shell and place a pat of butter on top. Sprinkle with garlic powder and Parmesan cheese. Broil until edge of oysters curl. Serve hot. Can also add crumbled bacon if desired.

Bonita carefully folded each of Candy's recipes and placed them in her evening purse on her way to bid her hostess farewell. Hannah could probably use them, although Bonita hardly served anything she had partaken at another's home. Hannah was sometimes at her wit's end looking for new menu items to serve as Bonita never liked to repeat anything she had previously offered her guests.

Bonita located Candy. As she began her good-byes, Candy's butler produced her black diamond mink as if from thin air.

"Mrs. Martin, thank you so kindly for the invitation to your soiree. I have enjoyed myself immensely. I do hope you and your dear mother will do me the honor of visiting very soon. I'll call in the next few days. I have something terribly important I wish to discuss with you. I'm sure it's something you will

find interesting and I know you will be able to give me so much advice, if you are so inclined."

"I'm intrigued," replied Candy. "I'll look forward to your call. Thank you for coming. Good-night."

The butler held the door and Bonita stepped out the front door into the nippy evening air as Alphonso pulled the Rolls up to the foot of the steps. He left the engine running and disembarked to hold Bonita's door.

"Oh, Alphonso, I had a wonderful time this evening. Mrs. Martin had some positively fabulous guests. Maria Shriver and Arnold Schwartzenegger were there."

"I seen him in *The Terminator*."

"Well, I saw him in the flesh tonight. He's more handsome than I thought and oh my, what a physique, but he smokes those nasty cigars non-stop. Maria is a handsome woman, not what I would call pretty. She has the Kennedy jaw, but her hair is lovely and she's quite outgoing and friendly. Senator Strom Thurmond was there too. He's more ancient than God and the old fool loves the young girls, but I'm sure nothing he does makes any difference. He's an institution in South Carolina and will be in office until the day he dies," Bonita sighed.

"Was there any other folks from South Carolina there?" Alphonso asked.

"Not that I'm aware of. Why?"

"Oh, I guess I's jest a l'il homesick. Thass all."

"I'm sorry, Alphonso, but South Carolina is no longer in our vocabulary and I hope you can get it out of your mind. I have no intention of ever going back there and I certainly hope you don't mention to anyone that we came here from there."

"No'm, I don't. I knows you hates it. I'll be fine. I jest thinks about it ever' onct in a while," Alphonso said more cheerfully as he pulled in to the wrought iron gates of Villagio.

11

Darling Huxtable

Darling was a small town gal from a nothing background, but she was intelligent and had gone to a nowhere college on a scholarship. Reasonably attractive, she had an awesome body and young men stood in line to take her out in the fifties when she had attended college in Richmond, Virginia. One of the young men was a law student and after weeding through her various suitors, Darling decided he would be the one to win the prize. She slept with him and got pregnant. BD, as his friends called Braxton David Huxtable, proposed and he and Darling were wed. When BD passed the bar, he returned to his native Spencer, Tennessee, and hung out his shingle.

Darling gave birth to a son and two years later to a daughter. She joined the Junior Woman's Club and the Garden Club and enrolled each of the children in the Spencer Montessori School at the age of two. BD worked long hours and Darling soon tired of playing housewife and mother with little time with her husband.

She bought flowers almost daily at a store owned by a local man who was married to a lovely woman and was the father of three teen-aged sons. Darling liked the florist's looks and began wearing more and more revealing outfits when she went to his shop, the largest florist shop in Van Buren County. She had managed to exercise and retain her excellent figure after giving birth to the two babies. A flirtation began between the housewife and the florist, although to Travis, the florist, it was innocent.

Darling shopped in his store practically everyday and spared no expense as to the flowers and floral arrangements she selected. Unlike some of Travis' customers who pinched a penny until it bled and bought only the least expensive flowers, Darling purchased with abandon. Not only was Travis interested in the amount of money Darling spent on each of her visits, but she was also a good-looking woman. Lastly, he didn't want to lose her business to one of the two relatively new chain-store operations in town that sold flower arrangements to go.

Darling often arrived in the spring and summer to make her purchases in short shorts, halter-tops, and high wedge sandals. All the landscaping boys, the plant manager, and the other employees would signal each other when they saw her pulling into the front lot. Usually, Travis would hear them calling to each other or see them signaling and would make sure that he was near the front door to greet his best customer.

On one of Darling's shopping trips, she mentioned to Travis that BD was out of town on a case. She invited him to drop by for a drink that evening. As luck would have it, Travis' wife Estelle had an Altar Society meeting at the Spencer Episcopal Church that night. Travis agreed to stop by for a drink.

Darling fed the children early, gave them quickie baths, read them their stories in double-time, and turned out their lights. She took a shower, applied a light veil of Chloe Silk all over her body and stepped into a harem style negligee as the doorbell rang.

"Who's that, Mommy? Is Daddy home?" Little BD called.

"No, Daddy's not home. Mommy has company. Go to sleep."

"Who is your company, mommy?" BD yelled again.

"It's not anyone you know. Now go to sleep and don't come downstairs. Be a good boy, BD, and Daddy will bring you a surprise when he comes home," Darling hastily called as she flounced down the stairs.

"What will he bring me?"

"BD, stop yelling! You're going to wake up your sister. Go to sleep."

"He won't wake me up. I'm still awake. Who's coming, mommy?" came from Ann Lisa's room.

"Hush, both of you! Go to sleep."

Darling pulled the front door open and said softly, "Hello, Travis. I'm so glad you were able to come."

"Me too," Travis said as he gazed upon Darling in her harem outfit. A superior man would have turned around and left right then. Better yet, a superior man would not have come in the first place, but Travis was there and after seeing Darling he wasn't about to leave. Darling's home had such familiar fragrance. It was almost like being in his shop. There were literally flowers everywhere.

The children didn't come down. Travis and Darling had several drinks. Darling didn't offer any hors d'oeuvres. Both grew a little tipsy and the evening ended in Darling's bedroom. Their affair had begun.

Darling and Travis became besotted with each other and made love whenever and wherever they could. Often, they resorted to the large cooler in the florist shop. Soon so many of the employees had been elevated to manager positions that there were hardly any employees left to go out and plant shrubs for customers. Their promotions had nothing to do with the abilities, but rather coincided with whether they happened to need something from the cooler when Travis and Darling were heating up the refrigeration unit. All of Travis' employees were aware of what was going on and they didn't hesitate to pass the gossip around.

About a year after their torrid affair began, Darling found herself pregnant. She still slept with BD occasionally, but she really couldn't remember the last time they had sex. Frequency didn't necessarily have anything to do with her memory. Darling felt that sex with BD was so boring she could hardly recall it the day after anyway. She thought it would be wonderful and so romantic to have her lover's baby and BD was so busy and so consumed by his law practice, she was sure he wouldn't be suspicious.

Estelle, Travis' wife, mother of three teenagers who was sure her childbearing days were over, also found herself pregnant within days of Darling's news. Travis obviously wasn't shooting blanks. The baby boys were born within weeks of each other and to this day could pass for nearly identical twins. Everyone in Spencer comments on their likeness. Ridiculously enough, the two young men are friends, and if they have noticed their resemblance have not commented on it—at least not in public.

BD and Darling are much sought after socially as are Travis and Estelle to a lesser degree. The couples often vacation together. It seems that BD and Estelle are none the wiser about what's going on while everyone else in Spencer is in the know. Bets are sometimes placed on whether Darling and Travis will "disappear" for awhile at approximately the same time, how long they will be gone, how near in time the two will appear again, etc.

The longest they were gone at the same time was at a beach party at Candy Martin's home when both ostensibly left the throng to use the surrounding woods as emergency facilities. It would seem they would have gone into Candy's house, only two hundred feet away to relieve themselves, however such was not the case. Both of them, apparently, became disoriented and couldn't find their way back to the noise and revelry for almost an hour.

Darling's fling with Travis didn't deter her from being one of the social leaders in Spencer. She was very active politically and with the arts and she was fervent campaigner against smoking. Although she and Lydia Henley were acquaintances and Lydia rarely smoked in her presence, whenever Darling had the opportunity, she would tell Lydia that she could smell cigarette smoke the moment Lydia walked into a room. Darling would then further elaborate on how Lydia's designer clothing was being ruined by cigarette smoke and that she really didn't see why Lydia spent all that money at the hairdresser's when the odor of the smoke permeated her coif. Lydia always smiled and looked pointedly at Darling's voluptuous hips when she said, "Well, Darling, we all have our vices, don't we?"

That would usually shut Darling up because she was never sure if Lydia might know something about her on-going affair and the paternity of her second son.

At a garden club meeting a few weeks after Bonita was settled in her lakeside home, Lydia and Darling were seated next to each other. Lydia raved about Bonita Roberts whom she'd met at the Peabody and who was now a resident of Spencer. Darling agreed to have Bonita to tea.

"She doesn't smoke, does she?" Darling asked Lydia.

"No, dear. She's a non-smoker, like you."

"Good. Then I'll definitely invite her for tea. I'll call her this afternoon as soon as I get home."

"You'll love her," Lydia said with a smile.

Darling would see about that. She actually cared for women very little, but she was anxious to meet this Bonita person who apparently was taking Spencer by storm.

12

Isaac Kahn

He was originally from Yemen and was Jewish. Born into a poor family, he had escaped from his homeland and family at an early age and hired on to a freighter. He eventually made his way to America, land of opportunity. A young man adept with his hands, Isaac had landed a job in California working for a construction firm. By the time he was thirty, he owned the company and set about performing huge condominium conversions all over Southern California. He made a fortune.

He married a nice Jewish American Princess and they had four children while he continued to stockpile money. A bright young man, he was slick in his business operations. Each time, he purchased an apartment building or hotel he set up a new corporation for its condominium conversion. Then he made the building cosmetically beautiful by painting all of them pale blue with navy trim—his trademark colors. The lobbies of the buildings were all fabulous with lots of marble, gold, chandeliers, and winding staircases. He patched up any plumbing or air conditioning problems, carpeted the hallways, made the swimming pool and health club areas first class and then he hired an army of sales agents to blow out the unimproved condo units at top prices.

He also conveniently owned an in-house construction company to perform the necessary renovations on the condos for the new owners. The condo board was developer controlled until enough buyers owned space. Then he would appoint one owner to the board who essentially had no voice, but it made the other owners happy. Reserves were put aside for a new roof, air-conditioning system and repairs. When a building was ninety per cent sold, he turned the whole operation over to the owners and left a skeleton crew there to sell the remainder of the units. The corporation folded so it had no assets and therefore had no money if and when the condo owners later decided to sue.

By that time, he had moved on to another building where he'd start a new corporation. Eventually, the California Condominium Board caught on to what Isaac Kahn was up to and pulled all of his licenses. This forced him to move out of the state and to pursue his condo conversions elsewhere. He chose Nashville.

Once in Nashville, Isaac purchased his first building and started his operation all over again, but smooth operator that he was, he was unable to save his marriage to Hava and his children elected to stay with their mother in California. He built a two-story penthouse for himself atop his first purchase in Nashville and determined to live it up. Who needed that old broad he had married? Isaac, from then on, always had a young chick on his arm and some of them could have definitely been his ticket to jail so young were they. He made millions again with his scheme and at the age of forty-five, decided to take life easy.

Isaac retired from his condominium conversions. He continued in another line of work in which he had made his first fortune, but then Isaac realized he had more money than he could ever spend and decided to go almost completely legit. He kept his hand in one extremely lucrative enterprise, but at arm's length.

One of his fondest desires was to be accepted by society and to hob-knob with the true blue bloods, the aristocracy of the Old South. It would be the crowning glory to his life for a small-town Yemen boy who had literally pulled himself up by his bootstraps while walking on the wild side in his business dealings.

He changed his name to Isaac Kahn, spent a small fortune on reconstructive maxiofacial surgery and five years before Bonita's arrival in Spencer, purchased the last available piece of land on the lake and constructed his fifteen-thousand-square-foot-Greek-Revival-mansion.

Isaac had never fit in with the social set in Spencer. He was regarded with suspicion. He looked Jewish and because his given and last names certainly sounded Jewish, the Southern society folk steered clear of him as there remain pockets of anti-Semitism in the South even today. He also chose to live quietly, but always seemed to generate gossip about all of the young people, both male and female, who were guests at his home.

He could be seen on any given day squiring young people to restaurants and clubs in town. And often, the townspeople would notice big vans heading through his wrought iron gates. They also noticed a number of strangers in Spencer. Whenever anyone asked about the identity of the strangers, one of the locals was sure to respond that they were guests of Mr. Kahn's.

Isaac had spent most of his time moving and shaking to make the big bucks. Now that he wanted legitimacy in Spencer, he wasn't exactly ostracized but he was rarely invited to anyone's home unless it was for a charity function where a large donation secured an invitation. Oh, he was always included on the charity ball invitation lists and any functions at the Spencer Country Club, which he had joined, but privately no one included him. More than anything, the poor little boy from Yemen wanted to be socially accepted.

When searching for some particular objects d'art for his home, Isaac was referred by an antique dealer to Precious. He called her immediately. Fortuitously, Precious was at home that afternoon. After discussing Isaac's ideas and plans for his home and learning what he desired, she was able to locate a gigantic gold leaf elephant that Mr. Kahn wanted for his bar.

Next, Precious searched the entire East Coast until she located a fabric Isaac approved. He wanted voluminous yards of the fabric to tent his great room to simulate a nomadic desert tent of the upper class Yemen Bedouins. Lastly, Precious unearthed authentic antique paneling from a razed Episcopal Cathedral in England for the walls of Isaac's elevator to his private suite. Precious was at Isaac's estate "Les Enfants," a little word-play on his part, two and three times a week helping him make selections and assisting him in finding hard-to-locate items.

At first, their relationship was entirely professional. However, once when Precious was doing some work in the library, she came upon a book filled with graphic pictures of young boys in all sorts of sexual positions. She commented to Isaac about the book later and he said it was the equivalent of the Kama Sutra for pedophiles. To allay any concerns she might have, he told her it was an extremely rare volume and worth a great deal of money. He explained to her that he was an eclectic collector and possessed numerous rare items of many types and art forms.

Precious accepted the explanation, although she was absolutely intrigued by the tome, given her interest in young boys. Over ensuing weeks as she rambled about the mansion, often alone, she found more books and a collection of video tapes with erotic titles that made her think there was more to Mr. Isaac Kahn than he wanted her to know.

Several evenings, Precious was still at Les Enfants when cocktail hour approached. On one occasion, followed by numerous others, Isaac asked her to have a drink with him. Precious agreed and soon they became friends of a sort.

Isaac told her about his failed marriage, how he missed his children, and the feeling he had that there was a touch of anti-Semitism in Spencer. Aafter many cocktail chats, Isaac confessed that he longed to enter the inner circle of Spencer society, but had no idea how to go about it. Precious didn't offer any advice at the time, but she kept his desire at the back of her mind. One never knew when one might wish to grant a favor to get something in return.

Little did Precious realize how very involved she was to become with Isaac Kahn. He was the most successful producer and distributor of child pornography east of the Mississippi.

13

Bonita's Social Secretary—Raven

Bonita was becoming so busy with her many social functions. After visiting or receiving any type of gift or foodstuff, she always sent a note on her monogrammed vellum stationery. Lists of menus served at each of her social functions at Villagio had to be recorded just as the outfits she wore to each and every event were catalogued. Another list was necessary to keep track of the jewelry she had worn where and when.

Additionally, there were the guest lists—those she wished to invite to future functions, and a list of those who had entertained her and to whom she needed to reciprocate. With all of this information needed on hand and readily accessible at any given moment, Bonita decided she needed someone to help her with it. A social secretary could assist her with her correspondence and keep her apprised of her daily schedule because there was quite a bit more societal activity here than in Montiac.

Bonita placed an ad in *The Spectator* for a pleasant, amiable secretary with computer skills. Duties would include screening phone calls, handling note writing, keeping her calendar, contacting caterers and florists, and arranging her two yearly trips to New York where she visited the designer houses to select her season's wardrobe.

Raven was born in Spencer and had lived there all her life. A beautiful creature, she was blessed with midnight black hair that hung in ringlets. Her green eyes were dramatically offset by a deep olive complexion and full, pouty lips. She had been educated in the finest schools in the South due to her father's largess and had only recently returned to Spencer after obtaining her undergraduate degree.

Raven was quite close to her mother after having been extremely wild and unmanageable during her teenage years. She and her father, however, had never formed any type of bond. They appeared to regard each other as two strangers who happened to occupy the same house.

Raven had never known either set of her grandparents. She knew her mother was originally from South Carolina, but her mother never discussed her family. When Raven was young and other children had spoken of going to *Nana's* in the summer or for holidays, she had questioned her mother about her grandparents.

Her mother simply said that she and Raven's father were estranged from their families. When Raven asked what *estranged* meant, her mother responded that she would understand when she was older. Well, Raven was older now, but she didn't understand anymore about the situation than she did as a child and her mother still would not discuss the subject with her.

Raven thought her mother seemed sad and faraway, but she was a good mother and she idolized her only child. She was still quite beautiful. Often they were mistaken for friends, but never for mother and daughter, nor were they ever mistaken for sisters for they looked nothing alike except for their eyes. Raven's mother had blonde hair and was fairly complected as was her father.

Raven often wondered as she grew into womanhood if she were adopted. Once when going through an old roll top desk in the attic, she had come across a book of documents and had seen her birth certificate. She had indeed been born to her mother, however her father's name did not appear on the birth certificate, but Raven was too young at the time to think anything of that fact.

Raven and her family did not live on the lake, but shared a large and comfortable home in town where Raven's mother busied herself with her mammoth rose garden, volunteer work at the hospital, her book club, and duplicate bridge games several times a week. Monday through Friday, Raven's father went to his office from which he administered the business of his five department stores all located in Southern states.

During Raven's teenage years, she had fallen in with a group of local girls who were party girls. They drank, experimented with drugs and shared their sexual favors eagerly and randomly. Nothing Raven's parents tried stopped her outrageous behavior. They sent her away to boarding school, but as soon as she came home she hooked up with the wild ones again and started acting erratically.

Raven became addicted to Ecstasy to the point where her generous allowance could no longer cover her habit. She began asking those whom she graced with her sexual favors for money, but that too soon proved deficient for the increasing amount of the drug she craved.

Eventually, two of her wayward friends convinced her the three of them should take off for Miami Beach to explore the lifestyle of South Beach, Mecca for sexual freedom, wild parties, obscene behavior, and every illegal drug known to man. Raven stole five-hundred-dollars from her mother's purse and she and her friends took off on their great adventure.

Within days of arriving in *paradise on earth*, Raven's money was gone. While sitting at a bus stop in tears, she was approached by an attractive older woman who asked her if she had ever considered modeling. The bench Raven had selected was on Eighth Street beside the News Café, located in the modeling district of South Beach, the place where all the beautiful people congregate. Raven replied that she hadn't.

The woman said she had a beautiful face and figure and she would like to take her to meet Mr. Perl. She further said Raven could be making big money within a few days. The naïve girl agreed and went with the stranger without advising her low-life friends of her whereabouts. She was taken to a penthouse apartment on Millionaire's Row, a section of Collins Avenue between the Fontainebleau Hotel and the upper sixties. There Raven met Ike Perl who poured her coffee while they chatted.

Raven didn't remember anything of the conversation when she awakened to see a large clock on the wall opposite her. The last thing she remembered was meeting Ike. That was over ten hours ago. She must have slept all that time.

Glancing around, she saw that she was in a luxurious contemporary bedroom. Gradually, she focused on the fact that her hands and feet were tied to the head and foot of the king-size bed. She attempted to free her hands, but was tied too tightly, so she began to scream. Almost immediately, there was a buzzing sound in her room and the door to her *prison* slid open. Ike entered and came to her bedside.

"Hello, Raven. Did you have a nice nap?" he asked.

"Why am I tied up? What are you doing to me? Let me go!" Raven screamed hysterically.

"Not so fast. Let's talk first. In our earlier conversation, you told me that you were interested in coming to work for me. Don't you remember?"

"No, but whether I said I was interested or not, I didn't agree to be tied up."

What Raven failed to understand was that she had already completed her first assignment for Ike. His modus operandi was to send his scout, the attractive woman who approached Raven, to lure young girls to his penthouse. Once a girl was brought in, he conducted the interview while serving the victim coffee laced with sodium penothol. Under the influence of the drug, any girl would continue to respond and seemingly act normal, but would have no memory of what had occurred while she was under the influence of the powerful drug.

After a few short moments, Ike would escort the young lady to one of his six bedrooms, all equipped with electric doors that locked from the outside when closed and opened only from a control panel in his palatial bedroom/office. Cameras were strategically and permanently mounted and a camera crew was in readiness.

The young male actors in Ike's employ would then enter and engage in all types of sexual acts with the young lady whose inhibitions were in limbo because of the ample amount of the drug imbibed with her coffee. Raven had not been sleeping for ten hours. She had been the featured ingénue in a porno film.

Ike untied Raven, who immediately bolted for the sliding door that had automatically closed when Ike entered the room. It could only be opened now with the remote control concealed safely in Ike's right trousers' pocket.

"Raven, come sit here on the bed next to me. I have something to show you," Ike said in a seductive tone.

"No! You let me out of here. My father is a very important man in Tennessee. My parents will be looking for me. I'll have you arrested," Raven spat.

"Perhaps, but first I have something to show you," he said calmly.

When Raven refused to sit, Ike reached for the TV remote on the bedside table and engaged the VCR. Music swelled and a group sex film began. Raven turned her back to the set. Ike told her she should take a look.

"I don't want to look at porno films with you, you perverted old creep!"

"Oh, this isn't just any old porno film. It stars my latest find. My newest *model*," Ike purred.

Raven turned, glanced at the television, and almost passed out. On the screen in full living color, she was tied to the bed in the room where she now stood. A man was on top of her and another was over her with his penis in her mouth. Raven started gagging and threw up all over Ike's two-hundred-dollar-a-square-foot Berber carpet. Ike, unperturbed, continued to sit on the bed watching the film.

When Raven seemed to be in control, Ike said, "Do you think your parents would like a copy of this film, Raven? If you give me their address, I'll be happy to send them one."

"No! Please don't send that to my parents," she whimpered.

"I thought not. Now, in our earlier conversation, you confided in me that you were partial to a particular drug. Ecstasy, I believe. Is that right?"

"I've tried it."

"Oh, I think you've done much more than try it, Raven. You see, the drug in your coffee is a truth serum. Sodium penothol. Have you ever heard of it? I know all about your love of Ecstasy and why you're down here and how you've sold your body to get more of the drug. I want to make you happy. There will be all the Ecstasy you want and need at your disposal. Right now, I want you to get some rest because tomorrow, Chana will take you shopping. Your personal bathroom complete with Jacuzzi and hot tub is right through there. After you've had your bath, leave the clothes you have on at the door. Chana will bring you some beautiful nightgowns. You're going to be leading a life of luxury from now on, Raven. So relax, enjoy, savor Miami Beach." With that, Ike rose, walked to the sliding door, hit the remote and exited the room. Raven raced for the opening, but the heavy door was too quick for her. It slid shut in her face.

Raven didn't know what to do. Her hands were tied more literally than when she had been bound to the bed. She could never allow her parents to see that horrible film—they wouldn't be able to bear it.

Resolutely, she entered the opulent master bath and proceeded to bathe and wash her hair. She was exhausted. She'd sleep and tomorrow, she would try to figure a way to extricate herself from this nightmare. As Raven sponged her body and washed her glorious hair, the hidden cameras installed in each of the penthouse's bathrooms silently rolled and filmed her every move.

Raven toweled off and returned to the bedroom. Four magnificent nightgowns were displayed on the bed. On the bedside table, there was a bottle of frigid designer water, a Waterford crystal glass, a bowl of fruit, a platter of finger sandwiches and enough Ecstasy to keep the inhabitants of a small town high for a month.

Raven remained a guest/employee of Ike's for six months. That was the usual length of time he kept young ladies in his *employ.* During that time, Raven was treated to the finest and most expensive designer clothes Miami Beach had to offer. She was wined and dined by Ike and sported on his arm, but he never so much as touched her in anyway other than to offer his arm to escort her. She was high almost all of the time as Ike made sure to keep her more than adequately supplied with drugs.

Raven's parents had no idea where she was. They had filed a missing person's report with the police. There was an all points bulletin out for her. Her two trashy friends had returned to Spencer many months before and had come clean with their parents, but they told Raven's parents and the police repeatedly that they had no idea where Raven had gone. They said all of them were going to the News Café to attempt to get someone to buy them something to eat since their money had run out. While they were dressing in their cheesy motel room they couldn't afford another night, Raven had said she was ready and that she would meet them at the café. When they arrived, Raven was nowhere in sight and they didn't see her or hear from her again.

The police scoured Miami Beach, but no one knew Raven nor recognized her from the picture they showed. Raven was a blonde now. Chana had called in hairdressers Raven's second day at the penthouse and they had cut, bleached, and styled her hair. Raven also was never in South Beach as Ike had her safely hidden away on Millionaire's Row and when she went out with him, it was always to private parties in penthouses or at private clubs. Gofers brought the designer clothes for Raven to select under Chana's watchful eye. Raven was never allowed to go out alone. There was no phone in her room. In fact, she was not allowed out of her room alone. Chana, Ike, or one of Ike's flunkies accompanied her.

At the end of six months, Ike tired of Raven, as he did of all *his girls*. Besides, she had been captured on film in every position and sexual situation imaginable and he was ready for new blood.

One morning just as Raven awakened, she heard the buzzing of the sliding door. She looked up and saw Ike.

"Good morning, Raven."

"Hello."

"Are you homesick?" Ike asked her gently.

"Of course. I've told you everyday since I was brought here that I want to go home."

"Are your parents going to supply you with your drugs?"

"No. I want to stop taking them. I can do that."

Ike chuckled, "Oh, just like that?"

"Yes, just like that," Raven proclaimed.

"Well, good, because today you can go home if you wish," Ike said as he placed a brown paper sack on the bed.

"I can? Just like that I can go home?" Raven asked.

"Just like that."

"I don't understand," Raven said completely baffled.

"I've made forty-six movies of you, Raven. They're in distribution all over the United States. I don't need you anymore. I do wish to warn you, though, that if you tell anyone where you have been or incriminate me in any way, I will have you terminated. You know what that means, don't you?"

She nodded.

"You are not to take anything with you that I bought, not even one lacy bra or one pair of thong panties. Here are the clothes you wore here. Get dressed. Chana will come for you shortly."

"What about my pay? You said you were employing me."

"Your pay? Your pay was all the clothes I lent you, over seventy-five thousand dollars in Ecstasy, the meals I provided for you, and the money I spent on your hair. Your biggest paycheck is what I'm giving you today, Raven. I'm giving you your life. Your parents have never been able to find you. You could be out in the ocean feeding the sharks, you know? That's your pay. Now, be a good girl and get dressed," and with that, he left.

Raven opened the bag and put on her clothes. Chana buzzed the door open and came in. She and Raven went outside to the waiting limousine and were driven to Eighth Street in South Beach where Raven was let out of the car in front of the bench where she had first met Chana. She had no money and no clue what to do. She was sure of only one thing at that moment. She could never tell anyone about Ike. If she did, he would have her killed.

She walked to the pay phone in the News Café and placed a collect call to her mother. Two hours later, she walked to the Western Union office to sign for the money wired to her by her parents. She caught the shuttle to Miami International Airport and flew to Nashville. Her relieved and jubilant parents greeted her!

Raven explained to them that she could tell them nothing or it would put her life in danger. While her parents wanted to know exactly where she had been and what she had been doing, they finally laid the matter to rest as Raven became more and more upset when they questioned her. Her panic and anxiety bordered on terror. The police were another matter. They questioned Raven for hours on end until her father intervened and said that Raven was home and that's all that mattered. He told them to close the investigation. She had been a missing person and now she'd been found. Case closed.

Raven's two friends who had accompanied her to Miami Beach contacted her to ask where she had been, but she wouldn't tell them anything either. She also told them that she no longer wished to see them or party with them. Raven came clean with her parents about only one thing—her drug use. They arranged for her to be admitted to a very expensive and very discreet rehab center where she spent several painful months kicking her habit.

When Raven recovered, more than a year had passed since she had begun her great adventure by running off to Miami Beach. She left for her freshman year in college where she majored in art history. A model student and a model daughter for the next four years, Raven graduated and returned to Spencer for the summer before pursuing a position in New York City in September.

The first day of her second week at home, Raven awakened and realized she was going to have to do something to stem the boredom. One could lie at the club pool, play tennis, and eat light novelle cuisine luncheons only so often. She couldn't stomach the thought of wasting the entire summer in those pursuits.

After rising and showering, she stood in front of the bathroom mirror as she toweled her curls. Once she had dried her hair sufficiently for it to finish air-drying and fall in natural ringlets, she stared into the mirror for perhaps the ten thousandth time. *Where did I come from? I don't look anything like either of my parents. My coloring isn't even the same as theirs.*

Raven no longer questioned her mother about her concern, for she had come to realize when she asked her mother anything relating to their dissimilarity to each other or about her family, her mother became visibly upset. Raven tossed her head and decided not to think about it anymore for now. She quickly got dressed and ran down the stairs toward the kitchen.

No one was around, so she poured herself a cup of coffee and picked up *The Spectator* and turned to the classified section. Bonita's advertisement caught her attention.

Her mother came through the back door with a basket laden with exquisite roses from her garden.

"Good morning, dear. Did you sleep well?"

"Yes, thank you."

"What are you going to do today? Going to the club? Have a tennis match scheduled?"

"I don't think so. I've decided I don't want to spend the entire summer relaxing. I'll go crazy. I was looking at the classified ads. Listen to this," Raven said and read the advertisement aloud. "I think that's something I would like to do for the summer. I've heard about Mrs. Roberts. It would be fun to be at her huge mansion taking care of her correspondence and appointments. I think I'll apply," Raven said.

"If you wish. It would give you some money of your own. It's only part-time, you'd still have time to enjoy yourself."

"I'll call right away," Raven said as she sprang from her chair and headed for the phone.

"Hello. Roberts' residence," Hannah said as she answered the phone in the kitchen of Villagio.

"Hello. My name is Raven Keyes and I'm calling in response to Mrs. Roberts' ad for a social secretary."

"Jest a minute. I'll fetch Miz Roberts."

"Hello, Miss Keyes? This is Bonita Roberts."

"Mrs. Roberts, I've just read your advertisement and I'd like to make an appointment to come and apply if you haven't already filled the position."

"Wonderful. How's tomorrow afternoon at two o'clock?" Bonita asked.

"That will be fine. I'll see you then," Raven answered.

"Do you need directions?"

"Oh, no ma'am. I know where you live. I'll see you at two. Thank you."

"I'm looking forward to meeting you."

"I'll look forward to meeting you also, Mrs. Roberts."

"Tomorrow then, Miss Keyes. Good-bye," Bonita said as she replaced the receiver in its cradle.

She liked the sound of Raven's voice and was delighted the young woman knew where she lived. Apparently her plan was working. Soon everyone in Spencer would know just who she was and where she lived.

14

Desiree Compton

Desiree reached for her tenth cigarette of the day although it was only nine o'clock in the morning. She pushed the button on her nightstand next to her massive bed to signal her maid Maggie to bring more coffee. She had been extremely busy since she awakened at five o'clock. She had made lists, looked up phone numbers in her Rolodex and prepared the speech she was going to make to each of those on her list when she began to ring them up shortly after ten o'clock. There was an election coming up for a new judgeship and Desiree wanted to make sure her candidate won.

Maggie, blacker than a thousand midnights in a cypress swamp and almost wider than the doorway, entered Desiree's room with a silver coffee pot. She poured Desiree her sixth cup of the morning and placed the pot next to the overflowing ashtray.

"I'll just empty that ashtray for you, Mrs. Compton."

"Thank you, Maggie."

"Are you ready for your bath? If you are, I'll draw your water and help you in now."

"No, I'll bathe this afternoon. I have phone calls to make this morning," Desiree responded.

"Would it be all right if I order the groceries to be delivered before you get started, ma'am? If you could make a list of what you want, I'll place the order and be off the phone shortly."

"Certainly. Let's see. What shall we eat this week? I tell you what, Maggie. I don't really feel like concentrating on a grocery list now. You make it out and order it to be delivered. Just make sure you get smoked salmon, escargot, and caviar. How is the champagne supply? You'll have to order those things and the champagne, if we need it, from *our* little specialty shop. So, run along and make those two calls. I have tons of work to do."

"Mrs. Compton, you know the doctor doesn't want you eating those rich foods and the last time he came he told you absolutely no more champagne. You're not supposed to be smoking those cigarettes either. You have emphysema and gout. The smoking is bad for the first and the rich food is bad for the second. You aren't going to get better if you don't change your lifestyle," Maggie said with authority.

"Maggie, I've had emphysema and gout for years and cigarettes and diet don't make either of them worse. Now run on and place those orders. I need to get on that phone," Desiree said with equal authority assisted by the fact that she wrote Maggie's weekly paycheck and it was a handsome one.

"Yes ma'am," Maggie said meekly as she left the room.

Desiree Compton, attired in a black lace peignoir, reached over to a tray on her bed for her brush and mirror. She set the mirror on its legs and brushed her long salt and pepper hair. Then she applied her favorite "Fire and Ice" Revlon lipstick, a little foundation and a fine dusting of translucent powder. Although she was nearing seventy, she was quite a handsome woman. Even though those receiving her phone calls would not be able to see her, Desiree liked to look her best when she spoke to those on her list about one of her projects. She felt that if one looked good, one projected one's attitudes, wishes, demands, and collections of paybacks in a better light.

She had not been downstairs in her enormous house or out of her bedroom for ten years except to enter her large bathroom on Maggie's arm. For all intents and purposes, Desiree was an invalid. The slightest exertion caused her to have severe shortness of breath eventually bringing on an attack similar to those suffered by asthma patients. Since she had foreseen her fate as her emphysema worsened in her fifties, Desiree, an architect by trade, had designed and built her home while she was still mobile, but with her growing fragility in mind.

Her large home on the lake was Gothic in design on the exterior, but the inside was completely modern with spacious airy rooms. The main level consisted of an expansive great room with an open floor to ceiling fireplace. A sunroom, windowed on three sides, was on the other side of the gray stone fireplace with a beautifully appointed and fully equipped kitchen adjacent to it. There was also a game room plus three bedrooms, each with its own bath, and a library fully stocked with rare volumes and all the latest best sellers. The second floor, accessible from the first by not only a grand staircase, but also by an elevator large enough to hold six people at a time, consisted entirely of Desiree's suite. It included a sitting room, her boudoir, and an almost gymnasium-sized bathroom with Jacuzzi, a round glass enclosed shower stall with seating inside, a colossal closet with built-in drawers, shoe racks, sweater cubbies, and mirrored doors inside and out.

If one were to wonder why someone who knew she was going to eventually become bedridden would design such a home, that person didn't know Desiree. She loved her privacy, and she wanted seclusion on the upper level. However, she also loved to entertain and her illness had not stopped her from doing so. Almost every Sunday, she held a *salon*, she called the gathering, which actually was an open house where her guests had full use of all of the facilities the downstairs had to offer. Between the hours of two and four o'clock in the afternoon, guests were brought up in twos and threes to Desiree's suite where she held court, however invited guests were summoned at ten o'clock in the morning and were expected to stay until eight in the evening. They could peruse the library, swim in the Olympic-sized pool in the summer, shoot skeet on her shooting range, play croquet, practice their short strokes on her putting green, roam her magnificent English gardens or try their hands at billiards or table tennis in the game room.

A lavish spread of heavy hors d'oeuvres was always on hand as was the finest champagne available. Mixed drinks were served too plus a delectable buffet dinner was laid out at precisely six o'clock every Sunday evening that she entertained.

Desiree's two favorites that she insisted be served every week were caviar pie and ahi tuna.

CAVIAR PIE

Make egg salad with chopped, hard-boiled eggs and celery bits, mustard and mayonnaise. Make sure the egg salad is firm. Mold into a ball. "Ice" egg salad with softened cream cheese. Make indentation in top of cream cheese and spoon in one small jar of black, red, or gold caviar. Serve with Carr's Water Crackers.

AHI TUNA

Brush fresh, pink tuna steaks with butter and press sesame seeds into flesh of fish on both sides. Place in very hot frying pan and sear on both sides. Remove from pan and slice thinly. Serve with pickled ginger, wasabi sauce, thinly sliced red onions, light soy sauce, and toast points.

Desiree did not use her *salons* to discuss any of her pet projects, but rather like the great society ladies of the late nineteenth and early twentieth century Europe, she preferred to discuss the arts and literature with her guests. She carefully selected those whom she invited and it was considered a great privilege to receive one of her invitations. Of course, there were regulars who came every Sunday unless they were ill or out of town. Those included Harcourt Ball and his mother, Candy Martin, and Precious.

Occasionally, Desiree condescended to invite Rhetta Robin Ricks, but the woman tired her so with her constant yammering and overwhelming desire to be liked. She was valuable to Desiree at times, because Rhetta Robin went to everything and knew everyone and could often persuade people to Desiree's way of thinking when Desiree was desperate enough to call on her to do so. Desiree was sure Rhetta Robin got people to agree with her simply to shut her up.

Desiree was originally from upstate New York and was from a modestly well-to-do family. A graduate of Sarah Lawrence, she had gone on to obtain a master's degree in architecture and had started her own firm in New York City at the age of twenty-six with a little help from her father's wallet. Her business success was almost instant as was her love life. A beautiful young woman, Desiree was courted by the most eligible and most wanted bachelors of the New York Four Hundred Blue Book Families.

Her first marriage was to one of the lesser-known Rockefellers, though lesser known, his financial situation was right up there with John D. and Nelson's. They were married for three years, and Desiree continued to conduct her business. They divorced citing irreconcilable differences. Desiree filed and was the recipient of a large settlement.

Six months later, she married another scion of a wealthy New York family, Martin Fleishman, a Jewish attorney, and they moved into The Plaza to live in his fifteen-room apartment. It was later purchased by Jacqueline Kennedy Onassis. That union lasted a mere nine months and once again, Desiree walked away with a huge sum of money and most of the new furnishings and artwork she had purchased when she remodeled all fifteen rooms.

Husband number three was Ansley Compton. She truly loved him and they were together five years during which time Desiree bore a daughter, Monique. Divorce soon followed after the birth of the child and Desiree received not only her customary mammoth settlement, but also alimony to the tune of ten-thousand-dollars a month and child support for Monique.

Two more husbands followed, but during her marriage to the fifth, Ansley Compton, who had not remarried and who had continued to be a part of

Desiree's life since he was the father of her child, passed away unexpectedly. Once Desiree had tired of the marriage game, she went to court and legally changed her name to Compton, thus keeping the name of the only man she had loved and sharing her daughter's surname.

Monique was everything Desiree could have desired in a daughter. She was devoted to her mother in addition to being a beauty, intelligent, athletic, compassionate, caring, and neat. She had never given Desiree one moment's trouble. The mother worshipped the child and if she could have had any wish at this stage of her life, it would have been to spend more time with her daughter. Monique met a Spanish count studying at Harvard while she was attending Radcliff and they had married two days after graduation. Since then, Monique had lived in Malaga, Spain.

When Desiree had been in good health, she had traveled to see her daughter several times a year, had helped renovate the Italian Renaissance mansion Monique and her husband Manuel occupied, and had played nursemaid to Monique after the birth of each of Desiree's three grandchildren. Now, bedridden, she was unable to go to Spain and Monique only came to see Desiree once a year. When she came, she stayed for two weeks and Desiree looked forward to her visit the other fifty.

She was very proud of Monique. The young woman was the epitome of motherhood, a perfect wife, and best of all a countess. Desiree got a lot of mileage out of that fact and always referred to her daughter as "The Countess" when speaking to others. She was also not above mentioning her visits to the palace of the King and Queen of Spain with Manuel and Monique when the occasion called for it. Sometimes, Desiree neglected to mention that she had been in her daughter and son-in-law's company when visiting the royals and referred to King Juan Carlos and Queen Sophia as simply *John and Sophie.*

Maggie came into Desiree's room and announced she had placed the orders and was no longer in need of the telephone. She had often asked her employer to put in another line because money was certainly no object, but Desiree maintained it was an unnecessary expense. Desiree thanked Maggie for letting her know the phone was free.

"Do you need anything, Mrs. Compton, before I start preparing your luncheon?"

"Perhaps a pitcher of iced water. I get so parched when I have so many calls to make."

"I'll bring it right up," replied Maggie, as she removed the coffeepot and once again took Desiree's ashtray and emptied it.

Desiree reached for her jeweled cigarette holder. She didn't use it when she smoked, but found that it was absolutely the best possible tool for tapping numbers on a touch-tone phone. She called the first number on her list.

"Mrs. Mapleton? This is Desiree Compton. How are you this morning? I'm calling to ask you to vote for a young attorney, who's relatively new to our area. He's running for a judgeship and I want to tell you all about him. He went to the University of Virginia and was the Editor of the Law Review there. He's from a fine, old Richmond family. He married well, has two children, and served as a clerk to Chief Justice Smedes. Prior to moving to Spencer, he was in private practice in Virginia and never once lost a case. He is fair, unopinionated, and I think he'll be a marvelous judge. We simply don't want that old fool Judge Rourke on the bench anymore. He's a corrupt old curmudgeon and he's letting all the drug dealers off with suspended sentences and even let that woman who embezzled money from the Spencer Union and Trust off last month. The best thing about my man, Royce Flanders, is that he's one of us. You know what I mean?" Desiree said all in one gush.

Mrs. Mapleton had never attended one of Desiree's *salons* and never would because she would never receive an invitation, but she was definitely a social climber and current President of the Spencer Garden Club. Desiree knew the woman would give anything to be included in her circle of friends, therefore she felt that the "He's one of us" was inspired and would make Mrs. Mapleton feel that she was a part of Desiree's world.

"He sounds like a fine candidate, Mrs. Compton, and I know what you mean about Judge Rourke. Maybe he's getting senile, huh? He certainly has made a lot of bad decisions lately. I'll be happy to vote for your Mr. Flanders and I'll pass your advice along to all of my friends. Will you be entertaining in your lovely home this Sunday?"

"Yes, I will, Mrs. Mapleton, and I do so want to have you come to one of my little Sunday gatherings. My social secretary has informed me that the lists are all made up for the next few months and the invitations have been sent, but I'll certainly have your name added to the list. Also, I may be having a little get together for Mr. Flanders and I sincerely hope that you will attend," Desiree replied.

"Oh, I'd love to, Mrs. Compton. Thank you so much for calling and you let me know when you'll be throwing that party for Mr. Flanders, you hear?"

"Definitely. Thank you so much, Mrs. Mapleton. You'll be hearing from me soon."

"I can't wait. You have a nice day now. I've written everything down you said about Mr. Flanders and I'll start my calls right now," Mrs. Mapleton simpered. The woman was so ingratiating. She reminded Desiree of a frightened, subservient dog lying on its back exposing its genitalia to a larger, more vicious canine.

"You do that. C'iao," Desiree cooed. The locals loved it when she threw in some foreign phrases.

Mrs. Mapleton would receive an invitation to El Arquitecto, the Spanish word for architect and the name of Desiree's estate, for the little gathering for Mr. Flanders. It was to be a fundraiser, but Desiree would not be inviting anyone of so little consequence as Mrs. Mapleton to her suite during that evening.

Her calls continued for several hours all in the same vein to the minor movers and shakers of Spencer and the surrounding towns. Desiree always made the promise to have those she called to one of her Sunday salons, but she never followed up on it. The locals fell for her line time and time again. She batted almost a thousand in getting any candidate she backed elected. Desiree enjoyed being the power behind the thrones of those she helped get elected. She could call on them and get practically anything she wanted. And she didn't hesitate to use that power when she had a desire.

Hers was a very boring existence, but quite a disciplined and structured one. On Mondays, Wednesdays, and Fridays, the masseuse arrived promptly at eleven o'clock in the morning to give her a two-hour full body massage. Tuesdays, she spent two hours in her private tanning bed secluded behind huge white doors on one wall of her bedroom. Because Desiree never went outside, she kept her naturally olive complexion tanned so as not to appear sallow. Friday afternoons, her personal hairdresser came to wash, dry, and style her long hair. Until fairly recently, the stylist had also colored it at regular intervals, but the past winter Desiree had been quite ill with the flu for a month and had foregone her beauty appointments. When she recovered, she noticed that she had a totally white streak of hair in the front. She decided she rather liked the look with the remaining salt and pepper hair, so she had dispensed with having it dyed. Her long sculpted nails were manicured weekly by the beautician while she sat under her hooded dryer. Desiree refused to allow a blow dryer anywhere near her head.

She kept abreast of everything going on outside her walls and read four newspapers daily including The New York Times. She was an avid watcher of CNN and Fox News and often amused herself by gazing at the security camera monitors that covered an entire wall of her room.

Desiree had security cameras located in each room of her house. She could look at the monitors in her room at any given time and see what was going on in practically every nook and cranny of the house. She especially enjoyed spying on her guests during the Sunday salons.

Desiree had landscaped her grounds for that the time she would be a semi-invalid. From her balcony outside her bedroom, she could view the English gardens, the swimming pool, the putting green, and in the distance—the shooting range. What she could not view from her room, she inspected weekly on a video filmed by the gardener. It included all areas not visible from her balcony and was taped each Monday. Desiree insisted that the date and time be displayed during the entire taping so she could make sure she was seeing how everything actually looked on that particular day.

With all of her technological equipment, Desiree refused to have anything to do with a computer, although she had purchased one for Maggie's use. She had also paid for Maggie to take a computer course via her kitchen monitor. Desiree was aware that Maggie primarily used the electronic device for playing solitaire, hearts, and Scrabble. Sometimes, in the evenings Desiree switched on the monitor of the camera mounted in Maggie's room to see her playing Tetras on the Game Boy she had given her the past Christmas. Desiree couldn't imagine anyone being so fascinated playing games with one's self. Upon viewing Maggie doing so, she would occasionally murmur aloud, "Well, there's my maid playing with herself again."

After placing calls to over fifty strategic gadflies, Desiree rang the buzzer signaling Maggie to bring her lunch after which she would spend an hour in the Jacuzzi and then dress in another beautiful negligee for her afternoon tea, cocktails, and dinner. She had given away or placed all of her street clothes, cocktail attire, gowns, furs, evening coats, shoes, and handbags in upscale consignment shops years ago. Her entire wardrobe consisted of negligees, peignoirs, lounging pajamas, and silk robes. Her slippers, which she rarely put on her feet, were legion and she had them in every color, texture, and fabric to match her various at-home outfits.

Each morning or sometimes in the afternoon, when Desiree decided on her attire for the day, Maggie was instructed to place the matching slippers next to Desiree's bed. Because her bedroom was completely carpeted in a plush Oriental custom woven to fit the room with Oriental throw rugs in the bathroom, Desiree seldom felt the need to actually wear the slippers. They simply looked nice next to her bed should she have any unexpected guests.

Desiree turned her thoughts to her upcoming Sunday salon. She had heard about the newcomer to Spencer. Lydia Henley had paid a visit and filled her in on Bonita Roberts. Desiree added Bonita's name to her list and planned to issue her an invitation soon. She didn't want to seem too eager to meet Bonita or have her think she invited just anyone new in the area that happened to own the largest estate on the lake. But truth be known, she was most anxious to meet Bonita Roberts. Desiree had known Joshua Roberts and his first wife and was sure she and Bonita would know many of the same New Yorkers. She looked forward to quizzing Bonita so recently arrived from New York City about her old hometown.

The other newcomer she had recently learned about was a Mr. Kahn. She wasn't sure yet whether she would include him or not, although Precious seemed to think he might be worthy of an invitation at some point and Precious had never steered her wrong. Desiree was soon to recall an old saw she had learned in business many years prior—"There's a first time for everything."

15

Ridge and Kd Dodd

Other relative newcomers to Spencer were Ridge and KD Dodd. Ridge was a Delta Airlines Captain and KD was his first wife, something of an anomaly in the airline industry. The couple and their daughter Jean Ann lived in a large, but homey log cabin almost completely hidden by trees some two thousand feet from the lake.

Ridge was actively flying for the airline and kept his own small Cessna on his private runway at the rear of the cabin. When it was time for him to fly a trip, he flew the Cessna to Atlanta and a 767 to its destination and back. Then he returned home in the Cessna.

Somewhat of a wheeler/dealer, Ridge was constantly getting involved in *get-rich-quick* schemes although he was making in excess of two-hundred-fifty-thousand-dollars a year and had made some excellent investments in the past. In his earlier years with the airline, he and KD had been Amway Distributors and had done quite well in that enterprise.

Later, Ridge had bought interests in farms out west, over the counter stocks in pharmaceutical companies, had speculated on real estate, and had even responded to and sent chain letters where each person is asked to send a dollar to each of the top five people on the list. When his name hit the top, Ridge was to get some twenty-four-thousand-dollars. Of course, he sent out his five dollars, but he never received a cent. Everywhere he had lived, anyone with any kind of hare-brained scheme always went to Ridge first, and without fail he bought into it.

KD, a former flight attendant, had kept her looks and was an excellent cook, an imaginative gardener, and kept her house immaculately. She was definitely not interested in the social whirl in Spencer and turned down practically every invitation she received. Her home was where she preferred to spend her time. She delighted in needlepoint, crewel, quilting, and watching movies with Ridge and Jean Ann on their new wide-screen TV.

Jean Ann, at sixteen, was the past state gymnast champion of Virginia, had already won the state championship in Tennessee and was destined to attend the nationals in Los Angeles later in the year. She loved her parents and enjoyed being with them having learned at a young age to fit in well with adults as she had no siblings with whom to interact. Although she dated occasionally, she was quite content to spend her evenings with either her mother when her father was away on a flight or with both of them when Ridge was at home.

Currently, Ridge was in the process of building a hangar for his Cessna and spent most of the daylight hours on his days off working on the project. Often, he had to go into town to Home Depot to get more supplies or to search for a particular screw or nail. On one of those forays, he met Isaac Kahn while waiting in line to check out.

Isaac and his houseboy/handyman Chang were in line holding all types of electrical cable.

"Well, looks like you're going to rewire all of Spencer," Ridge said to Isaac.

"Not quite, but I do plan to do some extensive rewiring to my house," Isaac answered.

"You live nearby?" Ridge queried.

"On the lake."

"Me too. Where are you located?"

"Oh, about three miles from here. I bought the Grayson's property, the last piece of unimproved lakefront property."

"Oh, yes. And built the mansion everyone talks about. I know where that is. How long have you been here now?" asked Ridge.

"Well, I bought the land about five years ago and built the house, but I only moved here about six months ago."

"I live about four miles up the lake from you on the same side. I have the log cabin," Ridge said.

"Oh, I haven't seen it, but I've heard about your hideaway. Sounds nice and secluded," Isaac responded.

"That it is. The wife and I like our privacy, but we do like to see other people once in a while too. You and your wife will have to come over for a drink," Ridge said smiling.

"I'm not married. At least, not anymore, but if the offer stands for a single, I'd love to come over sometime," answered Isaac.

"Love to have you. Let me give you my card. My number's on it," Ridge said as he extracted his walled and found one.

"Thank you. Here's mine. Let's definitely get together soon."

"It's a date. I go out on a trip tomorrow, but will be back in four days. I'll call you then."

"Where are you going?" Isaac asked.

"Oh, let's see, it's the first of June. I'm flying to Seattle. I'm an airline pilot. Seattle's where I'll be flying all this month," Ridge explained.

"A pilot? I always wanted to fly. Guess you hear that a lot?"

"Yep. Personally, I'm glad that not everyone who wanted to fly did or I might not have a job," Ridge said with a laugh.

"Oh, I'm sure you would, but if you're ever looking for a job, I keep a Lear Jet at the regional airport. I have a pilot on my payroll, but if you've ever interested, you could fill in."

"Thanks, but I can't fly for hire. It's a contractual agreement all pilots have with the airline, but I sure would love to fly that baby someday just to bore some holes in the sky. I'd be happy to pay for the fuel. I got my first type rating in a Lear, Ike," Ridge said excitedly.

Isaac's demeanor changed dramatically. He said, "What did you call me?"

"When?"

"Just now."

"I don't know. Oh, I called you Ike. That's a nickname for Isaac, isn't it?"

"I don't know, but my name is Isaac, not Ike. Please call me Isaac."

"Sure. I'm sorry. I'm always giving everyone nicknames. I'll remember to call you Isaac. Anyway, I'd love to fly that Lear sometime.

Isaac was immediately pleasant again and said, "Well, when you get back from your trip, let's plan on your taking her up."

"That's a definite. We'll work out a time to take the Lear up and then afterwards, I want you to come to the log cabin for drinks and dinner," said Ridge.

"Sounds like a plan," Isaac said smiling.

16

Bonita, the Countess and Desiree Lunch

Raven was hired, was in place, and was competently handling Bonita's social arrangements. She catalogued people Bonita wished to enlist in her plan, kept records of what Bonita had served at each of her social engagements, what she had worn, the jewelry she had allowed the people of Spencer to see at each outing, and the functions she had attended. Bonita had almost all of the information she required and almost all her ducks in a row. There were only three more people she wished to meet so that at a future date she could enlist their aid in her debutante ball strategy. They were Desiree Compton, Darling Huxtable, and Harcourt Ball. She decided on meeting Desiree first because she had not yet received a coveted invitation to one of the Sunday afternoon fetes.

Bonita tapped on the door to Raven's office, located off the kitchen, that she had given Raven complete autonomy to fill with any and all electronic equipment she desired and furnishings she needed to make her feel comfortable.

"Come in," Raven called.

"Hello, my dear. How is everything going?"

"Oh, fine, Mrs. Roberts. I'm working on a spreadsheet now and by this afternoon, I'll have everything ready so all of your bills can be paid online and you won't have to worry about writing checks."

"Splendid. I don't understand how all of that works, and I'm delighted I won't have to spend time going through bills and signing checks anymore. You can take care of all of that for me, right?"

"Of course."

"Would you be so kind as to give me Desiree Compton's phone number, Raven?"

Raven punched a key and within seconds gave Bonita the number.

"Absolutely amazing!" Bonita said.

"Computers are. I'd be happy to teach you how to find phone numbers or anything else you would like to know about the computer, Mrs. Roberts."

"No. I'm not interested in learning about the computer. That's why I have you, love. Besides, I'm going to be even busier soon and you'll have all kinds of lists to compile in that machine for me."

"Would you like for me to place your call to Mrs. Compton for you?

"Thank you, no, dear. I'll go into my study and call. Bye, now."

"Bye, Mrs. Roberts."

Bonita stopped before closing the door, "Be sure that you eat. Just tell Hannah what you would like for lunch and she can whip it right up for you."

"I brought my lunch, thank you."

"Well that is to cease immediately. I had no idea you were bringing your lunch. Hannah is a gourmet chef and I am your employer. I'll provide your lunch. No more brown bagging, Raven. Let Hannah know what you want and she'll fix it. All right?"

"Yes ma'am. Thank you."

"Thank you, Raven. You don't know what a help you are to keep track of everything. Bye, again," and with that Bonita closed the door.

In her study, she placed the call to Desiree.

"Hello, this is the Compton residence," Maggie answered.

"Hello. This is Bonita Roberts. Is Mrs. Compton available?

"Jest a minute, I'll see."

Bonita heard the receiver being placed on a table and footsteps. Several seconds later, Desiree said, "Hello, Mrs. Roberts. I've heard so much about you. You've apparently taken Spencer by storm and I'm so looking forward to meeting you."

Then why haven't you invited me to one of your Sunday things? "I'm so looking forward to meeting you too, Mrs. Compton."

"Desiree, please."

"Desiree. In fact, that is why I'm calling. I understand your daughter will be visiting you next week and I would be delighted to call on you one day while she's here, at your convenience of course, and bring a catered lunch for the three of us. Would that be acceptable?" Bonita asked humbly, not her usual manner by any means.

The old girl has cast iron gonads—that's for sure. But why not? I understand she's fairly interesting and she might provide some amusement for Monique, who

I'm sure gets bored sitting here in my boudoir attempting to entertain her bed-ridden mother. And I've heard rumors that Bonita is originally from Spain with some trace of royal blood somewhere. Monique would probably enjoy talking about Europe.

"What a lovely and generous idea, Bonita. Let me take a look at my book. How's next Wednesday? Say about 11:30? We can have a little champagne first and then luncheon."

"Perfect. I'll be there at 11:30 sharp. Are there any foods you don't like or is there something you and your daughter would prefer?"

"No chicken or fish. I prefer something in the beef line and I do take my large meal in the middle of the day. Indigestion at night if I eat too much then, you know? The Countess eats her large meal in the middle of the day, too, as is the European custom you know. When there, do as the natives do, yes? Also, I love sweets, particularly chocolate and I eat my dessert course along with my main course, so something decadent in the chocolate line would be deeply appreciated. Monique doesn't eat okra, cooked carrots, or salad. She also doesn't eat beef, chicken, or fish, so she'll need a vegetable dish but one without pasta. She hates pasta. And she's allergic to chocolate, so my dessert won't suit her. I hope I'm not being too much of a burden on you with all this."

Of course not, you old biddy. I'm running a restaurant here and can bring you anything your little heart desires. "Absolutely not, Desiree. I'm so glad I asked. What fun would a luncheon or dinner be if you were served a dish you didn't like or one that would cause your daughter an allergic reaction? I've written your preferences down and I'll be sure to adhere to every desire."

"Wonderful. I'll see you Wednesday at 11:30. By the way, Bonita, I absolutely adore butter mints, but no one can seem to find them anymore. Do you think you could find any butter mints for us to nibble after our meal?"

"I'll certainly try and I'm sure I'll be able to find them, Desiree."

"I can hardly wait. Thank you for calling and again, I'm looking forward to meeting you, Bonita.

"It's my pleasure and the feeling is mutual. I'll be there Wednesday." *What a spoiled woman. If she treats everyone this way, I'm surprised she has any friends, but her clout in the social circle here is legendary. I'll get Hannah and Alphonso on this immediately! I'll find the damned butter mints if I have to fly them in from Switzerland. Aha, Swiss chocolate, so much better than Godiva, which has become rather run of the mill. But wait until old Desiree tastes Hannah's double chocolate cake. Eats it with her entrée. She's insane. But, remember Bonita, you might need her.*

Bonita buzzed Hannah in the kitchen. When Hannah arrived at the study, Bonita instructed her about the meal she was to prepare for next Wednesday with everything ready no later than eleven o'clock. Hannah suggested Southwestern Swiss Medley for the vegetable dish and Filet Mignon Oscar for the beef dish along with Duchess potatoes, green beans Italienne, her homemade biscuits, and of course, the double chocolate cake. The potatoes and beans would also accompany the vegetable casserole. She thought a key lime torte for Desiree's daughter's dessert would do nicely because she didn't like chocolate.

"You never fail me, Hannah. Now, please go and tell Raven everything you're going to serve, give her the recipes, and have her put next Wednesday at 11:30 a.m. on that calendar thing she has in the computer. Tell her I'll need copies of the recipes to take with me that day. Also, I need her to find butter mints on that Internet she's always using. Tell her to order them and if they can't be delivered before Wednesday, find out how I can get them here by then including chartering a plane to collect them. I also want a list of the finest Swiss chocolates in Switzerland, not from Bergdoff-Goodman's, and I want the chocolates by Wednesday too."

"Okay. We is definitely out to impress somebody, ain't we?"

"We are, Hannah. And we always do, don't we?"

"Yessum. So far we's batting a thousand."

"And let's make sure, we continue to do just that."

Hannah left the study and went to Raven's office and knocked. Once in, she began giving Raven her list of "to dos" for the following Wednesday. Raven couldn't believe she had fallen into this position right here in Spencer. Working for Bonita Roberts was indeed a trip and she never knew what she was going to be asked to do next, but it was invigorating. The woman was a hoot! And the money she had was unbelievable and Bonita spent it like water gurgling down a waterfall—one the size of Niagara Falls to be exact!

At ten the following Wednesday morning, Alphonso returned from the small Spencer Airport where he had met a Bonita Roberts chartered jet carrying cargo of a two-pound tin of Swiss butter mints flown in from Switzerland the day before and transported from La Guardia Airport to Spencer, Tennessee, that morning. Total cost: $1565 per pound.

Bonita had decided against the Swiss chocolates after Raven could only find the authentic butter mints in Switzerland. Two candies from Switzerland wouldn't do. She had ordered Mrs. See's chocolates from California, her favorite when a resident at the Beverly Wiltshire and in the employ of Mr. Dubre. She was taking a chance that Desiree had never tasted them. In

Bonita's opinion, they put Godiva and Swiss chocolates to shame and at slightly over three-hundred-pounds, Bonita was unquestionably a chocolate connoisseur.

Bonita selected a Chanel to wear to her luncheon engagement accessorized with a black pearl choker, earrings, and pin. The black lizard pumps and clutch would go well with the outfit. She was sure Raven had the hostess gifts at the ready she had ordered for Desiree and the Countess. Bonita was giving the daughter a small diamond chip stickpin and Desiree a lavishly appliquéd satin bed jacket. She was determined to not only impress the two women, but also to overwhelm them with her generosity and to dazzle them with her wealth.

Hannah had been instructed to have the food ready at exactly eleven o'clock and to pack it in individual carriers for the trip to Desiree's. Hannah would be accompanying Bonita to warm the food in Desiree's kitchen, should it need it, and to serve the luncheon. Alphonso had already stowed the Royal Doulton china, the Wallace sterling flatware, and the Baccarat crystal goblets, including water, wine, and champagne flutes, along with the Philippine pena cloth tablecloth and napkins in the trunk of the maroon Rolls.

At precisely quarter after eleven o'clock, Bonita and her entourage proceeded to the car for their short trip from Villagio to Desiree's. Once in the car, Hannah and Alphonso exchanged knowing glances at the lengths to which "Miz Bonita" would go to get what she wanted.

Hannah and Bonita ascended the steps to Desiree's imposing front door while Alphonso began gathering everything to be taken into the house. Hannah rang the bell and stepped back behind Bonita. A lovely woman of perhaps thirty-five opened the door. She was bare-footed and dressed in designer jeans and what appeared to be a man's oversized shirt.

"Hello. You must be Mrs. Roberts and right on time too. I'm Monique. Welcome. Won't you come in?"

"Monique, this is my maid, Hannah. She will be making the final preparations and serving us lunch today."

"How nice. It's Maggie's day off, so that'll be perfect. We have a dumbwaiter, Hannah, so you can just put everything on that in the kitchen and I'll haul it up."

"Oh, Hannah doesn't mind serving, do you, Hannah?"

"No ma'am. That's what I's here for."

"Oh, no, that won't be necessary, Hannah. Just put it on the dumbwaiter. This is going to be just a casual little meal."

That's what you think, Countess Monique. And you certainly are dressed for the occasion. I can't imagine her coming to the door barefooted dressed in jeans after the food order her mother placed.

Alphonso approached the steps with his first load.

"Just take it around to the back and I'll open the kitchen door. Hannah, would you like to follow me?" Monique asked.

As Alphonso headed for the back door, Hannah trailed after Monique. Bonita was left standing alone in the foyer. Not a usual situation for her, Bonita had no idea what to do. She had not been invited to follow the countess and she had no wish to see Desiree's kitchen, but she also had not been invited to enter any other room from the foyer, so she simply stood there.

After a few interminable minutes, Monique called from the kitchen, "Oh, Mrs. Roberts, go on up. Come straight into the great room and turn right. Those stairs go up to mother's room. She's expecting you."

Desiree quickly tapped the button to close the automatic sliding doors over the banks of monitors. She had thoroughly enjoyed watching Bonita's discomfort filmed by the foyer camera while Monique had left her unattended.

Bonita hoisted her immense bulk up the rather steep stairs haltingly. She hated stairs and always used the elevators she had installed at Villagio. She wondered why Desiree didn't have elevators; *they would certainly make more sense than stairs for someone who was practically an invalid. At least then, she could venture downstairs in her wheelchair.* Bonita paused a moment to catch her breath and then tapped at Desiree's door.

"Come in, Bonita."

Bonita entered the smoke-filled bedroom and she and the bedridden doyenne of Spencer society were face to face.

"Hello, Desiree. I'm delighted to finally meet you," Bonita gushed as she extended her hand.

Desiree took Bonita's hand in both of hers and said, "Have a seat, dear, right over there so I can see you well." She indicated a fragile chair, which Bonita sat upon with great trepidation. It didn't break, but it did creak and groan. "Perhaps that chair is not a good choice. Here, sit over here on this chaise, Bonita."

Bonita hears a whirring sound, "What's that noise?

"Monique coming up on the elevator to join us I think."

And she sent me up the stairs. Twit! Bonita moved to the chaise as Monique entered the room. "Mother, you should see the feast Bonita's maid Hannah has prepared. We're going to gain ten pounds eating lunch."

"I can hardly wait," responded Desiree. "Bonita, you and Monique have met. Monique is the Countess Ortiz and lives in Malaga. I'm sure you're familiar with it. You're from Spain originally I'm told."

"Yes, but I haven't been there for years."

As Monique sat on the end of her mother's bed, Desiree continued, "I heard from Precious Woodson that you were descended from the royal line. You and Monique have all kinds of things to discuss, I imagine."

"Oh, nothing like a countess. You know rumors are always rampant, Desiree."

"Where did you live in Spain, Bonita?" asked Monique.

"A little mountain town, Fuji liana. I'm sure you've never heard of it."

"Of course I have. It's not too far from the Costa del sol where we have our summer residence. I've been there often. Now where did you live there? I bet I know. In that beautiful chateau about halfway up the mountain as you enter the town from the valley, right?"

"Oh, no. We had a modest home. My father was very ill and we had to move him to a one-story home when I was quite young."

"You knew the Rivera family there, didn't you?"

Bonita quickly realized she was in way over her head. She had always used the little mountain town that no one had ever heard of as her "home in Spain" and here was someone who had a summer home only miles from it. Bonita had never been to Fuji liana in her life and certainly didn't know anyone there.

"That name sounds familiar, but Countess, you must realize I'm an old lady and I left Spain when I was merely fifteen years of age, so everyone I knew has been long dead, I'm sure."

"Well, the descendants of the Rivera's are still very much alive and are still the most prominent family in that section of Spain. What is your connection to the royal family? Manuel, my husband is King Juan Carlos' second cousin and inherited his title ten years ago when his father Count Ortiz passed away. Manuel is the seventeenth count in that line."

"That's fascinating. And how do you like living in Spain? Has it been a big adjustment for you since you are an American and were reared here in the States?" Bonita asked.

Monique graciously answered her and let her question drop, but she and her mother exchanged knowing glances. Bonita was not of royal heritage, Monique was positive, and since she didn't know the Riveras or anything about them, Monique thought she probably wasn't from Fuji liana either. She wondered why Bonita had made up the story.

As Bonita presented Desiree and Monique with their gifts, her phone was ringing at Villagio.

"Hello, Roberts' residence," Raven answered.

"Mrs. Roberts, please. This is Rhetta Robin Ricks calling."

"I'm sorry, Mrs. Ricks. Mrs. Roberts is not at home presently. May I take a message?

"Oh? Well, I need to speak to her concerning a matter of some importance. Do you know where I can reach her?" Rhetta asked.

"She's having lunch at Mrs. Compton's, but I'll have her call you as soon as she returns."

"Oh, that won't be necessary. I just figured out the problem myself. No need to have her call back. In fact, just forget I called. Silly me. Thank you," Rhetta said hurriedly replacing the receiver. Fortunately, she was already dressed for the day.

So Desiree Compton was entertaining at luncheon and she wasn't invited. Strange. She hadn't seen a single luncheon invitation to Desiree's in her refrigerator forays last week, but no matter. She could manage to drop by Desiree's while on the way shopping in only a matter of minutes.

Monique and Desiree exclaimed properly over their gifts both realizing that Bonita must want something desperately.

"Now, I would like to call down to Hannah to bring us up some champagne. You do have an intercom, don't you, Desiree? I've brought Kristal. I hope that's all right. Dom Perignon is so vin ordinaire these days, don't you think?"

Monique started for the door, "Sounds lovely, but I'll pop down and bring it up. No need to make Hannah come up."

"But that's why I brought Hannah, so she can serve."

"Bonita, Monique will fetch it. We don't need to be waited upon. Let's have a casual girls' lunch."

A casual girls' lunch indeed. You'd think you were eating at Le Cirque with the various requests you made, Desiree.

"Fine," Bonita said, but Desiree could tell she was miffed.

As Monique hit the bottom step, the doorbell rang. She opened it and there was Rhetta Robin Ricks.

"Monique. What a marvelous surprise! I didn't know you were in Spencer. I was on my way to do some shopping and thought I'd drop by to see if your mother needed anything while I was in town."

"Hello, Rhetta. No, we're fine. Got everything we need. I'm here for two weeks so I'm able to go out and get whatever provisions are required. I'll tell mother you stopped by though. That's so sweet of you. It's nice to know she has neighbors who'll watch out for her when I'm in Spain. Now, I know you want to get on with your shopping, so I'll see you soon."

"I'm in no hurry and since I'm here, I'd love to say hello to Desiree. Would that be all right?" Rhetta asked as she pushed past Monique and started for the elevator.

Monique stood looking after her with her mouth ajar. *Was there no limit to Rhetta's brashness? Apparently not!*

Monique headed for the kitchen as Rhetta tapped on Desiree's door.

"Come in, Monique. There's no need to knock. Oh, maybe she needs help with the tray. Bonita, would you mind opening the door?"

Bonita crossed to the door and opened it and there stood Rhetta.

"Well, hello, Bonita. I had no idea you were here. Desiree, I was on my way shopping and not knowing that Monique was here, I stopped to see if I could get you anything in town."

"Whatever for, Rhetta? You've never stopped to see if I needed anything before?

"Well, of course, I have, Desiree. Ask Maggie. I've stopped several times to see if you needed anything, but I've always seemed to come when you were resting. Well, Bonita, what brings you here today?"

"A visit, that's all."

"How nice. Bonita's really an asset to our little community, isn't she, Desiree? Mind if I sit here?" Rhetta said as she molded her skinny frame into the fragile chair Bonita had earlier departed. "So what's the topic of the day?"

"Bonita had started to tell us about her home in Spain. She's related to the royal family, you know?" Desiree explained.

"Oh, then you and Monique must be related by marriage. It's kinda like the South isn't it, where everyone's related to everyone else?"

"We haven't really discussed that, Rhetta," Bonita responded as Monique pushed open the door bearing a tray with the bottle of Kristal and three champagne flutes.

"Oh, Rhetta, are you still here? I'll go downstairs and get another flute. We were just about to have a little glass of champagne."

"That would be lovely. You're sure it's not too much trouble?" cooed Rhetta.

Monique didn't answer, but set the tray on a table beside the bed and left the room.

Bonita was aghast at Rhetta's behavior.

"Well, while Monique's gone to get another glass. I'll just pour this for the three of us," said Rhetta as she crossed to the table and filled the glasses with bubbly. She passed one to Desiree, another to Bonita, and then took the other herself. "Well, chin-chin," Rhetta said as she hoisted her flute and took a sip.

Bonita and Desiree both stared at her.

"Try some. It's delicious," said Rhetta.

"I thought we'd wait for Monique," Desiree said and there was ice in her voice.

"Oh, how thoughtless of me! This is wonderful champagne. Where did you find it, Desiree? Not in Spencer, I'm sure."

"Bonita brought it, Rhetta. She also brought a delectable, I'm sure, luncheon we are about to enjoy after we have the champagne. So after Monique returns and we have our drink, I'm sure you'll need to run off and do your shopping."

"I'm not looking for anything particular. Just shopping, you know. I'm not in any hurry whatsoever."

Monique entered the room with a champagne flute, unlike the other three, since Bonita had brought only three with her. "Well, I see you've started without me," Monique said with a smile.

"Only Rhetta has," Desiree said. "Pour yourself a glass, dear, and let's drink a toast to our benefactress for this lovely champagne and the delicious luncheon forthcoming."

"Here, here," said Rhetta.

Bonita was absolutely stunned into silence. She could not believe the crassness of Rhetta, the daughter of the former governor and someone whose name was in the society notes every week in the little Spencer newspaper.

After another half hour of chitchat mostly instigated and facilitated by and participated in by Rhetta, Bonita had had enough. Just as she was about to announce that the luncheon must be served before it was ruined, there was a knock on the door.

Monique opened the door and Hannah stepped into the room, "Scuse me everybody, but Miz Roberts, I got to tell you, if I don't serve this here food we brought over here in the next few minutes, it ain't gonna be fit to eat." At that instant, Hannah spied Rhetta. "O law, Miz Roberts, you told me to prepare food for three people. There's four here. I didn't bring enough place settings or nothing for four people."

Desiree and Monique were delighted by Hannah's comment. Reluctantly, Rhetta rose from her seat and said, "There's no need to worry about that, Hannah. I simply dropped by to see if Mrs. Compton needed anything from town. I'll be going now."

She handed her flute to Hannah, told the ladies good-bye, and headed for the door slowly. It was obvious she didn't want to leave and hoped any or all of them would insist she stay. Rhetta had no such luck. Hannah had saved the day!

After Hannah showed Rhetta to the door and began to serve the sumptuous feast, Bonita said, "What in the world got into Rhetta? I've never seen anyone behave like that."

"Nothing got into her, Bonita. Rhetta does this all the time. She's always showing up everywhere uninvited. I'm only amazed that she left. I'm sure none of us would have been so impolite as to ask her to leave and if Hannah hadn't blurted out what she did, Rhetta would be sitting right here eating with us, regardless of whether her place setting matched ours or not and regardless of whether there was enough food for her or not."

"I had no idea. She's written up in the *Spectator* Social Notes every week."

"That's because Hunter Kimble, who writes the social notes, is Rhetta's first cousin and whatever Rhetta calls in to her, Hunter faithfully puts in the paper since her father and the former governor were brothers. I think Hunter is constantly hoping Rhetta will part with some of her mother's family money she inherited. The governor's family and Hunter's don't have a sou."

"I see," said Bonita thinking she probably would eliminate Rhetta from her debutante plans.

The remainder of the afternoon passed in a reasonably pleasant manner except when either Desiree or Monique attempted to steer the conversation back to Bonita's heritage and Spain. Bonita successfully managed to squirm out of each question and was sure the two women were impressed with the gifts, the champagne, the exquisite luncheon, Hannah's double chocolate cake, Mrs. See's chocolates and the damned Swiss butter mints. They were!

When the luncheon was consumed and everything was packed up, and Bonita, Alphonso, and Hannah were back in the Rolls heading for Villagio, Monique again entered her mother's bedroom, flopped on the bed and said, "Mother, I'm going to do a little investigative work. I intend to find out who Bonita Roberts is and where she came from and how she got here. What do you think?"

"I think that's a wonderful idea, darling. Now, hand me that tin of butter mints. They're delicious, aren't they?" as Desiree reached in for another handful.

HANNAH'S DOUBLE CHOCOLATE CAKE

1 cup boiling water
4 ozs. unsweetened chocolate
1 stick sweet butter
1 t vanilla extract
2 cups granulated sugar
2 eggs, separated
1 t baking soda
½ cup sour cream
2 cups less 2 T unbleached, all purpose flour, sifted
1 t baking powder

Preheat oven to 350 degrees, Grease and flour a 10" tube pan. Pour boiling water over chocolate and butter, let stand until melted. Stir in vanilla and sugar, then whisk in egg yolks, one at a time, blending well after each addition. Mix baking soda and sour cream and whisk into chocolate mixture. Sift flour and baking powder together, add to batter, mixing thoroughly. Beat egg whites until stiff, but not dry. Stir a quarter of the egg whites thoroughly into the batter. Scoop remaining egg whites on top of the batter and gently fold together. Pour batter into prepared pan. Set on middle rack of oven and bake 40 to 50 minutes or until edges have pulled away from pan and cake tester inserted in center comes out clean. Cool in pan 10 minutes, unmold and cool completely before frosting.

FROSTING

2 T. sweet butter
¾ cup semisweet chocolate chips
6 T heavy cream
1 ¼ cups sifted confectioner's sugar
1 t vanilla extract
1 T brewed coffee—the secret ingredient that makes the chocolate mouth-wateringly *ontorious*—one of Hannah's made-up words—*translated means delicious.*

Place all ingredients into heavy saucepan over low heat and whisk until smooth. Cool slightly, add more sugar if necessary to achieve a spreading consistency. Spread on cake while frosting is still warm.

FILET MIGNON OSCAR

Filet Mignon for each person to be served
Crabmeat (1 pound per 4 people)
Hollandaise sauce (2 cups per 4 people)
Lightly steamed asparagus (3 stalks per person)

Cook filet mignon to desired doneness. Top with warm crabmeat, Hollandaise sauce and 2 asparagus spears. Divine!

DUCHESS POTATOES

Bake potatoes in microwave until done—approximately 8 minutes per potato. When potatoes are done, cool until they are comfortable to work with and cut an oval out of top of each potato. With a spoon, scoop out inside of potato and place in bowl. Add milk, butter, salt, pepper, and horseradish (or garlic may be substituted) to taste, whip to make mashed potatoes, and return to shell. Before serving, place all potatoes on baking sheet and warm in oven.

Once Bonita had returned home, Hannah asked Bonita, "Miz Roberts, is you mad at me for what I said to Miz Ricks?"

"Mad at you? Absolutely not, Hannah. I loved it! She is the crassest person I've ever known. Did you know that Desiree Compton said she does this sort of thing all the time? She drops by or happens to be in the neighborhood and crashes people's parties all over Spencer."

"Ain't that somethin? I knows I oughta kep my mouth shut, but I didn't know what I was gonna do with only three place settings and not enuf food for four people."

"Don't give it another thought, Hannah."

Just then, Raven entered the kitchen with her lunch dishes. "I thought there were three for the luncheon, Hannah. Did you say you didn't have enough food for four?"

"There were only three for luncheon, Raven. Rhetta Robin Ricks *dropped by* just as Hannah was ready to serve and it didn't seem she was going to leave."

"Oh, Mrs. Ricks called for you this morning shortly after you left for Mrs. Compton's. I told her you were out and she asked where you could be reached because she needed to speak to you about something of the utmost importance. I told her I'd have her call you, but she said she needed to speak to you right away, so I told her where you were. Then she said she'd found the answer she needed and I needn't bother to tell you she called," Raven offered.

"Well, I never!" said Bonita. "She found out I was at Desiree's for a luncheon and decided to drop by and get in on yet another event. I heard from Desiree she does this type of thing all the time."

"Oh, I wouldn't know anything about that, Mrs. Roberts," Raven replied as she neared the kitchen door on her way back into her office. *Keep your mouth shut, Raven. Do not spread gossip. Mrs. Roberts will learn about Rhetta Robin Ricks soon enough. In fact, she got a firsthand look at Rhetta's behavior today. I wondered why she seemed so enamored of Mrs. Ricks who is almost a social pariah. She didn't know about Rhetta and how if she can't get an invitation to a social event, she simply shows up. That explains it.*

17

Party Time in Spencer

The following week, Precious Woodson entertained Bonita at a small dinner party and as luck would have it, among the guests were Harcourt Ball escorting his mother and Darling Huxtable with her husband BD. Bonita had ample time during cocktails and dinner to talk with both Harcourt and Darling and determined they would be affable to her plan. As far as Bonita was concerned, she had met everyone who was anyone in Spencer. She was ready to begin politicking for a debutante ball in Spencer featuring her at the helm.

Bonita instructed Raven to send invitations to Lydia Henley, Darling Huxtable, Precious Woodson, Candy Martin, Harcourt Ball, and Desiree Compton, although Bonita knew Desiree would be unable to come but felt it would be rude not to include her. The guests were to be asked to attend a wine and cheese discussion regarding Spencer. It was to be held at Villagio Saturday afternoon two weeks hence at three o'clock in the afternoon. Thoroughly efficient, Raven had the invitations in the mail within forty-eight hours.

On Monday morning, Rhetta Robin Ricks *dropped in* on Candy Martin and casually perused the space allocated to invitations on her sub-zero refrigerator. She all but suffered cardiac arrest when she read that Bonita Roberts was hosting a wine and cheese party to discuss something of importance to Spencer and that she was not included. Without finishing her Danish or coffee Candy had placed on the breakfast nook table for her, Rhetta told Candy that she must go.

"But you've only arrived, Rhetta. I thought we would visit for a few minutes."

"I'm sorry, Candy. I suddenly remembered that I must be downtown in only moments. I have to order invitations for my party."

"What party?"

"Oh, I'm having a colossal party at RickShaw next Friday night. Didn't I tell you?"

"No, you didn't. Next Friday night and you haven't mailed the invitations yet!"

"There was a mix-up when I ordered them, but they're ready now. I must go. I'll look forward to seeing you next Friday at my party," Rhetta said as she practically ran out of the back door to her car.

"What kind of party is it, Rhetta?" Candy called as Rhetta was about to shut the car door.

"Oh, you'll see. It's going to be smashing!" Rhetta answered since she didn't have a clue what type of party she was going to give. She started the engine and left in a cloud of dust.

I can't believe she didn't invite me. She liked me. I could tell. She told me she had an idea and wanted to include me. What could have happened? I have to go to that wine and cheese. I only hope I can get some kind of invitation done today. I'll get River to help me address them tonight and tomorrow, I'll have Randy personally deliver them to my invited guests. He won't mind. I'll send him to rent him a tux and hire a limousine for him to drive around to deliver the invitations. He'll probably welcome not having to work on the lawn for one day. When Bonita receives my personally delivered invitation to the most elegant party Spencer has ever seen, she'll invite me to her wine and cheese the next day. I just know it! Yes! A theme. I have to have a theme. What would be spectacular? A masked ball? No, overdone. What? What? Hurry, Rhetta. You have to have a theme before you order the invitations. A luau, that's it, on the lawn sloping down to the lake at RickShaw. Gigantic multi-colored tents, pigs roasted in the ground all day, and leis flown in from Hawaii. I'll hire sailboats with colored sails to come into shore to take the guests for a cruise on the lake. I'll find sarongs for Corinne, River and me, and flowered Bermudas for Trace with complementing Hawaiian shirt, in good taste, of course. I can pull this off. It's coming together. Get ready, Spencer! Little Rhetta Robin Shaw Ricks is going to entertain you like you ain't never been entertained before!

Rhetta entered the print shop and demanded to be helped immediately. She offered the printer double his usual fee to have engraved invitations ready for her to pick up at six o'clock that night. She roared back to RickShaw and compiled her list of invitees. She called New York and placed orders for her flower and decoration requirements at Farrar's, the florist Bonita always employed. She insisted upon orchid leis flown in from Hawaii and they had to be fresh, fresh, fresh! She wanted one hundred of them in every color of orchid that was available. She agreed to purchase first class tickets for all of the employees who would have to come to Spencer on such short notice to ready RickShaw for the social event of the season. The caterer everyone in Nashville used was her next phone call and she doubled the usual fee there too. The catering staff was to arrive the day before to be ready to get pigs in the ground early Friday morning. She called a local motel and made reservations for all of them. She had to put this together and quickly. Cost was not something she intended to let stand in her way. Next, she called a Nashville booking agency to line up a band. She got the group she wanted and ended up paying double for them too.

By six o'clock, she had things well under control and left to pick up the invitations. When Trace drove in from Nashville later that evening, Rhetta and River were at the dining room table addressing envelopes with calligraphy pens.

"What's going on?" Trace asked.

"Big party. You and Mom are having a luau next Friday night. It's going to be spectacular! Mom's somehow managed to get 'Southern Comfort' to provide the tunes. That's for after dinner. During the feast, she's hired wandering musicians to strum the guitar and mandolin," River answered excitedly.

"I haven't heard anything about a luau, Rhetta."

"I decided today. We haven't had a party in eons. Your dinner's in the oven. I'm pretty busy here right now, Trace," Rhetta responded.

Trace went to the kitchen, dismissed by Rhetta, and wondered how he was going to manage to pay for whatever she was cooking up because he knew it was going to be expensive. Rhetta had that "I don't care how much money this is going to cost" look in her eye.

Rhetta called Randy, her gardener and a rather handsome young man who was working his way through graduate school, and told him to go to *Dusk to Dawn Formal Wear* and rent a tux and to charge it to her account. Next, he was to rent a limousine from the Volunteer Hotel in Spencer and be at RickShaw at nine o'clock the next morning with the limo to personally deliver invitations. Randy agreed and thought for probably the thousandth time what a lunatic Rhetta Robin Ricks was. He did relish a day off from the constant care of the massive RickShaw lawn in the hot sun, but dressing in a tuxedo and driving around the lake delivering invitations didn't strike him as an exactly fun-filled day either. He wondered what Mrs. Ricks would think of next?

"Favors. I forgot about favors. I have to order favors!" Rhetta suddenly screeched as she and River laboriously continued to address envelopes.

"I think the orchid leis will suffice for favors, Mother."

"Absolutely not! I want to give each guest a favor. It must be something they can take home with them, something that will last, and it should be something they can use or wear for years to come. What goes with a luau? Think, River."

"I don't know. Pearls maybe?"

"That's it! Pearls! You're brilliant! I'll order a cultured pearl bracelet for each of the ladies and a pearl encrusted money clip for each of the men. And I know exactly how to make the presentation," Rhetta trilled.

"How?"

"You'll see. I'm going to keep that a secret so even you'll be surprised."

Trace came into the dining room with his tie undone and his shirtsleeves rolled up eating a roast beef sandwich.

"Now, Trace, why are you eating a sandwich? I left a lovely piece of roast in the oven with all the vegetables to accompany it so you would have a proper dinner," Rhetta scolded.

"I'm eating a sandwich because I wanted a sandwich. Now, what is all this activity about and why wasn't I told about a party next Friday?"

"Isn't it the most wonderful idea, honey? We're going to have a luau complete with roasted pigs cooked all day in the ground. I'm having leis flown in from Hawaii. Oh, I must remember to call Nashville Party Goods and order a thousand of those little umbrellas for drinks. I've already arranged for the caterers, the bartenders, the wandering musicians, the tents, and the band. And I've called the marina to bring over fifteen of those little sailboats with the colored sails. Right at sunset, they'll cross the lake and put in at our dock to take guests out for a short cruise. Won't it be divine, Trace?"

"River, would you mind going up to your room for a few moments? I need to speak to your mother privately."

"Sure, dad. I'm tired of doing invitations anyway," River said as she jumped up and fairly raced up the stairs.

"Trace, I need River to help me finish these. They must be ready by nine in the morning so Randy can hand deliver them."

"Rhetta, have you taken complete leave of your senses?

"And what is that supposed to mean?"

"What it means is that I have told you repeatedly for the past six months that we cannot afford your extravagances. Malpractice insurance is just about to break me. I'm still paying for equipment in two offices and it's time to give several members of my staff annual raises. I'm inundated with bills for this house and the one in Nashville. You spend money like its water and I cannot continue to pay all of the bills you keep piling up. And now, after all of those discussions where I thought maybe you were beginning to understand our financial situation, you're planning a party with caterers, bartenders, Randy hand delivering invitations, and I heard you mention cultured pearl favors. Where do you think I am going to get the money to pay for all this stuff?"

"Oh, Trace, you'll figure something out. You're one of the most successful doctors in Nashville. I know you're salting money away every month and that you're investing in the market. You have plenty of money."

"I don't, Rhetta. Why won't you listen to me? We are living in a house of cards. If anything happens, everything, including my practice, will collapse," Trace said somberly.

"Trace, we as leading members of the community and you as a professional man who is so well respected, are obligated to entertain. Think of all the parties we attend. Why, if we don't reciprocate, people will begin to talk. I'll economize next month. I promise, Trace. But you have to understand, this party is of the utmost importance right now. Believe me, after this party, I'll have gotten what I want and I won't need to entertain for eons. Now, please call River back down here so we can finish up. That's a dear." Rhetta delivered this entire monologue to her husband without once looking up, so engrossed was she in her addressing chore.

"Rhetta, have you heard anything I've said to you?"

"Of course I have, darling. Next month my motto will be save, save, save. Promise."

Trace threw his hands up in desperation and went to the stairwell and called River. When River returned to help her mother, Trace stepped out onto the wraparound porch and gazed out at the lake created by Fall Creek Falls. He wondered what it was going to take to make Rhetta understand that they had to curb the spending. He was practically tapped out. Trace didn't realize at that moment the staggering amount of the bills Rhetta would be piling up in the next two weeks for her spur-of-the-moment luau. Her little party would run in excess of $150,000.

Randy arrived promptly at nine the next morning in the hired silver limousine and a rented Ives St. Laurent tux. He looked fantastic! Rhetta was quite pleased. She handed Randy a box containing the invitations with a map directing him on the route to deliver each of them. Rhetta instructed him to ring the doorbell at each residence and to ask to speak to the addressee. If possible, he was to personally place the invitation only in the hands of the invitee. She stressed that this was imperative in the case of Mrs. Bonita Roberts of Villagio. Just as Rhetta finished her instructions, a flower truck from the local florist pulled into the circular driveway. The driver got out with two boxes and gave them to Rhetta. She opened the boxes and gave her approval of the cymbidium orchids within. She signed for the flowers and sent the driver on his way. Handing the boxes over to Randy, she told him he was to hold an orchid atop each invitation as he presented it to each invitee. "The pink ones are for the ladies and the white ones are for the gentlemen. If a couple is presented with an invitation, make sure you place two orchids, one pink and one white, atop the invitation. All right, Randy?" Rhetta instructed.

"Yes ma'am."

"When you've made all the deliveries, I want you to come back here before returning the car, all right?"

"Yes ma'am."

"Thank you, Randy. I'll see you in a few hours."

"Okay. I'm on my way."

"Good. Drive carefully. Bye-bye." Rhetta said with a wave as she headed for the front door. She could hardly wait for Randy to deliver the invitations and get back to RickShaw, so she could interrogate him about the reactions of her invited guests. She especially wanted to hear about Bonita's response. Rhetta was convinced that within moments of Bonita's delivery of the luau invitation, she would receive a call from Bonita inviting her to the wine and cheese gala at Villagio the day after the luau. It may be a little costly, but Rhetta had to be included in Bonita's plan for Spencer. At present, it was the most important thing in the world to her.

Randy turned into the gates of Villagio and pulled the limousine to a stop at the front portico. He retrieved a pink orchid from the florist box and Bonita Roberts' invitation. Placing the orchid atop the invitation, he mounted the front steps and rang the doorbell. A few seconds later, Hannah opened the door.

"Yes?"

"Good morning. My name is Randy and I am in the service of Mrs. Rhetta Ricks. Is Mrs. Roberts in?" Randy asked with a slight bow.

"Yes she is, but she ain't dressed for the day yet. Is there a message?"

"I should like to speak with her personally if that is at all possible."

"Well, it might be possible in 'bout two hours, but it sure ain't possible now. Miz Roberts is still asleep. What you got there? I'll give it to her," said Hannah.

"Mrs. Ricks would really like for me to give it to Mrs. Roberts personally. I don't mean to offend, but those are my instructions."

"You ain't offendin' me. If you want to give it to Miz Roberts, come back in a couple of hours," Hannah said and shut the door.

Randy went to the car and decided to deliver all of the other invitations and return afterward to personally hand Bonita's to her. Delivering these invitations was going to be a royal pain. He had to drive hither and yond, backtrack, wait for the invitees to get themselves to the door, and answer all manner of questions from them all while burning up in a tuxedo in the hot Tennessee sun.

Finally, he finished with the deliveries and thankfully returned to Villagio to dispatch the final envelope. Once again, he picked up a pink orchid, the last one and rather puny at that after sitting in the unrefrigerated box for almost three hours, although the limousine air conditioner had been on all the time. Randy mopped his brow with a handkerchief he pulled from his back pocket, ascended the stairs once again, and rang Bonita's doorbell.

The door opened and there was Hannah.

"Hello again. Is Mrs. Roberts available? I have a delivery for her," Randy said in his most commodious manner.

"She's here and she's awake and she's dressed. I told her you had been here before with a delivery from Miz Ricks and she told me to take it from you when you come back," Hannah explained.

"Could you ask her to please come to the door or could you allow me in and show me to her so that I could hand this invitation to her myself? It would mean a great deal to me. Mrs. Ricks was very specific in her instructions."

"I can ask her to come to the door, but she won't. Believe me, I understands about employers. I been with Miz Roberts since before you was a gleam in your daddy's eye and if she says for me to take that envelope, she ain't comin' to the door. I'm sorry as I can be," Hannah said kindly.

"And you can't show me in to hand it to her?"

"I reckon I could, but then I'd be in the doghouse with her. She told me to take it from you."

"Well, all right. I've given it my best shot. I'll tell Mrs. Ricks that Mrs. Roberts was unavailable," Randy sighed.

"Guess that's what you'll have to do then," said Hannah. She reached out and Randy placed the envelope with the orchid atop it in Hannah's outstretched hand.

"That's a pretty flower. What is it?" Hannah asked.

"Some kind of orchid is all I know. Thank you and you'll make sure Mrs. Roberts gets this right away?"

"I'll take it to her right this minute. I promise. Thank you and I'm sorry she won't come to the door, but when she makes up her mind, she ain't about to change it."

"I understand. Thank you. I'll be going now," and Randy returned to the limousine to drive back to RickShaw to Rhetta's ranting about how he had failed to follow her specific instructions, how disappointed she was in him, and yadda, yadda, yadda!

Rhetta saw the limousine approaching and ran out the front door to meet Randy.

"What did everyone say? Did they simply love it? Weren't they dying? Tell, tell."

"Oh, yes ma'am. Everyone was quite impressed. They asked me who I was, why I was wearing a tuxedo, where I had rented the limousine, and who was my employer. Then some opened the invitation right there at their front doors. Others took it inside. The ones who opened it were really impressed. All of them said they planned to attend and what a lovely idea it was. Your idea was a real hit, Mrs. Ricks."

"What did Bonita say?" Rhetta asked excitedly.

"Who?" Randy asked even though he knew exactly whom Rhetta meant.

"Mrs. Roberts at Villagio, the old Briggs' mansion. It used to be Brigadoon.

"Oh yes, Villagio. Mrs. Roberts was not available. I left the invitation and the pink orchid with her maid."

"With her maid! I told you explicitly that you were to place it in the hands of Bonita Roberts! You imbecile!"

"Ma'am, I went there first thing, but the maid told me that Mrs. Roberts was asleep. I left and made all of the other deliveries and then returned to Villagio. The maid came to the door again and told me Mrs. Roberts was unavailable."

"And you just took that for the gospel truth and gave her maid Hannah Bonita's invitation?" Rhetta fumed.

"No ma'am. I told Hannah, I didn't know her name, that I had specific instructions to give the invitation to Mrs. Roberts. I practically begged her to ask Mrs. Roberts to come to the door. She told me she wouldn't. Honest, Mrs. Ricks. That's exactly what happened."

"And how did the maid know Mrs. Roberts wouldn't come to the door? What time were you there? Was Mrs. Roberts still in bed? It's the middle of the day."

"No ma'am. The maid told me Mrs. Roberts was up and dressed and that she was in the house."

"Then why couldn't she come to the door?" Rhetta almost screamed.

"I guess she could come to the door. Hannah said she wouldn't come to the door."

"And why not?"

"I don't know. The maid said she had told Mrs. Roberts I had been there earlier and that I had a delivery from you and that I had been instructed to deliver it to her personally. Hannah said Mrs. Roberts told her to get it from me. And that's the honest truth, Mrs. Ricks," Randy explained.

"Did you ask if the maid would show you into the house so you could hand it to Mrs. Roberts? Did you think of that?" Rhetta sneered.

"I did. I asked Hannah if she would allow me in and show me to Mrs. Roberts so I could personally give her the invitation, but the maid said if she did that she would be in the doghouse. She apologized and everything, but she said I had to give her the invitation. Those were her instructions from her boss. She understood that I had mine, but there was nothing she could do. I can understand that, can't you, Mrs. Ricks?" Randy asked.

"No, I cannot. I told you to something and you didn't. What do I care if her maid gets in trouble? I wanted you to hand that invitation and that damned orchid to Bonita yourself."

"What could I do, Mrs. Ricks? Knock the maid over and wander through the house until I found Mrs. Roberts? I think she may have been really angry then."

"All right. All right. Take that tuxedo and that limousine back and then come on back here and start on the lawn. That invitation was to a luau here next Friday and you've got a mountain of work to do before then," Rhetta instructed.

"Yes ma'am, and I'm sorry, Mrs. Ricks. I truly am. I did my very best. Everyone who read the invitation was really impressed. I know your party will be the talk of Spencer and I'm sure Mrs. Roberts will attend."

"You better hope she does, Randy, because if Bonita Roberts' fat ass isn't sitting on my deck next Friday in a sarong big enough to tent a house overrun with termites, you're going to be out of a job!" As Rhetta uttered those last few words, Randy thought he heard her growl.

Rhetta was fit to be tied. She stomped into the house and placed a call to Villagio. Raven answered. Rhetta demanded to speak to Bonita immediately. Raven placed her on hold and told to Bonita Mrs. Ricks was on the phone. Bonita told Raven to inform Rhetta that she was suffering from a horrid migraine and was resting at the moment, but she would return her call later in the day permitting she recovered somewhat. Rhetta slammed the phone down when Raven repeated what Bonita said word for word.

Within seconds Rhetta's phone rang. She picked it up and sweetly said, "Hello."

Desiree Compton was calling to tell Rhetta how lovely her invitation was and how much she appreciated being included, but that of course she would be unable to attend.

"But I am so looking forward to hearing all about your luau, Rhetta. Please call me first thing Saturday morning and describe every detail."

"Well, the Countess will be able to attend, won't she?" Rhetta was really looking forward to entertaining royalty and having cousin Hunter write up that little blurb for the local paper. She was also planning to place a little tidbit about the party at her summer cottage in the Nashville papers and she would surely want to add that the Countess Ortiz was in attendance at RickShaw.

"Oh, I'm sure she'd love to attend, dear, if she were going to be in Spencer, but she's leaving on Sunday to return to Spain."

Rhetta was crushed. Was nothing going to work out for this party? She was spending a veritable mountain of money and having to listen to Trace complain vehemently on his nightly phone calls to her from Nashville.

"I'm so disappointed, Desiree. But thank you so much for calling and I'll be sure to fill you in on every little detail. Now, don't forget to put Trace's and my name on your list for a Sunday real soon, okay?"

"I'll be sure to do that, dear. *When pigs have wings after your last little drop in during Bonita's visit.* Thanks again. Bye now."

Rhetta sat down with her head in her hands. The phone jangled again. Grabbing it, Rhetta cooed, "Hello."

"Rhetta, what a caution you are! This is Darling Huxtable and I'm calling to thank you for such a lovely invitation and the orchids. Such a novel idea. You're so sweet to include us, but we won't be able to make it. BD and I will be at the annual bar association conference in Nashville until Saturday morning. We'll be back in time for Bonita's wine and cheese. I'll look forward to seeing you there and hearing all about the luau. Thanks, love. I know your party will be a smash! Bye, dear."

Rhetta burst into tears almost before she could hang up the phone. Darling can't come to my party, which just has to set Spencer on its ear, but she can hustle right back from Nashville and the bar association conference to have wine and cheese with Bonita. And that big, fat, filthy rich sow didn't invite me, but you wait, Darling, because you're damned right about one thing. You better believe you'll see me there—one-way or another!

18

Precious and Isaac

Precious was at Isaac's house overseeing the draping of the great room with yards and yards of fabric she had purchased to make his dream come true of simulating a Bedouin tent in the desert within the walls of his mansion. She had enjoyed her shopping spree for Isaac immensely since money was not an object. He had given her carte blanche to spend whatever was necessary. Precious delighted in telling her friends that Isaac Kahn had given her an unlimited expense account for his new decorating project and she had exceeded it.

In addition to the water-stained Moiré silk embroidered with fourteen-carat gold threads, Precious had selected Roman style velvet chaises and divans to adorn the immense room. Gold water pitchers on golden trays would rest atop carved, brightly painted Moroccan tables. The gold-leaf elephant she had earlier obtained for Isaac was to be the focal point of the cavernous room.

On her next trip to New York, she planned to put out feelers to find the perfect china to be placed in service for Isaac's dinner parties. She planned to suggest to him that he entertain lavishly once the room was complete and hire dancing girls dressed in layers of veils to serve a feast to be eaten with the fingers, as it is and was customary in Middle Eastern countries. The guests could recline on the chaises and divans while eating. She was tremendously excited about an object d'art she was expecting to bring back with her next time. Precious had located one of three remaining Roman vomitoriums in the world and was purchasing it with Isaac's money for the tented room. So what that she was mixing Roman and Middle Eastern cultures? Eclecticism was in. Precious was particularly impressed with the amount of the check she would be writing for the valuable marble urn, and she didn't expect Isaac to bat an eye. After all, he was a collector. He would be absolutely thrilled with the purchase.

After Precious had given detailed instructions to the crew she had assembled at Les Enfants to drape the great room, she wandered off in the direction of the kitchen in search of a Diet Coke, another of her passions. She had to pass through the library on her way. A large coffee table book resting on a library table caught her eye and Precious stopped to peruse it. It was child pornography at its apex. She had never seen pictures so graphic. As she continued to turn the pages, she didn't hear Isaac enter the room.

"Ah, I see you've found another of my treasures, Precious."

"I've never seen anything like this in my life. It's pornographic and yet it's arty."

"It's called erotica, Precious. Surely, you're familiar with erotica?"

"I guess not. This is beautiful. Where did you get it? I've never heard of this book."

"I'm a collector, remember? I have one of the largest collections of erotica in the world, I would imagine. I have Picasso's entire collection. Would you care to see it?" Isaac asked.

"Yes, I would."

Isaac slid the library ladder to the section he desired and climbed up so he could reach the highest library shelf in the library boasting fifteen-foot-ceilings. Retrieving a leather portfolio, he handed it down to Precious. She crossed to a leather sofa and carefully laid it on the glass-topped coffee table. Isaac joined her and opened the portfolio. Precious was absolutely entranced with Picasso's pen and ink erotic depictions. The two whiled away the afternoon looking at what most would consider *dirty pictures,* but what others consider one of the highest forms of art. Isaac showed Precious his Chinese and Indian erotica too. Before he was finished, he had taken Precious into a small room behind the library and shown her his figurines, teapots, urns, and pitchers all featuring erotica. Precious, with her vast knowledge of art, furniture, fabrics, objects d'art, and pottery was completely overcome with the enormity of her lack of knowledge about this highly sought after and greatly coveted art form. She simply couldn't wait to tell the people at Sotheby's about her find, but then what good would that do her? She knew Isaac would never sell any of it.

"Isaac, you have such a magnificent collection, but who ever sees it? Have you ever thought of selling any of this? You could ask a fortune for each piece."

"I *paid* a fortune for each piece, Precious. And why would I want to sell any of it? I spent years collecting it and as for who sees it, I do. Collectors are not interested in displaying their collections for others to see. A collector collects for his own pleasure. You are one of the few people I've allowed to see it. I'm happy to finds that you appreciate erotic art."

"It's fabulous! I adore it! I want some myself."

"Then you're in luck. You're in the business. You can start looking and making calls on your next Sotheby's trip. Some of your people there should be helpful in putting you on the right track to finding some good pieces."

"So could you. Will you put me on the right track to purchase some, Isaac?"

"Most of mine is from private collections. I don't buy from auction houses or catalogues, you understand?"

"Of course, I understand, but for instance did you travel to China to get the Chinese figurines and that exquisite teapot or did you buy them from a collector?"

"The teapot was actually a gift from a business associate, but enough about this collection for the moment. Let's check on the draping progress and may I offer you a libation?"

"That would be lovely. An ice-cold martini would be divine."

"Shaken or stirred, ma'am?"

"I think shaken. I always have them stirred. Why not live it up?" Precious responded with a laugh.

Isaac depressed a buzzer on the floor next to the foot of the leather sofa. Within seconds, his houseboy Chang appeared to take drink orders. In addition to her education in the world of erotica, Precious learned during cocktail hour that all those years she had partaken of stirred martinis had been squandered. Shaken martinis were fairly close to Utopia for a dedicated martini drinker.

At home that evening, Precious ate the dinner Lila prepared for her and then took to her room where she placed a call to a Sotheby's agent with whom she had become friends. The agent had no idea where to locate erotica, but advised Precious she would get right on it the next day. Precious racked her brain. If her agent, who was fabulous at ferreting out hard-to-find artifacts didn't know where to begin to look for erotica, she didn't know where to turn next. And then Precious had a brilliant idea!

I bet the boy would know where to find it. I'm sure he has access to all kinds of cheap pornographic literature, but sometimes people who know about the junk may have leads to the treasures. I need to call anyway as I'm going to be in the city next week to make sure I can book him. This time, I want him to come to my hotel. That lower East Side efficiency leaves a great deal to be desired. He's so delicious! I want him all to myself. How much is that going to cost? Let's see, at five-hundred-dollars per half-hour times twenty-four. That's twenty-four-thousand-dollars per day. That would certainly add up in a hurry, wouldn't it? You old fool! Why can't you be satisfied with men your own age? There are plenty of them sniffing around all the time, but no, you search for your lost youth with the hard bodies. So what? I'm not hurting anyone. No one knows and now you've become distracted again, Precious. Keep in mind this is a business deal. Call the boy and book him for several hours during your next trip and ask him casually if he knows anything about erotica and where you might be able to obtain some good quality pieces. It would be a perfect gift for Isaac once your project at Les Enfants is complete and with what he's paying you, you'll be able to afford a magnificent piece if one can be found.

Precious dialed and after three rings, an answer machine picked up.

"Hey, you've got the right number, but the wrong time. I'm busy right now, so either call back in a half-hour or leave your number and I'll get back to you then. Later."

A half hour. That means he's with someone else. I can't stand the thought. Precious, get a hold of yourself. He sells his body for a living. Did you think you were the first or maybe you thought you were so fantastic in the rack that after he had you, you would become theone and only. Right! But I want him so badly. I do want him all to myself. How could I possibly accomplish that? I'm going to New York twice as often as usual and seeing him a half-hour at the time. I want him longer than that. I'll call back right on the hour and schedule an entire afternoon with him in my hotel room for next week.

19

The Boy and His Uncle

The lead agent of the Child Pornography Detail of the Federal Bureau of Investigation glanced at his notes and began speaking to the newly formed task force, "Pornography is big business and generally, the making of and releasing of pornography is legal. Although it's been around for a long time, in recent years some of the biggest media companies in the nation have gotten into the porn business. Three Fortune 500 companies, through their cable television franchises, now peddle hardcore pornography. Many might be surprised to know that AT & T, Comcast, and General Motors are purveyors of dirty movies available on Echo star satellite television service and on Hot Network. These movies are not gauzily shot, romantic, or even morality versus immorality takes that are shown late at night on premium cable channels. These offerings are hardcore and downright raunchy. For the dedicated porn addict, the dirty movies offer easy access to their favorite form of *entertainment,* however they are pay-per-view. Some porn viewers are reluctant to order the garbage through their cable companies for fear of customer files not being handled in a confidential manner.

"Those addicted to child pornography, which is *not* legal, are relegated to ordering tapes and DVD's from direct distributors and receiving their parcels in plain, brown paper packages. This method, they believe, offers them anonymity. Additionally, they guarantee themselves the *pleasure* of being able to watch the garbage over and over in the privacy of their homes any time they wish. This is important to the sickos as many of them are married, leaders in their community, and seemingly model citizens, therefore they must indulge their addiction in private.

Because of constant, but less diligent federal intervention than you are going to use in pursuing these criminals, where indictments have customarily arisen and because of the producers' and distributors' fear of incarceration, great pains are taken to protect sources of child pornography. Often the place where the customer's order is placed for pornographic material featuring children has no geographic relation to the warehousing location of the films or to the company shipping the product to the customer."

The agent went on to explain exactly to the federal agents assembled in Washington, DC how this new task force was going to operate and how they were going to break up child pornography rings all over America. This particular area of pornography had reached epidemic proportions and the Attorney General wanted indictments and incarcerations immediately if not sooner.

Isaac had always been extremely cautious about the filming and distribution of his cash cow child pornography business and thus far he had aroused no suspicion, as far as he knew, from the authorities. He constantly changed addresses where his product could be ordered and locations where his films were warehoused. With the advent of the Internet, he had been able to successfully cover his tracks by always making sure that none of the websites where his films were available could be traced to him. Of course, he paid a great deal for that anonymity to various website providers. What he paid was a drop in the bucket to what he made in the illegal business, but it was a source of irritation to him since it detracted from his bottom line. Not computer literate himself, he didn't understand the nuances or the techniques necessary for covert computer operations.

What Isaac really wanted was someone whom he could trust to run a website for him that would be completely untraceable to him. He desired someone close at hand managing the site and keeping him apprised daily while allowing him to keep the operation at arm's length. And of course, he didn't want to have to pay anyone to design or run the site. He had pretty much given up on the idea of this wish ever being fulfilled.

Isaac's second desire was to retire from producing the films. Distribution was what Isaac wanted—that's where the real money was—and he was convinced that it could be covered up with Internet web sites. Distribution was where the real money was. Production was very shaky. Although Isaac himself, was never on location, he was linked to the production people and ultimately their paychecks came from his offshore bank accounts. He loved the money his dirty business provided him, but he wanted the best of both worlds. He wanted to retire from the production end totally while keeping the cash rolling in to his personal accounts. Thus far in his life, Isaac had somehow made his each and every wish come true. His child pornography business dilemma was proving his hardest to solve, but he knew that somehow he'd obtain this goal too. Once he was through with the ugly part of the business and was only taking in the money, he could concentrate totally on his ultimate goal—social acceptance by those who would have expected him to lick their boots when he first set foot on America's soil.

Though no one in Spencer had any idea of Isaac's involvement in child pornography, he had at one time been well known in pornographic circles, both nationally and internationally. Those purveyors of porn in his inner circle had also been aware of his impressive collection of erotica, said by many to be the largest collection in the world.

A lesser collector of erotica resided in a tenement building in Brooklyn and was the uncle of Precious' latest boy, Jesse. Jesse's uncle, Bartie, was a supplier of porn films to a few small time distributors since he had a ready-made actor and studio in his efficiency apartment with new *actresses* auditioning on an hourly and sometimes half-hourly basis. Bartie had installed a video camera complete with sound in the small apartment. It ran continuously twenty-four hours a day. Every few days, Bartie aired, edited, and spliced the tapes and *made* a new porn film starring his nephew Jesse and those ladies who had paid for his services during the last forty-eight hour period. Business was brisk, but Bartie longed to get into the big time and make the real bucks.

When Precious reached Jesse between engagements and *reserved* him for the entire afternoon two days hence, she also asked Jesse if he knew anything about erotica and where she might be able to obtain some of high quality. Jesse responded that he might be able to help her and asked when she had become interested in the art form.

"Oh, I'm not particularly interested myself, although I find it stimulating," Precious answered, "But I have a male friend in Spencer who has a huge collection. I want to find a gift for him. I've been decorating his mansion. He's paying me exorbitantly and I thought when I finished the project I'd give him a little gift."

"Really? What's his name?" asked Jesse.

"His name is Isaac Kahn. I really don't think he's anyone you would know, Jesse."

"You're right, I don't. I'll check with my sources and see what I can find. Maybe I'll bring some dirty pictures with me to your hotel when I come."

"Jesse, erotica is hardly dirty pictures, do you think?"

"I know it's artsy-fartsy, but I've seen some of that stuff. Just dirty pictures except somebody famous painted'em, that's all."

"Well I guess that's true," Precious said with a laugh. "I'll see you day after tomorrow at one o'clock. I'm really looking forward to it, Jesse."

"Yeah, me too. Gotta go now. See you then," Jesse said as he hung up.

"Uncle Bartie, that was the old broad from Spencer, Tennessee. She's hiring me from one o'clock Thursday until midnight. Big bucks for the Jes, huh?"

"Sounds good, kid. We'll have hours of flix."

"She wants me to come to her hotel."

"I don't like that, kid. You could get caught, you know? We've talked about this before. Besides, we'll miss all those hours of filming you with the old bag. Call her back and tell her to come here. You go to that fancy hotel and someone will start wondering why a young guy is hanging around there and pretty soon, its juvenile court city for you or worse."

"I'll have a reason to go there besides my services. I'll be delivering a package."

"What package?"

"She wants to buy some erotica," Jesse answered as he crossed to his computer.

"You told her I had erotica? What's the matter with you, Jesse? You got a death wish? You want us to get caught or what?"

"I didn't tell her anything about it. She asked me if I knew where she could find some erotica. She has a friend who likes the dirty stuff so she said. She wants him for him. It's a gift," Jesse responded as he hammered keys on his computer. "Well, what do you know?"

"Now what?"

"Come here, Uncle Bartie. Look at this picture I pulled up on the Internet. Who is that?"

Bartie took a few steps and leaned over Jesse's shoulder to look at the computer screen, "I don't know who he is, but he damned sure looks familiar. Who is it, Jesse?"

"Says here his name is Isaac Kahn and he lives in Spencer, Tennessee. This is an article from some piss ant newspaper called *The Spencer Spectator* about him buying some piece of property there and building—"

"A house. A house named *Les Enfants.* Now ain't that cute? Who does he remind me of, Jesse? It's on the tip of my tongue."

"Who has one of the largest collections of those dirty pictures you like so much in the world?"

"Ike Perl. Oh, my god, boy, you're right. It's Ike Perl. We have just hit the mother lode. But he looks different. What's different?"

"I think he's had plastic surgery. I bet he went under the knife and changed his name. Our boy is living in little Hooterville, Spencer, Tennessee, last left hand turn before the end of the world."

"And the old lady who loves getting banged by my nephew is a friend of his. We have to go slow on this one, Jesse. We gotta plan this one out real good 'cause when we get hitched up with Ike, we're gonna be in clover, boy! I gotta tell you, Jess, you are a man of many skills. You must screw like a bunny the way all those all broads are always sniffing around here like male dogs after a bitch in heat. You're one hell of a whiz on that computer too. Now, smart one, tell me how we're going to make this work."

"Give me some time to think. We'll put it together. Old Precious will tell me anything I want to know. I'll ask her a buncha questions about her friend, Mr. Isaac Kahn, model citizen, and we'll go from there. I can tell you one thing though, I bet the old broad will do anything I ask her as long as she can still get the rod."

So Ike, kiddie porn mogul, changed his face and his name and left Miami Beach, sin capital of the East Coast. He had dropped out of sight over seven years ago, but Bartie had known he was still in operation because Ike's films were unmistakable—they were the best because they were always the filthiest with innocent little children doing the unimaginable. The films were still available and new ones were coming out all the time, but neither he nor anyone he knew in the industry had been able to track Ike down since he suddenly disappeared from the porn scene. Bartie held high hopes for Jesse's learning anything from Precious that could somehow provide the catalyst for him to get hooked up with Ike's empire.

Bartie carefully reviewed his modest, but above average erotica collection, and selected an adequate Chinese octagonal mosaic tray. Each angle of the octagon was embellished with Chinese men and women in various sexual positions. Bartie had paid almost a thousand dollars for the piece and figured Jesse could squeeze maybe five grand out of Precious along with information about her friend Isaac Kahn. It greatly pleased Bartie that the icon of the porn world would be adding one of his cast-offs, to the tune of five thousand dollars from Precious' purse, to his erotica collection.

At noon on Thursday, Jesse boarded the "A" train for downtown Manhattan. He wore tan suede trousers, an off-white, long-sleeved, silk shirt open at the neck, tan socks and brown loafers. He looked every bit of his fifteen years of age. Tucked under his left arm was a handsome silver box Bartie had bought for five dollars from a jewelry store a few blocks from their apartment house. Earlier when Bartie handed Jesse the box that enveloped the erotica tray, he said, "The packaging makes all the difference, kid. Now remember, tell her the history of the piece just as I told it to you, and then start at five K. If she won't go that high, you can pretend to negotiate. I'll go as low as thirty-five-hundred-dollars, but then no more negotiating. Don't take a penny less than that, got it?"

"I got it, Uncle Bartie."

"And what else do you remember?"

"Find out everything I can about Ike."

"Yeah, but don't slip up and call him Ike. Call him Mr. Kahn. For God sakes don't let her get a clue you know anything about him."

"Don't worry. Now, I've got to go. Check you later, dude."

Jesse stepped off the train and transferred to another subway arriving a few blocks from the Mayflower on Central Park West at quarter to one. He walked slowly and checked out his profile in the plate glass windows of the stores along the way. At five to one, he entered the hotel through the large glass door held open by a doorman.

"Good afternoon, young man," from the doorman.

"Good day to you. Thanks," Jesse answered as he walked straight to the elevator bank. Jesse got in the elevator and pushed the button for the top floor where Precious had told him she had a suite.

At precisely one o'clock, Jesse tapped lightly on Precious' door.

"Coming," he heard her say and she opened the door.

She was dressed in slacks and some kind of fuzzy sweater, not at all what Jesse was expecting. He figured she would be in one of those slinky negligees or maybe even nude as she was always so hot to trot. Precious greeted him with a warm hug as if he were a young relative, offered him a seat, as she sat on a gold brocade sofa in the lavish, but old-fashioned suite.

"What have you got there, Jesse?" she asked.

"Some dirty pictures," he said, as he handed her the box.

Precious opened it and exclaimed, "Oh, it's gorgeous. Tell me about it."

Jesse relayed the *history* he was sure his Uncle Bartie had fabricated and he could tell Precious was absolutely intrigued.

"Where did you find this lovely piece, Jesse?"

"My uncle. He has a small collection of erotica. It took some talking, but I convinced him to sell you this piece."

"Well, I must have it. Mr. Kahn will love it. He has a teapot with similar art and I know he'll be thrilled with this. How much does your uncle want for it?"

"Five thousand dollars," Jesse said rather hesitantly. He thought the erotica stuff was just hard porn except it was done with oil paints or something. In the case of the tray, it was baked in an oven or a kiln or whatever those things were. But to Jesse, erotica remained just dirty pictures.

"Let me write him a check," Precious said as she rose to get her purse. "How do I make it out?"

"To Bartie Costlowe."

"Is that c-o-s-t-l-o-w?"

"With an e on the end."

Precious carefully tore the check from her checkbook and handed it to a rather stunned Jesse.

"Now I have some cola or beer if you prefer, but if you want beer, I don't want you to have too many. I wouldn't want to be arrested for contributing to the delinquency of a minor, now would I?" and they both laughed. "I ordered lunch earlier and it's warming in the oven. We can eat now or later, whichever you prefer."

"Thanks. I'd like to have one beer. That's all I'll have. I'm not a big drinker. And I think I'd like to have lunch now if it's all right with you," Jesse responded.

"That's fine," Precious answered and rose to cross to the kitchenette. As she did, she handed Jesse a stack of folded bills. "I've learned the rules and I know you prefer payment up front and in cash, so that bit of business is done and now we can enjoy ourselves until midnight."

Jesse put the money in his pocket without counting it. He had calculated how much she was going to be paying him for today, but he knew from his past trysts with her that Precious had also included a sizable tip. He hoped he didn't get mugged on the subway back to Brooklyn because with Uncle Bartie's check, he was going to have over ten grand on him.

Precious placed a tray will hot hamburgers, hot dogs, and grilled cheese sandwiches on the dining area table. She went back to the kitchenette and returned with another tray loaded with condiments, pickles, and a large bowl of French fries.

"I hope you like the selection," Precious purred.

"This is great!" Jesse responded as he dug in. He didn't want to tell her that he rarely ate junk food and was into energy shakes and protein boosters and Precious didn't want to tell him that she would diet for the next two weeks after eating the cholesterol delight.

"So you think Mr. Kahn will like that tray, huh?" Jesse said between bites.

"He'll love it."

"Have you known him a long time or what?"

"Not very long. He bought a piece of property on the lake in Spencer. Everyone who's anyone lives on the lake. Then he built this huge mansion, but he's not married and he hadn't hired a decorator. He has definite ideas about what he wants and he asked me to find a few pieces for him and I did. Soon, I was helping him decorate the entire house. He's from Yemen and he's cascading this gargantuan great room with moiré silk so it will look like one of the desert tents from his home country."

"So he's Jewish?" asked Jesse.

"I suppose so, but how do you know that he's Jewish if he's from Yemen?"

"I don't, but I do know that some Jews live in Yemen."

"How do you know that?"

"I spend a lot of time on the computer. I'm interested in a lot of things. I look up stuff all the time. Yemen is one of the countries I've looked up."

"Why would you look up Yemen?"

"Cause I got to "y" in the alphabet. I think up all the countries I can that start with each letter and look them up. I memorize stuff about each country. It's just something I like to do. Besides, you never know when one of those countries will come up in conversation—just like Yemen did today."

"Jesse, you are adorable and you're so smart."

"So what does your friend Mr. Kahn do for a living?"

"Nothing. He's retired, I suppose, but I'm not sure from what. Hardly anyone who lives by the lake in Spencer works. Most of them inherited their money, honey."

"Do you live by the lake, Precious?

"I do, in a home that's been in my family for generations. You would love it, Jesse. It looks like Tara. Do you know about Tara?"

"Scarlet O'Hara's home? Yeah, I know about Tara."

"Well The Woods, that's the name of my home, looks like Tara and it has a pool and tennis courts and beautiful manicured grounds."

"You have a swimming pool in your yard? I love to swim. The only place I've ever been swimming is at the YMCA pool and once at Fire Island when Uncle Bartie took me there a few years ago."

"You should come to The Woods. You could swim everyday."

"Are you inviting me to come?"

"I guess I am. I would love nothing better, but I don't know how I would explain you to the folks in Spencer."

"I could be your nephew."

"Everyone in Spencer has known me all my life, Jesse, and they know I was an only child and that I don't have any nephews. In fact, I don't have any living relatives."

"How about your pool boy then?"

"A live-in pool boy. What a novel idea!" Precious smiled.

The pure and simple fact was that Precious was absolutely intrigued with having Jesse come to live with her if she could think of some way to explain him. *What a perfect solution! I wouldn't have to make so many visits to New York and could have the delicious crumpet all to myself.*

Precious was brought back from her reverie with Jesse's question, "So do you and Mr. Kahn go to the same parties and stuff like that?"

"You certainly do have a lot of questions about Mr. Kahn, Jesse."

"I don't really have a lot of questions about him, Precious. I'm trying to get to know more about you. You told me he was a friend of yours, so I thought if I asked you questions about him, I could find out more about you. Then you wouldn't think I was prying."

Oh, yes, Jesse was good and slick well beyond his years. Precious all but melted into the sofa.

"Aren't you sweet? Actually, I don't attend parties with him. Mr. Kahn is really not into the social scene in Spencer, Jesse."

"Why? He doesn't like to party down?"

"I don't know about 'partying down,' but he hasn't been too well accepted socially in Spencer. It's a very provincial town, lots of old money, suspicion of newcomers, and that sort of thing," Precious explained. "But he does want to be included in the social scene. He's told me that. In fact, he practically asked me to get him into the right doors in Spencer so he would become accepted there by the *in* crowd."

"And did you get him invites to some of the bashes?"

"No, I haven't."

"Why?"

"I thought I'd get to know him better first. I don't want to be responsible for getting someone accepted by Spencer society and then have him turn out to be unacceptable," answered Precious.

"What would he have to do to be socially unacceptable?"

"I don't know. Maybe he's from a poor background. Maybe he was a gangster. Maybe he likes men. Maybe he likes young boys—"

"And that would make him socially unacceptable, but it's all right for you to like young boys?"

"Jesse, I don't like the turn this conversation is taking. Let's have our banana splits and talk about something else."

"I was only teasing you, Precious. It's different if a guy likes young boys. What would it take for you to get Isaac Kahn on the A-list in Spencer?"

"Nothing. I'd only have to suggest to some of my friends that he be included on their guest list for their next function."

"That's not what I meant. What would Isaac have to do for you for so you would get him those invitations?"

"I'm not following you, Jesse."

"He wants something from you. What is he going to do for you?"

"What are you talking about, Jesse?"

"Well suppose Isaac could do something for you that you really wanted. Suppose, for example that Isaac could make it possible for me to be able to come and live with you?"

"How would Isaac be able to do that?"

"I don't know. I'm just thinking out loud. Would you really like for me to come live with you, Precious?" Jesse said as he stood and moved behind her and began caressing the back of her neck and shoulders.

"I would, Jesse, but your coming to live with me is out of the question. Besides, even if I could work it out on my end, I'm sure your uncle wouldn't allow you to come."

"Yes, he would. Everything in Uncle Bartie's life is a business deal."

Precious was beginning to get excited now as Jesse moved his hands further down her back and began rubbing her with increasing intensity. "Are you saying that I could buy you from your uncle?"

"No way. Slavery's history, Precious. It is, isn't it? You don't still have slaves in Tennessee, do you?" Jesse whispered as he reached around and began to pull Precious' sweater over her head.

"Of course not, but you said a business deal. What business deal?" Precious asked between gasping breaths.

"We'll talk about that later. Let's get in bed. This will be the first time for us in a real bed, Precious," Jesse whispered again as he pulled the older woman to her feet and led her into the inner sanctum of her suite.

While Precious was in the throes of ecstasy and Jesse was performing to the best of his ability physically, his mind was going ninety miles a second. He was beginning to put together a plan. Isaac Kahn wanted to be in the social scene in Spencer. Jesse hoped that was extremely important to Ike. He figured it must be seeing as how he had gone straight and all. And Precious wanted Jesse to come live with her if there were some way she could explain having a young buck there all the time. And Uncle Bartie wanted into the child pornography game as Ike's partner drawing on Ike's expertise and distribution network. And Jesse and Uncle Bartie had tapes of Precious that would set the Spencer social set on its ass. All the ingredients were there. Now all Jesse had to do was to determine the correct proportions, mix them all together, and figure out how long to bake the concoction before it was ready to eat.

20

Meanwhile Back in Spencer

Rhetta was in bed with a migraine. Actually, Rhetta didn't have a headache at all. She was about to die of mortification. None of the people she needed and wanted to attend her luau had accepted. Only old fuddy-duddies and lesser asteroids in Spencer's galaxy of socialites were coming to her *party of all parties* and she had spent a fortune so far. She couldn't cancel. Trace yelled every time he spoke to her on the phone about the bills piling up and the big ones wouldn't arrive until after the gala. And Bonita still had not invited her to the all-important Saturday wine and cheese where she was going to lay out her grandiose plan for Spencer, whatever it was. To top it all off, Bonita had not returned Rhetta's phone call nor had she herself responded to Rhetta's hand delivered invitation. Bonita's social secretary, Raven somebody, had written on Bonita's embossed Villagio stationery that Mrs. Roberts would be unable to attend the luau. No explanation was offered.

Rhetta lay on her canopied bed with a cold cloth on her forehead trying to figure out a way to get Bonita to come. Maybe she should haul herself up, shower and dress, and call on Bonita. After all, she had entertained Bonita at RickShaw for tea, so it wouldn't be like she was barging in on her. Maybe she should take some flowers over and inquire as to whether Bonita was feeling under the weather since she wouldn't be attending the luau, only three days away.

Rhetta made the supreme effort and arose from her bed and readied herself. Once in the garage, she hit the automatic door opener and backed out. People were all over the lawn. The big multi-colored tent was up and the catering staff was setting up chairs and tables under it. Two men with shovels were digging a huge hole on the shore for the pigs that would be roasting there in forty-eight hours. She hadn't been able to get into her kitchen for two days because the catering staff had been there from six in the morning until six at night. All this madness, and no one of any consequence, would see all the effort or appreciate all the expense!

Rhetta drove into town and selected thirty sunflowers and had Travis arrange them in a bouquet tied with brightly colored raffia. She hurried out and pushed the accelerator to the floor in her rush to get to Villagio. As Rhetta approached the house, the maroon Rolls was coming toward her on the brick driveway. Rhetta pulled over to the right, stopped, and hit the automatic window. The Rolls stopped and Alphonso opened his window.

"Hello, Mrs. Ricks."

"Hello, Alphonso. I'm just on my way to call on Mrs. Roberts. I do hope she's at home and receiving.

"She's in the back seat, ma'am."

"Oh."

Since the back window did not open and the windows were darkly tinted, Rhetta couldn't see Bonita in the car. She couldn't believe Bonita's rudeness in not opening the window to speak to her. Not to be brushed aside, Rhetta threw her car into park and jumped out of the car and went to the back window of the Rolls. Still nothing.

"Miz Roberts, Mrs. Ricks is standing at your window. I think she wants to speak to you," Alphonso said with his head turned toward the back of the car.

Slowly, the back window opened.

"Hello, Rhetta. What brings you here?" asked Bonita.

"I got your note, Bonita, from your social secretary saying you won't be able to attend my little party and I thought you might be sick or something seeing as how you didn't write it yourself. I brought you something," and Rhetta moved back to her car and retrieved the sunflowers.

"How lovely. Could you take them up the house and ring the bell? Hannah will put them in water. I'm on my way to Nashville, dear, and I really must be going. I have an appointment at the Heavenly Spa for some maintenance work. You know how that is? Lovely of you to *drop by*. Thank you for the flowers. Alphonso, we must be going. Bye, Rhetta," Bonita trilled as both Alphonso's and Bonita's windows went up and the Rolls slowly started to move down the driveway.

Rhetta stood there with her mouth hanging open. She had never been treated so horribly in her life. Bonita wasn't sick and she hadn't explained to Rhetta why she couldn't come to her party *and* she had the audacity to tell Rhetta to take the flowers to her maid. Rhetta's immediate reaction was to throw them on the driveway, run over them a few times, and leave them there or not to take them to Hannah at all—she paid three-dollars-and-fifty-cents per stem for thirty damned sunflowers. But Rhetta was over a barrel. She couldn't make Bonita angry. She had to get her to that luau. Well, today was shot. She'd have to come up with another plan.

Rhetta returned to her car and drove the rest of the way up to Bonita's mansion and rang the bell. Hannah opened the door and Rhetta told her about seeing Bonita in the driveway and that Hannah was to put the flowers in water.

"I sure will, Miz Ricks. They's real perty."

"Do you mind if I come in for a minute, Hannah? It's so hot out here."

"Course not, Miz Ricks. Come on in," Hannah said as she held the door open wider.

"I'll jest go in the kitchen and get a vase for these, Miz Ricks," and Hannah started for the kitchen.

Rhetta followed her. Preparations were laid out in the kitchen and it was obvious Hannah was in the midst of stuffing pastry shells. *For the party Saturday, no doubt.*

"What are you making, Hannah?"

"Oh jest some stuffed shells."

"For a party?"

"No ma'am, they ain't for a party. Miz Roberts havin' a meetin' Saturday," Hannah responded.

"Oh, what kind of meeting, Hannah?"

"I ain't sure, Miz Ricks. Something about a cotillion or somethin' like that, I think."

"Who's comin'?"

"Now I don't know nothin' 'bout that. Raven's in her office. She handles all Miz Roberts' invitations and stuff. You can go ask her if you want." *But I sure hopes you don't.*

"Well, no, I won't do that. I don't want to be nosy," Rhetta said with a smile.

That's good. Hannah thought and almost said aloud.

The kitchen door opened and Raven entered with her lunch tray.

"Oh, hello, Mrs. Ricks. I didn't know you were here."

"I brought Bonita some flowers. After I got your note telling me she was unable to attend my luau this Friday evening, I thought maybe she was sick, so I came to visit and brought her some flowers."

"It's a shame you missed her. She left only moments ago," Raven said.

"I didn't miss her. We met in the driveway."

"Good, then you talked to her," Raven said as she put the dishes on the counter.

"Yes, but she didn't tell me why she can't come Friday night. Obviously, she's not sick," Rhetta had to refrain herself from shrieking.

"No, she's feeling quite well. She's on her way to Heavenly."

"So she said. So why can't she come to my party, Raven?"

"I wouldn't know the answer to that, Mrs. Ricks."

"Of course you would. You're her social secretary. Does she have another engagement? I'm not aware of anything else happening this Friday night," Rhetta said and this time there was definitely an edge in her voice.

"I'm sorry, Mrs. Ricks. Mrs. Roberts didn't discuss her plans with me for Friday evening. She merely instructed me to write a note to you with her regrets."

"I see. I guess you wrote the invitations or made the calls to those who are coming to her meeting Saturday, didn't you?" Rhetta questioned.

"Yes ma'am. That's what I do. Invitations, regrets, acceptances, lists, and so on."

"Who's invited?" Rhetta blatantly asked.

"I don't think I'm at liberty to give out that information, Mrs. Ricks."

"Why not?"

"'Cause it ain't none of her bizness, Miz Ricks, and it ain't none of yours neither. You knows we can't tell you who Miz Roberts has asked to her meetin'. We's employees and we can't talk about Miz Roberts' personal bizness. You tryin' to get us in trouble?" Hannah grumbled.

"Of course not. I was merely curious. I'm sorry, Hannah, Raven. I was only making conversation. Please forgive me. Now, I must be going. I have so much to do for my party Friday night. Before I go, would you mind if I just made a quick trip to the powder room?" Rhetta asked all smiles.

"Not at all. You can use the one right off from my office. It's through that door." Raven gestured. "Hannah, do you have any brownies left?"

"They's in the cupboard next to the Refridgidaire, Miss Raven. Help yourself."

Rhetta slipped though the door and was on the computer mouse like white on rice. She found the icon she thought was the right one and tapped the mouse. First try. There was Bonita's Wine and Cheese Meeting list of invited guests. Rhetta quickly scanned it and put her almost total recall into service. It took her only seconds. She closed out the folder, went into the powder room and flushed the toilet, washed her hands and returned to Raven's office. Raven was seated at her desk finishing the last of her luncheon dessert brownie.

"Thank you so much, Raven. I'll see myself out and again, I'm sorry. I wasn't trying to get you into any trouble."

"No problem, Mrs. Ricks. I'll walk you to the door."

Rhetta left the house. As she was driving away, she went over the list in her head_Precious Woodson_she wouldn't be any help. Lydia Henley had possibilities. Rhetta had known her forever. Darling Huxtable wasn't going to be back in town until the morning of Bonita's meeting. Candy Martin had always been friendly to Rhetta. Maybe Candy could say something to Bonita to get Rhetta invited. Candy was coming to her luau after all. Lesser luminaries were on Bonita's list too. The Hulbertson sisters, two old maids who were each at least as old as God and who had lived in Spencer since the creation or possibly before, were on the list too. *What in the world does Bonita want with those old dried up prunes*? Hannah said the meeting was to discuss a cotillion. Harcourt Ball was on the list and Albert Sloane. Why would men be invited to discuss a cotillion?

"No, no, no!" Rhetta said aloud, "There is something much bigger than a cotillion to be discussed Saturday evening and I *have* to be in on it, but how?" Rhetta knew this was one time she wouldn't be able to *drop by.*

By the time she returned to RickShaw, she was practically at her wit's end. She knew she'd have to call Candy Martin and ask her to please help her figure out a way to get Bonita to the luau. She supposed she'd have to tell Candy why it was so important. Rhetta didn't understand how everything had gotten so messed up. After all, she was the daughter of the former Governor of Tennessee and therefore should be on everyone's A-list. Here she was in little Podunk Spencer and she wasn't included on the list for a wine and cheese party that some newcomer was giving to discuss an idea for the little berg. She was a native of Tennessee for heaven's sake.

Rhetta passed Randy and his crew readying the grounds. She glanced down towards the shore where the caterers were spreading palms around the pit they had finished digging for the pigs. Once in the house, she had to sidle past the New Yorkers busily working on the floral arrangements and there was no need for her to attempt to set foot in her kitchen. At least eight people were in there pounding, chopping, mixing, and stirring. Rhetta wearily climbed the stairs to her bedroom and sat on the edge of her bed with her head in her hands.

Rhetta steeled herself to call upon Candy Martin's largess. She reached out for the phone as it rang. Rhetta waited for two rings and answered with a dulcet "Hello."

"Oh, Rhetta, I'm so glad I caught you. I know you must be busy, busy, busy. This is Candy Martin."

Please don't let her be calling to say she's not coming to the luau. "Candy, I was just about to call you."

"Well, you know, great minds and all that. I have the biggest favor to ask of you."

How fortuitous. She needs a favor. Now it won't be so difficult for me to ask her for one.

"Of course, Candy. You just tell me what I can do for you and consider it done," Rhetta practically cooed.

"I hate to ask this at the last minute and I do so hate it when this happens to me, but I received a call just moments ago. I have unexpected houseguests arriving tomorrow afternoon and they're staying through the weekend. I don't want to miss your party—it sounds so lovely and so festive. Would it be too much of an imposition if I brought them? I can't really tell them they can't come to visit because they're family. It's just one couple—cousins of mine."

"I'd love to have them. Please feel free to bring the couple. You didn't even need to call to ask about that, Candy."

"Oh, thank you, Rhetta. I'm sure you'll enjoy them. It's Sharon's daughter and her husband."

Rhetta ran through the litany of relatives of Candy Martin from Mainline Philadelphia. *Sharon's daughter. Sharon? Sharon Mortimer? Oh sweet Jesus, Princess Sharon's daughter. Which one? Who cares? A princess at her party! Thank you, thank you, thank you, Candy Martin.*

"What is Sharon's daughter's name?"

"Oh, I'm sorry. I didn't tell you which one. It's Alexandria. She's on husband number three now. I believe his name is Ruslan. Yes, Ruslan, that's what she said."

"Are you talking about Princess Alexandria, Candy?"

"One and the same. Sharon, although I never could bring myself to call her princess, was my cousin on my mother's side, you know. I told you that, didn't I?"

"Yes, you did. I'll be delighted to have the Princess and her husband. Should I make any special preparations? How do I introduce her? How do I address her? This is so exciting!"

"Just Alexandria. They've been in Philadelphia visiting the Mortimers and they're on their way to Miami Beach, specifically South Beach. Alexandria loves to party, but she's always been partial to members of her mother's family and drops by even for a few hours every time she's here in the states. I love it that they're going to be here for the whole weekend. And you're sure it's all right if they come to the party?"

"It's more than all right, Candy. It's fantastic! Thank you. I'll see you, the Princess, and her consort Friday night."

"We'll be there, but Alexandria doesn't expect any of that *Princess* stuff here in the states, so don't stand on formality, Rhetta. You know Sharon's husband Prince Alexander of Russia was in exile. He was known as a pretender to the throne in his homeland. We'll see you Friday and thanks. Bye," and Candy hung up.

Rhetta slammed the phone down and jumped up in the air as she gave a big yelp. Life was good. *The Princess of Russia, pretender/smender, she was a Princess, was coming to her luau right here in River City—wait until Bonita heard about that!* Rhetta bet the old cow would get her fat butt and her flabby tits to the luau now.

Rhetta dialed Bonita's number. Raven answered.

"Hello, Raven. This is Mrs. Ricks."

"I'm sorry, Mrs. Ricks. Mrs. Roberts isn't back yet."

"I hardly thought she would be, Raven, since I've only been home a few minutes. I simply called to tell you some exciting news I thought you might want to pass on to your employer. Princess Alexandria of Russia and her consort Ruslan will be guests at the luau. I thought if Mrs. Roberts can see her way clear, she may want to at least stop by for a few minutes and meet the couple."

"I'll certainly pass that on to her, Mrs. Ricks. Would you like for me to have her return your call?"

"That won't be necessary, Raven, I'm going to be quite tied up until the party. I have to run. Bye, now," Rhetta said breezily and gently replaced the receiver. *Two can play your game, Bonita. See, I don't have time for you to call me back. I'm going to be quite tied up. I'm about to entertain royalty. Yes!*

Rhetta made another call to Hunter the downtown newspaper office and then literally skipped into her oversized master bathroom, turned on steaming hot water, and poured in a hefty scoop of bath salts. She stripped off her clothes and sank into the tub. The *mouth of the south* at the *Spectator* had the word now. It wouldn't take long for all of Spencer to know about her guests who had seemingly dropped from heaven. Rhetta's work was done. She could relax.

Within hours, Rhetta's phone began ringing off the hook. Precious Woodson called to say she was leaving New York early the next morning to get back to Spencer in time for the party—would it be all right if she attended even though she had earlier sent her regrets? Darling Huxtable and BD had become so bored with the bar convention they were leaving that night after the obligatory dinner and would be able to attend the luau—such a precious and imaginative idea. Suddenly, all those who couldn't make it only days before were available and jumping in cars and on planes to attend what Rhetta was beginning to realize was going to be Spencer's party of the year.

All except one. By noon Friday Rhetta had not heard from Bonita. By four o'clock Rhetta gave up as she realized Bonita was not going to call her nor was she coming to the party. And if Bonita didn't come to the party, she wasn't going to include Rhetta in the planning session at Villaggio the next afternoon. All her scheming and all the expense was for naught. Perhaps not. The Princess of Russia was going to be there. That was reason to celebrate in itself.

Trace trudged up the staircase toward the bedroom after his long hot drive from Nashville. The air conditioner on his SUV had conked out about fifteen minutes into the two-hour run. Another expense! He didn't know when it was going to end. He was all but tapped out. What was going on here at RickShaw was unbelievable. There were caterers, florists, valets to park the cars, handmade, hand-appliquéd sarongs for Rhetta and the girls and he was sure there wasn't one fricking orchid left in all of Hawaii. Trace could not fathom how much this shindig of Rhetta's was going to cost, but he knew it was definitely going to approach or exceed six figures—and he didn't have the jack.

Rhetta entered the bedroom from the master bath wrapped in a velour bath towel.

"Hello, Trace, I'm so glad you're here. You look tired," Rhetta said compassionately.

Trace did a double take. It had been months since Rhetta had seemed to notice anything about him. She must have spent even more than he figured.

"I am. I'm tired and I'm hot. The damned air conditioner went out on the SUV. More money to be spent! How much is this damned party costing, Rhetta? There are people and flowers everywhere!"

"It's not inexpensive to entertain anymore, Trace. The days of having a few folks over for a little cookout are over. You're an important man in Nashville and you're married to the Governor's daughter. We have to entertain on a grand scale and I promised after this party, I'll economize."

"Former governor's daughter, Rhetta, and I know what your idea of economizing is. You'll only want to go to New York once a season to buy your designer dresses rather than twice and you'll have the maid cook one more night a week rather than going out, and oh yes, you'll only have your hair done once a week rather than twice. Is that what you mean by economizing? If it is, it's not going to be enough. We are in deep shit, Rhetta!"

"Trace, please lower your voice. The help will hear. Now, we'll pay for this and then I'll make big changes. I promise. Let's not argue tonight, Trace. This party is going to be so wonderful. The Princess is coming!"

"You told me and told me and told me. You've called me four times in the past day and a half, Rhetta, and you've told me about the Princess every time! So what? She sits on the pot like all the rest of us, doesn't she?"

"Trace, please don't be crude. Take a nice, hot shower. I'll call down and have a drink sent up for you. What would you like? A mai tai, maybe? That's the official drink of the party, but you can also have a Margarita, a pina colada, whatever you like. What'll it be?"

"I'll go get it. I just want a beer."

"Trace, could you do me a teensy-tiny favor tonight?"

"What's that?"

"Could you drink the bartenders' specialty drinks rather than beer?"

"Rhetta, beer is my drink of choice. You knew that when we met, when we dated, and when we married and it's still my drink of choice. I'm just a good old boy from the wrong side of the tracks, remember? And I want a beer," he said as he started for the door.

"Take a shower, Trace. I'll have a beer sent up."

"And not one of those micro-brews or foreign brands. Pabst Blue Ribbon, Rhetta."

"We don't have any Pabst Blue Ribbon. I didn't order any."

"You expect me to pay for all this silly-assed nonsense and you don't have any of my favorite beer for your high faluting shitball party? Well, I reckon I'll just go get in my hot as hell SUV and head for the convenience store and get me some of my favorite beer. I plan to enjoy at least one thing tonight."

"Trace, please. I'll get Randy to go get some Pabst. Please take your shower. Please, Trace. Tonight is so important to me. Please don't ruin it."

"You win, Rhetta. I'm tired. I'm hot. I have to get up and drive back to Nashville in the morning and I don't feel like going at it with you. Whatever drink you want me to have, you just have one of your highly paid minions bring it up. I'll drink it. I don't care."

"You have to drive back to Nashville in the morning?"

"Yes."

"Why? Tomorrow's Saturday."

"I know what day tomorrow is Rhetta. In one of your phone calls to me yesterday, I told you one of my patients from the nursing home had passed away and that her family asked me to be a pallbearer. The funeral is tomorrow afternoon."

"Couldn't you have declined, Trace?"

"Sure. I could have told the grieving family of a woman I cared for the past seventeen years that they were truly insensitive having the old bat's funeral on a Saturday since that's on the weekend and I have a home in Spencer two hours away. I could have told them I go there every weekend, and their having my patient's funeral on Saturday is extremely inconsiderate of my schedule. I could have added that my wife is throwing a party to compete with Truman Capote's Black and White Ball or Forbes Island birthday bash and that's it's inconvenient as Hell for me to attend the funeral, so screw them!"

"I'm sorry. I'll send down for your drink."

"You do that," and he headed for the bathroom.

"Trace, when you're finished, your new clothes for the party are hanging just to the left inside your closet."

"I don't need any new clothes. Why the hell are you buying me new clothes, Rhetta? I really do think you've completely lost your senses."

"Well, Trace, it's a luau. You can't wear jeans and an old golf shirt, which is your usual uniform here on the weekends. I got you a beautiful Hawaiian shirt, tasteful of course, and white trousers and leather thongs. You'll love it. And I ordered a lei specially for you that matches the flowers in the new shirt."

"I am not wearing a flowered shirt, Rhetta."

"Wait until you see it, Trace. You'll love it. I'll send for your drink."

Trace didn't hear the last part as he had already turned on the shower. He gratefully stepped under the hot water and wondered for the ten thousandth time how he had ever gotten himself into this marriage and this mess. He was Rhetta's puppet. He was completely hen-pecked and he no longer wanted any of the hen. He felt like a drone humming along doing whatever the Queen Bee wanted and paying for whatever struck her fancy. He couldn't do it any longer. But he knew that one more time, he'd shut his mouth and let her have her party. He'd wear the damned flowered shirt. He'd be a gracious host. He's give in this one last time, but then something had to give.

Rhetta hit the intercom button and requested that a mai tai be brought to the master bedroom right away, "And make sure it has one of those cute little umbrellas in it, and a chunk of fresh pineapple and a cherry. Thank you."

As Rhetta clicked off, the bedside telephone rang. She answered and when she heard the voice on the other end, she sank to the bed.

"Rhetta, it's Bonita. How are you, dear? Not too frazzled this close to party time, I hope?"

"Not frazzled at all, Bonita. I'm so sorry you won't be able to come," Rhetta said oh so sweetly.

"As it turns out, Rhetta, I've been able to make a few scheduling changes and if I'm still welcome, I'd love to come. I apologize for calling this late, but several people were involved and I've only just spoken to the last so that I could move things around and attend your what promises to be Spencer's party of the year," Bonita simpered.

"That would be wonderful, Bonita. Of course, you're welcome tonight and anytime. I never stand on ceremony, you know?"

Bonita bit her tongue not to respond to that one. "Good, then I shall see you at the appointed hour. Goodbye, dear."

"Goodbye, Bonita. See you soon," Rhetta said as she hung up the phone.

"Oh, how sweet it is!" Rhetta sighed.

"How sweet what is?" Trace asked as he came back into the bedroom.

There was a tap on the door. Rhetta retreated to the bathroom as Trace, in a terry robe, went to the door and took his mai tai from a dark young man clad in a loincloth and a lei.

"Thanks," Trace said and shut the door.

Rhetta raced into the room, "Wait, don't take a sip yet. I want to see it. Oh, that's perfect! Isn't it a pretty drink, Trace?"

"A beauty, Rhetta. And it doesn't taste bad either. Now where are those new duds you want me to wear?"

"I'll get them." Oh, thank you, thank you, thank you. Trace has calmed down. He's going to wear the new clothes. Bonita's coming. Princess Alexandria and Ruslan will be at my house, right here at RickShaw. I don't care what it's costing. It's worth it!

21

The Luau

Five handsome, tanned young men in loincloths and leis stood opposite five voluptuous tan young women clothed in gaily-flowered sarongs and leis around their necks and orchids behind their left ears in readiness for the guests to arrive. As the various cars and limousines began closing in on RickShaw, it looked like a commercial were being shot for Rolls Royce, Mercedes, BMW, Jaguar, and Lexus. There were no Chevrolets, Oldsmobiles, or Fords to be seen.

As a car pulled up to the Porte cochere of RickShaw, two uniformed valets rushed to either side of the car to hold the door for the departing passengers and then the one on the driver's side whisked the vehicle away for the next arrival in line. The guests stepped onto a palm-strewn pathway where the beautiful, tanned young people, employed especially for the occasion, waited with orchid leis. One of the beautiful girls kissed each gentleman on both cheeks and put the lei around his neck while one of the handsome young men did the same to the female of each couple. At the end of the pathway, Rhetta and Trace stood under a fiber optically lit hut complete with thatched roof.

Trace looked quite debonair in his white Hawaiian shirt decorated with huge magenta flowers. His complementing orchid lei almost perfectly matched the magenta leather thongs Rhetta had specially ordered for him. Trace had almost rebelled when he saw the shoes, but once again he had zipped his lip and given in reminding himself that this was the last time he was going to do what Rhetta wanted. Rhetta was in her glory in a white sarong, appliquéd with red and yellow flowers in a diagonal down the front. The dress set off her tanning salon bronze skin tone perfectly. Her orchid lei was a mixture of yellow orchids and red ones, the rarest of all orchids, and she had made sure there was not another red orchid any closer to her than Maui. Rhetta also had one of the rarities in her hair. Her shoes were white shell sandals accented with a silk red and yellow orchid on each.

Once the guests were welcomed by their host and hostess, they passed through the hut onto the rolling front lawn of RickShaw where there were four more huts. Two of them housed bars and two were hors d'oeuvres stations. Closer to the water sat a gigantic multicolored tent in which tables with brightly colored cloths were arranged to accommodate six persons at each. Tropical fruits were attractively arranged in the center of each table including pineapples, coconuts, mangos, and papayas on which orchids had been tastefully placed here and there. The fruits and the orchids on each table surrounded a mini-volcano emitting smoke. Since the tropical fruits had to be shipped in and the mini-volcanoes were custom-made, the cost of each centerpiece was in the neighborhood of two-hundred-dollars. Thirty tables awaited guests. Fiber optic lighting, another horrendous expense, was woven around the tent's poles, around the stage where the band would soon be playing at twenty-five-hundred-dollars an hour, and along the edge of the dance floor especially erected for the gala. The pearl favors at a cost of seventy-five-dollars each were next to each place setting encased in a hinged, bleached, and glittered oyster shell, ordered from Louisiana's Gulf Coast and commanding almost as much expense as the favors themselves. Oyster shells are the result of the oyster being shucked and shuckers don't leave the shells hinged, therefore Rhetta had paid for the live oysters, their delicate removal to keep the shell hinged, the bleaching and glittering process and the shipping. Oyster shells are not lightweight cargo.

The sterling silver place settings and the Baccarat crystal Rhetta had rented gleamed in the glow of the fiber optics. Everything was even more perfect than Rhetta had imagined.

On the lake's shore, men in loincloths and leis were demonstrating the Hawaiian fishing method by throwing nets into the water. Although the men caught nothing, some of the guests were enjoying watching. Musicians strolled the grounds playing the banjo and guitar and hula girls in grass skirts swayed to and fro offering hula lessons to anyone interested. The aroma of the roasting pigs wafted through the air as others employed for atmosphere and ambiance pounded taro to make poi on an imported tree stump at the water's edge.

When almost everyone had arrived, Rhetta saw Candy's chauffeur swing Candy's classic Mercedes into the drive. She could hardly contain herself. She was about to meet Princess Alexandria of Russia. No one in Spencer would ever be able to top this. As the car slowed to a stop, Bonita's Rolls appeared. Rhetta didn't know whether to shit or go blind.

Princess Alexandria emerged from the car. She was in a white halter jumpsuit and she was absolutely stunning. Ruslan came behind the car and extended his arm to her and then waited for Candy to get herself arranged and offered his other to her. The three of them stepped onto the palm pathway for the lei presentation. Bonita was assisted from the Rolls and was immediately behind them. What a horror she was! She looked as if she had a very large tablecloth wrapped around her girth and it was a strapless tablecloth at that. With her pendulous bosoms, the strapless thing was not a pretty sight. Gobs of fat hung from her upper arms and the mountains of flesh above the strapless *tablecloth* made every man there realize there definitely could be too much of a good thing! Giant black silk orchid earrings that could have doubled for chandeliers in a small house hung down below her quadruple chins and of course, she was totally made up with the iridescent blue eye shadow, the black pencil thin eyebrows and the ubiquitous pale pink lipstick. Her bleached coif was pulled back in a cascade of curls secured with more black silk orchids. On her feet, she sported black sequined sandals adorned with black orchids.

As the Princess and her party approached Rhetta, Rhetta curtsied and said, "Your Royal Highness, it is such a pleasure to have you at our little old party at RickShaw tonight."

Princess Alexandria extended her hand, "Please Rhetta, call me Alexandria and please, no curtsy. This is my husband Ruslan and of course, you and Cousin Candy are friends. It's so kind of you to allow us to come. We surprised Candy with our visit so we do so appreciate your hospitality and your generosity."

Ruslan bowed to Rhetta and she thought she might faint. Candy took Rhetta's hand and thanked her again for allowing them to come. All of them said their hellos to Trace and then it was Bonita's turn.

"Rhetta, what a lovely do. Everything looks so gorgeous. I'm so happy I was able to rearrange my calendar to be here," Bonita said as she looked over Rhetta's shoulder at Princess Alexandria.

"It's my pleasure to have you, Bonita. I'd like for you to meet my husband, Dr. Ricks, but Trace to you. Trace, this is Mrs. Roberts."

"Bonita, please. How do you do, Dr. Ricks?"

"Trace. I'm fine, Mrs. Roberts. Glad you're here. Belly up to the bar and get yourself a drink," Trace said with a grin.

Rhetta laughed loudly and nervously, "Let me get you a libation, Bonita," as she passed in front of Trace and shoved her elbow into his side. Rhetta thought she might die of humiliation. She steered Bonita to the bar where the Princess contingent was holding court and took ultimate pleasure in introducing her to Her Royal Highness, the Princess of Russia *in exile, of course, but that was never mentioned.* Again, Alexandria asked Rhetta to simply call her Alexandria, but before the evening was over, Alexandria gave up. Rhetta did not miss one single opportunity to introduce *Her Royal Highness.*

The party went off without a hitch. Everyone came and any who had earlier sent regrets apologized. Rhetta was in heaven. Her party was a sensation. Princess Alexandria was a hit. She was so down to earth and so gracious. The music was perfect; the food was divine, and when the hired sailboats with the brightly colored sails hove into the RickShaw pier just at sunset Rhetta thought she had never seen anything more beautiful.

By the end of the evening, Rhetta was in such fine fettle she had completely forgotten her purpose for the party—to get an invitation to Bonita's wine and cheese the next afternoon. When things were winding down and the guests were leaving, Rhetta was again in the fiber optic lit hut saying her good-byes. Bonita approached Rhetta and gave her a big hug and thanked her profusely for including her. She then whispered in Rhetta's ear,

"I'm having a few people over for wine and cheese tomorrow afternoon at three o'clock to discuss a little idea I have. Perhaps you and that delightful husband of yours might find time to stop by?"

"Oh, thank you, Bonita. Trace has to be back in Nashville tomorrow, so I know he won't be driving back in the evening. Tell you what. I'll call you in the morning. Just let me check my book, but I think I'm free," Rhetta smiled as she extended her hand to another departing guest.

Bonita was aghast. Rhetta had brushed her off and she knew Rhetta wanted to come to her wine and cheese so badly she could taste it. That's what the phone calls and the flowers and the interrogation of Raven and Hannah had been about. Bonita wouldn't be a bit surprised if Rhetta hadn't given this party just to get herself invited tomorrow afternoon. If Candy Martin hadn't saved the day by having Princess Alexandria surprise her with a visit the same weekend as Rhetta's party, Bonita wouldn't have come on a bet. The party had been a smash though, Bonita had to admit, and beautifully arranged. Rhetta certainly hadn't scrimped on anything. In her magnanimity, Bonita had decided to go ahead and invite Rhetta. She found it appalling therefore that Rhetta acted as though her invitation were of no consequence!

22

Trace Leaves and Precious' Guests Arrive

The next morning after Trace left in Rhetta's car as he refused to drive two hours back to Nashville without any air conditioning, Rhetta called Bonita, who answered the phone herself. She told her she would be delighted to attend her little fete that afternoon. Rhetta asked if she could bring anything.

Bonita told her that it would be a simple and casual and thanked her for the offer to bring something. Bonita thought how bourgeoisie Rhetta was. For heaven's sake, she hadn't invited her to a potluck dinner. After the phone call, Bonita returned to her notes for her planned presentation concerning the future of the young ladies of Spencer.

A few short miles away, Precious finished the coffee Lila had served her in bed. She was exhausted. After running all over New York and her delicious afternoon with Jesse and then rushing back early after getting a call from Darling Huxtable that Princess Alexandria was going to be at Rhetta's party, Precious was beat. She had enjoyed meeting the Princess and it was a good thing too since she had canceled her Friday afternoon with Jesse. He had sounded quite upset when she told him she had to go back to Spencer. She hoped he had been peeved because he wasn't going to see her, but common sense told her that more than likely he was disappointed he wouldn't be making several thousand dollars.

Precious looked at the clock. It was only ten. She decided she would take a nap. Later, Lila could come and do something with her hair so she could start getting ready for Bonita's do. Just as she fell asleep, Precious considered she may be getting too old for all this jet setting and partying.

Before her breathing had settled into a steady rhythm, there was a knock at her bedroom door.

"Lila, I'm napping. Wake me in a few hours. I want you to try to do something with my hair before I dress for Bonita's party."

"Miz Woodson, there's a man and boy at the front door."

"Who are they?"

"I don't know. I ain't never see them before, but they says you knows them and they wants to speak to you. Says it's real important."

"And you don't know who they are, Lila?"

"No ma'am."

"Probably some Jehovah's Witnesses or something. Tell them I'm unavailable. Wake me in time to get ready, Lila."

"Yes ma'am."

Precious was settling herself on her down mattress a second time when there was another knock. This time, Lila came into the room.

"That man and that boy says they ain't gonna leave 'til you come down there. They says they knows you from New York. They said to tell you it's Bartie and Jesse."

"Bartie and Jesse. That can't be! What do they look like, Lila?" Precious said as she virtually jumped out of the bed.

"The man look like he's 'bout fifty, balding, and a little heavy. His clothes look like he's a pimp or something. The boy's good-looking with dark eyes, hair and skin. Bartie says Jesse's his nephew."

"Invite them in, Lila. Take them out to the sunroom and get them some tea or something. I'll be down as soon as I can get myself together. And Lila, after you give them some tea, come back here and see what you can do with my hair. Hurry!"

Precious dressed as quickly as she could and waited impatiently for Lila to return to pull her hair into an elegant French Twist that only Lila could manage. When Precious attempted the hairstyle, she always felt she looked like a washerwoman. She lit a Vanity Fair and took two puffs before she realized she already had one going in the ashtray. She was a nervous wreck as she contemplated the reason Bartie and Jesse were on her doorstep here in Spencer. Maybe they had come for Jesse's money she thought. He had been quite upset she wasn't going to show. She didn't know the protocol, but perhaps she hadn't canceled in time and it was like a doctor's office—she still owed for her missed appointment.

Lila tapped on the door.

"Come in, Lila. Do something with this hair."

Lila entered and within minutes Precious appeared as if she had stepped from a chic hair salon.

"Who those people, Miz Woodson? They talks funny."

"Mr. Costlowe's a business associate from New York, Lila, and Jesse is his nephew. They don't talk funny. They merely sound funny to you because of their New York accents."

"I heared people from New York talk before and they don't sound like them two. They sounds like gangsters on the television set," Lila grumbled.

"I can assure you they're not gangsters, Lila. Now while I go down and tend to our guests, I want you to take the car and go into Spencer and pick up a few things at the grocery store."

"We don't need nothing. I went to the store yesday before you came home."

"I need some vitamin pills, Lila, and I need two cartons of Vanity Fair. And I'm sure we need tonic and soda."

"No, we don't. I got your vitamins. They're in your medicine cabinet. I got two cartons of them fancy cigarettes too and they's in the freezer where you likes to keep them and we got plenty of tonic and soda, Miz Woodson."

"Then go and get eggs and ham and milk and bread, Lila."

"Miz Woodson, we don't need any of them things."

"Lila, I want you to leave while I talk to these gentlemen, please."

"Why? In all the years I's worked for you, you ain't never wanted me to leave before. You afraid of them men, Miz Woodson?"

"Of course not. I simply have to discuss business with them," Precious answered as she started for the door leading to the upstairs hallway.

"Business that you don't want me to hear nothin' 'bout?"

"That's right, Lila. Now please understand and go to town for something, anything, but leave for a little while."

"You sure you's gonna be all right?"

"I'll be fine. Just go," and Precious left the room and headed down the stairs for the sunroom. She entered to find Bartie and Jesse lounging on the furniture watching television and drinking iced tea.

"Mr. Costlowe and Jesse, what a surprise! Whatever brings you to Spencer?" Precious turned to watch Lila leaving by the front door. Once the door closed, she said, "Do I owe you money, Jesse?"

Both of them had risen when Precious entered the room and both were smiling broadly.

"No, Precious. Why would you owe me money?"

Precious relaxed somewhat. At least this wasn't going to be a shakedown.

"Well, I had to cancel our appointment and because I had to give you such short notice, I thought perhaps you wanted your fee."

"I understood that you had to leave. I don't want a fee," said Jesse as he crossed to Precious and gave her a hug.

"We decided to come down to see you, Mrs. Woodson, because Jesse and I were both planning to present a proposal to you yesterday, but when you had leave suddenly, we didn't get a chance. It's a matter of some urgency. We didn't know when you'd be back in the city, so we booked a flight to Nashville and rented a car and drove to Spencer and here we are."

"It must be a matter of some urgency then. Well, let's all have a seat and hear this proposal," said Precious graciously. She could not begin to imagine what type of proposal Bartie and Jesse would wish to make to her.

"Do you have a DVD player, Mrs. Woodson?" Bartie inquired.

"Yes, right there. It's incorporated in the television set. Why do you ask?"

"I brought a DVD with me that you might be interested in seeing later on and I wanted to make sure we would be able to watch it together. Now, here's the proposal. I want you to introduce me to your friend Isaac Kahn."

"And why do you want to meet Isaac Kahn, Mr. Costlowe?"

"Let's say we have similar interests."

"Oh, the erotica? I haven't had a chance to give him the piece I purchased from you as yet, but when I do, I'll certainly ask him if he wants to meet you personally and perhaps see the rest of your collection," Precious offered.

"The erotica is not the common interest I'm talking about here, Miz Woodson, and I don't really care whether he wants to meet me or not. I want to meet him and I want to meet him today," Bartie said. Precious took note that his voice and manner had changed significantly. He was no longer asking, he was demanding.

"Mr. Costlowe, I'd have to have a reason to introduce you. What am I going to say to Mr. Kahn? I want to introduce you to my house guests, my business associates, what?"

"You don't tell him anything. You take me to his house and introduce us, that's all."

"I insist on knowing why you're demanding this of me, Mr. Costlowe. I don't owe you anything. Jesse says we're square. Why do you think I'll drop everything and take you to meet Mr. Kahn?"

"I think it's time to watch this DVD, Precious," said Bartie with a sneer. Precious did not miss the fact that for the first time he had addressed her by her given name.

Bartie removed a DVD from his pocket and crossed to the television set and inserted it. He took the remote from the console beside the television and adjusted the volume. Precious sat staring at the set wondering what in the world she was about to see. When the scene opened, she realized she was looking at Bartie and Jesse's efficiency in Brooklyn. As soon as she recognized the setting, she saw Jesse stride across the room and open the door. The next thing she saw was her own image. She realized she was seeing herself the first time she went to Jesse's for an assignation. Suddenly, the picture started moving rapidly as Bartie scanned through several minutes.

"We'll skip this part and get right to the meat of our little film," Bartie said.

As Precious watched Jesse remove her clothes, she understood what was happening. Everything she and Jesse had done on the efficiency sofa had been taped. Bartie was blackmailing her.

"Turn it off!" Precious screamed and Bartie immediately complied. "I want that DVD, Costlowe, and I want all the copies! Name your price."

"This DVD and any copies I have are not for sale, Precious, not for money anyway. I'll give you this DVD after you introduce me to Isaac Kahn."

"And if I do, I get all the copies?"

"There aren't any copies, Precious."

"I don't believe you."

"I'm sorry you don't, but it's the only one. Promise."

"Jesse, is it the only one?" Precious asked.

"Yeah. He hasn't made any copies. I'm sorry, Precious. You seem like a nice lady, but Uncle Bartie and I are in business, you know?"

"Why is it so important for you to meet Isaac Kahn, Bartie?" Precious asked. She decided to drop the formality of calling Bartie Mr. Costlowe. Her aristocratic manner and attitude had obviously had no effect on him, nor had it helped when she referred to him merely by his last name alone without the mister. She may as well sink to his level. After all, he had a DVD that possibly negated any attempts she might make at claiming an aristocratic, genteel, or ladylike background.

"I told you. We have similar interests."

"And all I have to do is introduce you to him and I can have that DVD?"

"Perhaps."

"What do you mean perhaps? You said you'd give it to me if I introduced you," Precious snapped.

"Now don't go getting all het up, Precious. I believe I'm holding all the cards in this game. You might have to do one more teeny little thing before I relinquish this valuable commodity I have here."

"And what would that be?"

"You told Jesse that Kahn wanted respectability. He wants to be included in the social scene here, right?"

"Yes."

"And you can arrange that, can't you, Miz Society Matron of Spencer, Tennessee?"

"I suppose I could get him invited to some of the right places."

"Then that's the other thing you'll have to do, because I mean to do some business with Mr. Kahn and that'll be one of the carrots I'll dangle in front of him. If he sees things my way, you'll get him into the right homes and mingling with the right people."

"But then he'll think I'm mixed up with the two of you, Bartie. I don't want Mr. Kahn to think that I have anything to do with your wanting to enter into a business deal with him, especially when I'm not aware of what business it is."

Waving the DVD in front of her face, Bartie said, "I believe you are mixed up with us, Miss Precious. Now why don't we head on over to Les Enfants for our introduction?"

"I have to leave Lila a note. Shouldn't I call Mr. Kahn and tell him we're coming? He may not be receiving at the moment."

"Nah. No phone call. He'll be receiving after we're introduced," Bartie chortled.

"Receiving means whether he's accepting or seeing guests, Bartie. If he's not receiving, you won't be getting your introduction," Precious explained.

"That's not my problem, Miz Asterpoop. If he's home, you're gonna make the introduction. I don't care whether he's *receiving* or not. Maybe he'll be interested in *receiving* after I send him this DVD," Bartie said menacingly as he waved it in her direction.

Precious wrote a note for Lila and placed it on the hall table.

"I'll go upstairs and get my purse," Precious said as she hurried up the stairs.

She returned quickly with a purse the size of a small suitcase. The three left by the front door. Jesse held the back door of the rental car open for Precious.

"Thank you, Jesse."

"Yes ma'am," said Jesse as he climbed into the front seat.

My god, he's beautiful. I love to look at him. Precious, you old fool, he's blackmailing you. Bartie is dumber than dirt and Jesse's as smart as a whip. Which one of them came up with this scheme, do you think? And Jesse knew that camera was running every second he was with you and you're sitting here mooning over him and how beautiful he is. You're nothing but a sick old bitch. And how am I going to get out of this? I can introduce them to Isaac. That's simple enough. I have the erotica tray I bought from Bartie with me. I'm not as dumb as you think, boys. I didn't have to get my purse. I had to get this satchel to hold the tray. I'll go in first and give the tray to Isaac and then I'll tell him about Bartie's superb collection—

what do I know? I've only been introduced to this artwork myself, so even if his collection sucks, I might think it's fabulous and then I can introduce Bartie and Isaac. Then I'm out of it. No, wait, I'm not out of it. Bartie wants me to insinuate Isaac into Spencer's social scene. What does he care about Isaac's social life? There are obviously things here I don't understand. But wait! I can do that. Isaac is reasonably attractive. He has good manners. So he's a Jew, so what? So are the Barkleys and everyone includes them and likes them. Isaac has more than enough money to impress all the once-had-the-old-money-but-now-it's-gone-but-I've-still-got-my-good-name crowd and if Spencer society accepted Bonita Roberts—she had looked like an over-the-hill prostitute at Rhetta's luau last evening, they would accept Isaac Kahn. Besides, just because I get Isaac invited to some parties and into the right homes doesn't mean I'm responsible for him. I'm Precious Woodson. My name is as old or older than anyone else's here and my word is golden. This will be all right. Once I have that DVD, it'll be okay. I don't think Jesse lied to me. I believe it's the only DVD. I'll do this. I'll get that disc and this chapter will be over. Au revoir, Jesse. You were the best I've ever had, but our little arrangement has come to an end after today. And thank god they're not making Jesse come to stay with me at The Woods, part of the deal!

About the same time Precious and the Costlowe boys were entering the gates of Isaac Kahn's estate Les Enfants, Trace Ricks was pulling into the parking lot of the Euclid Funeral Home in Nashville. He somberly entered the chapel and extended his condolences to the family members gathered there before retreating to the back room where his late patient's remains rested and where he was to meet the funeral director to receive his instructions.

It wasn't long before the other pallbearers arrived and were assembled in the viewing room. The director led the family members in for the final viewing of their loved one and then sealed the casket. Trace heard his patient's daughter whisper to her husband, both of whom he had met when he arrived, "How are we ever going to pay for this?" Her husband shook his head.

Trace was confused. Mrs. DeLancy had been quite well off. He had made numerous investments for her and in fact, only a few months ago, she had appointed him guardian of her estate. He wondered now why she hadn't appointed her only child. At any rate, he felt compelled to go to the couple and tell them that there was more than sufficient money to pay for the funeral and a fairly nice lifestyle for both of them for the rest of their natural lives. At that moment the funeral director gestured to the pallbearers to come and lift the coffin. The family members lined up behind them to follow the pallbearers bearing Mrs. DeLancy's remains into the chapel for her last hurrah.

Mrs. DeLancy had been a practicing Catholic all her life so her funeral was quite lengthy in that it was a funeral Mass. For a while, Trace, who was not a religious man at all, thought a little about the sweet little old lady. She had first come to him seventeen years before with minor ailments. Most of his elderly patients had very little wrong with them and were more than willing to have Medicare pay for doctor visits primarily to have someone to talk to who actually listened to what they had to say or appeared to anyway.

He had examined Mrs. DeLancy, listened to her ailments, real and imagined, commiserated with her when she had to have her twenty-two-year-old cat euthanized, and made house calls on her when she suffered from the vapors. When she voluntarily moved into the nursing home, Trace had called on her within hours of her arrival and he continued to call on her weekly during her ten-year stay there.

She had confided in him, asked for portfolio recommendations, insisted that he invest money for her and recently had made him guardian of her assets that exceeded three million dollars. As Trace thought about the time he had spent with Mrs. DeLancy, he recalled when he had gone to see her to sign the guardianship papers with her attorney, the attorney had told her that the next thing she had to do was make out a will. Mrs. DeLancy agreed, but Trace recalled asking her about the will only weeks ago and she still hadn't gotten around to it.

Trace ruminated during the rest of the service and by the time Mrs. DeLancy was laid to rest in the moist earth of the Spencer Faith Episcopal Church Cemetery, Trace had decided against telling her daughter how well off she was. Perhaps there was no will. Trace had full authority to deal with Mrs. DeLancy's money. No one was keeping an eye on him. Although he had actually made money for her, who knew that but him? He had been good to Mrs. DeLancy. She herself had told him she felt he was like a son to her. She would want him to have something for all he had done for her.

Who would know if he took just a little of that stack? Her daughter and son-in-law would still have a pile of money and he could pay off some of Rhetta's never-ending debts. It wasn't really a crime in Trace's mind and even if it were, it was a victimless one. Mrs. DeLancy certainly wouldn't know and there would still be plenty of dough for her daughter and husband.

Trace made sure to wipe the tiny smile from his face and somberly walked in procession with the other pallbearers as they each placed a boutonniere on Mrs. DeLancy's coffin before it was lowered into the ground for eternity.

23

The Meeting

Precious was no fool. She had to comply with Bartie's and Jesse's wishes and introduce them to Isaac Kahn. How she wished she had held to her prior convictions and never entered that chat room on the pornography web site. While Jesse had provided her with the best sex of her life, nothing was worth the price she was having to pay now. If she didn't get her hands on those tapes, these two guys could ruin her. And how was she ever going to know if she had the only or all of the copies? She could see months, years, perhaps the rest of her life dealing with these blackmailing low-life thugs.

Once outside, Precious suggested Bartie and Jesse follow her to Les Enfants in their rental car. "As soon as I've introduced you and given Isaac his gift, I'll excuse myself and come home. Before I leave Les Enfants, I want that tape and Jesse and I want your word once more that there are no copies."

"That's the only one, Precious. We aren't trying to shake you down."

"You're not? That's exactly what you're doing, Jesse."

"Yeah, I guess it is, but Bartie only wants your introduction to Isaac and then he'll give you the tape and we won't bother you anymore, right, Bartie?"

"He's right, Mrs. Woodson. I'm not a blackmailer. I'm a producer. I don't think you'll be able to leave right away, however. You're part of the deal. Kahn wants into the social world here and you're going to have to guarantee him that. You have two roles to perform before you get your tape back with your best performance ever on it—the introduction and seeing that Kahn gets into the *in crowd.*"

"All right. Do you want to follow me or shall we go together?"

"I think together," Bartie said, as he opened the passenger door to Precious' Jaguar.

As they pulled into the driveway of Les Enfants, Precious said, "Why don't I go in alone and present Isaac with his gift and then come out and get the two of you?"

"Bad idea. I don't know how well you know Kahn. For all I know, you'll tell him the whole deal. We're all going in at the same time."

"Fine," Precious said. She was resigned. There was no way she was going to get out of this. She pulled the car to a halt in front of Isaac's house.

Jesse jumped out from the back seat first and held Precious' door for her.

"Thank you, Jesse."

"You're welcome. I like you, Precious. This'll be okay. Just do what Bartie says and this'll soon be over."

"I hope so, Jesse," Precious answered. She was on the verge of tears.

"Get your purse, Ms. Woodson. You left it in the car."

Precious reached in for her purse containing the handsomely wrapped tray for Isaac. They climbed the steps together and Bartie rang the bell.

Chang opened the door, "Good morning, Ms. Woodson. Mr. Kahn will receive you in the great room."

"Thank you," Precious said as she headed through the center hall to the room she had decorated.

As she entered, Isaac stood up and crossed to her, kissing her on both cheeks, "Hello, Precious, I missed you."

"Thank you, Isaac. Allow me to introduce Mr. Barton Costlowe and his nephew Jesse Costlowe. Bartie and Jesse, this is Mr. Kahn."

Pleased to meet-yous and *how do you dos* followed and then Isaac invited everyone to have a seat and instructed Chang to serve coffee and croissants.

"I found a gift for you in New York, Isaac," Precious said as she handed the package to him.

"There was no need for you to bring me a gift, Precious," Isaac said as he took the package and placed it on the sofa next to him, "You've done so much for me. Gentlemen, Ms. Woodson decorated this great room for me. Didn't she do a superb job?"

Bartie and Jesse looked around and nodded although they felt they had fallen into the set for the *Sheik of Araby*. Bartie didn't particularly care for the style, but he had enough of an eye to tell that everything in the room had cost a small fortune.

When the coffee and croissants arrived, Precious excused herself to use the powder room.

"So what brings you two to the little town of Spencer, Mr. Costlowe?" asked Isaac.

"We're here to hopefully conduct a little business, Mr. Kahn," answered Bartie.

"I see. Well, there's not too much business conducted in sleepy Spencer, I'm afraid."

"The business we're interested in is definitely not conducted in Spencer. We're sure of that," said Bartie.

"I'm afraid I don't understand. If the business you're interested in conducting is not in Spencer, then why are you here to conduct it?" asked Isaac.

"Being a business man yourself, I'm sure you know that often people don't conduct business in the same place they live," Bartie said with a smile.

"True. What is your business if I may ask?" questioned Isaac.

"Same as yours."

"I'm retired."

"That's what I hear, but I know that's not true. You might say I am a connoisseur of your product, Mr. Kahn, and it's still very much in the marketplace."

"I'm afraid you've lost me, Mr. Costlowe," Isaac responded calmly, but Jesse noticed a slight twitching in the muscle of Kahn's jaw.

"I'm in the pornography business same as you."

Isaac's eyes widened, but he didn't respond.

"You were the biggest and the best, Mr. Kahn, Isaac, or shall we cut to the chase and I call you Ike?"

"Who are you?" Isaac asked as he stood.

"You already know my name. I have some of my films out there in distribution, but I don't have your network, your warehouses, or your financial resources. I do, however, have something you want, Ike."

"And what is that?"

"I have unlimited resources for children to star in your flicks. Children completely removed from you. I have contacts and I have no problem being the front man. You can provide the moolah and get back into the business in a big way and do it all absolutely incognito."

"I'm doing that now."

"Obviously not. I found you."

"Yes, you did. And how did you?" Ike asked.

"That's a long story."

"And how is Ms. Woodson involved?"

"She fell into our lap."

"And if I don't want to make a deal with you?"

"Then I guess I'll have to let certain authorities know about sleepy little Spencer and one of its stalwart citizens, Ike Perl, *the Porno King*, who has undergone reconstructive surgery. But as I understand it, not a stalwart enough citizen to be included on the Spencer A-list," Bartie answered.

"Done your homework, huh?"

"Here's the entire deal, Ike," Bartie began. Over the next forty-five minutes, he explained everything to Ike. Bartie had carefully thought out the entire arrangement with Jesse's help as Jesse was really the brains behind the deal. Jesse, however, never said a word during the negotiations.

"And finally, since you seem to like Ms. Woodson, I'll tell you her part in all of this. We have some rather compromising tapes of Ms. Woodson. Rather than seeing those become public property, Ms. Woodson would like to own them herself. In exchange for our copy of the tape, Ms. Woodson agreed to introduce us to you. She has further agreed to make sure you are introduced to the social scions here in Spencer. Finally, she has given us her guarantee that she will get you into all the hallowed mansions for Spencer's important social functions. You'll be accepted, Ike. Respectability will be yours," Bartie concluded.

"Who'll deal with the orders?" Ike asked.

"I imagine you'd want someone nearby so you could kinda keep an eye on that aspect, wouldn't you?" Jesse spoke for the first time.

"I would, but I know nothing about computers. I'm paying a flaming fortune for hidden web sites now."

"No web sites. Much too dangerous," Jesse responded with commitment.

"Just an ordinary email address. Set it up as an embedded link. People who want the products are computer literate believe me. I can tell you how to do this so it won't be discovered. In fact, I can do it for you from Brooklyn."

"No way. I'm keeping my finger on the pulse of my business if I should decide to go along with your proposal."

"I don't see how you can afford *not* to go along with our proposal," Bartie said menacingly.

"Bartie, when you threaten me with going to the authorities and telling them who I am and where I am, you think I can *not* afford to go along with your proposal. I can afford or not afford whatever I like. You know who I was, so you're also aware of some of my connections. I wasn't and am not in the kindergarten supply business. I'm in the pornography business. In case you haven't noticed, there are people associated with that business who have mob connections. I could make a phone call right now and you and your nephew would be dead before you left Spencer and no one would ever know who did it or even who you were. Now, do you want to keep talking or would you like to do a little listening?"

Isaac Kahn was gone. Ike, the hood, was back. Bartie decided he'd like to a little listening.

A deal was struck. Ike would be running the show and Precious would be introducing him to Spencer society. Ike's profile would be low in the new deal, but he'd have the final say, and he would figure out how the ordering process was to take place. He may or may not tell Bartie and Jesse how he arranged it when it was up and running.

"Now that we've concluded the business you hoped to conduct here in Spencer, where is Precious?" asked Ike. He called to her, "Precious."

She entered the room. "Isaac, I am so sorry."

"For what?"

"For getting myself into a position where I was forced to bring Bartie and Jesse into your home."

"No problem, Precious. Now that the gentlemen understand how I run a business, I think we're going to get along fine. You've actually done me a favor, Precious, and I understand you're going to do me another."

"Introduce you to Spencer society?" Precious asked.

"I've already been introduced to them. Now, I wish to be a part of them."

"I'll see to it," said Precious. "In fact, if I may use your phone, I'd like to make a call and get you an invitation to a little event that's taking place this afternoon at three 'clock if you're going to be available then,"

"Certainly. Whose little event is it?"

"Bonita Roberts is having a small, but very important, wine and cheese tasting."

"Bonita Roberts. Perfect."

While Precious was on the phone, Isaac told Bartie and Jesse that he saw no need for them to remain in Spencer. He wanted them on the next flight to New York and he would contact them the following Monday via cell phone. He instructed Bartie to get a cell phone if he didn't have one and to call him with the number first thing Monday."

"I have a cell phone, Ike."

"My name is Isaac, but for you, Bartie, it's Mr. Kahn. Got that?"

"Yes sir, Mr. Kahn. Here's my cell number," said Bartie as he handed Isaac a business card.

"Where's your car?" Isaac asked.

"At Ms. Woodson's house," Jesse answered.

I'll have my man drive you there now so you can hot foot it back to Nashville and get on a flight. Do I need to show you to the door?" from Isaac.

"No. We know where it is. This has certainly been a pleasure, Mr. Kahn. I know you'll be happy with our arrangement especially when you see the quality of work I'll provide for you," said Bartie as he and Jesse headed toward the hallway.

"One minute, Bartie," Isaac said as he grabbed his upper arm.

"Yes?"

"I believe you have something that belongs to Ms. Woodson."

Bartie reached inside his jacket pocket and extracted the DVD and handed it to him.

Isaac put it on the sofa, then looked back at Bartie and said, "And it better be the only copy—or you'll sincerely wish it was."

"It's the only one. I swear, Mr. Kahn," answered Bartie.

"Good. See you," Isaac said as he resumed his seat on the sofa and turned toward Precious dismissing the two men.

Jesse turned and caught Precious' eye as she was on the phone. He waved to her.

Precious raised her hand in return and then brushed a single tear from her eye.

"Oh, that would be lovely, Bonita. We'll see you at three. Bye-bye." Precious hung up the phone. "Would you like to call for me at two forty-five this afternoon to attend Bonita's little fest, Isaac?"

"I would be delighted, Precious."

"I am *so* sorry."

"Don't mention this ever again. This meeting never took place. You don't know those two men. Here's your DVD. Now, let's open my gift."

Isaac was elated with the tray or he appeared to be. The erotica was actually not that good, but it was worthy of being part of his lesser collection and Isaac certainly didn't want Precious to know she had given him something not of the highest quality. He hoped she had not paid a small fortune for it.

Precious was greatly relieved. Isaac appreciated the gift and he was such a gentleman. She wasn't sure what transpired when she had excused herself since she refrained from listening at the doorway. She had decided the less she knew about what was taking place in that great room between Bartie, Jesse, and Isaac, the better off she would be.

"Have they left? They came with me in my car."

"I had them driven to your place to get their car. They'll be gone when you get home and they're leaving Spencer right away," Isaac responded.

"I don't want to know what this is all about, do I, Isaac?"

"No, you don't. Now, you go on home and I'll be there to collect you right on time. What is the purpose of Bonita's function this afternoon? Strictly social?"

"Actually, no. There's more to it than that. She has a proposal for Spencer. I think I know what it is, but I'd rather not say right now in case I'm way off base. If she is able to put together what I think she's planning though, you'll certainly want to be a part of it."

"And how did you wrangle me an invitation?" Isaac asked with a wicked smile.

"I simply told her you had been here for a while, but had been involved in closing down your final business arrangements and in working on your gorgeous mansion and now you were ready to become involved in community activities and to entrench yourself in the social world. I also mentioned your obscene wealth," Precious said with a laugh. "Although Bonita has all the money in the world but a quarter, she's impressed with wealth equal to or greater than hers."

"Thank you, Precious. I'll look forward to seeing you later and to dazzling Mrs. Roberts with my obscene wealth," Isaac said as he rose and walked Precious to the front door and outside where he held her car door for her.

Precious drove away feeling much better than when she had driven up a few hours before. She had the DVD. She had been assured there were no copies. Isaac didn't seem upset with her. All she had to do now was to make sure he received all the important invitations until he was unquestionably accepted as a member of Spencer society. Just that and of course, she had to give up Jesse.

24

Bonita's Proposal

Bonita checked the refreshment table on the sun porch although she didn't know why she always made a last check. Hannah never made a mistake and always followed her directions down to the minutest detail.

The cheeses were arranged on trays each with its individual domed glass cover. There was Cambozola, a delicious creamy double molded French cheese, a combination of soft Brie and Camembert. A wheel of St. Andre, a beautiful-looking triple-mold cheese that melted in the mouth was on another platter. Next to it was Bel Paese, an Italian semi-hard cheese that was perfect with the Volpolicella Alphonso would be serving later in the evening.

Lastly, placed on yet another ornate platter was Canadian Black Diamond cheddar, a nutty, white cheddar that would be so splendidly offset by the St. Emilion to be served. Besides the imported cheeses, a variety of pates, stuffed mushrooms on a hot tray, artichoke/crab quiche, stuffed cherry tomatoes, fresh Beluga caviar at fifteen-hundred-d0llars a pound, French bread, Belgian flatbread, and complementary crackers, there were several chilled white wines ready for the guests. Tulips filled several priceless vases around the porch. They had arrived this morning at the small Spencer airport after being shipped over from Holland especially for Bonita's casual little fete.

The *hostess with the mostess* was particularly pleased her order of Riedel wine glasses had arrived in a timely manner. The expensive glasses cost between fifty and one-hundred-fifty-dollars each and were made by the Riedel Company. Bonita was aware that the company and real wine connoisseurs believed each wine variety called for a slightly different wine glass. Each Riedel glass was fine-tuned for a particular wine to enhance its subtleties and to evoke the robustness of each particular grape. According to the folks at Riedel, the shape of each piece of their crystal was solely responsible for the intensity, the quality, the color, the legs, the bouquet, and anything else about the wine poured in it. Although Riedel boasted twenty different shapes, Bonita had ordered one of each for seven wines to be poured at her wine and cheese. The glassware alone had set her back a little over seven-thousand-dollars.

As Bonita checked her image in the center hall mirror, she wondered for the fourth or fifth time about Precious' earlier phone call asking if she could bring Isaac Kahn. Bonita had met Isaac on a few occasions, but she hadn't seen him at any of the numerous parties she had attended in Spencer since her arrival.

She wasn't aware that he was a part of the social scene, but Precious had said he'd been busy. It was so unlike Precious when she kept Mr. Kahn's wealth. Her behavior had bordered on the gauche. Bonita couldn't get a fix on it yet, but she was suspicious about Precious' sudden interest in Isaac's social significance. It occurred to her that maybe they were *seeing one another.* She had heard Precious was helping him with his interior decoration and Precious was quite an attractive woman. Bonita decided that was it. They were an item and Precious simply wanted Isaac to be brought into the inner circle.

She fluffed her hair and decided she looked good. Gray was the color Bonita had chosen to wear today. The crepe pantsuit draped nicely on her, she thought, and the gray lambskin mules matched perfectly. Giant opals at her neck and on her ears displayed just a hint of color accented by the hues of the tulips. Bonita was gazing at her reflection for another reason this particular day. For the very first time, she had deviated from fluorescent blue eye shadow and was wearing a soft matte gray to compliment her outfit.

Aloud, she said to the mirror, "Well, I guess it's all right, but my eyes don't stand out as well as with the blue."

As Bonita continued her myopic inspection, she heard a door behind her open. Bonita turned and there was Raven.

"Hello, dear," Bonita said as she turned away from her favorite image.

"Hello, Mrs. Roberts, I hope I'm not late. I had trouble getting my car started."

"You're right on time, Raven. I hope you don't mind my asking you to come to work on a Saturday."

"Not at all. What would you like for me to do today?" Raven asked.

"As you know, I'm having a little wine and cheese tasting, but I'll also be presenting a proposal to some of the leaders of Spencer society. After we've imbibed a little, I'd like you to record the minutes of the meeting."

"Fine. I'll be in my office. Have Hannah call me when you need me."

"Absolutely not. I want you to attend the party. If my proposal is accepted, there'll be a ton of work for you to do. Hopefully those here today will be a part of the committee or board or whatever is decided, so I want you to get to know all of them. You're a guest in addition to working."

"Thank you. Am I dressed all right?"

"You're perfect, my dear. With that hair, those eyes, and your gorgeous figure, whatever you wear, you'll always look perfect," Bonita said with a beneficent smile on her face.

"Thank you. Is there anything I can do now, Mrs. Roberts?"

"Not a thing. Hannah and Alphonso have everything under control. Why don't you go out to the sunroom? The other guests will be here shortly and then we'll pour wine and begin."

"All right, if you're sure there's nothing I can do."

As Bonita nodded, the doorbell rang and Hannah emerged from the kitchen to answer the door. Darling and BD Huxtable were the first to arrive. Bonita greeted them warmly and showed them to the sunroom where she introduced them to Raven. The Huxtables were followed by Candy Martin and soon all of the invitees including Precious and Isaac were assembled.

Alphonso entered the sunroom and stood behind a table laden with several varieties of wine.

"Before Alphonso pours, I would like to ask all of you to note that the jalousies have been opened in order to allow in plenty of fresh air. Two of my friends are smokers and as you can see there are cigarettes, lighters and ashtrays throughout the room. I ask all of you to allow Lydia and Precious to be comfortable if they should desire to smoke. There'll be no *going outside* to enjoy a cigarette at Villagio. And now Alphonso, why don't you pour our first selection?" Bonita said grandly.

Alphonso expertly uncorked an especially procured Chilean Pinot Grigio that Bonita found pleasing to the palate as she extolled its virtues. As the guests sipped, Hannah passed the appropriate cheeses and hors d'oeuvres to compliment the wine and the palate.

Bonita, the small town Texas Mexican gal, was many things and quintessential hostess was at the top of the list. Before long, there was a general hub-bub in the room and everyone was thoroughly enjoying themselves. Precious was thrilled with Isaac's social skills and the guests were receiving him quite well. A natural wit, Isaac had them in stitches with his funny, but not off-color, jokes.

Following the official tasting when the guests had selected their wine of choice and most were sitting talking quietly, Isaac crossed to Raven and said softly, "Hello, Raven. Long time no see."

"I beg your pardon?"

"I said, long time no see."

"Yes, I heard what you said, Mr. Kahn, but I don't think we've met before. Have we been introduced at the club perhaps?"

"No, we met much longer ago. In Miami Beach."

The mention of Miami Beach caused a cold chill to run down Raven's back, but she knew she hadn't met Mr. Kahn there. "I'm sorry, you must be mistaken. I was in Miami Beach many years ago, but I don't think we met."

"We did more than meet. Are you still hooked on Ecstasy, Raven?"

A sledgehammer to her head could not have caused more pain or shock. Raven knew instantly who he was. She started to feel physically sick and turned ashen before Isaac's eyes.

"Don't do anything stupid like faint, Raven. We don't want any of these fine people here to know that we have previously met, do we? Now put on a big smile. Better yet, laugh like I told you one of my funny stories." Isaac said purposefully.

Raven glanced around and saw no one was paying attention to them, but she let out a sorry half-hearted laugh.

Bonita heard her and looked over at Raven and Isaac and said to Precious, "I had no idea Mr. Kahn was so humorous. He has made the party. Tell now, Precious. Are the two of you seeing each other romantically?"

"Heavens no, Bonita. I've helped Isaac find fabrics and objects d'art and assisted him with his Bedouin great room. You should see it."

"I hope too. With his social skills, I imagine he will reciprocate and have all of us to Les Enfants in short order."

"I'm sure. No, there's nothing romantic. I've simply gotten to know him and now that's he's free from his business ventures and his interior decoration is almost complete, he has the time to socialize. I thought your gathering this evening would be the perfect entrée for him into Spencer society. I hope you don't think me presumptuous to have asked if he could attend," said Precious.

"Absolutely not. I find him quite charming. Also, I'll be interested to hear his take on my proposal. What businesses was he in?" Bonita asked.

"You know I've never asked him," Precious said and she realized she hadn't, but after what had occurred earlier today with Bartie and Jesse, she wasn't sure she wanted to know.

"What are you doing here at Mrs. Roberts' party, Raven?" Isaac asked.

"I'm her social secretary. She asked me to come take notes at the meeting she's having shortly."

"I see and do you work out of the house here?"

"Yes."

"And you have access to a computer?"

"Yes."

"Excellent. I may have a little job for you too. I'll let you go now, Raven, but we'll be in touch. It's lovely to see you again," Isaac said to her with a slight bow before he crossed to Precious side and asked, "Precious, may I refill your glass?"

"That would be lovely, Isaac."

"And may I get anything for you, Mrs. Roberts?"

"Bonita, please, Isaac. No, thank you. I think I'll ask everyone to refill their glasses and then I'd like to conduct a little business."

That's the second time I've heard that phrase today Isaac thought as he headed for the wine table to refill Precious' glass. I hope this little business is more pleasant than the last. But I'm sure the business Bartie and I discussed will be quite pleasant and quite lucrative now that they know I won't stand for their shake-down plans. Ike, no Isaac, always runs the show. No one tells me what to do. Not now, not then, not ever. And then I find that sweet Raven lives here in Spencer and works for Bonita Roberts as her social secretary and has access to her computer. And, to top all that off, here I am amidst Spencer's social elite and doing quite well impressing them, I would say. How sweet it is! This may well go down in the annals of Isaac Kahn as his luckiest day!

Bonita began her pitch with flowery compliments about Spencer and elaborated a few minutes on its rich history. Then she told a little about each individual present. When she came to Mr. Kahn, she explained she knew he had been involved in several businesses, but didn't know what they were. Isaac replied modestly that he had dabbled in construction and had been the angel for a few films.

"Films, my, my, Mr. Kahn. I don't usually tell this, but when I was quite young, I starred in a few films in Hollywood."

The guests asked her the names of them and Bonita quickly pooh-poohed them with, "Oh, they were years ago. I'm sure they're not available anymore. I wasn't a major star or anything. It was a short chapter in my life, but it was fascinating. What sort of films did you produce, Mr. Kahn?"

"Art films," answered Isaac. He did not amplify his response.

Bonita moved on as she didn't want to broach that subject. There were art films and there were art films. She was sure anyone as respectable as Mr. Kahn hadn't been involved with *dirty movies*, but she decided the art film genre would be better left untouched.

She wished she hadn't said anything about her short-lived film career. That's what had gotten her into trouble in Montiac. That stupid old biddy friend of Celestine's had met Bonita at Darlene's party and the husband kept thinking he had see her somewhere before. Somehow he found her old films and made the connection between her and Joshua Roberts prior to their marriage. The whole nasty story of Bonita's life as a prostitute in residence at the Beverly Wiltshire had been told at the Magnolia Ball by Celestine through that disgusting, horrid doll Anthony.

No, better not to discuss the film industry this evening. Wine had loosened her tongue or she would never have mentioned it. She was going to have to be more careful. Bonita to make a debutante ball in Spencer a reality and she didn't want any backlash from Texas, Hollywood or Dorchester County, South Carolina.

Once Bonita set the stage with her knowledge of and compliments about darling little Spencer and then made the guests aware they were sitting among others as influential and wealthy as they, she laid out her plan. Spencer needed to have its own debutante ball.

She understood that young ladies from Spencer were asked in Nashville, but speculated on how wonderful it would be for those same young ladies to debut in their hometown. Once the ball became well known, it would be more prestigious to debut in Spencer than to go to the city where the young ladies knew no one.

Bonita had the contacts in the publishing world through her late husband and could get press in the Nashville and Knoxville newspapers. While Spencer was already a social center because of its well-known retirees, a debutante ball would elevate it to social Mecca of Van Buren and surrounding counties in the great state of Tennessee.

Rhetta jumped right on the bandwagon then. "As all of you know, my daddy is the past Governor of the State of Tennessee, and I think this is a wonderful idea. Bonita, I want to volunteer to do whatever I can to see that this fabulous idea of yours comes to fruition. My girls will naturally be invited in Nashville, but I want them to debut in Spencer too."

Private conversations ensued and there was general chitchat. Candy Martin asked what would be involved. Bonita started to answer when Isaac stepped forth and offered, "I see merit to your idea, Mrs.—ah, Bonita, however I think there are some who would think a debutante ball just for the sake of a debutante ball is quite shallow. There are people in great need only miles from the center of town. Money that would be spent on gowns, flowers, invitations and parties could be better spent helping those less fortunate than we."

Bonita glared at him. If she had known that Precious was going to bring someone who would not be one hundred per cent behind her proposal, she would not have consented to issuing him an invitation. She gave money to charities. This didn't have anything to do with that. This was about another Magnolia Ball and about Bonita heading up the debutante committee and about Bonita becoming *THE* social dowager of Spencer. *Why didn't he shut up about the poor people?*

With an expert eye for nuance and changes in expression from his filming ventures, Isaac realized he had irritated his hostess. She had mistaken his statement for disagreement to her proposal. He continued, "On the other hand, if we were to incorporate assistance for those less fortunate and the proposed debutante ball, I think we would meet with no resistance, but would be hailed as champions of the poor."

Bonita quickly recovered. He wasn't opposed to her idea—maybe he had a better one. "What are you saying, Isaac?"

"I'm suggesting we establish a charitable foundation. The proceeds from the debutante ball would go to the foundation and those moneys would be distributed to the needy in the area. Of course, there will need to be a board set up to oversee the distribution of the money," Isaac explained.

"What a wonderful idea!" Harcourt Ball, the attorney chimed in. I'd be interested in serving on such a board myself.

"I'd like to start the foundation off with a little seed money, Mr. Ball. I'll donate fifty-thousand," Isaac volunteered.

"That is extremely generous, Isaac. Put me down for the same, Harcourt," Bonita exclaimed. Lydia Henley nodded to indicate she was in for the same as did Candy Martin. Harcourt said he too would donate fifty-thousand-dollars. Soon everyone in the room, with the exception of Rhetta, had spoken and each had pledged fifty-thousand-dollars. All eyes were on her, so Rhetta took a deep breath and cleared her throat. "Of course, Trace and I will be donating that amount also," she said. *In for a penny, in for a pound as the Gov always said, but where in the hell am I going to get that money?*

By the end of the evening, Bonita was floating on a cloud. Those in attendance had agreed to proceed with first setting up a charitable foundation. Harcourt had agreed to draw up all the necessary papers at no charge. Lydia Henley had agreed to serve on the board and to head the committee to oversee the distribution of funds. Bonita was to proceed with her plans for the ball and to chair the selection committee. Bonita volunteered to serve as mistress of ceremonies after explaining she had previous experience in that realm from her days in New York. She was unquestioned and it was agreed she was to be the mistress of ceremonies. It was further decided to hold the initial ball during the Christmas holidays. Since it was already May, there were mountains to move, but with the assemblage of movers and shakers she had assembled, Bonita knew there would be no problem.

The question was raised as to where the ball would be held. Bonita responded it would probably have to be at *The Volunteer*, the only hotel in Spencer, or perhaps it could be held at the club with a large rented tent added to the clubroom currently used for large social events.

"Or we could move it out of town a little," volunteered Isaac. "Are you familiar with that big cave a few miles away?"

Everyone nodded.

"It so happens I bought that property recently. What could be more newsworthy than a debutante ball in a cave?"

Objections arose of its being too cold, not having electricity, no parking area, how would refreshments be served, what about a sound system, where would the orchestra be located, was there enough space for a dance floor, etc. Isaac stopped everyone in their tracks. "Let me take care of the cave. If you would like it for a venue for the debutante ball, I will have central heating and air conditioning installed, a sound system, a kitchen, a lighting system and a parking area built. We'll have a bigger and better ballroom than Nashville's *Peabody*."

Bonita was speechless. He truly must be obscenely wealthy. She could not fathom what Isaac's generous offer would cost.

Once again, Rhetta rose to the occasion, "Mr. Kahn, that is so sweet of you. And as my daddy, the *Gov*, always said 'Never refuse a generous offer.' I think we should set a time for all of us to go to the cave and look it over. Then we can put our final stamp of approval on Mr. Kahn's offer. My heavens! I can just see it now—a debutante ball in a cave that's been made into a ballroom bigger than anything in Nashville. This is so exciting! Now, Bonita, I want to serve on the selection committee with you. After all, I know just everybody and their backgrounds here in Spencer."

"Thank you, Rhetta," said Bonita graciously. That wasn't the place Bonita had in mind for Rhetta, but she had to remember Candy obviously liked the woman. Candy had attended Rhetta's luau and she had brought the Princess. Bonita was sure she could tone Rhetta down and stop her from crashing parties. With Rhetta on this very important committee, she wouldn't need to do that anyway as she would be assured an invitation to anything in Spencer and its environs of social note.

After the business was concluded until a meeting set for the following week, Hannah appeared with a sheet cake decorated with fresh magnolias. Across the cake the words *Spencer's Magnolia Ball* were emblazoned in red frosting letters.

The guests were too polite to comment on Bonita's obvious presumptuousness.

"Magnolia Ball? Is that what we're going to call it?" Darling asked.

"It's merely a suggestion. The magnolias here in Tennessee are lovely and I thought it would be appropriate," said Bonita.

"But they're not in bloom in December?" said Rhetta. "Maybe it should be the Poinsettia Ball or the Amaryllis Ball?"

"They're not native to the area, Rhetta," commented Candy. "The iris is our state flower, Bonita. Perhaps the Iris Ball?"

"Sounds like an eye disease to me," Isaac quipped, as he surreptitiously winked at Bonita, as everyone laughed.

Harcourt asked Hannah if she had made the cake and when Hannah nodded, Harcourt spoke, "Let's eat the cake. We can decide on the name later. Hannah's cakes are the best and I bet you have some of that wonderful coffee out there in the kitchen too, don't you, Hannah?"

"I does, Mr. Ball," Hannah answered beaming. "I's about to bring it out in the samovar right now."

As the guests enjoyed their cake and coffee, Raven asked Bonita if she might be excused to go home. "I'm not feeling well, Mrs. Roberts."

"Oh my! You should have told me, Raven. Of course you may go. Thank you so much for coming. I hope you got everything down that transpired at the meeting."

When Raven nodded, Bonita continued, "Would you like Alphonso to take you home?"

"No, I'll be all right to drive. Thank you. I'll be here Monday."

"Don't come in if you're feeling poorly. You can type those notes up anytime before the meeting next Thursday."

"It's only an upset stomach. I'll be here Monday. Good night."

As Raven crossed toward the center hall, Isaac excused himself and followed her. "Leaving so soon, Raven?" he asked.

"I'm not feeling well."

"Oh? I'm sorry. May I walk you to your car?"

"Please don't."

"I insist. Wouldn't want you to pass out on the way to the car, would we?" Isaac took her arm and ushered her out the front door. He gallantly held the car door open for her. "I'll be in touch, Raven. Good night."

Raven spun gravel as she pulled away. She didn't know what she was going to do. Ike Perl in Spencer after all these years. She had almost pushed the Miami Beach fiasco to the back of her mind and here he was. She would never have recognized him although she had felt a little jolt when she first heard his voice. Even his mannerisms weren't the same as the monster she remembered.

She knew he still had the tapes he filmed of her when she was his prisoner for six months. It would kill her parents to see them.

And she wondered why he had asked if she had access to a computer and why he was going to be in touch. Raven didn't like this, but she had no idea what to do about it. She couldn't tell anyone. It was obvious Ike had undergone plastic surgery. He was living in that big mansion Les Enfants, the irony not escaping her, and was *Mr. Respectable.* Raven pulled the car over to the side of the unmarked country road. She opened the door and jumped out and threw up on the macadam.

As Isaac returned to the party, he announced, "I tell you what I'd like to do. I'd like to match what's been pledged by everyone this evening, so we can really get this ball rolling." There was silence in the room. Then everyone erupted with applause at Isaac's seemingly boundless generosity. His wealth must be incalculable. As the others upped their donations, Rhetta felt ill. She knew she couldn't pledge anymore. She was already way out of her league with the fifty-thousand-dollars she *donated* that she didn't have. Trace was definitely going to kill her! He may wish to hire someone to do the job, but he wouldn't be able to afford the luxury.

And so a debutante ball, the arrow to be shot from the bow of some nebulous foundation, was born in Spencer, Tennessee the brainchild of a former prostitute and primarily funded by a producer of child pornography. With credentials like that, the as yet unnamed ball would no doubt soon emerge as the social highlight of the Southern states!

25

Trace Shocks Rhetta

Rhetta was extremely apprehensive. Trace was due at RickShaw any minute. She had finished going through all the luau bills and was appalled to learn she had spent almost one-hundred-fifty-thousand-dollars on a party simply to get an invitation to Bonita's wine and cheese where she had pledged even more money for Spencer's possible debutante ball. She had no doubt at all about it—Trace would kill her. She had planned to partially defray the party expenses with twenty-five-thousand-dollars of the money her parents had left her when they passed away within six weeks of each other. That left one-hundred-twenty-five-thousand-dollars plus her pledge she had to get from Trace. She couldn't begin to imagine how she was going to tell him and she couldn't put the bills on hold. If she didn't pay them immediately, word would spread all over Spencer.

Rhetta cringed as she heard the gravel crunch under Trace's tires as he pulled to a stop in front of the *cottage.* She quickly crossed to the fridge and removed a frosted mug from the freezer and a Pabst Blue Ribbon from the other side and poured it for her returning husband. Trace entered all smiles and caught Rhetta up in a bear hug.

"How you doing, Beautiful?" he asked after planting a big kiss on her.

Rhetta was amazed. It had been years since Trace had actually seemed glad to see her, much less hugged her or kissed her passionately on the mouth other than in the throes of abandon in their bed when, infrequently, they engaged in sexual intercourse.

"I'm fine, Trace. How are you? I'm glad to see you. And you look so good. Usually by the time you arrive, you seem so tired."

"Not today. I took the afternoon off and played a round of golf before driving out. I feel better than I have in years," he answered as he accepted the mug of beer and took a sip. "Good job, Rhett, Pabst Blue Ribbon."

"I went to the store this morning and got it for you special," Rhetta said with a smile.

"Thank you. I know this plebian beer goes against your grain, but remember you married a simple old boy from the wrong side of the tracks."

"A simple old boy who's the smartest man I ever met and who became the best doctor in all of Tennessee," Rhetta said. She picked up her Margarita and asked Trace if he'd like to sit on the deck and watch the sunset.

"Great idea. Where are the girls?"

"They're still at the club. They're helping with the children's carnival. They should be back in about an hour and then we'll have dinner. Are you hungry now?"

"Nope. An hour will be fine. Let's go enjoy the sunset."

Once settled on the deck, Rhetta decided it was time to *carpe diem*. She hadn't seen Trace in this good a mood for as long as she could remember. "I finished calculating all the bills for the luau today, Trace, and I went way over budget."

"Well, honey, you always do. That's one of the things I can always count on in my little Rhetta."

He didn't seem angry. He's actually teasing me about my spending habits. Maybe I should drop the whole bomb right now before he morphs into the Trace who always complains and yells about how much money I spend..

Before she could speak, Trace said, "In thinking about the food, the booze, the tents, the orchids, the favors, hiring the boats, the limousine, the invitations, yadda, yadda, yadda, I estimate you spent about two-hundred-thousand-dollars. How close am I?"

"Oh, Trace, I didn't spend anywhere near that much. The bills came to one-hundred-twenty-five-thousand-dollars"

Rhetta was still planning to use twenty-five-thousand of her own money to pay for the party because she also had to tell Trace about the debutante ball pledge to the foundation she had made.

"That's good news, Rhetta. Go ahead and write the checks. I know you want to be prompt paying the bills so the old biddies don't start gossiping about the doctor and the former Governor's daughter who don't pay up on time. Pay the bills with Nashville checks. I'll transfer the money to the checking account on Monday."

Rhetta was feeling light-headed. She wasn't sure if it was from her second Margarita, as she had already had one before Trace arrived to bolster her courage, or his complete reversal of attitude. She couldn't believe he wasn't screaming bloody murder about her extravagances as usual.

"Trace, did you rob a bank?" Rhetta asked with a chuckle.

Trace's demeanor changed in a flash. "Why did you say that?"

"I was kidding, sweetie. Usually, you get so upset with me for over-spending and you're being so nice."

"No, I didn't rob a bank and it seems to me that rather than casting aspersions upon me, you would be thankful there's enough money to pay for your nonsense, Rhetta. Your whole world revolves around Nashville and Spencer *society* and what invitations you can wrangle. You are the shallowest person I know. Sometimes, I ask myself why I stay married to you. One reason only—my girls!"

Rhetta felt her world spinning out of control. *Trace has never spoken to me like that. Oh, he's bitched about my spending habits, but he's never said I'm shallow or mentioned my pursuit of social functions. Now he says he wonders why he stays with me.*

"Trace, I was teasing you. I know you didn't rob a bank. It's just that you usually get so upset with me and you're being so nice about the money I spent on that silly party. I won't do it again. I promised you that before the party. It was important to me at the time, but I won't do it again. I won't!"

"Yes, you will, Rhetta. Again, and again, and again! It's okay. I knew who and what you were when I married you and I do love you. Sorry. Your remark about robbing a bank hit me the wrong way. I know how important socializing is to you. Forget what I said. I'll transfer one-hundred-twenty-five-thousand to the checking account on Monday and that'll be the end of this discussion."

As Trace spoke, Rhetta breathed a sign of relief. "Well, there is one more little bill. I went to Bonita's wine and cheese party and she has this marvelous idea."

Rhetta proceeded to fill Trace in on the whole debutante ball/foundation idea and the money that Isaac Kahn was donating and what Bonita and the other invited guests were going to contribute. Then she mentioned how she hadn't wanted to appear cheap or unconcerned about the poor of Van Buren County when everyone else pledged fifty-thousand-dollars each, so she had agreed to donate the same amount.

"Okay, so my estimate on the luau was off by seventy-five-thousand, but then you pledged fifty-thousand for a foundation to provide the legitimacy for a debutante ball in Spencer, which has to be one of the truly dumbest ideas I've ever heard. At any rate, I was only twenty-five K off of what you need for this month excluding the household bills for here and the manse in Nashville. I'll transfer one-hundred-seventy-five-thousand to the checking account on Monday. Now can we stop talking about money, which seems to have been the major topic of all of our discussions for eons, refresh our drinks, and get ready for dinner? I'm suddenly starving. Shouldn't the girls be here any minute?"

"Any minute. I'll go in and finish up dinner, but first, I'll get you another beer." Rhetta crossed to the freezer and got another frosted mug and poured the Pabst. She knew any moment she was going to awaken from this very pleasant dream and Trace would start screaming about her exorbitant ways.

While Rhetta fussed in the kitchen, Trace headed for the rec room, grabbed the remote, and turned on the big-screen TV. He settled into his recliner and truly relaxed for the first time in months.

It had been so easy. After calling Mrs. DeLancy's attorney and making sure she had not left a will, Trace transferred one-million-dollars of Mrs. DeLancy's assets to his personal account. He waited a few days and contacted the attorney again telling him that as guardian of Mrs. DeLancy's assets, he had liquidated her accounts and was prepared to present her heirs with a little over two-million-dollars.

The attorney was stunned as he had no idea his client had been worth that kind of money. He assured Trace he would contact Mrs. Delaney's next of kin. And he did, post-haste.

Friday morning, Mrs. DeLancy's daughter and son-in-law called on Trace at his Nashville office to personally thank him for all he had done for the deceased. They thanked him especially for handling her money and for contacting the attorney and turning it over to them since they would have never known about it if he hadn't told them. Trace enjoyed his warm, fuzzy feeling. He was a doctor. He loved to make people feel good and Mrs. DeLancy's offspring and her son-in-law definitely felt good. Trace did too. He had one-million-dollars and no one was the wiser and no one had been hurt. Life was good!

Of course, Trace made one very large mistake. Rather than harping on Rhetta before paying her bills and pledge under protest, he had turned into *Mr. Wonderful.* Rhetta would go through that million faster than the Roadrunner could outpace Wiley Coyote.

And, as is always the case, once Trace had *borrowed* Mrs. DeLancy's money, it became second nature to him to *misplace* various sums of the moneys he invested for his other patients. Or when they, like Mrs. Delaney, made him guardian of their assets, it seemed all right to make transfers to his own account and to spend their money personally.

Most of the patients who gave Trace *carte blanche* were suffering from pre-senile dementia or were in the throes of Alzheimer's and many of them had either no relatives or distant relatives who had no interest in them. Trace was available at their beck and call and they loved him.

Therefore, he was able to take their money with no qualms of conscience. Before long, Trace was a multimillionaire; Rhetta was spending with abandon and without recriminations, and all was well with the Ricks' family-for the moment!

26

Separate Plans Set in Motion

Harcourt Ball set about establishing a charitable foundation to serve as the cornerstone of Bonita's debutante ball while Isaac had Chang make calls to solicit bids for converting his Falls Lakes cave into a ballroom. Meanwhile, Bonita and Lydia called on Desiree to solicit her ideas of those who should be contacted about the charitable foundation and all the good works it would accomplish. Desiree had done her homework and presented the ladies with a copious list of organizations and groups for them to contact.

"In fact, since I do nothing but lie in this bed all day, I'll be happy to make the calls and set up speaking engagements for you at their meetings, Bonita. Will you be available to speak also, Lydia?" Desiree asked.

"Well, I'm available, but I think we would all be better served by having Bonita do the speaking since this whole wonderful concept is her idea," Lydia responded.

"Fine, but Bonita, I do hope you will take this in the manner it's given. There are still some old-timers in Spencer who will view you as a Yankee upstart come-here, so it may be a good idea to have Lydia, native daughter, accompany you to meetings. I certainly don't mean to offend you," Desiree said softly.

"And you certainly don't, Desiree. I've been here long enough to understand there is still a great deal of provincialism in Spencer. I think it's a wonderful idea for Lydia to go with me. That is, if you have no objections, Lydia."

"I'd be delighted, Bonita."

"Then I'll start making calls as soon as the two of you provide me with your schedules, girls."

"I'll have Raven call you this afternoon, but don't let my schedule prohibit you, Desiree. Unless it's something of the utmost importance, I can cancel. We really need to get the backing of the community so we can press forward, don't you agree, ladies?"

Both women nodded.

As these preparations were progressing, Isaac was giving a great deal of thought to Bartie's and Jesse's business proposal. With the new age of electronic technology, orders for the pornography would be practically instantaneous. Customers ordering products nowadays provided their credit card numbers via the Internet, so their money would be in Isaac's account immediately. He saw the possibility of millions of dollars a year. Jesse had said he could set up a simple email address to handle orders on a remote computer with his hacking abilities. The only catch was that someone who operated the *hacked* computer should be aware of what was going on since there would be thousands of "hits" per day when orders came in.

Isaac wasn't sure he understood about hacked computers or remote access or IP numbers or all the other gibberish Jesse had spouted to him, but he was sure of one thing and that was that Jesse knew what he was talking about. Precious had confirmed that Jesse was some kind of computer genius guru geek.

Isaac began to formulate a plan. He knew all the other producers of child porn that put out what he considered quality material. They would be more than happy to distribute their products through him. He had the experience and although he didn't have his old name of Ike Perl anymore, as soon as he spoke to the other producers and reminded him of some of his four-star productions, they would realize that Isaac Kahn was now the number one name in kiddie porn. So quitting production himself and getting good quality crap was no problem. And the kid said he could hide the whole operation on someone else's computer if there were someone using it in the know.

Now, isn't all this a great coincidence? Isaac thought. I want to get out of the production business and go legit—well almost legit. Legit enough so I won't be at risk. I also want to be accepted socially. Why is that so important to you, Ike? Isaac. It's important because I came from nothing. In Yemen, people spit on me. I came here with nothing and I worked and scraped and lied and stole and did whatever it took, but I finally made it and I made it BIG! I've got more money than I can ever spend. Then why do I want more? It's a game now! If I know how to make it and I don't have to put forth much effort, why not?

Now along comes Precious who can provide me with the entrée to the social world and lo and behold, she's into little boys and has gotten herself caught on a DVD. The little boy she stars with on screen and his uncle want to get into the big-time kiddie porn distribution business and somehow put together what Precious tells them about me when she buys me that clap-trap tray from Bartie. The computer whiz-kid types my new name into some cyber database and badda,

badda, bing, comes up with a picture of Isaac Kahn in the Spencer Spectator. Even with the reconstructive surgery I've had, Bartie recognizes me. They put the move on poor old Precious. But, hey, what they're suggesting is good. It'll work. All we need is a remote computer with someone who operates it knowing the deal. And who might that be?

Once again, lovely Lady Luck looked down from whatever mountain she hales from and decided to beknight dear Isaac Kahn with her favors. She dropped sweet little Raven right into my lap. Raven operates Bonita's computer and Bonita's computer is the perfect remote access tool for Jesse in Brooklyn. Raven will know something's going down, but I can guaran-damn-tee she won't say a word. No suspicion will be cast when I have to speak personally with Bonita on occasion concerning this foundation/debutante nonsense, so I'll easily have access to Raven and can get reports about the "business." Meanwhile, Jesse can tap in anytime he wants to. I guess it's time to give the Brooklyn contingent a call and see what we have to do to get the ball rolling.

Bartie and Jesse awaited Isaac Kahn's phone call in their tenement apartment. They knew he would call. The deal was too good for him to pass up.

Jesse had long ago learned practically everything there was to know about computers. He had been hacking for years and could get into almost any computer. The only ones he had not been able to gain access to thus far were the World Bank, the FBI, and the Pentagon. Other than those, he could access any computer he wanted. He knew all the web sites to visit to download hacking tools and he knew how to cover up the log on any given computer to show he had entered it.

All Jesse needed was the go ahead from Isaac that he was going into the kiddie porn distribution business with Bartie. When that word came, Jesse was ready to set up an elaborate ordering site on whatever computer Isaac designated. Once the business was up and running, Jesse could link another gazillion computers to the designated one so fifty or one hundred or even more hired peons could spend eight hours a day taking orders. Those orders would be relayed to the warehouses Isaac set up. Jesse also planned to attempt to explain to Isaac that there was another and even better way to distribute the trash. He had yet to tell Isaac about the process of downloading where the customer could have his product immediately since Isaac and Bartie would have the customer's money instantly from the credit card companies.

Isaac picked up the phone and called Bartie. "Hello."

"Yes?"

"You know who this is?"

"I do."

"It's a go. You and your partner fly down here tomorrow and we'll work out the details."

"Right," and there was a click as Bartie hung up the phone.

Isaac had instructed Bartie during their initial meeting that names were never to be used and that nothing about the business was to be discussed via telephone.

"That was Ike, I mean Isaac, Jesse," Bartie said as he turned to Jesse, hard at work on the computer. Jesse was between sexual engagements at the moment.

"And?"

"And, what do you think? It's a go. He wants us to fly down tomorrow. Call Jet Blue and book a flight."

"I'll do it on the computer."

"Whatever. Is there anything you can't do on that thing?"

"It won't cook the food.; I have to order in and I haven't figured out a way to turn it into a portable toilet yet, but other than that—" Jesse responded with a grin.

"You're amazing, kid! And don't think you aren't going to be handsomely rewarded for your part in this. You found Ike, I mean Mr. Isaac Kahn, through Precious and your computer skills and you convinced Isaac. If he didn't think he could hide all this with your hacking skills, he would never have gone for the deal. I'm cutting you in for fifty percent of everything we make. You'll be a multi-millionaire by the time you're eighteen."

"Suits me. Then I'll be able to stop screwing old women."

"Right on, but get those plane tickets, because since neither of us are millionaires yet, you have an appointment in twenty minutes," Bartie reminded him.

"I'm on it," Jesse answered. "What time do you want to leave?"

"Get an early flight. Reserve a rental car too. We'll get there early, conduct our business and fly back here tomorrow night. I don't think it's a good idea for us to hang out in Spencer too long, do you?"

"Nope. I'll take care of it."

"Good. I gotta go out. Don't want to be here when your *date* arrives."

"Very funny, but you won't mind watching later on, will you?"

"Jesse, my boy. You know I don't enjoy watching, but someone's got to edit our new releases."

"Sure, I forgot," said Jesse as he winked at his *favorite* and only uncle.

27

Isaac, Raven and Ridge

Desiree set up speaking engagements for Bonita with the Kiwanis, the Rotary Club, the Rotaryanns, the Lions' Club, the Woman's Club of Spencer, the Animal Welfare League, the local Red Cross Chapter, and Meals on Wheels. She then moved on to schedule the Spencer Hospital Auxiliary, local churches, the Interfaith Council of Van Buren County, and the scholarship committee at the county high school. Next she called the alumni association of the elite St. Brigitte's Academy for Young Ladies located about ten miles outside of town and the boards of the Spencer Soup Kitchen and the Spencer Shelter. Lastly, she resorted to everyone else she could think of who might be interested in helping those less fortunate. All were receptive and Bonita and Lydia were scheduled to speak every weekday for the next several weeks.

Raven was filling in squares on the computer calendar she had devised for Bonita's activities. She wondered how Bonita could keep up such a pace at her age and particularly at her girth. In addition to her forthcoming speaking engagements, Bonita had an assortment of teas, luncheons, and brunches she didn't plan to miss and finally, she had been feted with an invitation to Desiree's forthcoming Sunday salon.

Raven began to type up a copy of Bonita's schedule for the coming week for Hannah had to know where she was going so she could assist Bonita with planning her wardrobe and make sure that whatever creation she decided to shroud herself in was at the ready. The doorbell rang.

Hannah rushed to answer it and Raven flinched when she heard her say, "Why, hello, Mr. Kahn. Miss Bonita ain't here right now. Was she 'spectin' you?

"No, she wasn't, Hannah. As a matter of fact, I'm here to speak to Raven if that's all right."

"Sure is, Mr. Kahn. She's right in here," Hannah said as she gestured toward Raven's office door, which stood open. "Raven, Mr. Kahn's here to see you."

Raven came to the door and Hannah turned toward the kitchen. Then she stopped and said, "You want me to bring y'all some iced tea or something, Miss Raven?"

"No thank you, Hannah, I'm sure Mr. Kahn won't be staying long."

"I'll be in the kitchen if you needs me."

"All right. Mr. Kahn, what can I do for you?" Raven asked outwardly composed and looking him straight in the eye, but inwardly feeling ill.

"May I come into your office, Raven? Perhaps we should shut the door?" Isaac said softly as he crossed in front of Raven and entered her office. Raven followed and Isaac gently closed the door.

"Won't you have a seat, Raven?" he asked full of congeniality.

"I don't think so. What do you want?"

"Merely to tell you that you and I will be conducting a little business together."

"No, we won't. I don't want anything to do with you. I want you to leave now, Ike, or Isaac or whatever your name is."

"You always were a feisty one, weren't you, Raven? You know, you got to stay a lot longer in Miami Beach than most of my girls. I always liked your gumption. I hardly think, however, that you are in a position to ask me to leave or to tell me that we're not going to conduct a little business together. You know I still have numerous tapes of you. Let's see—how many were there?"

"I don't remember."

"Think your parents would be interested in seeing them? They might like some *home movies* of you when you were a teenager. You think so?"

"No!"

"Then I suggest you take a seat and listen to my little business proposal."

Raven sat down defeated.

"I'm going to need to use this computer."

"I can't let you use this computer. It's not mine. It's Mrs. Roberts' computer."

"I know that, Raven, and Mrs. Roberts will never know a thing about my using it. Everything that needs to be done will be done remotely. It won't affect you or your work in the least, however there will be numerous "hits" per day on the web site so you simply need to be aware that someone else is using it."

"What are you going to do?" Raven asked.

"That's none of your concern. I'll inform you when my operation is in place. And now, I know you have a lot of work to do what with the foundation that's being set up and Bonita's social engagements. I have a lot of work to do too. You know I'm having the cave made over into a ballroom for this affair."

"I know. I was at the meeting."

"So you were and what a pleasure it was to see you again, Raven. And now I must be going. Please give my regards to your boss lady and tell Hannah I said good-bye." With that, he exited Raven's office and left by the front door.

Ridge, the pilot Isaac had befriended at the Home Depot, had three weeks off before his next trip. When Isaac returned to Les Enfants, Ridge was getting out of his car.

"Hi, Isaac. Long time no see."

"Hello, Ridge, how are you?"

"Doing good. Have some time off now and thought I'd come over and help you with that recessed lighting you were talking about. I've been working on a hangar for my plane out at General Aviation, but it's about finished up now, so I'm free. Is this a good time for you? I called earlier and you weren't in. I had to go into town and was on my way home, so I thought I'd stop by and see what we're talking about here."

"It's a good time. Come on in."

The two men entered the mansion by the front door. Chang was in the foyer almost immediately.

"Hello, Mr. Kahn. Can I get anything for you?"

"I'd like some iced tea. How about you, Ridge?"

"Sounds good. It's a hot one out there, isn't it?" he asked.

"Everyday is hot here in the summer, I think," Isaac agreed.

Isaac took Ridge through the house showing him what he wanted to do as far as lighting went. He had plans for recessed lighting in the great room and he wanted to use stage lighting, ellipsoidals and fresnels in some of the other rooms. Ridge found that odd.

"Why do you want to use stage lighting in your home, Isaac? It's none of my business. It's your place. I'm just wondering."

"Ridge, do you know anything about stage lighting? A pink gel on a fresnel can make the ugliest woman in the world look like Julia Roberts. I want stage lighting so my female guests will always appear at their very best. I especially want it in the powder room off from the great room. Every one of my female guests in Spencer will think she's the most beautiful woman in the world," Isaac responded with a wink.

"Very clever, Isaac."

"Also, with stage lighting, dimming can be much more dramatic than with ordinary dimmers and run-of-the-mill lighting. One must always be conscious of special effects when throwing a social extravaganza."

"I see. Are you getting ready to enter the social whirl of Spencer and environs, Isaac?"

"I already have, my boy, already have—and what a whirling dervish it is. But, I didn't want you to come over and do this work for me. I'll hire an electrician. I merely wanted your opinions on some of my ideas."

"Hey, I'm not a licensed electrician, but I love messing around with this kind of thing. I can do the work for you and then you can have it inspected by a licensed electrician. I can save you a fortune," Ridge said.

"I'm always interested in saving a fortune. Where do we start?" Isaac asked as Chang reappeared with iced tea. He served the frosted glasses complete with sprigs of fresh mint and slices of lemon from a sterling silver tray as he handed each Isaac and Ridge a monogrammed linen cocktail napkin. He placed a platter of sandwiches, a tray of assorted pickles and relishes, and a bowl of bagel crisps on the table between them. Lastly, he placed a fork and luncheon sized plate before each of them.

"Will there be anything else, Mr. Kahn?"

"No. Thank you. That's all for now."

"Boy, this is some glass of iced tea! I didn't know we were going to get lunch too."

"Well, I'm hungry and I hope you are. Chang is excellent. He's been with me for years. He probably checked his watch and realized it was noon—that's my regular time for lunch even though I didn't realize it was that late or that I was hungry."

"Looks great!"

"Then let's dig in," Isaac said.

As the men ate, Ridge told Isaac they should start with a blueprint of everything that he wanted done in the way of lighting. Ridge said he would check out all of the circuit boxes and trace the existing lighting and then they'd be ready to start. He said he'd get on it right after lunch and probably by late afternoon, he could have a list ready of what had to be ordered.

"Sounds like a plan," Isaac said as both men remembered their initial conversation where that same phrase had been used.

"And when are you going to fly me around in my plane?" Isaac asked.

"Say the word. I'd need to take it up first with an instructor to make sure I'm checked out in it and then we'll go wherever you like, but I'd only be going because I'd love to fly that bird," Ridge responded.

"I'll pay you for your time."

"Absolutely not, Isaac. I told you I can't accept money for flying except with the airline. It's in my contract. I'd just love to fly your plane."

"When shall we go?"

"What do you want to do first? Lighting or flying?" Ridge asked.

"How about lighting today and flying tomorrow?" Isaac asked.

"I'll call out to General Aviation at the airport and make sure I can get an instructor to go up with me early in the morning and then we'll take her up in the afternoon if that's all right with you?"

As Isaac began to speak, they said in unison, "Sounds like a plan."

The men shared a laugh together and continued chatting until they finished their lunch. Isaac showed Ridge where the recess lighting was to go and exactly what he wanted where while Ridge made a primitive blueprint he planned to take home and fine-tune. Before he left, he was able to provide Isaac with a list of lighting supplies to be purchased.

Prior to his departure, Ridge called General Aviation on his cell phone and fortunately was able to set up a check ride with an instructor the following morning in Isaac's Lear jet.

When he had terminated the call, Ridge turned to Isaac, "We're in luck. I can get the check ride in the morning and we can take her up in the afternoon. Don't forget our first discussion. After we take that baby flying, you're coming out to the cabin for drinks and dinner with KD, Jean Ann and me, right?"

"Have you checked with Katy?" Isaac asked.

"It's not Katy, Isaac. It's a "K" and a "D." And I don't need to check with her. She loves to cook and we'd love to have you. Tomorrow night, okay?"

"Sounds great. Give me a call after the check ride and I'll meet you at the airport. I want to take a look at that hangar you're building too."

"You got it. Give a ring out there to tell them you've okayed my taking a check ride in your plane, okay?"

"I'll call right away. See you tomorrow afternoon, Ridge."

"Should I give our classic response? Sounds like a plan."

They both chuckled and Ridge left *Les Enfants* for the cabin. He, KD, and Jean Ann had one of their favorite family nights planned—grilling out on the huge deck and then watching a first-run movie on their wide screen.

28

The Costlowe Boys in Spencer

At ten o'clock the next morning, a sporty yellow convertible turned into the gates of *Les Enfants.* Bartie and Jesse had arrived to finalize the business plan with Isaac Kahn.

Isaac himself opened the door when they rang the bell. He glanced out at the rental car.

"Nothing like keeping a low profile, boys," he commented.

"We couldn't resist, Mr. Kahn. When I saw that baby on the rental lot, I knew it was the car for us. We don't have much opportunity to ride in a convertible in Brooklyn."

"Yeah, well, you don't want to be arousing any undue interest here, but I guess it'll be all right this time. You won't be coming to Spencer again in the near future. From now on, we can conduct our business by FAX. I got you one," and Isaac handed them a FAX machine in its original box. "That's how we're going to communicate from now on unless there's an emergency. Then use the cell, but no names and no business discussions. Come on in the great room and let's sit down and you explain this computer jazz to me, Jessie."

Jessie explained about web sites and IP numbers and how they could be traced. He again suggested a simple email address with an embedded link was the way to go. After several hours of explanations and questions from Isaac, Isaac said, "Then I think the way to go is for me to go into the Internet Access business."

"That's a great idea because if the FBI locates the email address we use, the first place they'll go is to the Internet Service Provider, ISP in the vernacular, to get the IP number of the computer. If you own the company, that gives us another layer of protection, but do you have any idea what one of those companies will cost to get it up and running?"

"Not a clue," answered Isaac.

"Probably hundreds of thousands of dollars and the competition is fierce."

"Let me work out the details, Jessie. I'm buying an Internet Access company. What I've gathered from your three-hour tutorial is that I need to buy one before we set everything else in motion. I've located the computer for you to use. It belongs to Bonita Roberts and is in her home right here on the lake and I know her social secretary who is the only one who uses the computer."

"How are you going to keep the social secretary quiet?" Bartie asked.

"That's none of your concern, Bartie. I've taken care of that. Once I own the Internet Company, I'll see that Mrs. Roberts' computer uses it. Now, let's discuss the rest of our plan and I want to see some pictures of these children you've lined up for the flicks. You brought them, didn't you?" Isaac asked Bartie.

"Right here," and Bartie opened his briefcase to display a leather portfolio of children from ages three to ten.

At two o'clock as the Costlowes and Isaac were concluding their business discussion after enjoying one of Chang's sumptuous luncheons, Isaac's phone rang. It was Ridge.

"All ready to fly the bird, Isaac?"

"Sure. How about we fly her up to La Guardia?"

"Fine. Any particular reason?"

"I have some guests who flew in for the morning. We can take them home."

"Okay, I'll go file a flight plan."

"Excellent. We'll leave now and return their car on the way to the airport and meet you at the hangar in forty-five minutes," Isaac answered.

Isaac clicked off and said, "Well, boys, that about ties it up." He shook hands with both of them and said, "You follow me out to the airport. We'll return your rental car and then Ridge and I will fly you back home."

"Who's Ridge?" Jesse asked.

"A friend. He's a Delta pilot, but we're going to fly you back in my Lear jet."

"You have a Lear jet?" Jesse asked excitedly.

"I do. Now let's get going."

Jesse was beside himself. He and Bartie were going into business with a man who owned a Lear jet. A fully loaded new Lear jet would set someone back about twelve or thirteen million dollars. Jesse could not begin to comprehend that kind of money. Bartie, on the other hand, seemed to be in a trance. He had a big smile on his face. Bartie was thinking of the money that was going to come rolling in. He and Jesse would soon be living in a mansion a la *Les Enfants.* No more tenement living for them and no more renting yellow convertibles—they'd be able to buy one or fifty if they wanted. If Bartie had been a religious man, he would have offered up a prayer for dropping Precious Woodson into sweet, little, Jesse's bed.

29

Darling's on the Road

Darling brought her car to a screeching halt in front of Desiree's home. She was fifteen minutes late—at least that was still fashionable. She had planned to be on time, but her morning had been a harrowing one. Practically at dawn, she had left Spencer to drive up to Nashville to visit BD's mother who was a resident of the Hermitage Retirement Home there. It was a lovely old restored plantation and was the *in* place for one's final home before his or her permanent one at the Episcopal Cemetery or so it was harked to be. Darling wasn't all that sure.

When she had entered Berniece Huxtable's private room that morning, the old lady was lying upon her soiled sheets screaming at the top of her lungs. Darling quickly ran to the nurses' station and summoned an aide to change her mother-in-law's clothing and bedding. Once that emergency had been handled, Darling sat next to Berniece's bed and attempted to begin a conversation.

"Where's BD?" Berniece demanded. "Why do you always come and I never get to see my only son?"

"He's very busy, mother. He wants to come, but his clients keep him so involved. I'm sure he'll be here Sunday."

"Like you were sure he'd be here last Sunday and the Sunday before that? He didn't come, you know?"

"I know, mother. I promise he'll come this Sunday."

"That's all right. My only son and a lawyer and he can't come to see me. I had a little financial business to take care of and I needed assistance, but I got it all squared away all by myself."

Mrs. Huxtable was worth several million dollars and BD had been planning to go to see her at his earliest convenience, but he hated the drive to Nashville. He did work long hours and on Sundays, his only day of rest, he had a hard time making himself go to see his critical and overbearing mother.

"What did you square away, mother?"

"It's none of your concern. I wanted to talk to BD about it, but he's too busy so Dr. Ricks took care of everything for me."

"Dr. Ricks?"

"Oh, he's the most wonderful man. He took care of me before I was forced to come to this God-forsaken hole. He comes to see me two and three times a week. He's very busy too—Dr. Ricks is—but he always has time to come and visit me. He's never in a hurry to leave either like you are."

"Mother, I'm not in a hurry to leave."

"Oh, you're not? You've been here for fifteen minutes and you've already looked at your diamond watch twice."

"I have a luncheon engagement."

"Oh, my, a luncheon engagement. That's certainly important. Where is it?"

"In Spencer. I'm having lunch with Candy Martin at Desiree Compton's home."

"Then you're dumber than I thought you were. Why in hell would you drive to Nashville in the morning when you have a luncheon engagement in Spencer? You could have come another day," the old lady almost screeched.

"This is the only day I could come this week. I left very early this morning, mother, so I'd be able to visit with you."

"Well, you could have spared yourself the trouble. I don't even like you, Darling. I never did. And you can tell that son of mine he doesn't have to come anymore either. Dr. Ricks will handle my affairs."

"Mother, what are you talking about?"

"What I'm talking about is that in case you haven't noticed, I'm not going to be around much longer and I've been trying to get BD to write up my will and handle some of my other financial affairs for over a year. But he's never had the time, so I turned everything over to Dr. Ricks.

He's made some wonderful financial decisions for me in the past. Yessir, he's made me a pile of money in investments. So, I made him the guardian of my accounts and gave him my power of attorney.

He called an attorney and made the arrangements and brought the attorney, who apparently isn't as busy as my own son, here last week and I dictated my will. Yesterday, Dr. Ricks and the attorney came back and I signed it. It's witnessed, legal, ready to go and in the vault at *my* attorney's office as we speak. Pass that on to BD for me, will you?" the old lady said with the tiniest hint of a sadistic smile.

"Oh, mother, you shouldn't have done that. BD will be so upset."

"Oh dear. It didn't matter to him that I have been upset. So he'll just have to be upset, I suppose. Now, go on home, Darling, or to your luncheon or to hell for all I care. I'm tired and I don't want to talk to you anymore," and with that Berniece heaved her body over on her side facing away from her daughter-in-law.

"Mother, BD and I will both be here Sunday. Would you like for us to take you to the club for lunch?"

"No, I wouldn't, and I don't want either of you to come. Leave me alone. That's what you've been doing ever since I moved here anyway."

Darling picked up her purse and started for the door.

"Oh, and one more thing, Darling," Berniece rasped.

"Yes, mother?"

"Don't call me mother. I've always hated it when you did that. I'm not your mother and if I had been, I would have drowned you at a very early age."

Darling left the room and shut the door firmly and soundly, just a little short of slamming it. Once in her car, she hit the speed dial on her cell. BD's secretary answered.

"Put BD on Carla."

"He's with a client, Mrs. Huxtable."

"I don't care if he's with the Pope. Put him on the phone."

"Yes ma'am."

"Darling, I hope this is important. I'm in the middle of a big negotiation here."

"Oh, it's important all right. I just left your old bat of a mother. I've told you over and over to come up here and see her, but you're always too damned busy. Well, you're going to be sorry because the bitch has made Trace Ricks the guardian of her accounts, has given him power of attorney, has gotten a lawyer in Nashville to write up her will and his signed it with witnesses. For all I know, she named Trace Ricks her executor. There, BD, is that important enough to interrupt your big negotiation?"

"You must be mistaken, Darling. Mother would never do such a thing."

"Well unless she's developed Alzheimer's since my last visit, she told me that's what she's done."

"We'll both go up Sunday. Tell her we'll take her to the club for lunch."

"I can't tell her anything. I'm on the road. She told me to leave. She told me to tell you not to come Sunday or any other time. She doesn't want to go to lunch at the club. She wants us to leave her alone. She says that's what we've always done since we forced her into the Hermitage. She furthermore told me that she's never liked me and that she's always hated it when I called her 'mother.' So, BD, lunch at the club is not going to fix this one. Just thought I'd let you know."

"All right. We'll discuss it when I get home tonight."

"And what time will that be? You know how I hate these important discussions after midnight."

"I have to go, Darling. I'm really tied up here and I don't need your sarcasm. Thank you for the heads up and I'll see you tonight. I'll be home by seven. That's a promise," BD said and rang off.

Darling threw the cell phone onto the passenger seat. *I should have thought of telling him about something like this long ago. Home by seven—that'll be a first. Who does that old bitch think she is? BD is her only child AND he's an attorney. The very idea of her retaining another lawyer and what the hell is this with Trace Ricks? He's her doctor and he's made her a lot of money in investments? There's something rotten and it ain't in Denmark—it's in Nashville!*

Never fear, Berniece, I'll get to the bottom of this. There are many things your attorney son can do—like having you declared incompetent, you disgusting old crone who shits herself. This isn't the first time I've walked in on you lying there in your own crap. You've done it before. You lie there and soil yourself and then scream for someone to come, but you didn't ring your buzzer when you had to go, did you? Pathetic old bitch, what a way to get some attention—shitting all over yourself, so the nurses will have to spend ten minutes with you cleaning you up. Why don't you just die and be done with it?

Darling's mood improved as she got closer to Spencer. As her visit with Berniece, dragon lady, had been cut short, she would have forty-five minutes to spare before she was to be at Desiree's. That would give her ample time to go to the florist shop to select a beautiful arrangement to take to Desiree as a hostess gift. She'd have it placed in one of the Oriental vases Travis sold and then Desiree's maid wouldn't have to bother with arranging it. While one of the lesser florists did up the flowers, maybe Travis could make a delivery in his van and she could accompany him. The van was one of their favorite places for a tryst since it had no windows in the back.

Once at the florist shop, where Travis met her at the front door, Darling selected a lovely blue and white ginger jar and told Travis' right-hand man she was going to Desiree Compton's for lunch and that Desiree had a large number of Oriental accents in her home. Darling ordered a traditional three-pieced Japanese floral arrangement featuring baby orchids. As she finished her instructions, Travis asked her if she had a few minutes. He said he needed to go out to a customer's home to take a look at an area where they wanted him to plan and landscape a typical English garden.

"Your own garden is so lovely. Perhaps you might be able to give me some pointers and ideas," Travis said with a wink.

"I would be delighted, Travis," Darling said as she turned to the flower arranger and said, "I'll be back shortly."

"Yes ma'am, I'll have it ready for you," the lesser floral designer responded.

Travis and Darling headed for the van.

Forty minutes later when Darling arrived at Desiree's, she said to herself *you always stay too long at the fair, Darling, and look at your hair.* As she glanced in the rearview mirror, she noticed that not only did her hair resemble a rat's nest, but her eyeliner was also smeared down the front of her left cheek. *Thank god Travis had gone in and gotten the arrangement and brought it to her car so none of his employees had seen what a mess she was.*

Darling moistened a tissue with a little good old-fashioned spit and got the black mess off her cheek and quickly reapplied liner. She combed her hair and reapplied lipstick, grabbed the arrangement, and hopped out of the car to ring Desiree's bell.

Candy Martin opened the door for her. "Well hello, so glad you could make it."

"I'm so sorry I'm late, Candy. I had to go to Nashville this morning to see Berniece and then I had to run by the florist to pick up this arrangement I'd ordered for Desiree."

"No problem. We had a sip of champagne while waiting for you. I just came down to see if I could help with anything in the kitchen. Those flowers are lovely. Desiree's waiting for you."

The two entered the elevator and ascended to Desiree's boudoir where she was ready to hold court. Darling offered the same excuses to Desiree, who accepted them graciously, while casting a knowing eye in Candy's direction. The floral arrangement was a dead giveaway as to Darling's whereabouts and why she was late for lunch.

Darling ceremoniously placed the arrangement on Desiree's dressing table with a sigh, "Isn't it lovely? I especially wanted something with an Oriental flair since you have so many Eastern accents in your home," Darling gushed.

"It is truly lovely, Darling. Thanks ever so, but you know you didn't need to bring anything. It's been ages since I saw either of you and I simply wanted you two gals to come over and chew the fat," Desiree said between raspy coughs.

"Haven't given up the cancer sticks yet?" Darling asked.

"It's my only vice, dear," Desiree responded as she lit yet another cigarette.

Desiree was the only person who ignored Darling's furtive pleas not to smoke in her presence and Desiree was the only person Darling tolerated feeding her addiction. After all, the woman was bedridden—what other pleasure did she have?

While the ladies lunched, they discussed Bonita's debutante ball plans. Desiree allowed as how she was having everyone on the various committees at her Sunday salon and that she hoped both of them would be able to attend. Candy and Darling readily accepted the invitation and commented on how much fun the salons were. Desiree practically purred.

The conversation moved on to some small town gossip items, what social functions were upcoming, Bonita's horrid taste in clothing even though her outfits were couture and outrageously expensive, her exquisite jewelry and her seemingly unending supply of money.

Darling stifled a yawn and Candy asked if they were keeping her up.

"Not at all. I find the conversation very stimulating and luncheon was delicious, Desiree. I must have that soufflé recipe. No, I'm sleepy because I got up at the crack of dawn this morning to drive to Nashville to visit Berniece."

"Heavens, Darling, you've already been to Nashville and back today?" Candy asked.

"I have. I go to see the old bat once a week, although BD hasn't been for over two months, but I don't think I'll be having to go anymore."

"Why not? Is she approaching the end?" Desiree asked.

"One can only hope," Darling replied with a laugh. "No, that's not the reason. Today, she told me how she never could stand me and she didn't want me to come to see her anymore. She also told me how much she hated it when I called her 'mother.'"

"Well that ungrateful old biddy—as sweet as you've been to her," Candy remarked.

"And to no avail. She's been asking BD to come up for weeks to do her will, but he's been so busy, he hasn't had a chance to get up there. Anyway, today she informed me that because her only son hadn't had time for her, she had gotten Trace Ricks to recommend an attorney and she's written her will and signed it with witnesses. She also told me she's made Trace the guardian of her accounts and given him power of attorney. She extolled his virtues and said how he had made her a lot of money in investments. What is a doctor doing handling nursing home patients' money?"

"That *is* odd," commented Desiree.

"It certainly is, but you know these old folks really love their doctors. I guess she gave some money to Trace and asked him to invest it for her in a particular stock or bond?" Candy asked.

"That's not the impression I got from what she said," answered Darling, "And besides, she has a broker."

"I say that's odd because last week I had a call from my friend Lorena. She's at the Hermitage too. She was telling me how Trace Ricks had done so well for her in the market. You know Lorena has no heirs. She and William never had children and they were both only children so there are no nieces or nephews either. She mentioned in passing she was thinking of giving Trace Ricks her power of attorney. We were beginning to discuss that possibility when a nurse came in and Lorena had to ring off. She had to go down to X-ray for some test. Odd though, isn't it? I wonder how many of these nursing home residents are giving Trace free access to their money?" Desiree queried.

"Well, however many there are, he must be making money for them. Certainly there haven't been any complaints, I suppose," Candy offered.

"I've never known how Trace and Rhetta do all they do. He was from the wrong side of the tracks, you know, and while the Shaws left Rhetta some money, they certainly didn't leave her a fortune. Governor Shaw was in public service most of his life. They didn't really own a house until after his two terms as governor. Rhetta's mother came from some money, but I don't think Rhetta was left millions by any means," said Darling.

"I couldn't believe it when she pledged fifty-thousand-dollars at Bonita's. I've never heard Rhetta anxious to give to anything before. In fact, there are those who refer to her as *Rhetta Robin Take-Everything-Free-You-Can-Get Ricks*," Candy chuckled, "But she has a good heart. I've always liked her. Her luau was fabulous, Desiree. She must have spent close to two-hundred-thousand-dollars."

"That's what I understand. I'm sure Trace is still paying for equipment in his office and his new building plus they have the two houses to support and all those medical bills for the slow child," Desiree said next.

"Rhetta inherited RickShaw, Desiree," Candy explained.

"I know, dear, but she's redone practically every inch of it from what I hear," Desiree countered.

"True, she has. I think we simply need to chalk up these older ladies giving their assets to Trace as a symptom of their loneliness and their love for the handsome young doctor," Candy replied.

"Perhaps," said Darling, "But you better believe BD is hotfooting it to the Hermitage this Sunday. He'll get to the bottom of this. He's Berniece's only child. I can just see her cutting BD out of her will—the spiteful old bitch!" Darling said and she was definitely losing control.

"Now, Darling, don't get yourself all agitated. Berniece adores BD—she'd never cut him out of the will," placated Desiree.

Candy poured a splash more champagne in each of their flutes and ever the peacemaker said, "I think we've exhausted this subject. Let's move on to something more pleasant. Tell us your plans for Sunday's salon, Desiree."

And Desiree complied. Before the ladies left, Desiree handed them both copies of Maggie's luncheon soufflé.

MAGGIE'S NEVER-FAIL SOUFFLE

1 pie shell—can be homemade or purchased already made Bake pie shell at 450 degrees for 15 minutes.

Whip the whites of three eggs until they form soft peaks. In another bowl mix 8 ozs. of cheese (Monterey Jack, mozzarella, and cheddar are all good ones to use) and ½ cup milk (non-fat is all right.) Fold cheese and milk into whipped egg whites and pour into pie shell. Bake at 350 degrees for 30 minutes. Perfect every time and yummy!

30

Isaac Retains Harcourt

Isaac made an appointment with Harcourt Ball. He told him he had a business idea he wished to discuss. When Isaac arrived, Harcourt's secretary showed him into the attorney's office. Isaac felt he had walked through a wormhole in space and been catapulted back in time a few hundred years. Harcourt's office looked exactly as Isaac imagined a formal study in an old Southern mansion to look. Completely paneled in dark walnut, bookshelves covered three walls filled with handsome leather bound volumes. The massive partner's desk was constructed of gleaming mahogany. Seating for clients consisted of a maroon velvet settee and matching Queen Anne chair—all original pieces Isaac was sure. His recent interest in interior decoration had given him knowledge of the field through Precious' tutoring.

Harcourt rose from behind the desk and extended his hand to Isaac, "Hello, Mr. Kahn."

"Isaac, please."

"Isaac, have a seat. What can I do for you?"

"I want to purchase an Internet provider," answered Isaac.

"I think you can do that on your computer, Isaac," Harcourt responded.

"I don't mean one to use on my computer, Harcourt. I want to purchase the whole service. I want to own the Internet access service and sell it to other people."

"I see."

"And I want you to do the research and find out what's involved and make the deal work."

"You are a man of few words, I see."

"I like to cut to the chase."

"It's my understanding that this is a highly competitive field," Harcourt offered.

"Price is not a factor."

"I gathered as much at Bonita's meeting. How's the cave operation coming?"

"Everything's going fine there, I think, but back to the question at hand. Can you do this for me?"

"I'll get on it right away," Harcourt answered realizing that where business was concerned, Isaac was not interested in small talk and was certainly not the same witty, entertaining individual he had been at Bonita's. Perhaps that's why he was so obviously successful.

"Good. How long do you think it will take before we can be up and running?

"I have no idea, Isaac. Let me do some preliminary fact-finding first. Let's say I'll get back to you next week. Will that do?"

"I want to get this thing activated and going ASAP!"

"I'll be in touch next week. I'll get right on it."

"Do you want a check now?"

"Heavens, no. Let me see what I can do. We'll discuss finances later. I'm sure you're good for it," Harcourt said with a smile.

"I am. Time is of the essence though," Isaac said and he returned Harcourt's smile.

"Your real estate background is showing, Isaac. Realtors are always using that *time is of the essence* phrase."

"I have done a little real estate business in my time," Isaac answered. "Well, don't let me keep you. I'll look forward to hearing from you next week," Isaac said as he rose, crossed to Harcourt, extended his hand, shook Harcourt's, and exited through the double walnut doors leaving Harcourt's inner sanctum.

Isaac's next stop was several miles outside of Spencer where he checked on the progress being made at the cave. The renovations were costing more than he had spent on some of his condominium conversions, but unlike those enterprises, he could completely write this one off on his taxes. Isaac was always looking for ways to shelter income and to get write-offs, so the cave project was good.

Donning a hard hat, he met with the field supervisor and got an update on the progress being made. Everything was going according to plan and it looked as if the renovations would come in very close to the estimate Isaac had been given when he put the job out for bids. That, in itself, was amazing!

He drove back to Les Enfants where he had a meeting with Ridge about the lighting design for his great room. As he pulled in the driveway, he saw that Ridge was already there.

Entering the house, he called out to his pilot friend.

"I'm in the library, Isaac," Ridge answered.

Isaac entered the room to see Ridge engrossed in a large tome.

"This stuff is fascinating," Ridge said as he rose to shake Isaac's hand.

"What do you have there?" Isaac asked.

"I think it's child pornography, but it's beautifully done. The book is called *The Art of Children.*

"One of my favorites and yes, it is beautifully done. It's not child pornography, Ridge. It's erotica. I have a rather large collection. Are you familiar with erotica at all?"

"Sure, I used to have the biggest collection of *eight-page-bibles* of any of the kids on my block."

"Not trash, Ridge, erotica."

"The two seem a little similar, Isaac, except mine were poorly rendered cartoons and these look like Rembrandt painted them."

"I see I'm going to have to educate you on this topic. How about a drink?" Isaac asked.

"Nope. I'll pass. I have the sketch for the new lighting design all worked out, so I want to go over that with you. Let me put this *erotica* away and we'll get started."

Isaac and Ridge spent the next hour or so reviewing Ridge's very thorough and seemingly complicated plan for Isaac's lighting with Isaac asking questions and making suggestions. After he had made a few changes, Isaac gave his approval and said he would put out bids for electricians to get started on the job.

"I'd really like to do it for you, Isaac. I'm not a licensed electrician, but as I mentioned before, I could do the work and then you could have a licensed electrician come in to green tag the work. You, as the owner of the property, can get any permits we might need, although I don't think any are necessary as this is an existing home, but it's always better to check. I'd have to work on it on my days off—that's the only catch and you might want the job done as soon as possible."

"I'd be happy to have you do it, Ridge, but only if you'll let me pay you," Isaac said.

"No pay. I really enjoy this type of work. Besides, what are friends for?" Ridge asked with a smile.

"Then I'll go see the building inspector Monday and see what permits are necessary, get them if we need them, and you can start whenever you like. I have an account at all of the major hardware stores and I'll call them and tell them you'll be charging electrical materials and supplies to me. I really like your design. It's exactly what I had in mind, but I had no idea how to go about sketching it and I have even less of an idea how to implement it."

"It'll be an interesting and challenging project. I'm looking forward to it and whenever I get tired and need a break, I'll go into the library and check out some more of that *fine art*."

"Help yourself. And now how about a drink?"

"I don't mind if I do," Ridge accepted.

The following Tuesday, Ridge began work on the lighting in Isaac's mansion and he did exactly as he said he was going to do. Whenever he needed a little break, he went to Isaac's handsomely appointed library and perused a volume of erotica of which there were several hundred. He learned quite a lot about the questionable art and he learned even more about Isaac.

Isaac was gone most of the time Ridge was working as he was caught up in the cave renovations and also in some major colossal business deal he was putting together, so Ridge pretty much had the run of Les Enfants. Chang was always around to fix him lunch, snacks, or a soft drink if he wanted anything to eat or drink, but other than when he rang for the servant, he never saw him.

After scanning through the books, Ridge turned to the DVD's filling one entire wall of the bookshelves surrounding the room. There were classics galore and Ridge amused himself with watching *Citizen Kane* over a week's period. *The Manchurian Candidate, Rear Window*, and *On the Waterfront* were his next choices. He avoided *Debbie Does Dallas, Deep Throat* and *Behind the Green Door*, all of which he had seen during his bachelor days.

As he was skimming over titles on one of his breaks, he came across one of interest, *Tom Decking' Jane*. Ridge burst out laughing as he recalled the jokes he and his friends had made in high school about the old Dick and Jane primers. He recalled how they would make up raunchy titles like *Dick and Jane Do Spot, Jane Dicks Spot*, and *See Spot Dick Jane.*

Still chuckling, Ridge inserted the DVD and sat back to watch. He had no idea what was in store. As the credits rolled, Ridge thought his eyes were deceiving him. Children no older than six or seven were involved in explicit sex acts. He quickly turned off the overhead projector, removed the DVD, and returned it to its plastic case. Ridge thought he might throw up.

What in the world was Isaac doing with that piece of trash? Erotica, an art form, is one thing, but what I just saw is nothing but smut. It's child pornography plain and simple. And child pornography is illegal. It must be a fluke. But Isaac is such a man's man, I can't imagine him being interested in child pornography. Maybe, I'll just check out a few more of these provocative titles.

For the next half-hour or so, Ridge inserted DVD after DVD and each one was more graphic than the one before. They were definitely child pornography.

As he slipped a DVD into its holder, Chang came in and asked if he were ready for lunch.

"No, thank you, Chang. I'm not feeling too well. I think I'm going to knock off for today. Tell Mr. Kahn I had to leave early, okay?"

Ridge got in his car and drove to his log house. He wasn't sure what he was going to do. He certainly didn't want to associate with someone who was a pedophile, but he couldn't put Isaac and the kind of person he imagined would have such trash in his home together as one person. He determined he'd have to go back to Les Enfants the next day and confront Isaac. He'd ask him about the dirty kiddie movies. There must be a reasonable explanation, but what could it possibly be?

31

Hell's Apopping in Spencer

Bonita thanked Alphonso for his ministrations and discreetly slipped him a one-hundred-dollar-bill as he rose from her pink enveloped bed in the master suite and reached for her robe. Alphonso had known his mistress would be calling on him that morning for his extracurricular services. She always seemed to need sex prior to one of her big committee meetings. Alphonso supposed sex relaxed her.

"Will there be anything else, Miz Bonita?" Alphonso asked as he zipped his trousers.

"Yes, Alphonso, could you please go and present my debutante plans to the Van Buren Junior League today?" Bonita said with a twinkle in her eye.

"If you wants me too," Alphonso answered matching her twinkle with amusement in his eyes.

"I believe you would, wouldn't you? You have been one of the greatest finds of my life, Alphonso, and I want you to know how much I appreciate all of your skills."

"Thank you, ma'am. Now if I don't need to be preparin' a speech to give to the ladies for you, I think I better be getting' back to my regular schedule."

"You do that. I'll be ready for you to drive me in an hour."

"I's goin' to polish up the Rolls right now," Alphonso said. He exited Bonita's bedroom and gently closed the door.

Today was the big one. Bonita had sold her idea to every organization she and Lydia had presented it to, but she had been warned about today's group. Desiree, Lydia, and Darling said this would be the hardest sell yet primarily because the snooty broads in the Junior League would be upset that they had failed to come up with Bonita's debutante ball idea. Bonita had to admit she was more than a little nervous. With all her money, her past social status in Dorchester County, before *the unpleasantness* as Bonita had come to think of her downfall, and all of her social graces, it was at moments like this when

Bonita recalled her roots. She was very good at faking her background, but every once in a while, her past reared its ugly head and Bonita had to steel herself to remember that she was Bonita Roberts, society matron. If only she hadn't been reduced to a laughing stock in South Carolina. She lived in fear that somehow the people here would learn of her disgrace.

"But enough of that," Bonita said aloud to herself. "Get yourself into that tub. You're going to wow the snotty bitches today. Remember, my dear, you are the widow of the venerable and obscenely wealthy Joshua Roberts, and you are a power to be reckoned with. You have a clean slate here. Everything will be fine."

As Bonita prepared to lower herself into her scented bath, the phone rang. She knew either Hannah or Raven would answer it, so she carefully stepped into the tub so as not to cause a tidal wave. Bonita laid back and let the hot water and the essential oils do their jobs. As she felt her tightened muscles relax, there was a knock on her door.

"Yes?" Bonita answered testily.

"Miz Bonita, you has a important phone call," Hannah called through the closed door.

"Not now, Hannah. I'm in the bath."

"It's Miz Lydia. She say she has to speak to you this minute."

"All right. Come in and bring me the phone," an exasperated Bonita answered.

Hannah passed the phone to her. Bonita said, "My goodness, Lydia, I hope you're not canceling on me. You're a member of this group. I need you to go with me."

"I can't, Bonita," Lydia sobbed into the phone.

"Why not? What's the matter? Are you crying?"

"Yes, I'm crying, and I can't go with you today. I'm sorry," Lydia responded and then she hung up.

"Lydia? Lydia?" Bonita fairly screamed into the phone. "Hannah, where's that redial button? I don't have my glasses on. Lydia hung up on me. Hit that button and call her back."

Hannah pushed the button and gave the phone back to Bonita. It rang and rang, but Lydia didn't answer. Bonita threw the phone onto the pink tiled floor. Hannah picked it up and thought to herself once again that the phone must be the strongest ever made since Bonita routinely tossed it on the hard tiles in her almost daily fits of pique. Once again, it had survived.

"Hand me a towel, Hannah, and get my robe. Of all the days for Lydia to have an attack of the vapors. She simply has to go with me today," Bonita screeched as she rose from the tub and wrapped her folds of fat in the voluminous bath sheet Hannah provided. The Porthault velour bath sheet barely met in front between her two pendulous breasts. Bonita in a bath sheet was not a pretty sight!

"Hannah, go downstairs and tell Raven to keep trying Lydia's number until she answers and then transfer the call up here to me. Come right back up and help me get dressed. What in the world am I going to do?"

This was another of Bonita's idiosyncrasies. She had a buzzer to the intercom beside her bed she frequently engaged when she wished to speak to Raven. When she gave a directive to Hannah however, Hannah had to haul her tired old bones down the stairs to Raven's office and then haul them back up. The maid prudently decided this might not be a good time to mention this fact to Bonita.

"Now, Miz Bonita, you jest calm yourself right down. You's made your speech to every kit and caboodle in Van Buren County 'cept these ladies. What you so upset about?"

"These are the most important ones I'm going to be speaking to, Hannah. If they don't go for the plan, I'm sunk."

"No, you ain't. Mr. Kahn's already got that cave about ready for the ball and you's got your committee for selectin' the girls. You's got the charities lined up that's gonna get the money and the foundation is in place. What you worried about?"

"I'm worried because I want everyone to accept this idea wholeheartedly. We're definitely going through with it, but if the Junior League doesn't approve there will be a stain on the ball. They'll go running their mouths and gossiping and maybe won't accept if their daughters are invited. You wouldn't understand, Hannah. The Junior League is of utmost importance to my plan. Lydia is a member. I need her there today."

"I'll go tell Raven to keep trying her and I'll be right back to help you dress. Do you want me to bring you some of your green medicine?"

"Yes, Hannah, thank you and hurry," Bonita answered. She sat at her dresser table and smeared at least a tablespoon of foundation on her wrinkles, undereye pouches, and overly enlarged pores. She was already feeling better because Hannah had remembered the green medicine.

Some thirty years ago, one of her johns was a doctor who had *visited* her on a regular basis for several years. When she told him about the little anxiety attacks she sometimes experienced, he provided her with a prescription for a mild tranquilizer. It was a green liquid in a cough syrup type bottle and it was the most wonderful drug of which Bonita had ever partaken. One tablespoon in water would calm her down in a matter of moments. She had the prescription refilled over and over.

When the doctor told Bonita he was moving to the East Coast to practice at Sloan-Kettering, Bonita asked him how she could continue getting the wonderful medicine. On his last call on her, he presented Bonita with a case of twenty-four bottles. She took doses sparingly as she always wanted to have some on hand. Bonita had no idea what the ingredients were since the bottles were not labeled.

She had smudged the fluorescent blue shadow on, lined her eyes, and applied her false eyelashes by the time Hannah returned with the medicine. Bonita gratefully gulped it down and asked Hannah if Raven had reached Lydia.

"Yes ma'am. Miz Lydia answered the phone, but when Raven asked her to hold for you, Miz Lydia say she can't talk and hung up again."

"What in the world is the matter with her? Well, I can't spend my time worrying about her. I'll be late. I'm wearing the pale blue ensemble today, Hannah."

"I'll get your underclothes first."

Hannah placed a pale-blue hammock-sized brassiere on the bed for Bonita along with the matching barrel-sized panties and mammoth slip. Next to them, she carefully arranged a pair of queen super plus pale blue panty hose.

Then she headed for Bonita's warehouse sized closet and removed the dust cover from a pale blue linen tent and its complementary mosquito net. That's what Hannah thought the outfit looked like from the first time she saw it. It was a Vera Wang and Vera's palm had been greased quite sufficiently for her to make one of her usually petite designs in gargantuan size. Over the shift, which would look darling on a size ten and under, was a full-length outer garment of loosely woven macramé.

Hannah held the satin hanger high so as not to let the expensive material touch the carpeted closet floor. She reached up in the vast shoe collection for the pale blue peau de soie Dolce & Gabanno shoes and their forty-five-hundred-dollar corresponding clutch purse, which could barely hold a comb and a lipstick.

Bonita finished her makeup session and moved over to the bed where she began her dressing routine. The phone rang. Hannah picked it up. After she answered, she listened for quite a long time.

"Yes'm she's here. Miz Bonita, it's Miz Desiree."

"Tell her I can't talk now. I'm getting ready to speak to the Junior League."

"She knows that. I think you'd better speak to her."

Bonita impatiently took the phone, "Hello, Desiree. I hope this is important because if I don't keep moving, I'm going to be late. You know this engagement is imperative to our plan?"

"I do, Bonita. Have you spoken to Lydia?"

"Yes, she called in hysterics and said she couldn't accompany me. What in the world is the matter with her?"

"Nothing much. Randolph has been out of town for the past week supposedly bestowing grants for the Henley Foundation. He returned home last night with a bimbo he met in Atlanta and told Lydia she has one week to be out of the house and that he's filing for divorce and marrying the bimbo, his soul mate, the love of his life. He ensconced the bimbo in one of the guest rooms at the plantation."

"My god! That can't be true!"

"It's all over town. I think it might be wise to postpone your speaking engagement. I'm sure most of the Junior Leaguers will have heard the news. You know how gossip spreads here. As Lydia is a member, this might not be the most opportune time to have to explain her absence. Call them right away and feign dire illness or whatever you have to do."

"You're sure that's the right thing to do?"

"I'm positive. Then get yourself over here this afternoon. I'll call the other committee members and we'll have a meeting and decide what our next step will be in light of this disaster."

"All right, I suppose," Bonita said, but with none of her customary assuredness that whatever she did was always the right thing.

"I'll call you back shortly, Desiree. What time shall we meet this afternoon?"

"Two o'clock. C'iao, love."

Bonita pushed the buzzer next to her bed and was immediately connected via intercom to Raven.

"Raven, I've suddenly taken ill. I was in the midst of getting dressed for my engagement with the Junior League and my stomach began roiling. I simply cannot go today. Please call Mrs. Tilleston, the president, you have her number, and offer my abject apologies and ask her to please reschedule me for their next meeting. Thanks, dear."

"Miz Bonita, what you up to now? You ain't sick?" Hannah chided.

"I think I may be. Lydia's husband Randolph came back into town last night after a business trip. He brought some Georgia peach he met on his business trip with him and gave Lydia one week to vacate the plantation. He told her he wants a divorce and is going to marry the slut whom he claims is his soul mate. Stupid old fool!"

"Lawsamercy, white folks is plumb nuts! You want me to put these here clothes back in the closet?"

"No, I'll go ahead and get dressed. I have to be at Desiree's at two o'clock. I may as well dress and have lunch and then I'll go on over there. I tell you, this is one fine kettle of fish."

"That must be why Miz Lydia was crying when she called and insisted on talkin' to you, huh?"

"Definitely."

"Too bad she didn't tell you what was wrong so you could tell her how sorry you was, ain't it?"

"What?" Bonita answered distractedly.

"I said it's too bad she didn't tell you what the matter was so you could tell her how sorry you was, ain't it? You would have told her you was sorry, wouldn't you?"

"Hannah, stop jabbering. Hang the clothes up. Of course I'm sorry for her, but I don't think you realize the ramifications of this whole mess. I have to get the Junior League to go for my plan. I've explained to you how important that is."

"More important than someone who's been a good friend to you finding out that her life as she know it is over and done?"

"Her life's not over, Hannah. She's a very attractive woman and she'll get a huge settlement. She's been married to lover boy practically since she stepped from the cradle and he's worth a flaming fortune."

"A huge settlement! Is that all you thinkin' bout, Miz Bonita? What about the man she love betrayin' her?"

"He isn't betraying her, Hannah. All men go through these phases. You, of all people, should be aware of that. If men didn't wander, we wouldn't have spent thirty years in the lap of luxury in Los Angeles, would we?"

"No ma'am." Hannah picked up the clothes to help Bonita dress as she shook her head. Hannah was concerned about Bonita. *Miz Roberts don't seem to care 'bout nothin' or nobody anymore 'cept herself and that society bidness.*

After lunch and a retouch to her makeup, Bonita summoned Alphonso to drive her to Desiree's. When she arrived, Candy Martin was pulling in the brick driveway. Rhetta's car was there as was Marietta Ball's. Precious drove up and after the three ladies air-kissed, they entered the house and headed for Desiree's boudoir.

Greetings were exchanged and then Desiree asked if anyone had heard from Darling Huxtable. No one had.

"I called her this morning, but she didn't answer. I left a message on her machine. I was hoping she would have returned home and gotten it. It would be good if all of us were here to discuss our next move."

At that instant, the doorbell rang. The maid scurried to the door. Those upstairs heard loud voices and the elevator door slam shut. Someone was ascending. Desiree breathed a sigh of relief. Darling had gotten the message after all.

Estelle, the wife of Travis who owned the local florist shop, entered the room.

"Well, hello, venerable members of Spencer society. I'm here to tell you that one of your chosen will not be attending your meeting this afternoon and I'm not talking about Lydia. Darling has been detained. Would you like to know why?"

Everyone's eyes were riveted on Estelle, whose hair was a fright. She wore no makeup and was in faded jeans and a denim shirt. Her dirty feet were clad in flip-flops.

"Because her tits are probably frozen off by this time."

There was an audible gasp in the room. Surely, Estelle, whom none of the assemblage knew well, had come unglued.

"Now you're probably wondering how I could possibly know that, aren't you? I mean about Darling's tits. Well, you see, after lunch, I was out in my garden. I love to work in my garden. It's the main reason I still have my sanity. My garden is. Anyway, I noticed a few bare spots where I've been planning to plant some pretty perennials. You see, most of the time when I'm out in my garden and see a bare spot, I soon become engrossed in another project and before long it's time to go in and cook dinner for that fat assed husband of mine."

Candy Martin stopped her and said, "Why don't you sit down, Estelle? You're obviously distraught."

"Oh, am I? Well, good. I'm so glad you think I'm obviously distraught because I am definitely distraught."

Then moving closer to Candy and fairly spitting the next words in her face, Estellecontinued, "This afternoon I decided I wasn't going to get involved in anything else. I was going to seize the moment and go right down to Travis' shop and get some plants for that bare spot. I didn't put on any makeup. I didn't comb my hair. I didn't change my clothes. I simply got in my car and headed for the shop. Iparked out front and I went through the front door. I didn't see any funeral sprays being arranged, but there was certainly a funereal quality inside. Every employee in the place stopped dead in his tracks and stared at me.

Now, I know I look a fright, but I've gone down to the shop other times looking just as I do now. No one spoke to me and when I looked from one employee to the other, they averted their eyes. I asked one of them point blank where my husband was and he shrugged. I glanced around and saw a few others anxiously looking towards the cooler, so I marched myself right over to it and opened it. The stupid shits were in the cooler with no lock on their side of the door. Anybody could have walked in. Well, anybody did! Me!"

"Estelle, what on earth are you talking about?" Rhetta asked.

"I'm talking about Darling Huxtable, that bitch, Darling who always pretended to be my friend. Travis and I took vacations with Darling and BD She spent half her time at my house. Now I know why. I'm talking about Darling Huxtable and my fat assed husband. I hope her tits have frozen off. She was in that cooler *naked* as the day she was born on her knees in front of fat ass and he was naked too. She was performing, I believe the Latin word is *fellatio,* on the big dumbshit right there in the flower cooler in the middle of the florist shop at one o'clock in the afternoon.

So I just dropped by to tell you Darling won't be coming to the meeting today. You would think she would be real upset when she was caught *inflagrante delicto* with my husband, but the first words out of her mouth were about how now she was probably going to miss her meeting at Desiree's. I told her I'd be happy to come by and give you all the news that she wasn't going to make it. I'm sure she didn't think I would, but then I guess fat ass didn't think I'd be coming to the shop today either, did he? Well, that's it. Gotta go," and she tore out of the room.

The elevator engaged and descended. The front door closed. There was absolute silence in the room as a car door slammed. The next sound came as a complete surprise to everyone assembled. A gunshot rang out. Bonita moved to the window and looked down at the parking area in front of Desiree's house into the moon roof of Estelle's car that was in the fully open position.

"My heavens, Estelle's shot herself!"

There were shrieks and moans and sounds of disbelief as everyone rushed to the window to look out. Neighbors began pouring out of their houses heading in the direction of Desiree's house. In the midst of all the confusion, the phone rang. Desiree answered. When she screamed, the ladies turned toward her. Desiree placed the phone in the cradle.

"Before Estelle came over here, she shot Travis and Darling in the cooler. She walked in on them, said her piece, left the cooler, went to Travis' desk, took the gun he's always kept there out of the drawer, walked back into the cooler and shot both of them in cold blood. Then she did an even more amazing thing. She picked up two flats of perennials and took them with her to her car."

"For the bare spot. Are they dead?" asked Precious.

"That was Harcourt on the phone. He said Darling died instantly. Travis is in critical condition at Baptist Hospital. They're trying to stabilize him to airlift him to Nashville."

"Well, Lydia's news certainly pales next to this, doesn't it?" remarked Bonita.

Everyone in the room looked at her askance.

"What I mean is, we were all so upset about poor Lydia, and now look what's happened to Darling and Travis and Estelle. Desiree, you should call the police. We'll stay until they've arrived and questioned us and then I think we need to postpone this meeting," Bonita said, suddenly realizing she had made a faux pas and therefore jumping on the offensive and taking charge.

Maggie, Desiree's maid, came flying into the room, "Oh Lawd, Miz Desiree, Miz Estelle done kilt herself in the driveway. There's blood dripping out the car door."

"I know, Maggie. I'm calling the police now," Desiree responded in her calmest voice.

As Desiree dialed and the others headed for the stairs, police sirens were heard approaching. Within seconds, a black and white police car pulled into the driveway.

32

Southern Social Functions—Funerals!

Once the cursory investigations conducted by the Van Buren County Sheriff and the Spencer Police Chief were concluded, Darling's family and Estelle's family along with Spencer's elite moved into *funeral mode* with all the planning and preparations to be made for the two women's final hurrahs. Though Travis remained in the hospital, he was recovering well from his gunshot wound, was removed from the critical list, released from ICU, and moved to a private room. Although he received many floral bouquets, mostly from his own florist shop, and several visitors, he was shocked when he looked up and saw BD Huxtable standing at the foot of his bed.

"Hello, Travis."

"Hello, BD, I'm so sorry about Darling," Travis said as he looked away from his lover's husband's face.

"I'm sure you are, as am I. I'm here to talk to you about funeral arrangements. I imagine you're going to bury Estelle at Trinity?"

"Yes."

"Darling is to be buried there too, so I suppose, in light of the circumstances, we should plan the funerals for different days, don't you think?" BD asked.

"Yes, I think that would be best."

"Darling's wound was in the chest and she therefore can have an open casket. What is the situation with Estelle?" BD asked gently.

"I haven't seen my wife's body since I was only released from ICU yesterday. It is my understanding the casket will be closed. She shot herself in the temple."

"I see. Well, then, I was thinking of having Darling's body in our home for the viewing. That is, if you wish Estelle's body in the closed casket to remain at the funeral home until her services."

"I haven't discussed the arrangements with the children yet, but I think it would be best for Estelle's body to remain at the funeral home. Just prior to the funeral, the casket will be placed in front of the altar at the church. The family will not be able to process into the sanctuary behind her pall-covered casket since she committed suicide."

As Travis spoke those words, he began to cry and soon was sobbing, "I'm so sorry, BD. There's nothing I can say to you to make amends for what I have done. I never meant for anything like this to happen. I loved Estelle. My children hate me. You hate me. Lovely Darling is dead and it's all because of me. I wish Estelle's bullet had killed me too."

BD laid his hand on Travis' leg to offer him comfort, but he had no words for the man, his dead wife or Darling, BD's unfaithful wife, all of whom had made him a widower. BD loved Darling. He hadn't suspected her infidelity and hadn't realized anything amiss in their marriage. A workaholic, he provided for Darling and their children handsomely and he believed he was a good husband. BD was doing much soul-searching himself. He was an intelligent man and couldn't fathom how a situation had gotten so out of control that two people were dead and he had never been aware of a problem.

"Try to get some rest, Travis, there are trying days ahead," BD said. With a final pat to Travis' leg, BD turned and left.

The *telewoman* system in Spencer worked at a geometrical progression and soon everyone in Spencer was aware that Darling would be *lying in state* in her living room while Estelle's closed casket would be in the chapel at Tolman's Funeral Home. Estelle's services were to be held at Trinity on Tuesday at two o'clock in the afternoon. Darling's funeral would take place there the following afternoon at three.

The electric meters in Spencer were set awhirl as local housewives and the maids of the Spencer elite turned on ovens and burners and began to boil pounds of potatoes and dozens of eggs for homemade potato salad and deviled eggs. Ovens were jammed with cakes, pies, cookies, brownies, homemade bread, rolls and biscuits. Iron skillets were brimming with chickens frying in a combination of lard and butter. The local delicatessens had to call in special orders to their suppliers for more meats and cheeses to prepare the *funeral tray orders* they had received in anticipation of the receptions to follow the two approaching funeral services.

And when the women of Spencer weren't cooking or instructing their maids on what to cook, they were on the telephone rehashing the events at the florist shop, in Desiree's bedroom, and in her driveway. Lydia Henley's bad news had been shoved to a back burner. Shootings were so much more titillating than run-of-the-mill infidelity!

Bonita, who felt she was already fairly well embraced by the community, became an overnight celebrity in that she had actually seen Estelle in her car an instant after she killed herself. She was more than happy to elaborate to anyone who asked, with the appropriate touch of shock and sympathy, what she had witnessed. She was able to embellish the story with a full and complete accounting of what Estelle had done and said in Desiree's bedroom immediately prior to her self-inflicted death. The phone at the Roberts' household rang almost constantly. Even people Bonita hadn't met called to hear the *particulars* first-hand.

Raven shook her head more than once as Bonita took call after call. She found it highly unusual because Bonita rarely took calls but preferred to have Raven take messages. Then Bonita returned the ones to those she condescended to speak to at a set time each afternoon. For the past few days Bonita had taken each and every call and had talked at length to anyone and everyone who wanted to hear her story.

Monday, Bonita buzzed Raven and told her to hold her calls for the rest of the afternoon. She was readying herself to attend Estelle's wake at the funeral home.

"Be sure to take the number and the name of the caller so I can return the call in a timely fashion, dear," Bonita reminded her.

Bonita buzzed Hannah in the kitchen and asked if Alphonso had left with the first trunkload of food she was dispatching to Estelle's home.

"He left a half hour ago, Miz Bonita. He done took potato salad, deviled eggs, four fried chickens, green beans, that pineapple, lime Jell-O, cream cheese, coconut, gelatin mold thing I makes, a chocolate cake and a bourbon pecan pie."

"Splendid, Hannah. Thank you for making all those delights. What will you be getting ready for the reception after the funeral tomorrow?"

"I'm gonna bake a ham, make biscuits to go with it, sweet potato puff, seven-layered salad, fresh butter beans, and a five-layer coconut cake. Is that all right?"

"It sounds divine. Have Alphonso deliver the second load about eleven in the morning so it'll be there in time to set out after the funeral. You did remember to include one of my cards this morning, didn't you?"

"Yes'm and Miz Raven's already got the one ready for tomorrow. It's right here on the shelf starin' me in the face so's I won't forget."

"Thank you, Hannah. I'm getting into my bath now, so I'd like you up here in about an hour to help me dress. That's a love," Bonita said as she released the intercom button.

Alphonso had entered the kitchen after returning from his mission of mercy in time to hear Bonita's last few words.

"She's a demandin' one, ain't she?" Alphonso asked.

Hannah, who had food preparations covering every counter in the oversized kitchen said, "I'm used to it. Miz Bonita's been a godsend to me. I loves to cook and I gets to do that plenty and I dearly loves to help that woman get dressed. Now, I likes it cause sometimes the get-ups she wears is jest plain funny, but in her day, Miz Bonita was a great beauty. You shoulda seen some of the beautiful things she wore. I loved getting out all them fancy nightgowns and pig-nor things."

"You mean you helped her dress at night 'fore she went to bed too?" Alphonso asked.

Hannah realized she had slipped and said too much, "Yes, I did. But those nightclothes ain't the only pretty things she had. She had gowns like queens wear and lawsamercy the shoes that woman had. Everything in her closet was plumb gorgeous. Her clothes now is very expensive and of the finest material, but Miz Bonita has gained a few pounds since she was in her glory days," Hannah said with a smile, hoping she had successfully covered her slip of the tongue when she mentioned dressing Bonita in lingerie.

"Um-hmm," Alphonso nodded, "And what time she want me to take over the loada food tomorrow?"

"Eleven o'clock so it'll be there in time to be set up for after the funeral. The funeral gonna be at two o'clock. That's gonna be some sad time. Four teenaged boys without their momma and then the humiliation they's gotta feel. Their daddy been doin' the nasty with Miz Huxtable and their momma killin' Miz Huxtable and herself plus she tried to kill their daddy too. The messes people does get themselves into. It's a downright shame, ain't it, Alphonso?"

"It shore is, Hannah. Ain't you glad we works for Miz Bonita? We's so busy *steppin' and fetchin'* we don't have time to think about gettin' into no trouble like that."

"There won't never no possibility of that with me. I ain't never wanted no man, Alphonso. Oh, I ain't one of them women what likes other women, but I jest ain't never been interested in no man. 'Course I been taking care of Miz Bonita since I's twenty years old, so I ain't never really had no time to be interested in one," Hannah answered.

She guessed Alphonso didn't think she knew what went on between him and Miz Bonita. Hannah recalled when Bonita first approached Alphonso with her *extra duties* proposal. Hannah had been so worried Alphonso might talk, but the arrangement had gone on for years in South Carolina and she knew it continued here and so far as she knew Alphonso's lips were sealed even if his zipper wasn't. Hannah liked Alphonso and she believed he was a good man. He probably went along with Miz Bonita's proposal because she paid him so good anyway and then with his extra duties, she paid him even more. Hannah wondered sometimes what Alphonso was enjoyin' in his life. He didn't have no outside social life that she knew of other than when Miz Bonita called him upstairs. Hannah saw Miz Bonita nude almost daily when she helped her with either her bath or to dress and she thought Alphonso must have a mighty strong constitution or be so horny he would screw the crack of dawn if he could get it up for the likes of that.

Hannah broke out of her reverie and told Alphonso to have some tea and uncovered a platter of brownies, "Sit down and have a snack, Alphonso, while I finish up here so I can go help Miz Bonita get dressed for the viewing."

Bonita, meanwhile, was drying off her mounds of flesh. That done, she donned a velour robe and peered into her mirror surrounded with pink lights. She wasn't sure she liked the little flip on the side that new girl, supposedly fresh from Sassoon's in New York, had insisted upon when she had gone to the only beauty salon in Spencer the upper crust set foot in—*Curl Up and Dye.* Bonita thought it was such a tacky name, but it was by far the very best salon in Van Buren County.

The new girl, Sissy, had convinced Bonita a little flip on the side would make her look younger and she said it was all the rage in New York. Bonita had agreed, but now she had second thoughts. She reached for her brush to see if she could do something about it when she realized it would be hidden under the black cloche she planned to wear.

Bonita loved hats and even though they were no longer de rigueur, she wore them at every opportunity hoping to inspire others to do the same thereby bringing them into style once again. She felt that an outfit only looked complete when accompanied by a hat. So many customs of good breeding had gone by the wayside. It was up to those who spearheaded society to make sure the good customs and traditions remained intact.

Hannah tapped softly on Bonita's door and entered with a flowing black two-piece ensemble Bonita had earlier selected to wear that evening. Hannah had taken it from the closet to steam any wrinkles away. She hung it on the antique gold leaf coat rack in Bonita's bedroom and headed for the lingerie chest where she removed a black lace bra, black panties and black, sheer nylons.

Hannah had hinted to Bonita several times in the past few years that maybe a girdle was in order, but Bonita wouldn't hear of it. Hannah had finally given up. Bonita continued to stuff her face and to pile on the pounds and Hannah came to realize that a girdle wouldn't be of any help anyway to Bonita's once ravishing figure. Hannah giggled as she thought to herself that it would be like putting a rubber band on a sow's belly.

"Did you say something, Hannah?" Bonita asked.

"No'm. I jest had a tickle in my throat."

"I hope you're not coming down with something with all that food that has to be prepared," Bonita said as she continued to dress.

"Don't you worry yourself. I ain't comin' down with nothin' and the food's gonna be ready. Now, don't you look nice!" Hannah exclaimed knowing that once she had paid Bonita a compliment, her mistress would forget about anything that had to do with her and her tickling throat.

"Thank you, Hannah. You really do have an eye, you know, after all these years we've spent getting dressed together."

Bonita took one more turn in front of the Cheval mirror and then swathed in black from head to toe, she descended the stairs where Alphonso waited to escort her to the waiting Rolls. He drove her to Tolman's Funeral Home where she instructed him to wait.

Bonita entered the chapel looking as if she were a bereaved widow. She slowly walked up the center aisle to Estelle's casket and laid a black-gloved hand on it and wept a few crocodile tears. Everyone assembled in the chapel turned to stare, for there was great concern and sympathy among the mourners for Bonita. After all she had seen Estelle's body right after the grisly act. It didn't occur to any of them that Bonita hardly knew Estelle and that they had never been friends or even acquaintances for that matter. Bonita, ever the aspiring movie actress, played the grief-stricken role for all it was worth.

After paying her respects, Bonita took a seat on the front row in the little chapel. Within minutes, she was surrounded by people patting her hand, offering their condolences, and asking about the spectacle in Desiree's driveway. All spoke in hushed tones, as did Bonita, while she bestowed upon them her now memorized and mesmerizing blow-by-blow account of the events of the previous Thursday afternoon.

When Travis arrived on crutches with his four sons, Bonita was the first to offer them her condolences. Travis thanked her profusely for all the food she had sent that afternoon. Bonita assured him there would be more arriving the next day and asked if she could be of any assistance in helping with the reception to follow the services. Travis thanked her and told her everything was under control.

The widower moved to the right side of the casket and stood flanked by two of his sons on either side shaking hands and receiving those at the viewing. He looked both grief-stricken and uncomfortable for he knew everyone there was aware of the circumstances of Estelle's death, Darling's death, and why he was on crutches. He felt so sorry for his boys. They knew everything too and he knew the loss of their mother was horrible for them and that they blamed him, but at the moment they had nowhere else to turn. He hoped that somehow, someday he would be able to make this all up to them, but he didn't have any idea how. He was responsible for their mother's death. How could they ever forgive him?

In Spencer, everyone turned out for funerals, but Estelle's brought more people than usual. Typically only those people who knew the departed attended viewings and that accounted for a large number of people since Spencer was a small community and practically everyone knew everyone else. Estelle's viewing drew spectators and curiosity-seekers from all over the county. More than a thousand people filed through the chapel that evening.

The funeral directors knew if that many attended the viewing typically considered a somewhat private function, the funeral itself, traditionally a public event, would attract even more. They spoke quietly in the foyer outside the chapel about speaking to Travis regarding additional tents outside Trinity Church since the weather-guessers were predicting another scorching hot day tomorrow. It would be nice to have protection from the sun for the overflow crowd sure to be present at the service.

During the two hours set aside for the viewing, Precious Woodson, Candy Martin, Trace and Rhetta Ricks, Harcourt Ball and his mother, Isaac Kahn, Ridge and KD Dodd, and Raven and her parents were among those paying their respects. A few minutes before the viewing was scheduled to conclude, a hush fell over those congregated who were now standing in small groups conversing since the gathering had taken on a cocktail party atmosphere.

Everyone looked toward the door of the chapel. Lydia Henley had entered. A very subdued Randolph followed a few steps behind. They moved to the casket, bowed their heads and then greeted Travis and Estelle's sons and took seats. No one ventured near them, but conversation immediately broke out again. Except for Travis and his sons, everyone had forgotten about poor dead Estelle. They were now speculating on what was going on with the Henleys. Where was the bimbo? Was she still in town? Did Randolph still expect Lydia to move out?

Of course with Randolph sitting right there next to her, none of her close friends of which Bonita considered herself one, could approach Lydia and ask her outright about the current situation at Henley Plantation. For a while no one ventured near the couple. Finally, Bonita excused herself from her conversational group and walked over to them.

"Lydia, how lovely to see you. Hello, Randolph. How are both of you? I'm so glad to see you. Lydia, I'm especially happy to see you after you had to cancel the Junior League meeting Thursday because you were feeling poorly."

"I'm feeling much better now," Lydia answered Bonita. She had a big smile on her face. Lydia knew exactly what Bonita was doing and she loved it.

"It's such a shame about Estelle, isn't I? And Darling? Two homes without mothers and poor BD and poor Travis. So much tragedy from a little fling, don't you think?" Bonita said looking directly at Randolph.

"It's horrible!" Randolph said, "We've never had anything like this happen in Spencer or in all of Van Buren County that I recall."

"Well, I must run, but it was lovely to see both of you. Of course, I'm sorry it was under these circumstances. Will you be at the services tomorrow?"

The Henleys nodded.

"I'll see you then. Lydia, do you think you might be able to accompany me to the Junior League meeting when they reschedule?" Bonita asked.

"Certainly, Bonita. I'm so sorry I had to cancel Thursday, but you know at our ages, we have these little hiccups now and then. I'm sure I'll be feeling fine when the meeting is rescheduled and you can definitely count on my accompanying you."

Bonita and Lydia air-kissed and squeezed hands and Bonita made her exit. She wondered what Lydia had said to Randolph. It was obvious she had put the fear of god in the old coot. *Good for her!*

Alphonso was waiting beside the Rolls for Bonita. He opened her door and got her settled in the back seat. As soon as they pulled away from the funeral home and were moving with the traffic pattern, he asked, "Miz Bonita, who was those folks with Miz Raven?"

"Her parents. Raven introduced them to me. Lovely people."

"Miz Raven sure don't look like neither one of them. They is fair and she is dark. Is she adopted maybe?"

"She's never mentioned it. But you're right, Alphonso. She doesn't look like them. I thought they were both quite attractive. Did you see them up close?"

"No ma'am. Miz Raven came over and spoke to me but they was already at the door. Her momma did turn around and glance my way and I seen she was real pretty. It jest struck me strange that they was blonde and had such light skin and Raven has that olive-colored skin and her eyes is almost black," Alphonso commented.

"Well, to my knowledge she's not adopted, but I'm certainly not going to ask her that. You know some people who adopt children never tell them? I've never understood that, but each to his own. I'm glad this is over. So sad. I feel so badly for those boys. Teenagers without their mother and the stigma of her suicide. I'm sure they're going to have rough days ahead," Bonita sighed.

"I reckon so," Alphonso agreed as he headed for Villagio. He couldn't stop thinking about Raven's mother. Although he had seen her only at a distance, he could tell she was beautiful and there seemed to be something familiar about her, but what could that be? Alphonso had never seen her before.

The next day when Alphonso delivered Bonita's offerings for the reception to Travis, he saw Raven's mother again. She was coming out of the front door as Alphonso was pulling into the driveway. Once again at a distance, Alphonso was struck by her beauty.

After he deposited the food in the kitchen and started back, he again had the haunting feeling that something about her was familiar. He quickly dismissed it. He had a list of errands to accomplish before he went back to collect Bonita to take her to the funeral. He couldn't spend his time daydreaming. Alphonso chalked the déjà vu off to the fact that he had always been appreciative of good-looking white women. In his youth when he was with friends and had expressed appreciation for a white woman, his fellow blacks had teased him and called him "Uncle Tom."

Fifty years before when Alphonso was a young boy, misigenation had usually been one way—upper class white men and attractive high-yellow servants. It was highly unusual for a black man to see a white woman socially much less to marry her. A black man who *messed* with a white woman in the South in Alphonso's youth was setting himself up to be hanged.

The chauffeur completed his errands and was back at Villagio in time to drive Bonita to the funeral. She glided down the front steps of the mansion to the waiting Rolls and Alphonso had to turn away to keep her from seeing his amused expression. She looked to him like a picture of the Wicked Witch of the East he had once seen in a children's book in Bonita's library. His employer had on a big black picture hat slightly pointed at the top with a black veil over it covering her face. She was completely in black. The only thing missing were the red shoes, but then Alphonso thought *Dorothy ain't here and she don't need to go back to Kansas, so I reckon Miz Bonita don't need the red shoes.* He wished he could chuckle aloud, but ever the commendable servant, he shut the door and moved into the driver's seat to take his boss lady to her destination. He did not chuckle and he said not a word unless Bonita spoke to him.

Fortunately Travis had agreed to tents outside the church as it was overflowing. There were hundreds of floral arrangements in the sanctuary, one more beautiful than the other. The most spectacular was the spray covering Estelle's casket. It had not been there the night before at the viewing. There had been a small bouquet of violets, no doubt flown in as they were not in season, from her boys adorning Estelle's casket then. Someone had commented they were Estelle's favorite flowers. Today, a spray of magnolias, gardenias and baby's breath covered the coffin in the form of a large heart. Red roses had been jaggedly placed in it to make it appear the heart were broken. Word at the reception later was that Travis had gone to his shop that morning and had insisted on arranging the spray, delivering it and placing it on Estelle's casket himself.

A sound system was in place at the cemetery so everyone could hear the final rites as the crowd was so large and so widely dispersed over the sloping hillside where the venerable were buried overlooking their beloved Spencer.

After the benediction, the Trinity priest announced Travis and his sons would be receiving guests at their home following the service. That afternoon hundreds, many of whom had never laid eyes on Estelle, walked on her carpets, sat on her chairs, and ate the foodstuffs provided by the Spencer townspeople from her china using her sterling silver utensils.

Those who knew Travis and the boys expressed their condolences again upon their arrival, but turned quickly to the bar and the groaning dining room table and began to party down. Receptions following funerals in the South are parties, plain and simple, and many go on into the late hours of the night or even the wee hours of the morning. Travis was relieved when his last guest left at a little after seven o'clock. He knew most of them were heading to BD's house for Darling's viewing and would be attending her services the next day.

Travis didn't know what to do. BD hadn't come to Estelle's funeral, but then Travis nor anyone else had expected him to be there. Estelle had killed his wife. But what was Travis to do? He had been involved in a love affair with Darling. That affair was the reason both his lover and his wife were dead. He wanted to be able to pay his respects to Darling, but he didn't want to further upset BD. He certainly didn't want to cause any grief to BD's children, one of whom he was sure was his own son.

He decided not to attend Darling's funeral, but he would send an arrangement. Darling had fancied orchids. He'd make the arrangement himself and he'd sign the card from the boys and himself. The orchids would have to suffice for his presence. He hoped Darling would understand why he couldn't be there. He was sure she was looking down on him that very moment.

Travis shook his head to clear his thoughts. If he believed Darling was looking down on him, he wondered where Estelle was. Somehow, he didn't feel the two women were in the same place, but then he supposed heaven or the other place were both quite large. Travis sat in his LaZy-Boy recliner with his head in his hands. Again, he wished Estelle's bullet had killed him too, but he had to keep going for the boys. How had a little piece of tail on the side developed into such a tragedy? He probably knew twenty guys who messed around and nothing like this had ever happened to any of them.

While Travis pondered and wept, the rest of Spencer offered their condolences to BD, hugged his children, remarked on how beautiful Darling looked, and partook of white wine and light hors' d'oeuvres at the Huxtable residence.

HANNAH'S PINEAPPLE, LIME JELLO, CREAM CHEESE, COCONUT, GELATIN MOLD THING

1 small package lime Jell-O
4 pineapple slices
4 cherries
2 8 oz. packages cream cheese
1 large can crushed pineapple drained
1 8 oz. package shredded coconut
1 package Knox gelatin

Mix small package of Jell-O according to directions and pour into lightly greased bundt pan. Arrange pineapple slices with cherry in center of each in Jell-O. Chill until set.

Mix softened cream cheese, Knox gelatin, coconut and drained pineapple and spoon on top of set Jell-O in pan. Chill for at least 4 hours. Run hot water on outside of pan and invert on decorative platter. Slice like cake to serve. Delicious and very pretty as green Jell-O with pineapples and cherries is now on top of mold. Keep any leftovers refrigerated.

HANNAH'S SWEET POTATO PUFF

Large can sweet potatoes—drain and wash
½ cup brown sugar
½ cup sugar
1 stick butter
2 eggs
1 ½ t vanilla extract
4 oz. pecans

Melt stick of butter and beat eggs. Mix all ingredients except nuts with mashed sweet potatoes. Spread in Pyrex baking dish. Bake at 350 degrees for 30 to 40 minutes. Remove from oven, sprinkle with pecans and serve.

Rhetta and Trace were at Darling's funeral and at the reception following where they quietly made the announcement to their close acquaintances they were leaving the following afternoon for a trip around the world. Everyone was duly impressed. When Bonita asked Trace how he was going to manage leaving his practice that long, Rhetta quickly informed her he had hired two new doctors for his rapidly growing practice and they would be handling the patients until their return. She also informed everyone that they would be traveling alone. A live-in couple would be taking care of the girls while they were gone.

Candy Martin and Precious Woodson soon had their heads together gossiping about the seemingly sudden wealth of the Ricks' family. While Rhetta and Trace had always managed and Rhetta had spent freely on her daughters, they rarely entertained except for the lavish luau. Rhetta's gifts for engagements and hostess gifts were usually on the cheesy side or when they were lavish, many suspected they were the result of that age-old custom called *regifting*, where one rewraps and gives away a gift previously presented to them.

For the past few months it seemed there was no end to Trace's resources. Rhetta spent a fortune at *Ulterior Motifs*, the interior design shop in Spencer, redoing every room at RickShaw again! She and the girls had been to New York to design houses for new wardrobes and Rhetta had let everyone know she was having the house in Nashville completely refurbished also.

Rhetta, herself, didn't know where all of the money was coming from and why Trace had stopped complaining about her spending habits. It seemed nothing she asked for was too much. He simply wrote her a check or told her he would deposit the money in her account. Rhetta wasn't going to ask any questions. She was in pig's heaven. While her family had always had a good name, perhaps the most important attribute in the South, they had never been fabulously wealthy, something of which Rhetta had always dreamed. She'd had to make do while presenting a picture of wealth to both of the communities in which she dwelt. Those days were over and Rhetta and Trace were happier than they'd ever been.

Trace, of course, was raiding all of the accounts of the old ladies who made him the guardian of their accounts or who gave him cash to invest for them. He had spent hundreds of thousands of dollars of other people's money. Several of the old ladies had passed away and none of their heirs were the wiser. Trace had found it so easy to steal money. After the first few times it became second nature to him. Most of the old ladies who placed their complete trust in him hadn't had a visitor for months or in some cases years. Their families paid little or no attention to them, but he was always there for them. He went to the nursing homes of assisted living facilities at their beck and call. Trace was convinced he deserved their money and they, if the truth be known, wanted him to have it.

He wasn't too concerned about leaving his practice in the hands of his two new hired associates either as he hardly ever saw patients in his office. He spent the major portion of his doctoring workdays traveling from one nursing home to another checking up on his wealthiest and loneliest patients.

As the reception wound down and the Spencer elite began to leave, Bonita had a moment with Lydia.

"What in the world did you say to Randolph? Did you threaten him, Lydia?"

"Of course not, Bonita. Randolph loves his money and his land more than life itself. I simply reminded him that I would take him for every cent he had. I told him I would fight him tooth and nail and I reminded him that he hasn't been able to get it up for years and how long did he think the bimbo would stay with him. I suggested to him he tell her she would be required to sign a prenuptial agreement, which the old fart hadn't even considered. Anyway, he does love his money, so he went straight to her and told her she would be required to sign a pre-nup once I was out of the way. She was gone within the hour. I almost felt sorry for him. Randolph believed the twit actually cared for him, I think. Old fools are the worse fools, Bonita, but I've known the fool since he was young and he's my fool. Besides, I love him. All is forgiven and I'm sure I won't have any more surprises from Randolph. After I got over the shock, the whole thing kind of amused me. Randolph has never done anything to the left or right of the path of absolute normalcy, so it was probably good for him. It was definitely good for me. I *condescended* to remain with him after he had mortified me," Lydia said with a chuckle.

"You are something, Lydia. I'm so glad everything is all right with the two of you."

"Oh, things are better than all right, Bonita. I plan to get a lot of mileage out of this."

Randolph joined Lydia and all said good night as they moved to their respective cars.

Isaac Kahn was at his car door when Ridge approached him.

"Hello, Ridge. Will you be at Les Enfants tomorrow to work on the lights?"

"Isaac, there's something we need to discuss," Ridge answered.

"Is there a problem with the lighting?"

"No, but I have a problem."

"What is it? Is there a way I can be of assistance?" Isaac asked.

"There definitely is. You know, when I'm working at your house, I take little breaks. I started watching some of your videos and DVD's and Isaac, I'm a little confused about some of the films. They're child pornography. I mean this stuff is really graphic with young children. I have to be honest with you. It bothers me and it bothers me that you would want to watch that trash."

"Ridge, I'm a collector. The child porn films are part of my erotica collection. They're an art form."

"Isaac, those films are not art. They're filthy. Young children are being sexually abused. How can you have that filth in your house?" Ridge continued.

"All right, Ridge. I'm sorry to have tried to insult your intelligence. Let me be entirely truthful with you. I invested in a film company a while back. I had no idea pornography was one of their genres. I was sent a copy of each film the company produced. I watched a few of the films and some were pornographic. While that's not my idea of entertainment, pornography is legal as I'm sure you know and as far as my investment went, the pornography films were the biggest moneymakers.

"After a while, so many films were coming in so quickly, I ceased to watch them. One title did intrigue me so I watched it. It was one of the films causing you concern and it caused me great concern also especially because I was a principal in the company. I am no longer involved with the company but I kept all the films to turn over to my attorney within a short time as I am suing the corporation. Those films are evidence.

"Please keep all of this confidential. I wouldn't want the lovely people of Spencer to know I was ever involved in such a smutty operation. It was my own fault for not doing proper research and putting money into a corporation I had not fully explored, but it was at a time when I was heavily involved with other business and I didn't do my homework properly," Isaac explained.

"I can't tell you how relieved I am, Isaac. I was really beginning to have questions about you. I hope you didn't lose any money."

"On the contrary, I made a great deal of money, but I don't want or need to make money at the expense of precious little children's exploitation. I'm completely out of it, Ridge, but please don't let this go any further," Isaac beseeched.

"I won't say a word. I've had my share of business deals gone sour myself. Sorry about your problem with that trash, Isaac, but thanks for confiding in me. I'll be over tomorrow."

"I'll look forward to seeing you, Ridge," Isaac said as he got in his car. From the open window, he said, "And Ridge, I have hundreds of movies for you to watch on your breaks. I'll have Chang box the evidential ones up first thing in the morning so you won't get one of them by mistake."

"Thanks. See you tomorrow," Ridge called as he joined KD and walked to his car. He was greatly relieved now that Isaac had explained the reason for the smut in his library. Meanwhile, Isaac was smiling to himself. *I can hardly believe it, but I think old Ridge bought my story. You haven't lost your touch for lying on your feet, Ike. Damn it, I mean Isaac!*

Cars began moving out of Travis' driveway. The funerals were over. Spencer would talk about Darling and Estelle and Travis for another week or so, but then would move on to the next order of business or the next tidbit of gossip. And as luck would have it, they were going to have a mountain of tidbits upon which to chew!

33

Plans for the Ball Proceed

Bonita and Lydia met the following week at Simpson's, an upscale tearoom, for a light luncheon to go over their notes prior to the presentation for the Junior League. Lydia filled Bonita in on some of the members and gave her pointers as to which of them might be a hard sell. Bonita took notes with her gold Cross-pen and listened carefully to every word of advice from Lydia.

At quarter of two, Alphonso pulled up in front of the restaurant to collect the ladies and take them to their meeting. Lydia looked lovely as always in a pale pink Chanel suit with matching Jimmy Choo shoes. Her tote was a Vera Bradley of the same shade of pink as the suit and was covered with deeper pink roses. Her only accessories were a rock-sized diamond hanging from a gold chain around her neck, her two-carat stud earrings and her Patek Philippe watch.

Bonita was in her signature shade, iridescent blue, with matching shoes, purse, and hoses. Everything she had on including her underwear was from the House of Versace. She was accessorized to the hilt with pale blue freshwater pearls at her ears and around her neck in addition to a large lapis brooch pinned precariously above her right fist-sized nipple. She resembled an oversized dyed Easter egg.

Lydia was amused by Bonita's ensemble as she was most of the time with Bonita's selection of outfits, but Lydia was not the least bit concerned. She had apprised several of the ladies of Bonita's vast wealth, social standing, and Spanish heritage including her descent from royalty. No one would be disparaging about Bonita's bulk or her choice of blue on blue on blue. The kind of money Bonita possessed could cover up lack of taste, lack of class, lack of couth, lack of education, and even piles of shit! And if it couldn't, it could guarantee silence so none of it would be mentioned.

The presentation was a complete success. The Junior League members were thrilled with Bonita's proposal of a Spencer debutante ball. The establishment of a foundation to make charitable contributions was the icing on the cake. The social function could masquerade as good works. Every single member wanted to become involved. They waxed poetic about how in years hence it would be more prestigious for one to debut in Spencer than in Nashville of Knoxville. They fairly wallowed in delusions of grandeur.

Bonita perched atop cloud nine. Isaac had told her the week prior the cave remodeling was almost complete. Harcourt Ball and Lydia and now the Junior League would have all of the charities identified in short order. It was time for Bonita to name those fortunate souls to serve on the selection committee, the chosen ones who would decide on the young ladies to be invited to debut at the first Spencer Ball.

A name for the ball hadn't been decided upon by the committee yet and Bonita desperately wanted it to be another Magnolia Ball. She felt reasonably sure she would be able to overcome any objections to her suggestion as she had come up with the idea and had done most of the work convincing the people of Spencer it was a wonderful idea.

Back at home, Bonita told Raven to call a meeting of the original committee. Reports were to be given on the establishment of the foundation, the amount of money donated thus far, and the progress on the cave. She would be giving a report on the clubs to whom she had spoken. She told Raven to suggest to each person they have officers in mind for the foundation. They would need a president, vice-president, secretary and a treasurer. Bonita further instructed Raven to inform each board member that she would refrain from holding an office. Her positions would be chair of the selection committee and emcee of the event itself. She further planned to school the young ladies prior to the ball itself, so as not to have an embarrassment like that horrid Mandy and her entire white trash family in Montiac, South Carolina.

While Bonita was making her plans for a committee meeting, Isaac was meeting with Harcourt Ball and putting his Internet business in place. Harcourt had been thorough in his research and Isaac was preparing to purchase a small local Internet service that had not been operating in the black. He was prepared to pay top dollar for the fledgling company and Harcourt was sure the offer would be accepted.

"Then let's get the ball rolling, Harcourt. Make the offer today and I'm ready to settle immediately. I'll have the money wired to their account at settlement."

"I think you can get it for a lot less than four million, Isaac."

"Fine, offer whatever you want and of course, make me the best deal, but I'm willing to go up to four million. See what they say. Call me this evening if you get through to them. I want to get this show on the road right away, Harcourt."

"I can see that you do. I thought you were retired, Isaac. Why in the world do you want to buy an Internet service that hasn't been able to make a dime?"

"I'm bored and computers and the Internet are what's happening now. We old folks have to stay up with the times, don't we?" Isaac answered as he took his leave.

He returned home to find Ridge working diligently on the great room lighting. It was really coming together. He would have to think of something special to do for Ridge. He absolutely refused to take any money for all of the hours he spent making Isaac's lighting design into a reality.

"Hello, Isaac. KD and I are hoping you'll be able to come over to the cabin after I finish up here for the day and have drinks and dinner with us."

"How nice. What time do you think you'll be wrapping up?"

"About four-thirty. Is that good for you?"

"Sounds fine. Let me tell Chang I won't be here for dinner this evening. I'll go change and make a few phone calls and then it'll be time to shove off. Thank you. I'm looking forward to getting to know your lovely wife better."

"She's a prize and a fantastic cook. You'll love whatever she fixes. She prepares a gourmet meal every night. It's a wonder I'm not as big as Bonita Roberts," Ridge said with a laugh.

"That is one large lady, isn't she?" Isaac asked.

"With the bank account to match, I hear," Ridge responded.

"She's definitely got a lot of money, that's for sure. I'll be back shortly," Isaac said and hit the button on the elevator to retire to his private suite.

Ridge hit speed dial on his cell phone and told KD Isaac would be joining them for dinner.

"Good. I made Basque chicken for dinner."

"My favorite. I know Isaac will love it. See you soon, honey."

KD had spent the major part of the morning preparing the chicken dish after Ridge left for Les Enfants. It didn't matter to her whether Isaac came for dinner or not. She and Ridge enjoyed the dish and she liked making it.

BASQUE CHICKEN

1 T paprika
2 T salt
1 T white pepper
1 T black pepper
1 T onion powder
1 T garlic powder
1 T dry basil
1 T thyme
½ T oregano
¼ T nutmeg
3 lbs. chicken
1 lb. peeled shrimp
2 T olive oil
2 cups lean diced ham
1 ½ cup onion
¼ cup flour
1 ¼ cup white wine
2 cups chicken stock

Mix all of the seasonings together and then separate into thirds. Roll chicken in 1/3 of seasonings and sauté chicken. Roll ham in 1/3 of seasonings and then sauté. Sauté onion. Add flour, then wine, then chicken stock and remaining 1/3 of mixed seasonings.

Place chicken, ham, onions and juice in a casserole dish and bake about twenty minutes at 350 degrees. Add shrimp, mix together, and bake for 15 more minutes at 350 degrees.

KD usually served the chicken mixture over diced boiled potatoes and served green beans on the side. Her amusement about the recipe was that it was a favorite dish of Basque shepherds who traditionally stayed out in the highlands for as long as nine months at a time. Where in the world did they get all those spices? Did they take them with them in anticipation of making the dish? She could fathom that the shepherds may have come across a stray chicken and may have even slaughtered a pig to get the two cups of diced ham, but for the life of her, she couldn't figure where the gourmet shepherds had found the shrimp.

At any rate, both she and Ridge loved the dish and she hoped Isaac would too. All the other times she had served it, her shepherds' recipe had received rave reviews.

KD didn't do anything the ordinary way. Her green beans would not simply be boiled with a little butter and salt and placed next to the yummy chicken dish.

KD'S GREEN BEANS

2 lbs. green beans snapped and rinsed.
Boil green beans with one stick of butter and a T of salt and leave crunchy.

Mix ¼ cup olive oil and ¼ cup Balsamic vinegar. Stir in 2 t. oregano and 2 t. basil. Transfer hot beans to frying pan sprayed with olive oil and sauté for a few minutes and then pour dressing on and serve.

KD melted eight ounces of cream cheese in the microwave while she diced a small onion. She mixed the onion with the softened cream cheese and added a pound of lump crabmeat and a tablespoon of lemon juice. She covered the dip with a layer of shredded cheddar cheese and popped it into the oven while she went to the bedroom and ran a brush through her hair and applied some lipstick.

Back in the kitchen, she checked on the crab dip and began setting up the bar. She filled the ice bucket, got out the glasses, sliced up a lime, put olives in a small bowl and made sure there were stirrers available. As she returned to the oven to take out the dip and place it on a tray surrounded by crackers, she heard Ridge pull up out front. She hastily crossed to the table and added another placemat, linen napkin and place setting.

The men entered and Ridge introduced Isaac to his wife.

"Hello, Mr. Kahn, we met at the reception after Darling Huxtable's funeral I believe."

"We did, KD, and please call me Isaac. Where is this lovely daughter I've heard so much about?"

"It's Wednesday, Isaac. She goes to her gymnastics class every Wednesday and spends alternate Wednesday nights with her friend Alicia. Next week, Alicia will spend the night here with her," KD explained.

"I understand she's a state champion in gymnastics," said Isaac.

"She is. We're very proud of her. She'll be attending the national competition in Denver next month," KD answered.

"I'll be rooting for her as I know everyone in Spencer will," Isaac offered.

"Thank you and now let Ridge fix you a drink while I check on dinner," KD said as she headed for the kitchen.

"It smells wonderful," Isaac called as he crossed to the bar.

"What's your pleasure, Isaac?" Ridge asked.

"A vodka martini if you have the makings."

"Got you covered. You like it dry?"

"I do, just open the vermouth near the vodka. You don't need to pour any in the glass," Isaac responded and Ridge laughed.

"Olive?"

"Two if you don't mind," Isaac answered. He crossed to the south wall that was virtually one huge window and looked out at the wooded area beyond. "You're really in the woods here, aren't you?"

"Sure are. We love it. It's remote and quiet and we have no close neighbors so we can make all the noise we want, but we're actually quite close to town and all the necessities," Ridge explained.

The two men sat in the large lodge like living room. KD joined them shortly bearing the crab dip. Ridge placed her frozen Margarita in front of her and the three chatted amicably until it was time for dinner. Isaac was extremely impressed with KD's dinner. He complimented the chicken dish several times and when she served her signature Sweet German Chocolate Pie, Isaac said he thought he had died and gone to heaven.

SWEET GERMAN CHOCOLATE PIE

1 4 oz. sweet cooking German chocolate
¼ cup butter
1 2/3 cups=13 oz. can evaporated milk
1 ½ cup sugar
3 T cornstarch
1/8 t salt
2 eggs
1 t vanilla
1 9" deep dish unbaked pie shell
½ cup chopped nuts (pecans are best)
1 1/3 cups flaked coconut

Melt chocolate and butter stirring well until blended. Gradually blend the milk in with sugar, cornstarch and salt. Thoroughly beat in eggs and add vanilla. Blend chocolate mixture in and pour into pie shell. Combine cocoanut and chopped nuts and sprinkle on top of mixture in pie shell. Check after ten minutes to make sure top is not browning too quickly. If it is, cover with aluminum foil. Bake at 325 degrees 45 to 50 minutes. (Can also use two 8" unbaked pie shells and make two pies with recipe.)

Isaac patted his stomach and told KD once again what a wonderful cook she was and complimented Ridge on his fine catch. He agreed with him that he didn't know why Ridge wasn't as big as a house if he ate like this every night.

"I promise you, Isaac. This was not a company meal. KD feeds me like this every night I'm home. It's really difficult for me when I fly trips and have to eat airline food."

"And what else do you do to occupy your time while Ridge's away besides cooking, KD?" Isaac asked pleasantly.

"Well, I have a teenager at home so she keeps me busy, but I love to garden and I sew and do needlepoint. I belong to a few clubs in town and my book club keeps me busy too. We've been reading rather large tomes of late. Mainly, although I know this probably isn't the most politically correct statement to make these days, I am a housewife and a mother. And I enjoy it!"

"Bravo!" Isaac said. "It would be nice if more women felt that way, in my opinion, and you know this politically correct business is really getting out of hand. Do you know I read recently where *The Old Man and The Sea* can't be taught in our public schools anymore because it's age discrimatory. That's ridiculous as far as I'm concerned."

A lively discussion among the three of them followed for about an hour and fortunately they were all on the same side of the fence so there were no raised voices and no one was offended. It was a most enjoyable evening for all of them. Isaac left for Les Enfants shortly before ten o'clock wined, dined, and sated.

He enjoyed socializing with normal, nice people. His foray into Spencer society was a success. Harcourt was doing his job. He would soon be the owner of an Internet service. Then Jesse could work his magic on Bonita's computer. Raven would keep her mouth shut. Bartie and Jesse would make films. Jesse would oversee the orders to be sent to Isaac's warehouses and money would roll in. Isaac thought about the money. He had all he could possibly ever spend and more than enough to leave his children. He wondered why he wanted more.

Because you came from nothing and you never had a damned thing. You pulled yourself up out of the Yemeni desert and you did whatever you had to do to make it. And now you have. You have the mansion. You have Bonita Roberts thinking you're an angel. You have Precious making contacts for you. And you won't get caught, so why not? Besides, Precious thinks you hung the moon since you got her ass out of a crack. All's right with the world, Ike Baby! Isaac! You've done good! As he drove home, he hummed a few bars of *If They Could See Me Now!*

34

Phone Calls, Deaths and Salon *Plans*

Everyone in Spencer was talking about Trace and Rhetta. They were conjecturing about how the Ricks were having any time to sightsee or to enjoy their trip as practically everyone in Spencer had received at least three post-cards from them. Rhetta really wanted everyone to know she and Trace were seeing the world and having a *mahvelous* time.

Trace's practice hummed along with the two new doctors and he kept in touch through emails on a daily basis. The couple was in their suite in Paris' Georges V and Rhetta was packing as that afternoon they were leaving on the Orient Express for Istanbul. Trace was checking his email when he read something that caused him to feel a little unsettled. Mrs. Baines, one of his nursing home patients, had suffered a fall. There had been a number of calls to Trace at his office. Mrs. Baines wanted him to come immediately. Trace crossed to the room phone and dialed an outside line and connected to the international operator. He placed a person-to-person call to Mrs. Baines at the hospital. Momentarily, the elderly lady's weak voice came on.

"Mrs. Baines, this is Trace Ricks. What have you gone and done? I can't leave you for a minute. How are you feeling?"

"Trace, you need to come home. I'm not doing well at all. I broke my hip and they set it, but I feel terrible. I don't like the doctors here. They're not taking good care of me. I need you, Trace. I had the nurse call my daughter. She's coming tomorrow from California. I don't think I'm going to make it."

"Of course you're going to make it. Now, I'm leaving this afternoon for Istanbul on the Orient Express and then a week after that, I'll be home. I'll be next to your bed the minute I get to Nashville," Trace said soothingly in his best bedside manner.

"I'm not sure I can wait that long, Trace."

"Don't you dare stand me up. We have a date, Mrs. Baines. Now, you take care and I'll see you before you know it."

"What shall I tell Delilah about my investments, Trace? She's going to be asking me all kinds of questions."

"Tell her you've been making money hand over fist and you have, you know. Everything's fine with your investments. There's nothing she needs to know. You have a will. Your financial affairs are in perfect order."

"All right. That makes me feel better. Hurry back, Trace."

"I'll be there before you know it," Trace said sweetly as he hung up.

"One of your patients, Trace?" Rhetta asked.

"Yes, Mrs. Baines. She fell and broke her hip. I'm sure she'll be fine but she's feeling lonely and she doesn't like the doctors at Memorial. She wants me to come home right away."

"We're not going to have to give up our trip on the Orient Express, are we?"

"Of course not, Rhetta. I reassured her. Everything is fine. I'll give her doctor at Memorial a quick call to check on her. I'm sure she's exaggerating her condition."

Trace spoke with the doctor at Memorial who assured him Mrs. Baines' operation had been a complete success. They had pinned her hip and she was expected to make a full, but slow recovery. She was in reasonably good shape for her age. The doctor said she was a little cantankerous and she was asking for her Dr. Ricks all the time, but everything was under control. Mrs. Baines was not in a life-threatening situation. Trace thanked the doctor and hung up.

He wanted to make sure there was no chance of Mrs. Baines cashing in her chips while he was half way around the world for he had practically depleted her cash reserves for this trip, but that would be of no great concern to him if he were in Nashville. But things could get sticky if she died while he was out of the country. Another of his patients had passed away recently and Trace had quickly covered some missing funds from her accounts with another patient's money. Mrs. Baines' daughter was aware of her mother's financial situation so Trace knew from the outset he eventually would need to replace any money he *borrowed* from the old lady's account.

"Is everything all right?" Rhetta asked.

"Hunky-dory," Trace replied as he planted a kiss on the back of Rhetta's neck.

Rhetta giggled. She couldn't believe her good fortune. This handsome man loved her. He hadn't been able to get enough of her during their trip. They spent luxurious mornings in bed, partook of *afternoon delights*, made love before going to sleep and he bought her everything in sight. Rhetta had always known that one day her ship would come in and she had known from that first day she met him that Trace Ricks would be a fantastic doctor. Her ship had arrived and her fantastic doctor was making more money than Rhetta had ever allowed herself to covet.

The porter knocked on the suite's door to tell them their transportation to the train depot was waiting downstairs. He was ready to take down their luggage.

"Oh, Trace, I'm so excited. The Orient Express. This is going to be so fantastic!"

"It is indeed," Trace answered as he opened the door for the waiting porter.

As the Ricks prepared to board the luxury train in Paris, Candy Martin was on the phone to Desiree in Spencer.

"Desiree, Candy here. You wanted me to let you know when the Princess would be in town again. She called this morning and will be paying me a short visit a week from this Sunday for the afternoon and night. She's popping by on her way to the Islands for a round of parties with the jetsetters."

"Perfect, Candy. The Countess will be in residence that same weekend. My daughter is arriving for an extended stay the Saturday prior. What a lovely salon we shall have ten days hence. I'll put Maggie to work immediately getting out the invitations and I'll look forward to seeing both you and Alexandria. It'll be nice for things to get back to normal after those dreadful deaths, won't it?" asked Desiree.

"It certainly will be a change. Shall I bring mother, Desiree, or would you rather not have to watch your cameras every minute to see what she's putting in her bag?"

"Oh, do bring her, Candy. I won't even bother to watch. I know whatever she *borrows* you'll return the following week. Besides your mother has exquisite taste. I know I have something of value if she decides to deposit in her bag," Desiree said with a tinkling laugh that deteriorated into a rasping cough.

"I'll let you go, dear. I can tell I'm tiring you," Candy cooed to Desiree as she replaced the receiver.

Once Desiree had finished her coughing attack, she summoned Maggie and planned the guest list for her forthcoming afternoon of entertainment. She included Bonita, the Ricks because she thought they would be back in town by then, Isaac Kahn, Precious, Lydia and Randolph, Harcourt and Marietta, the Hulbertson sisters, and various and other sundry friends and neighbors. She told Maggie that not only would the Countess be visiting, but that Princess Alexandria of Russia would be attending the salon also. She instructed Maggie to contact that amusing black fellow who had played the piano at one of her gatherings a few years ago.

"I think it might be nice to have some live entertainment this time, Maggie. Now let's talk about the menu."

Maggie dutifully made out Desiree's list. She didn't bat an eye when Desiree mentioned the royalty. Maggie had practically raised Desiree's daughter single-handedly and the fact that she was now a countess didn't impress Maggie one bit. She faithfully read the *National Enquirer* every week and she *was* looking forward to seeing the Princess of Russia in the flesh, but she didn't want Miss Desiree to know she was at all impressed by her guest list. Maggie had seen the rich, the poor, the pariahs, the wannabes, the scandalous, and everything in between at Miss Desiree's parties. She wondered what excitement would occur at this one for it seemed something interesting always happened at Miz Desiree's Sunday afternoon get togethers.

Maggie copied Desiree's requests for the menu word for word and mentally made the grocery list simultaneously. Desiree wanted Maggie to serve lamb sauté, shrimp and rice balls, and cheese balls Sorrento style.

"I think we need to serve something that will stick to their ribs, Maggie. Make a big pot of navy beans to go with the sauté. The last few salons when we've served only hors d'oeuvres, it seems many of our guests have become a little tipsy. Of course that's always amusing, isn't it?" Desiree asked.

"I reckon," Maggie responded as she continued to write.

LAMB SAUTE

4 lbs. lamb—best pieces to use are neck, shoulder, leg and shank. Remove fat and sauté in olive oil.
1 t sugar
1 large onion chopped
2 lb. tomatoes, peeled and diced
1 large T flour
8 oz. white wine
1 cloves garlic chopped
1 bouquet garni (parsley, 2 bay leaves, sage, and thyme)

Sauté lamb, take out of pan, sauté onion. Add sugar when onions are light brown. Two minutes later, add tomatoes and then two minutes later, add wine, bouquet, salt and pepper. Add lamb. Let simmer 1 ½ hours. Put lamb in fridge. Let it sit until next day. Remove fat from broth. Rewarm right before ready to eat. Serves 8.

SHRIMP AND RICE BALLS

Mix ½ cup tomato juice with one well-beaten egg. Add ½ cup dry bread crumbs, 1 cup cooked rice, 1 t chopped parsley, dash of salt and pepper, ½ t celery salt and 1 5 oz. can of shrimp mashed. Mix thoroughly; roll into finger lengths; wrap each roll with half a slice of bacon and fasten with toothpick. Broil, turning frequently to brown evenly. Makes 30 rolls.

CHEESE BALLS, SORRENTO STYLE

½ lb. Mozzarella cheese
2 T fine bread crumbs
1 egg
1 t chopped parsley
½ cup flour
oil for deep fat frying

Soften cheese in microwave. When soft enough to handle easily, mix with breadcrumbs, egg, and parsley and blend well. Shape into balls size of walnuts, roll in flour, and fry in 2-inch deep hot oil until golden color. Yields 12 balls. Serve hot as a side dish or for cocktail tidbits either hot or cold.

Desiree listed a number of dessert items for Maggie to prepare and she told her to order Moet Chandon champagne. Maggie was to set out the Spode china and the Waterford crystal for the event. Desiree kept copious notes about each of her salons so she knew the Delph china and the Baccarat crystal had been her choice last time.

Maggie left Desiree's room with her lists of instructions and set out writing the invitations on her mistress' embossed stationery. The invitations took no time at all because Desiree's parties were so well known that all Maggie had to write on each folded sheet was "Salon on Sunday and the date." Desiree never requested regrets or RSVPs. She was confident everyone would attend. Her invitations were highly coveted.

Another item of which Desiree kept track was what each of her female guests wore to her parties. She loved it when she went back through her notes and realized one or the other had repeated an outfit. Although Desiree's entire wardrobe consisted only of peignoirs and gowns, she made sure she was never seen at any of her salons in the same bedclothes twice. Desiree was quite interested to see the Princess' selection of attire for her party. One person of whom she didn't keep track was Candy's mother. Poor old thing wore the same old housedress practically everyday although Candy did manage to at least keep her mother clean.

Desiree called down to Maggie and added two more names to her list. She had decided to invite Ridge and KD Dodd. Lydia had mentioned what an attractive couple they were following the duet of funerals and Desiree had heard from Precious that Ridge was helping Isaac with a lighting design for his mansion. They might be an entertaining addition. Desiree prided herself on always gathering a good mix of guests.

The invitations were delightfully received and everyone in Spencer who was on Desiree's list planned to attend. Spencer matrons began at once to think about their attire for the afternoon as everyone at Desiree's parties attempted to outdo the other. Bonita retreated to her dressing room as soon as Raven handed her the invitation. This would be Bonita's first salon and she wanted to look her absolute best.

Rhetta and Trace landed at the Nashville Airport the Friday before Desiree's gala. Trace planned to go to their home in Nashville and spend the night before driving to Spencer the following day, but Rhetta insisted they go straight from the airport to RickShaw because she missed the girls so much. Trace had also planned to check with his service and to listen to his messages at the office while in Nashville, but the email the day before from his office staff said everything was running as smoothly as silk, so they drove to Spencer. Trace didn't give a thought to his promise to Mrs. Baines that he would be at her side within minutes of landing in Nashville. He'd go see the old lady on Monday. That would be plenty of time. Besides, he hadn't told her specifically when he was returning.

The Ricks arrived in Spencer at midnight amid shrieks from their daughters as Rhetta gave each of their daughters gift after expensive gift. After several hours of chatting and stories of their fabulous trip, Rhetta and Trace retired to their bedroom where the housekeeper had placed the mail in a basket next to the king-size bed. Rhetta glanced at the mail and espied what appeared to an invitation. She ripped it open and squealed!

"What's the matter, Rhetta?" Trace called from the bathroom.

"Nothing's the matter. We've been invited to Desiree's salon this Sunday. Oh, Trace, do you know how long I've waited to go to one of Desiree's salons? I'll wear one of my new ensembles from Paris."

Rhetta threw herself on the bed clutching the invitation to her breast. All of her dreams had now come true.

The doctor and his wife slept in the next morning recovering from their plane trip, jet lag, and the drive from Nashville to Spencer. At eleven when Trace arose, he phoned both his office and his service to check his messages. There was nothing of interest so he didn't bother to check his emails.

Rhetta awoke and began immediately to try on one outfit after another in an attempt to decide what she would wear to Desiree's the next day.

Trace had not heard any messages of interest on his office recorder or from his service because when Mrs. Baines daughter called his office early Friday morning to tell him that her mother had passed away, she had spoken with Dr. DeWitt, one of the doctors recently hired by Trace. Dr. DeWitt took down all of the information and immediately had one of the receptionists send Trace an urgent email. Unfortunately, the email was sent after Trace had boarded his flight and he didn't check them again all weekend.

In addition to the email, Dr. DeWitt left a message on Trace's answering machine at his Nashville home. He knew Trace was arriving that evening from his world tour. The young doctor never thought to call RickShaw and leave a message on that phone or with one of Trace's daughters.

Trace didn't use the remote number to check his answering machine at his Nashville home. Those messages would be of a social or civic nature. Rhetta could tend to those.

Mrs. Baines' daughter Delilah Smathers arrived from California eight days prior to her mother's death. She gently questioned her about the whereabouts of her will and her financial situation. Mrs. Baines was close-mouthed at first, but as her condition worsened, she confided that Dr. Ricks had been handling her financial affairs for quite some time and she had been making large sums of money through the doctor's savvy investments. When her daughter asked where her mother kept the receipts from the doctor's stock purchases and from her dividend proceeds, Mrs. Baines said she had never gotten any receipts.

"Dr. Ricks tells me every few weeks what he's purchased for me and how much I've made. He deposits the profits and the dividends into my account. I've given him carte blanche. He's wonderful, Delilah. Just wait until you meet him. He and wife are on a trip around the world, but he'll be back soon. He promised me as soon as he steps off the plane, he'll be right here beside my bed. He comes to see me every day when he's in Nashville. I hate the weekends because he goes to his Spencer weekend retreat, but he's here bright and early every Monday. There's nothing to worry about. My money is safe."

Delilah went immediately to her mother's attorney and obtained a copy of her will. She was her mother's only heir. She rested easier after she read it. Her mother had left everything to her. The amount was considerable plus her mother said the doctor had made investments that had increased her net worth. Delilah couldn't imagine her mother turning her assets over to her doctor no matter how wonderful he was. Mrs. Baines had always held the purse strings very tightly. Delilah supposed she should have visited her mother more often and paid closer attention to what was going on in the financial department, but after reading the will she wasn't concerned.

She stayed by her mother's bedside and watched her slip slowly away each day. On Friday morning, Mrs. Baines breathed her last. Delilah called the funeral home and began making arrangements immediately. She called her mother's attorney and informed him of her mother's death. Delilah advised him to proceed right away with whatever had to be done. She said she was planning on having the funeral on Monday morning and hoped to leave for California either Monday afternoon or Tuesday morning.

"As most of mother's assets are in cash, although she does have some stocks, this should be a relatively simple matter, right?" Delilah asked the attorney.

"I believe so. Your mother had a number of certificates of deposit also, but she had put your name on them, so you'll be able to take those and the cash right away as she named you executrix. There will be no penalty for early withdrawal of the certificates as there's a one-time death exclusion without penalty. I'll instruct your mother's financial advisor to sell her stocks or do you want to keep them invested?"

"I haven't decided yet, but go ahead and get all of the information together about the other assets. I'll probably arrange for a wire transfer to my bank in California."

"Very well. You have my deepest sympathy, Delilah. Your mother was a wonderful lady. Is there anything else I can do?" the attorney asked.

"Thank you. That's very kind of you, but everything is under control. My husband is flying in this afternoon and Wingate's Funeral Home is handling the arrangements," Delilah said through a few sniffles.

"I'll speak to you Monday then," replied the attorney.

Delilah turned her attention to the funeral arrangements. She wished Dr. Ricks were back. Mrs. Baines had thought so much of him. She knew how much it would mean to her mother for the wonderful doctor to be a pallbearer at her funeral.

Other patients who relied on Trace and his visits were missing him too. There must have been something in the air that weekend because another of Trace's patient/clients, Olivia Sanborne, passed away on Saturday. The distant relatives of the deceased were unaware of her relationship with Dr. Trace Ricks, although the staff at the nursing home informed them he was the physician of the deceased. They didn't see any reason to call the doctor. Their relative was already dead. They were not too interested in her anyway, but they were definitely looking forward to the reading of her will. Great-aunt Olivia had been loaded and these distant nieces and nephews were champing at the bit to get their hands on her loot. Every one of them was in town for the funeral and not a one had ever visited her in the eight years she had been a patient at the nursing home.

On Sunday morning, another of Trace's ladies, Matilda Mae Grimes, slipped into a coma. The nursing home staff called his office and left a message on his machine, but they did not call his service. There was no point in bothering the doctor on the weekend as there was nothing he could do for her. Monday morning would be time enough for him to know of her situation. The nurses knew that Dr. Ricks would come to the old lady's bedside first thing Monday morning once he received the message even though she would be unaware of his visit. He was so kind and sweet to all of the little old ladies and they adored him. The nursing home staffs throughout Nashville thought Dr. Ricks walked on water.

Desiree phoned Bonita and suggested she might want to bring Raven to the Sunday salon. She was sure there would be suggestions and ideas for the debutante ball bandied about and perhaps it would be good to have Raven available to take notes. Bonita agreed it was a splendid idea. She knew how thrilled Raven would be to be asked to Desiree's salon. She promptly informed Raven of her invitation and told her that of course she would be paid overtime for Sunday afternoon. Raven said extra pay wasn't necessary and she would be delighted to attend. She was even more excited after Bonita told her Princess Alexandria of Russia would be in attendance.

Isaac Kahn opened his invitation and was pleased to be included on Desiree Compton's guest list. Precious had explained to him that an invitation to one of Desiree's Sunday salons sealed one's acceptance into Spencer society. It was turning out to be a very good day. Harcourt had concluded his deal and Isaac was the new owner of the local Internet Company *VanBuren.net.* Harcourt had bargained hard and gotten the company for just under three million. Jesse had provided Isaac with a list of the equipment he needed to purchase and to rent. It included servers, switchers, dedicated telephone lines and a whole bunch of other electronic gizmos that Isaac had not the slightest knowledge of or interest in other than to achieve his goal of covering his tracks in the kiddie porn venture. He had been on his cell phone to Jesse several times during the day.

Once the equipment was delivered and in place in a building downtown Isaac had purchased, Jesse would hack into Bonita's computer and set up the email address for the order-taking portion of the operation. Bartie had hired eighty order processors who were located in different sites all over the county to start. They were ready to go to work as soon as everything was up and running. Jesse had assured Isaac this network was the way to go with all of them using the same main frame, Bonita's computer. Isaac had no idea what Jesse was talking about.

Ridge informed Isaac that sane morning that the lighting job was very close to being finished. He hoped to turn on all the lights for the first time that night for Isaac's approval. And the renovation of the cave was complete. Isaac planned to drive Bonita Roberts out there the next day to see her reaction to the cave ballroom created expressly for her debutante ball.

Isaac called Bonita Roberts to make sure she remembered their appointment. Raven answered and assured Isaac that Bonita was aware of the engagement and was expecting him to call for her the next day at one o'clock in the afternoon.

"Great. How are you doing, Raven?" Isaac asked.

"I'm fine, Mr. Kahn, but I'm very busy and can't talk right now," Raven responded in a monotone.

"Well, I'm glad you're fine. That little matter I spoke to you about a while ago will be taking place in the next week or so. Keep your eyes peeled, Raven."

"Yes sir. I have to go now. I'll tell Mrs. Roberts you called," and Raven hung up.

In the next week or so, Mrs. Roberts' computer was going to be hacked into and Raven knew Isaac Kahn was up to no good otherwise whatever he was planning he could do on it his own computer. She didn't know what to do. She felt a great deal of loyalty to her employer. Mrs. Roberts had been so good to her, but she couldn't tell her what was going to happen. If she did, Isaac would go right to her parents with those tapes. It would kill them. She had thought about quitting her position with Bonita and leaving Spencer, but she wasn't sure that would provide her with any protection. Isaac Kahn was evil incarnate and he'd show her parents the tapes then just for spite if she didn't follow his instructions precisely. She was trapped!

Bonita decided on her ensemble for the salon on Sunday. After cogitating on her wardrobe and getting Hannah's input, Bonita was going to wear a flowing emerald green caftan affair. She planned to retrieve her emeralds from the wall safe in her bedroom to accent the Dior original. At the moment, Bonita was trying out an iridescent green shadow on her eyelids. The blue wasn't going to do. It decidedly clashed.

Raven knocked on her door and reminded of her of her appointment with Isaac Kahn the next afternoon.

"Thank you, Raven. I remember. Come in, dear. Tell me what you think of this eye shadow?"

Raven thought Mrs. Roberts wore entirely too much make-up and often resembled a clown, however she would never say that to her employer.

"It's very green, isn't it?" Raven said softly.

"Very. Let me show what I'm wearing to Desiree's salon. That will give you a better idea," Bonita said as she swept into her closet and retrieved the caftan.

"It's beautiful, Mrs. Roberts. Who's the designer?" Raven asked.

"Christian made this for me exclusively. Don't you love it?"

"I do. The material is so lovely and what a divine color. The eye shadow is perfect, Mrs. Roberts. It's an exact match."

Bonita smiled, "I thought so too. I do hate to change from my usual blue, but it looked horrid with the emerald green. I'll be wearing my emerald necklace, ear bobs, and my emerald and diamond ring. You don't think that's too much green, do you, dear?"

"Of course not. And besides, Mrs. Roberts, emeralds go with anything especially emeralds as beautiful as yours. You have gorgeous jewelry."

"I do. Joshua loved to see me covered with baubles."

"I haven't seen a bauble among your jewels. They're all absolutely exquisite."

"Thank you, dear. Some afternoon, we'll look through them, and perhaps you can select a few pieces you'd like to have. I have no heirs you know and I don't think Hannah will need all that jewelry and it would look a bit odd on Alphonso."

"Oh, I couldn't, Mrs. Roberts. Besides, that's nothing you need to be thinking about now."

"One never knows, Raven. I could drop dead tomorrow. Any of us could."

"Well if anyone has to drop dead tomorrow, I certainly hope it isn't you, Mrs. Roberts," Raven responded.

"Oh, but you do have someone in mind I take it?"

"No ma'am, why do you say that?"

"You seem a little distracted lately, Raven. Is there something wrong?"

"Has there been a problem with my work, Mrs. Roberts?"

"Of course not. I've simply noticed you staring off into space several times and I wondered if something's troubling you. I hate to see a frown on that beautiful brow."

"Nothing's bothering me. I guess I was daydreaming. I'll make sure I don't do that in the future."

"I'm not criticizing you, Raven. Daydream all you want. I merely wanted to make sure everything was all right."

"Everything's fine, Mrs. Roberts."

"And is there a young man in your life?"

"No ma'am. You may have noticed there are not too many young, eligible men in Spencer."

"Well you must have some kind of social life, don't you?"

"Not much. I go to the club, play a little tennis and swim a little. I have some girlfriends who are still here, girls I knew in high school, but most of them are married."

"How boring it must be for you. Why do you stay in Spencer?"

"Mostly for my mother. She always seems so sad. I will be leaving the first of the year for a position in New York. You recall I told you that when you hired me?"

"Yes, but you've become such an asset, I don't know what I'm going to do without you. Perhaps if I gave you a very significant raise you would consider staying?"

"I'd love to, Mrs. Roberts, and I really love my job with you. It's exciting and interesting just keeping track of all of your social events, but at some point I'll need to get on with my life and move into a career position."

"There, how does that look?" Bonita asked as she capped her mascara and turned to show Raven her eye makeup.

"Very nice. You'll definitely be a hit."

"Well, thank you, Raven, for the message from Mr. Kahn. We'll talk more later. By the way, what do you think of Mr. Kahn?"

"What do I think of him?"

"Yes. I got the distinct feeling at the organizational meeting for the debutante ball you had already met Mr. Kahn. It seemed to me you felt quite uncomfortable around him."

"I'm sorry if I gave you that impression, Mrs. Roberts. I don't know Mr. Kahn. I really don't have any feelings for him other than he seemed very much behind your idea and it was generous of him to donate the use of his cave and to pay for the renovations."

"But you don't have any feelings for him personally one way or the other?"

"No ma'am. I must get back to my desk now, if you'll excuse me. I have several matters to take care of for the next committee meeting."

"Then run along, Raven. We'll speak again soon."

Raven closed Bonita's door and rested her head against it. She'd have to be more careful around Mrs. Roberts. The lady was definitely shrewd and obviously paid a lot more attention to her surroundings than Raven realized. She'd also have to watch herself around Isaac Kahn. She didn't want Mrs. Roberts or anyone else suspecting she had known Isaac previously, but how she longed to tell everyone what a fake *Ike* was and about his smut peddling.

Ridge was in the final stages of his work for Isaac. Things had progressed a little slower than he had planned because Isaac was at home all day. The man practically lived on the telephone with calls to his attorney, calls to someone in New York, and social calls. Although Ridge hadn't been intending to eavesdrop, he gathered Isaac had purchased the local Internet service. He couldn't imagine what Isaac Kahn would want with that. The man was computer illiterate.

When Isaac was talking on his cell phone to New York, he had wandered in and out of the great room. Ridge had picked up bits and pieces of Isaac's side of the conversation. He mentioned films several times and Ridge heard him call someone Jesse. He wondered if Jesse were Isaac's attorney's name—the one he was using in his suit against the kiddie porn people from the business venture he had talked about, but he discounted that. It sounded as if Isaac was talking to this Jesse person about new films and order taking. Ridge decided it was none of his business. He liked Isaac Kahn and what he was doing with an Internet service, films, and Jesse had nothing to do with him. Because of all the interruptions, Ridge didn't finish Friday. He told Isaac he would be back the next day and have everything ready to go by early afternoon.

"That'll be fine, Ridge. I'm taking Bonita Roberts out to the cave tomorrow afternoon to see the renovations. I should return about three o'clock. We'll pull all the drapes and try out the new lighting then."

"Sounds like a plan," Ridge said as he left for the day. He and Isaac both chuckled over the catch phrase they used with each other on a frequent basis.

The next day, Isaac drove up the impressive lane to Villagio at precisely one o'clock, disembarked, and rang Bonita's bell. Bonita opened the door herself dressed in beige slacks, walking shoes, a dark brown jacket and huge Jackie Onassis style sunglasses.

"I'm so excited, Isaac. I can't wait to see what you've done with the cave."

Isaac helped her into his car and they chatted for the twenty-minute drive to their destination. As they pulled around a curve in the hilly region outside Spencer, Bonita quickly inhaled. There in the middle of nowhere was a huge green canopy overhanging the opening to a cave. The canopy could have been on Fifth Avenue in New York City.

"My heavens, Isaac. You've really done this up right, haven't you?"

"I hope so, Bonita. Shall we?" and he held her door open and took her arm.

They entered the cave and Isaac reached to his left and flipped a switch. The parapet where they were standing was illuminated and Isaac guided Bonita to an elevator.

"You put in an elevator?"

"I did. It's a little precarious to get into the *ballroom* if one has to walk down the paths and some of the overhangs are very low. We wouldn't want the lovely young ladies to muss their gowns," Isaac explained.

When the elevator stopped, the door slid open and they stepped into a fairyland. Tiny, twinkling lights sparkled everywhere. Eighteen massive crystal chandeliers hung from a suspended framework in the cave's ceiling. A stage had been erected at one end of the huge room for the orchestra and the presentations of the debutantes. A complete central heating and air conditioning system had been installed along with running water. There were two fully equipped ladies' lounges and two men's rooms, a thirty foot long hand-carved bar, and a commercial kitchen. Bonita was speechless.

"So what do you think, Bonita?"

"I never dreamed you would do so much, Isaac. It's absolutely amazing. Perfect. Can you imagine the press we'll get from this? A debutante ball in a cave and one that makes the ballroom at the Sherry Netherland look seedy."

"Then we're good to go."

"We are definitely good to go, Isaac. I simply can't thank you enough!" and with that Bonita leaned over and planted a kiss on Isaac's cheek.

"Well, thank you, Mrs. Roberts."

"Bonita, please" she said coyly.

Bonita gushed about the cave and the renovations Isaac had designed and donated all the way back to her mansion. When they arrived, Bonita invited Isaac in for a libation, but he told her he would take a rain check. Ridge Dodd was finishing his lighting design at Les Enfants and he needed to be there for the initial turn-on that afternoon.

"Then I trust I'll see you tomorrow afternoon at Desiree's salon, Isaac?"

"You shall. I'm looking forward to it. Would you like for me to call for you so we can go together?"

"That would be delightful. What time shall I expect you?"

"Two-thirty? That should give us plenty of time."

"Two-thirty, it is. Thank you, Isaac."

Bonita went into her house in a state of euphoria Hannah met her at the door.

"I take it you liked what he done to that cave?" Hannah asked.

"You wouldn't believe it, Hannah. It's more beautiful than any of the ballrooms in New York City. We'll be the talk of the South. The press alone will be fabulous. No one's ever had a debutante ball in a cave!"

"It's good to see you so happy, Miz Bonita."

"I am delirious, Hannah, and if the cave weren't enough, I have a date."

"A date?"

"Yes. Mr. Kahn has asked to escort me to Desiree's salon tomorrow afternoon. He's arriving to pick me up at two thirty."

"Well, ain't you somethin'? A date? You still got what it takes, baby!" Hannah said grinning from ear to ear.

"I guess I must, Hannah. Besides I kissed him in the cave."

"Go on. You did what?"

"I was so impressed with what he'd done to that cave I forgot myself and kissed him."

"On the mouth?"

"No, Hannah, just on the cheek."

"Well, that's all right, I reckon."

"A date at my age. Won't the old biddies at Desiree's be flipping their wigs?"

"I 'spect so, but remember who you is, Miz Bonita. You is Mrs. Joshua Roberts, widow. You ain't back in California."

"I don't need reminding, Hannah, and hush your mouth. I have no intention of gracing Mr. Kahn with any sexual favors," Bonita tittered as she ascended the stairs to the master suite, but she was terribly excited. Bonita did dearly love men. She had never fallen in love with a particular one, but she did so much prefer them to women. Men were so simple, so straightforward, and so honest. Of course, their egos were fragile and they weren't particularly bright. Most of them were still looking for their mothers, but all in all, she'd rather spend her days with men anytime than with a bunch of women. Women talked out of both sides of their mouths, were forever making passive-aggressive comments, couldn't be trusted, and were all egomaniacs as far as Bonita was concerned.

It had been a long time since a man had shown an interest in her other than Alphonso for whose favors she paid. It felt good!

Isaac had gone off to collect Bonita for the trip to the cave neglecting to take his cell phone with him. It was Chang's day off and he was out. As Ridge was performing final tests on some of the lighting fixtures, Isaac's cell phone rang almost constantly. It wasn't programmed to receive voice messages, Ridge surmised. Finally, Ridge answered it as it was lying on the coffee table in the room where he was working.

"Hello. This is Isaac Kahn—" Ridge was planning to say "This is Isaac's Kahn's cell phone and he isn't here right now, but he should be back in about two hours."

Before he could make Isaac's last name possessive, a voice responded, "Jesse here. I hacked into the computer today. It's all set. Everything is a go. The orders are already rolling in. We're filming constantly and have other companies ready to provide product."

"I'll give Mr. Kahn that message," Ridge answered.

"Who is this?" Jesse demanded.

"My name is Ridge Dodd. I'm doing some lighting work for Mr. Kahn. He must have forgotten his cell phone. It's been ringing constantly so I answered it. I was trying to tell you it was his cell phone. He's out and should be back in about two hours."

"Tell him to call me as soon as he gets in," Jesse said and hung up.

Ridge glanced at the caller identification window, but the number calling was blocked. Ridge didn't like the sound of Jesse's call. Someone's computer had been hacked into and obviously Isaac was aware it was to occur. Films were in production and orders were pouring in. Jesse. That was the person Isaac had been talking to the day before when Ridge thought it must be his attorney when he heard Kahn mention films. Ridge suddenly realized Isaac had probably been lying about the kiddie porn films and a possible lawsuit. He decided he would tell Isaac upon his return that Jesse had called and nothing else. Ridge would simply wait and watch.

35

The Ricks' Trip and Desiree's Sunday Salon

Monique arrived Saturday afternoon for an extended visit with her mother. She was distressed to find Desiree more fragile than on her last visit plus her mother coughed all the time. Monique decided not to mention her concerns lest she cause her mother worry and Desiree was in such high spirits in anticipation of her salon the following afternoon.

"It'll be so exciting for all the Spencerians, Monique. Not only will a countess be in attendance, but also a princess. Who would ever think all that royalty would congregate in our little town?"

"Princess Alexandria is lovely, mother. I've met her several times before. She's a distant relative of Mrs. Martin's, isn't she?"

"Yes, Candy was her mother's Princess Sharon's second cousin. Candy's Philadelphia Main Line, you know?"

"So I recall. And what are you planning to wear tomorrow, mother?"

"One of my peignoirs naturally, but I haven't decided which yet," Desiree responded amidst a burst of deep rasping coughs. "I do wish I could get rid of this nasty cough. I can't imagine what's causing it," Desiree said as she reached for her second pack of cigarettes for the day.

"Me either, mother. Well, if you haven't decided what you're going to wear, perhaps I can help. I'll be right back."

Monique returned in minutes with two huge shopping bags of gaily-wrapped packages.

"What in the world is all this? I haven't forgotten my birthday, have I?" Desiree asked, but she was as excited as a young child when she saw all the gifts.

"Does a mother have to have a birthday for her daughter to spoil her a little? I picked up a few things for you here and there," Monique laughed as she handed Desiree a large box from Harrods.

"Harrods, one of my favorite of all stores! How I'd love to be able to go shopping there one more time. I can't wait to see what's in here," Desiree snickered as she ripped the wrapping off.

"Monique, it's gorgeous!" Desiree purred as she removed the ice blue satin gown with matching robe trimmed in dyed marabou feathers. "My decision's made. I'll wear this creation tomorrow. Won't I be stunning?"

"You absolutely will, mother, but there's more," and Monique passed Desiree another box.

"Mules dyed to match! Oh, thank you, Monique. I love them!" Desiree threw back her covers and sat up on the side of the bed and began to cough anew. Once the coughing fit subsided, she steadied herself by holding onto the nightstand, stood, and slipped her feet into the peau de soie mules trimmed in blue marabou feathers. "I'll definitely be the cat's meow tomorrow."

Monique presented her mother with other gifts. She had purchased a Calibre lighter for her, her favorite perfume, dusting powder, another gown and robe in pink and less fancy than the blue ensemble, and several best-selling novels.

"You're too good to me, dear, but I love all the gifts. What's that one?"

"Oh, I brought a little something for Maggie, and I'm not too good to you. I can never do enough for you, mother, after all you've done for me.

"Well, aren't we a mutual admiration society? And what are you planning to wear tomorrow?"

"I brought a little black number I picked up in Milan last month. I think you'll like it. It's an Armani. Plain black fitted pants and an off-shoulder tunic with a spray of pearls at the shoulder. Very Georgio."

"And did you see Georgio this time and is he still in love with you?"

"Yes and yes, and the fact he's still in love with me stands me in good stead. He always makes luscious designs for me and he never lets anyone, not even his staff, see them, so there are never any knock-offs. I love his clothes."

"And well you should as they are made expressly for you and look smashing on that figure of yours. I wonder what the princess will be wearing?"

"White, I assume. That's her signature color and speaking of good figures, hers is perfect."

"I'm looking forward to the party. I enjoy seeing what everyone wears almost as much as I enjoy seeing them. I'm so glad you're here for this one, darling, and that you're going to be staying for a while. I miss you so."

"I miss you too, mother, but I'll be here for a month, so we'll have lots of time together. Maybe I'll even persuade you to leave your room and go out for a spin in the car."

"We'll see about that," Desiree said.

Every female in Spencer invited to Desiree's salon was up Sunday morning at the crack of dawn to begin preparations for dressing for the party. Bonita was in a complete tizzy as she was not only attending one of Desiree's salons for the first time, she was also being escorted by Isaac Kahn. She was in the bath by eight o'clock in the morning getting her massive body ready to be swathed in the emerald green creation.

Precious Woodson called to Lila to come up to her room to help her decide how to wear her hair with the yellow and white tuxedo jumpsuit she planned to wear. Precious was accessorizing with the family heirloom pearl choker and earrings.

Candy Martin was wearing a brown business suit and no nonsense brown lace up shoes. Never concerned about fashion herself, Candy was attempting to convince her mother to wear something other than her housedress that resembled a burlap bag.

"Why do I have to dress up to go to Desiree Compton's house? She's going to be up there in her bed in a nightgown in the middle of the afternoon."

"She's bedridden, mother. She doesn't get dressed in street clothes anymore because she doesn't go out. I think it was very nice of her to include you. Everyone will be dressed to the hilt and Alexandria is here. Don't you want to look nice?"

"I'm ninety-two years old, Candace, in case you've forgotten. How nice can I look?"

"*Very* nice, mother. I'll style your hair and you can wear some of your beautiful jewelry. You have some lovely dresses. We'll get you bathed and then put on one of those pretty dresses and doll you up. Alexandria said she would help."

"I don't need either one of you to give me a bath and I can get dressed by myself. All right, I'll wear one of my pretty dresses, but I'll comb my hair myself."

"Fine. Shall I draw the bath for you?"

"I can do that too, thank you."

"Very well," Candy said and left her mother's room.

The old lady went to her bathroom and pushed the stopper down in the tub, then turned the water on full blast. She watched the tub fill and turned off the faucets. She reached in her linen closet and got out a washcloth. She removed her clothes, dipped the cloth into the tub, soaped it, and sponged off in front of her sink.

I'm not about to get in a bathtub. For heaven's sake, I could slip and fall.

Enid couldn't remember the last time she had taken a bath. That's why she wouldn't let her daughter help her. She'd been filling the tub and letting the water sit for years.

After she sponged off, Enid got out her dusting powder and patted it heavily all over her wrinkled, shrunken body.

Now today I took what I call a marine bath, Candy, 'cause you think Desiree's party is such an occasion. When nothing special is planned for the day, I only take a PTC bath—pits, tits, and crotch!

Next, she took out her teeth and plopped them into a glass of warm water. Picking up the washcloth she had already used all over her body, she washed her face. Thirty seconds later, she replaced her false teeth, put the lid down on the toilet and sat on it.

"Are you in the tub, mother?" Candy called from the floor below.

"Yes."

"Do you need me to wash your back?"

"No, I'm using my brush, thank you."

"All right. Call me if you need any help."

"I will."

Enid continued to sit on the toilet for about ten more minutes after which she removed the stopper from the tub and let the water run out. She stomped on the floor a few times so Candy would think she was getting out of the tub. Next she got a bath sheet, reached into the tub and generously sprinkled water all over it so it would appear she had toweled off. As the last of the water drained out, there was a knock at her bedroom door. She quickly wrapped the damp towel around her and said, "Come in."

"Now look at you, all clean. Didn't that warm bath feel good, mother?"

"It certainly did."

"Would you like for me to help you get dressed?"

"No and I can do my hair myself too. Now run along, Candy. Take care of Alexandria or get dressed yourself. I'm fine."

"I'm already dressed, mother, but I'll leave you now. You're going to look lovely."

"Um-hmm," she answered as Candy closed her door.

Enid returned to the bathroom and hung the towel over the shower rod. The shrewd old lady dipped the bath brush in the last remaining drops of water rolling out of the tub. Just in case anyone checked, she wanted to make sure everything appeared as if she had bathed in the tub.

She went to her lingerie chest and pulled out a raggedy old bra, turned it over this way and that, and decided it was fine. She had new bras Candy bought for her, but they weren't comfortable. They cut into her shoulders and rubbed her raw under her breasts. She positioned the rag, leaned over and stuffed her pendulous breasts into the material worn thin from years of use.

Next she reached for her *drawers* as she still called her underpants. They were roomy and resembled modern-day shorts. She glanced in the drawer and saw the Vanity Fair underpants Candy had bought her. She wasn't going to wear those things. They crept up her crotch and they were nylon or silk or something silly.

Good old white cotton drawers are the best and I never have any yeast infections like all these young people today. Who wants to wear those silly drawers?

Reaching again into her lingerie chest, she pulled out individual stockings. She sat on the side of the bed and pulled on first one leg and then the other. She knotted each stocking above the knee. She'd make sure she wore something long enough to cover them up or Candy would have her right back up here trying to convince her to wear a garter belt or worse yet those panty hose things.

Next she pulled a full white slip, a *petticoat* as she called it, over her head and padded toward her closet. Rifling through her dresses, she decided on a magenta one trimmed in lace and sequins. She had worn it to someone's wedding a decade ago. She got the dress on, but she couldn't zip it all the way. She'd have to ask Candy to do that.

Then she looked at her shoe racks. As she examined each pair of shoes to coordinate with the dress, she recalled how they hurt her feet. Finally, she pushed her feet into her everyday bedroom slippers. She rummaged through her jewelry case and attached rose stones to her ears and clasped the matching necklace around her wattled throat.

Enid sat in front of her vanity and combed her snow-white hair. She reached in a drawer and pulled out a rat, a contrivance made from real hair very popular in the thirties and forties, and proceeded to wrap her hair around it so the style resembled a pageboy hairdo. She took her eyebrow pencil and made one straight black line above each eye and generously smeared blood red lipstick across her face where her once full lips, now reduced to a thin straight line, had been.

Finally, she picked up her see-through tote, put her lipstick and comb in it, took a last look in the mirror, and left her room to join Candy and Alexandria downstairs.

Candy and the Princess glanced up as she descended the stairs looking like someone about to attend a masquerade ball, but even with the horrid make-up and the bedroom slippers, she looked better than usual. Both women complimented her profusely. Alexandria asked if she could go up and get the shoes she planned to wear so they'd be right there when they were ready to leave, but Enid said she had on the *shoes* she was wearing.

"All those other shoes hurt my feet. And besides Desiree will have on slippers too if she gets out of bed, that is. I'll be right in style."

"Fine, mother. You look very nice. Why don't you sit down for a few minutes? We won't be leaving for another half hour."

Her mother placed the tote bag on the coffee table and sat down on the living room sofa and immediately allowed her legs to fall open in the typical *old lady sitting position*.

"Mother, did you forget to put on your garter belt?" Candy asked.

"I didn't forget. I hate that thing and I'm not going to wear it."

"All right. It's all right, mother. Now, before we go, I want to remind you that although it may mean nothing to you, there are those in Spencer who are very excited when they receive an invitation Desiree's."

"I don't know why. I've been to bigger and better houses and grander parties in Philadelphia than anything I've ever seen here."

"I know you have, mother, but we're in Spencer now. This is a big event for those who live here. I hope you'll thank Desiree for inviting you today by *not* putting any of her possessions in your tote bag."

"What are you talking about, Candace?"

"Mother! You know almost daily I get calls about things you put in your tote bag and I have to go to the stores and pay for them. The last time you went to Desiree's, you put a Faberge egg and a cloisonné lighter in your bag."

"I did not! Alexandria, I am sorry you have to hear this nonsense from your cousin Candace. Candace, you must stop this! Alexandria is going to think you're nutty. Don't you think she's nutty, Alexandria? But my, my, don't you look lovely, my dear?"

"Thank you," replied the Princess.

Alexandria did indeed look lovely in a white, flowing, tea-length dress. It was high-necked, long-sleeved, and cut to the waist in the back with little strings attached on the sides, so Alexandria's beautiful tan back was exposed. She wore white sandal heels and pale yellow Topaz earrings and necklace.

"That necklace and those earrings belonged to your mother, didn't they?"

"Yes they did. I love them."

"They were our grandmother's. I remember playing with them when I was a little girl. My sister, your grandmother, got the topazes and I got these rose stones. I think they're smashing too, don't you?"

"They really are. I remember mother telling me about the rose stones. Great grandmother had some beautiful pieces, didn't she?"

"She had the most extensive jewelry collection in all of Philadelphia. Grandfather used to tease her and say he had never seen so much steel converted into precious stones. Your great grandfather owned Pennsylvania Steel and Ironworks, you know?"

"Yes ma'am. I think mother always missed her Philadelphia life when she was in France with father in exile, much more than her New York life as a famous model."

"I imagine she did. She was main line in Philadelphia, a debutante, one of the chosen, not like those upstart Kellys. In New York, she was just another pretty face. We were all so relieved when she stopped cavorting with all those male models and that nasty old photographer and married her prince."

"Mother, I think it's time to go now," Candace said pointedly trying to stop her mother from divulging all of the late Princess Sharon's secrets, real or imagined, to her daughter.

"What have I done now? Said too much? I don't know how or why you put up with me, Candace. First you accuse me of stealing and now you're trying to shut me up. Why don't you simply leave me at home? I must be an embarrassment to you everywhere we go."

"Hush, mother. Let's go out to the car."

"And by the way, Candace, you look like something the cat dragged in from the slums. You want me to look nice. Well, I do. Both of you said so and of course, baby Alexandria looks like a dream, but you look like the cleaning woman. Why don't you wear something pretty? You have a ton of money. You can afford anything you want to wear. You have two cases full of jewelry. I know. I gave it to you and what do you have on? A man's watch! No earrings, no necklace, old lady shoes, a business suit. You're not one of those women who likes other women, are you, Candace? Is that why you always look so masculine?"

"Mother, that is indeed enough! What in the world's gotten into you?" Candace asked on the verge of tears.

"Nothing's gotten into me. I'm ninety-two. Alexandria, I was ninety-two last week. I've decided it's high time I say what's on my mind. What do you think of that, Alexandria?"

"I think we need to get in the car so we won't be late for Desiree's salon," the princess answered diplomatically.

Candy got her mother situated in the car and started the engine.

And here we go. The Princess of Russia, me looking like a dyke according to my own mother and mother looking like a bag lady as usual. Desiree will be so delighted when The Redneck Royals descend upon her. We should learn to play instruments—Redneck Royals sounds like a good name for a band!

Meanwhile at Harcourt Ball's house, he was calling to his mother it was time to go. Marietta Ball came into the living room decked out in a lovely ecru haut couture ensemble.

"Is that what you're wearing, mother?"

"I'd planned to. Is there something wrong with this outfit?"

"Nothing. It's lovely, just as lovely as it was three salons ago when you wore it to Desiree's."

"I've worn this to Desiree's before?"

"You have. I've asked you repeatedly to keep track of what you wear to functions the way you keep track of what foods you serve and to whom when we entertain. You know Desiree and everyone else who was there last fall will remember you've worn that de la Renta before."

"I have to go change. How much time do we have?"

"Hurry. We'll be fashionably late if you change in less than ten minutes."

Marietta went to her bedroom and threw open the gigantic closet. She hoped to find something in the same shade that would be all right with her jewelry so she wouldn't have to start all over. She settled on cream Palazzo pants and a pale coffee lace-trimmed blouse. The jewelry and shoes looked fine. She grabbed her purse and met Harcourt in the living room in seven minutes flat.

"You look beautiful, mother."

"Thank you, dear, and thank you for remembering what I wore." She thought, for not the first time, how nice it was that her handsome, intelligent son paid so much attention to her clothing. Most men wouldn't have a clue as to someone's outfit at a function six months prior, especially their mother's.

Rhetta was decked out in red from head to toe. Her handkerchief-hemmed skirt was aflutter with ruffles as was her sleeveless elongated tunic top. She felt both elegant and lovely in her Paris original with garnets at her ears and neck. Her feet were adorned with red Italian leather sandal pumps. She carried a matching purse she had purchased in Venice.

Raven, who would have looked spectacular in a feedbag, selected a pale pink sundress and matching pumps and purse for the occasion. Her mother lent her a pair of pale pink pearls she had owned since she was sixteen.

KD Dodd, who was anything but a clotheshorse, donned beige linen slacks and a brown lace blouse. She wore plain brown pumps from Payless Shoes and gold stud earrings from the Piercing Pagoda at the mall. She didn't take a purse as she was a natural beauty and wouldn't need to reapply her makeup as she didn't wear any.

Various other Spencer matrons turned out in their finest and headed for their vehicles to descend upon Desiree and to be greeted by royalty.

Desiree was ready. She wore the ice blue peignoir from Monique. Her daughter had shampooed and set her hair. Her make-up was perfect. Resplendent in aquamarine jewelry, she was ensconced on satin sheets under a custom made velvet and sequined bedcover. Onyx bejeweled cigarette holder in one hand and Manhattan on her side table ready for the other, Desiree made sure her remote control was accurately set up for her viewing pleasure so she could watch her guests in secrecy. She hit the button to activate the screen to catch the action on camera number one hidden at the front entrance as she heard the doorbell chime. Rhetta and Trace were the first guests to arrive. Desiree was hardly surprised. Trace looked quite handsome and Rhetta was gorgeous in flaming red. Desiree nodded her approval.

Lesser Spencer social types including Mrs. Mapleton, the President of the Spencer Garden Club, whom Desiree at last decided had earned an invitation, were the next few clusters of guests to arrive followed by Bonita Roberts on the arm of Isaac Kahn.

I don't believe it. That old broad has snagged herself a date with the wealthy Mr. Kahn for my salon. And, my god, would you look at her. She looks like a giant receptacle where the Easter Bunny threw up. Where in hell did she get that green get-up? And look at the size of those emeralds. Gorgeous, but the one around her neck is the size of a hardball! Oh, my, green eye shadow! That's a first. I'll keep a close watch on what goes on between those two.

Ah, here comes Harcourt and Momma Ball. He's perfectly groomed as always and Marietta looks fine in her insipid shades. They'll do. Let's see, who's that? Oh, that must be Ridge and KD Dodd. Now she's a looker, isn't she? Same colors as Marietta, but she looks beautiful. No make-up, no purse, no expensive clothes, and she looks better than most of the other guests. I'll give her an "A."

Here's Candy looking like a dyke as usual. I wonder if she is. I've never heard of her making a pass at any females, but I've never known her to have a date and she does all that work with those Girl Scouts. I'll have to ponder on that at a later date. Ah, look at the Princess. Absolutely divine! Good, there's Monique to welcome her. Isn't that precious? She curtsied to the Princess. Oh, good lord, look at Candy's mother. She looks like a clown, but at least she doesn't have on her duty housedress. Oh I see she didn't give up the bedroom slippers and just so I wouldn't be disappointed, she's got the see-through tote bag. I'll watch with baited breath to see what she rips off from me this afternoon. Now, give credit where credit is due, Desiree. The slippers are pink and the dress is magenta. At least she wore something in the same hue.

Lydia looks lovely as always in a gold cocktail suit. A little formal for this time of day, but after what she's been through with old Randolph she can wear anything she wants. I'll have to find out what she said to him or how she threatened him. I understand the bimbo has hit the road. And there's darling Precious and doesn't she look precious in her yellow and white tux by Dolce and Gabanno? She has such a fabulous figure. Wonder why she's never married? She's always been a looker!

And who in the world is this lovely creature? Oh, that must be Raven Keyes, Bonita's social secretary. What a pretty girl! Simply dressed, but smashing!

Desiree switched to another camera in time to hear the piano player tap out the first bars of "Afternoon Delight!" How cute! An attractive man and one with a sense of humor. I think this is going to be a delicious afternoon. Now let's see, who shall I have Maggie send up first? Well, there's no question about it. I must receive the Princess first off. I wouldn't want to commit a faux pas in my own home.

Downstairs the guests were mingling, eating, drinking, and having a delightful time. Bonita saw Raven enter and called her over. Raven headed toward Bonita when she realized Isaac Kahn was by her side. She hesitated, but only for a second, and then plastered a big smile on her face. She was determined not to let Bonita think she didn't like Mr. Kahn.

When Princess Alexandria had finished her visit with the hostess, she came back to the large great room and Monique brought quests one or two at the time and presented them to her. Everyone conducted him and herself beautifully, although Rhetta was a little too effusive.

"Oh, my goodness! We're being presented to the Princess, Trace, even though we already met her at our luau. This is so exciting!" Rhetta said as Monique led her and Trace toward the Princess.

Before Monique could speak, Rhetta extended her hand to Princess Alexandria, a big no-no. The Princess offers her hand if she so desires, but one does not offer his or hers to her first. Princess Alexandria, familiar with Americans and their lack of understanding of royal protocol, graciously took Rhetta's extended hand.

"Hello, Princess. I'm Rhetta Robin Ricks. Y'all, that's you and the Prince, were at my, well Trace's and my, luau, remember? I'm sure I told you but just as a little reminder, my daddy was the former Governor of the State of Tennessee. Governors are a little like royalty here in the States, but of course you know that, don't you? I keep forgetting you were an American.

"And this is my husband, Dr. Trace Ricks—you've met before. Trace, you remember Princess Alexandria of Russia, don't you, honey? She's Candy Martin's cousin.

"Isn't that right, Your Highness?"

Before Princess Alexandria could answer, Rhetta continued, "Trace and I are just back from a trip around the world. We were in Nice. That's where you live, isn't it? The next time we're there, we'll have to drop by to see you and your Prince, Ruslan, isn't it, won't we, Trace?"

The Princess nodded. She couldn't believe the audacity of this woman. One did not *drop by* to see royalty. Everything was scheduled, but then Americans were so informal. The Princess hoped Rhetta was never in the south of France again for there was no doubt in her mind that Rhetta would attempt to *drop by*.

And so it went.

Ridge Dodd was talking with Harcourt Ball and some other guests when he noticed Isaac Kahn corner Raven. Kahn was in her face speaking to her forcefully while Raven appeared extremely uncomfortable. Later, when Ridge had the opportunity, he crossed to Raven and introduced himself. The two chatted for awhile and then Ridge said, "It's none of my business, Raven, but I saw you and Isaac Kahn talking a while ago. It seemed he was leaning toward you in a threatening manner. You seemed quite uncomfortable. Is anything the matter?"

"No. I don't recall he did or said anything threatening, Captain Dodd. If I looked uncomfortable, perhaps I didn't understand what he said because of the noise level. I'm here with Mrs. Roberts to take notes. You know she's planning a Spencer Debutante Ball. Mr. Kahn has renovated the cave he owns outside of town for the ballroom—" Raven raced on as if she had verbal diarrhea and Ridge realized if anything untoward had occurred, Raven was not going to tell him about it.

Desiree was without invited visitors in her bedroom suite at the time Isaac was talking to Raven and had witnessed the exchange. She zoomed the camera in and turned up the mike. She heard every word.

"Your computer was set up today, Raven. Everything's a go," Isaac whispered loudly to the girl.

"It's not my computer; it's Mrs. Roberts' computer."

"All right. Mrs. Roberts' computer, but you're the one who uses it."

"I hope whatever evil thing you've done is not going to interfere with my work."

"You won't notice a thing, but it's good to have you in place in case there's a snag, although I'm sure my man can take care of it from a distance. I guess you noticed you've changed Internet Providers. I bought the local access company." Isaac said.

"Yes. Fortunately, I hardly ever use the Internet. You do know I'm leaving in the fall to go to New York? I won't be working for Mrs. Roberts permanently. Then what are you going to do?"

"I beg your pardon, Raven? Are you telling me what you're going to do?"

"Yes," she answered quietly.

"Well you can scratch your plans for New York. You'll work for Bonita Roberts as long as I tell you to work for her," Isaac said menacingly.

"How much more do you want to do to me? You already practically wrecked my life once," Raven said with tears in her eyes.

"You think I almost wrecked your life? You do remember what I have? Don't you, Raven? And I could really wreck your life now."

"Why do you have to use Mrs. Roberts' computer?"

"One reason only, Raven. Because I want to."

"What are you using it for? I know it's something dirty and sleazy."

"You don't know anything of the kind and you don't need to know how it's being used. You're just handy in case there's a problem. If there is, call me right away."

"What kind of problem? You told me I won't even know what's happening on it so how will I know if there's a problem?"

"I thought you were computer literate? You'll just know. Now, I've gotta go make nice to the society types. I'll be in touch, Raven."

Desiree was intrigued. It was obvious Raven and Isaac Kahn had known each other prior to his coming to Spencer. It was even more obvious that Raven didn't like him. In addition, she was afraid of him and he was blackmailing her. Isaac Kahn had done something to or had someone do something to Bonita's computer and he had told Raven he was going to do it. She wasn't going to tell Bonita because Isaac was holding something over her head. Raven had accused Isaac of almost wrecking her life. This was interesting, juicy stuff. Desiree hadn't enjoyed herself this much in years.

When Isaac moved away from Raven, Desiree flipped to another camera and there was Candy's mother. The old bag was putting a Faberge egg in her plastic tote. *By damn, it's the same one she lifted before and it is the most valuable of my collection. The old broad's loony, but she still has good taste.* Desiree removed a pad and pencil from her bedside table and noted the egg to retrieve from Candy. She lay the writing materials on the bed beside her for she was sure there would be other items to add to the list before the afternoon was over.

On another screen, Desiree saw Randolph ogling Princess Alexandria. Lydia moved to his side and said, "Are you enjoying yourself, Randolph?"

"Yes, I am, dear."

"Well you're being a little too obvious staring at the Princess' back. Behave, Randolph, you've embarrassed me enough."

"Forgive me, Lydia. Would you like me to refresh your drink?"

"That would be lovely, Randolph."

Desiree guffawed. If any of Randolph's business associates around the world knew that he as one of the wealthiest and most powerful men in the world was under the thumb of Lydia, daughter of a tenant farmer, she wondered what they would think. Real life truly was stranger than fiction.

Desiree's microphone picked up a beep and she scanned the party room until she saw Trace Ricks remove his pager. He moved to a secluded corner and quickly punched numbers into his cell phone.

"Dr. Ricks here. You paged? Mrs. Baines? When? Why wasn't I notified immediately? Her daughter? Right now? Yes, I'll call her. Give me the number."

Trace crossed to Rhetta and whispered something in her ear and exited through the French doors onto Desiree's terrace. Damn, I would love to know what that's all about. I'll have to have a camera and microphone mounted on the terrace next. Think of all I could be missing.

The call was from Trace's service. Late Friday afternoon, Mr. Smithson, Mrs. Baines' attorney, called her daughter Delilah at the deceased's home to inform her that all of her mother's bank accounts had been closed. When Delilah asked how that was possible, Mr. Smithson said Dr. Trace Ricks, who possessed her mother's power of attorney, had closed them three weeks ago. Delilah Baines Smathers went ballistic! She called Trace's office and left numerous messages.

When her call wasn't returned by Saturday afternoon, she called the hospital and got the number of Trace's service. She called it repeatedly and left messages, but Trace hadn't informed the service he was in Spencer as he wasn't on call.

By Sunday morning, Delilah was at her wit's end. She called the service screaming and threatened the girl who answered with everything she could muster. The young girl assured her she would do everything in her power to get in touch with Dr. Ricks.

The girl called another of the doctors associated with Trace and explained the situation. Dr. DeWitt suggested she try Dr. Ricks' number in Spencer. When she called his Spencer home, River Ricks answered the phone and said her father could be reached on his pager.

She immediately rang Dr. Ricks' pager. Thus, Trace had been tracked down. Trace returned the call and learned of his patient's death and Mrs. Baines' daughter's numerous and angry calls.

He called Mrs. Baines' daughter.

"Hello, Mrs. Smathers. This is Dr. Ricks. Please accept my deepest sympathy on the passing of your mother. I am so sorry I was out of the country and could not be with her at the end."

"Skip the sympathy, doc. What have you done with my mother's money?"

"I'm sorry—your mother's money?"

"Don't give me the innocent bit, doc. Her attorney called the bank to get her accounts straightened out and you've closed them all. It seems you had my mother's power of attorney?"

"I did and I have closed out her accounts, but the only thing I've done with your mother's money is invest it. All of her money is intact. In fact, I've made her money. It was easier for me to make the transactions in my name, but I have kept a careful accounting of every penny of your mother's money. I will be in Nashville tomorrow and will cut you a check for the entire amount or have it wired to your bank whichever you prefer. I will go over the accounting with you too. I'd also like to attend your mother's funeral. What arrangements have been made?"

Delilah immediately calmed down. The money was safe. She was going to be able to get it the next day. "I'm sorry if I came on a little strong, Dr. Ricks. You know there are so many crooks out there today and it would have been very easy for someone to take advantage of my mother. I know she trusted you a great deal. When the lawyer told me the accounts were closed, I hope you can understand why I jumped to conclusions."

"Of course, now about the funeral?"

"Yes, the funeral is scheduled for one o'clock tomorrow afternoon and I know this is short notice, but it would have meant a great deal to my mother if you could serve as a pallbearer."

"I would be honored. Where is the funeral?"

"At Trinity Episcopal."

"I'll be there. Again, you have my deepest sympathy. Would you like to meet before or after the services to get the money and go over the accounting?"

"I'm hoping to be able to catch a flight back to LA late tomorrow afternoon, so morning would be better for me. Say at ten o'clock? Where shall I meet you?"

"Why not at my office if that's convenient? I'll have everything ready for you then."

"I think it would be better if we met at my mother's attorney's office if that's all right with you."

"Of course. That's Mr. Smithson of Smithson, Styles, and Noah isn't it?"

"That's correct."

"Fine, I'll see you at Mr. Smithson's office at ten o'clock tomorrow morning. Should I call him to make sure that's convenient with him?"

"No, I'll handle that. It'll be convenient, Dr. Ricks."

"I'll see you there at ten then."

Trace disconnected and leaned against the brick wall of the terrace. He'd have to leave tonight for Nashville. He had spent every dime of Mrs. Baines' money. There wasn't a sou left. He'd have to be at another patient's bank by nine in the morning. He'd use another of his powers of attorney and get enough money out to make Mrs. Baines' daughter happy. He was going to be up quite late making up accounting entries to satisfy her. Why hadn't he heard about Mrs. Baines' death before now? She'd been dead since Friday morning. Heads were going to roll over this. Trace collected himself and went back to the party.

"Rhetta, please don't be upset, but I'm going to have to leave now. I have to get back to Nashville immediately. One of my patients, Mrs. Baines, passed away. Do you want to leave with me or would you prefer to ask someone for a ride back to RickShaw?"

"Trace, Mrs. Baines is dead. What can you possibly do for her now? Why do you have to go back to Nashville tonight and leave this beautiful party now? If you must go to Nashville, you can leave once the party's over."

"I have to leave now, Rhetta. There are several things I have to take care of before the funeral tomorrow."

"What things?"

"Rhetta, leave boring details like this to me. I'm sorry to spoil your afternoon, but you can ask someone for a ride, can't you? I know you're having a wonderful time. You won't even miss me. Just let me go now without creating a scene, please, love!" and he squeezed her hand.

"All right, but I'm getting awfully jealous of these old ladies who are dying and taking you away from me," Rhetta said coyly.

"I'll call you tonight," Trace said as he kissed her lightly on the cheek. He bid farewell to the Princess, thanked the Countess for the lovely party, asked her to extend his thanks to her mother, and left. Desiree watched him from the instant he returned from the terrace through the French doors until he walked out the main entrance. She glanced at her watch. From the time of the phone call until his departure, seven and one half minutes had elapsed.

Something was definitely afoot. Trace wasn't going to see a patient. A woman had died on Friday in Nashville. Why did Trace have to go to there tonight and why did he have to leave immediately?

Desiree felt the plot thickening as surely as gravy thickens when the chef adds cornstarch. She wondered if the chef had stirred it in cold water first or if this plot were going to a lumpy one. Lumpy plots, unlike lumpy gravy or lumpy thighs, were the best ones!

Ridge approached Isaac and asked if he had returned Jesse's call.

"Yes, I took care of that. Thanks for the message. I'm sorry you had to take on phone duty while you were doing the lighting job for me," Isaac said effusively.

"No problem. I wouldn't have answered someone's cell phone ordinarily, but it kept ringing and ringing. It was starting to bother my concentration."

"I appreciate it and thanks again for the message."

Reaching out for Bonita's arm, Isaac pulled her over, "Ridge, I'd like to introduce you to Bonita Roberts. She's the grand dame who's come up with the idea of the Spencer Debutante Ball. I'm sure your lovely daughter Jean Ann will be an invitee."

"Hello, Captain Dodd. Indeed she will. Isaac has told me what a talented daughter you have. A gymnast, isn't she?"

"Not your run-of-the-mill gymnast either, Bonita. Jean Ann is the new national champion," Isaac added.

"Well congratulations to her and to you too, Captain Dodd. She's exactly the type of young lady we'll be inviting to debut here in Spencer."

"That's mighty kind of you, Mrs. Roberts. I'm sure Jean Ann will be thrilled to receive an invitation, but we'll leave the acceptance up to her. She definitely has a mind of her own."

"Oh, there's no doubt she'll accept. To be among the first group of debutantes in Spencer at the initial ball will be a great honor. Every young lady invited will accept, I'm sure."

"You don't know Jean Ann, but I thank you for planning to include her. It's a pleasure to meet you, Mrs. Roberts. Now, I best go see if KD needs anything. Can't wander too far, you know?" Ridge said graciously as he moved away.

Ridge checked on KD and then sought out Raven again. He had a gut feeling something was going on between her and Isaac and that it was not good. Ridge asked Raven if he could freshen her drink.

"No, thank you, Captain Dodd. I'm going to hold off since Mrs. Roberts may want me to take some notes for her. I want to have a clear head."

"You know I've just finished doing a lighting plan for Mr. Kahn at Les Enfants?"

"No, I didn't know that. I thought you were an airline captain."

"I am, but I love doing handy work. Isaac and I met at the Home Depot and I told him I'd do his lighting. He also has a gorgeous plane I've flown a few times. He's offered to pay me for my work, but I enjoy it and flying his plane now and then is more than enough pay."

"So you and Mr. Kahn are good friends?" Raven asked.

"Acquaintances, that's all. I got the distinct impression earlier that you don't like him one bit."

"I hardly know him."

"Me either, but while I was working at his house, I found some rather disturbing things."

"Such as?"

"He has a vast collection of pornography."

"I see."

"And pornography is legal, so that's no problem. Sometimes when I'd take a little break, I'd pull out some movies to watch. I pulled one out one day and was horrified by what I saw. It was pornography featuring children."

"How horrible! But why are you telling me this?"

"Because I saw the body language when Isaac was talking to you and you not only don't like him, but you're also afraid of him, aren't you?"

"No, Captain Dodd, I'm not. Thank you for your concern. Now I really must check with Mrs. Roberts to see if she has any work for me," Raven said as she moved quickly away from the pilot.

Upstairs, Desiree watched and listened to the Ridge and Raven exchange. Her ears pricked up when she heard mention of child pornography. *This is getting quite good! I must tell Monique to send Raven up. Maybe I can get her to talk about Mr. Kahn.*

Just as Desiree called down to Monique and requested to have Raven come up for a visit, Raven's cell phone rang through the air with a catchy little tune. She has programmed it to play *Happy Days Are Here Again* rather than a normal ring. Raven checked her caller identification and saw the call was from her home. She answered immediately to her mother's distressed voice saying her father had suffered a heart attack and was on the way to Spencer Memorial Hospital in an ambulance. Raven told her mother she would meet her at the hospital right away.

Monique approached Raven as she disconnected and saw the look on her face.

"Is everything all right, Raven?"

"No, it isn't. That was my mother, Countess. My father has suffered a heart attack and is on the way to the hospital. I must leave right away. Please extend my regrets to your mother."

"Is there anything I can do?" Monique asked.

Raven looked around and didn't see Bonita.

"Yes, could you please tell Mrs. Roberts what happened and that I had to leave?"

"Of course. Let me show you to the door," Monique answered leading the way.

Desiree notified Monique she would like to receive Precious. Precious entered Desiree's suite shortly after and gave her a Spencer air kiss.

"You look lovely, Precious, as usual. Have a seat. I want to ask you a question. What do you know about Isaac Kahn and child pornography?"

Precious almost passed out. "Why, nothing, Desiree. What is this about?"

"A little fishing expedition. I hear things, you know. Since you're the one who provided Isaac with his entrée into Spencer society, I thought you might be able to enlighten me about his child pornography business."

"I'm not aware of any child pornography business, Desiree. Child pornography is illegal. Isaac's only business of which I'm aware is his recent acquisition VanBuren.net. He hired Morgan Stansill to head it up. You recall I told you about meeting Susannah Stansill and that Bonita has asked her to serve on the deb committee."

"Why would Isaac Kahn, who says he came to Spencer to retire, suddenly want to buy an Internet company?"

"I guess there's money to be made in that business."

"He doesn't need any money, Precious."

"There are many people who don't need money who go into new ventures, Desiree. It's part of the game. Money is how one keeps score."

"Keep your ear to the ground, Precious. There's something mysterious and quite possibly illegal going on in Spencer and I have reason to believe your Mr. Kahn is in the eye of the hurricane."

"Desiree, you never leave your bedroom. Where do you get all your information?"

"Let's just say at El Architecto, the walls have ears," Desiree responded with an enigmatic smile.

36

Trace Chases the Money

Trace unlocked the door to his Nashville office building a little after seven that night and immediately went into his private office and began to *cook* Mrs. Baines' books. When she had given Trace her power of attorney, Mrs. Baines had a net worth in cash, certificates of deposit, and stocks of about six hundred-fifty-thousand-dollars.

Trace pulled up his expenditures on the computer screen. He had spent a little over a hundred-thousand-dollars on Rhetta's ridiculous luau. Another fifty had gone for Rhetta's pledge to the charitable foundation sponsoring the soon-to-be-held Spencer debutante ball. So far, she had squandered two-hundred-fifty-thousand-dollars on renovations to RickShaw plus the expense of the round-the-world trip and all the shopping. There was not a penny of Mrs. Baines money left.

Trace scrolled through the other accounts he controlled for by now he had the powers of attorney or the guardianship of some twenty of them belonging to his elderly and very trusting patients. *Aha! Olivia Sanborne. Boy is she loaded! There's several million there. I'll take the money from Peter, in this case Mrs. Sanborne, to pay Paul, Mrs. Baines' daughter Delilah. Since I told Delilah I had made some money for her mother, I'll make the total sum seven-hundred-two-thousand-dollars. Now, all I have to do is fabricate a list of investments and dates so I can present Delilah with a full accounting of her mother's money while it was under my care.*

Trace worked into the night. A little after midnight, his creative accounting was complete. The next morning, he'd be at Mrs. Sanborne's bank promptly at nine to withdraw some of her money to pay off Delilah. The spending of other people's money had become so second nature to Trace that he had absolutely no feelings of guilt, therefore he had no concern about being caught. His rationalizations had become so implanted he no longer believed he was doing anything illegal, immoral, or wrong.

Trace headed for home as soon as he finished the phony spreadsheets. He was exhausted. They'd returned home from their trip, driven to Spencer, gone to the party and now back in Nashville, he'd had to tax his brain. Trace left a note for the receptionist telling her he wouldn't be in until the next afternoon and closed the office without checking his messages. There would be plenty of time for that tomorrow after meeting with Delilah and attending Mrs. Baines' funeral as a pallbearer.

Maybe after that, he could get back to doctoring patients rather than spread sheets on the computer.

All went well the next morning with Delilah, who was in fact delighted with the sum of money Trace was prepared to transfer to her account. Mr. Smithson agreed everything was in order. He thanked Trace and told Delilah they would need to go over the details of probate. Trace said he would see them both later at the funeral and left.

It was almost noon by the time the meeting concluded. Trace went home, freshened up, changed into a dark suit, and headed for Trinity Episcopal and his pallbearer duties. He called Travis at the florist shop and ordered an expensive arrangement to be sent to Mrs. Baines' funeral from him and his staff. He served as a pallbearer for Mrs. Baines and managed to shed a tear or two when he offered his sympathies once again to Delilah. She insisted he come by her mother's home for the reception following. Trace made an appearance and finally returned to his office after three in the afternoon.

As soon as he entered, the receptionist told him he had fifty-two messages on his private line and that Mrs. Sanborne had passed away over the weekend. She also said a call had come in moments before from one of the nurses at Hillcrest. Cynthia Grimes had lapsed into a coma.

"Mrs. Sanborne died? She was fine when I saw her before my trip."

"All I know is what I heard on the answer machine, Dr. Ricks. She passed away Saturday morning. Her funeral is scheduled for tomorrow morning."

"Thank you, Hedda," Trace said and headed for his office.

Trace listened to the messages. He called the funeral home about Mrs. Sanborne and tactfully asked if there were any relatives in town for the funeral.

"Only fifty or so, Dr. Ricks. All of them are distant cousins and some grandnieces and nephews. One of the nurses at the home told me not a one of them had ever visited her or sent her a card or letter to anyone's knowledge, but they're all here now awaiting the reading of the will, I'm sure. I hear tell Mrs. Sanborne was quite well-to-do."

"Thank you. I'll be over later today to pay my respects."

"The viewing is tonight at seven o'clock. If you come then, I'm sure you can meet some of the vultu—er—relatives."

Trace turned on his swivel chair from the phone to the computer. *How eerie is that? Of all the accounts I could have selected, I chose Mrs. Sanborne's and now she's croaked.* Trace looked at spreadsheets again and made arrangements to move someone else's money into Mrs. Sanborne's account to replace what he had pulled out to give to Delilah earlier. It didn't occur to Trace that, like the pyramid schemes so popular in the seventies and eighties, eventually he would run out of people or money. And once again, it did not occur to him that he was either an embezzler or a thief.

37

Kiddie Porn Up and Running

Once Harcourt had completed the deal for Isaac to purchase the local Internet access company, Isaac bought a vacant building on Spencer's main avenue and had the equipment he purchased delivered there. Jesse handled the rental of phone lines and other parts of the operation Isaac didn't understand.

Isaac hired a few of the people from his old kiddie porn company and checked with some of his former business associates and found a CEO. Morgan Stansill was a man Isaac could trust plus he had a sharp mind for business and he knew computers and the computer business inside and out. Isaac offered Morgan a phenomenal salary, purchased him a large home in town, paid all of his moving expenses and promised him hearty bonuses plus a generous retirement plan.

Isaac also explained to Morgan what was going down and why he had purchased the Internet access. Morgan was to protect the IP number on Bonita's computer. He was also to change the number frequently and if any investigation ever arose about the computer and its use, Morgan was to figure out a way to cover it up. For promising to and convincing Isaac he was capable of doing all that was required of him, he was to be paid a cool million per year with tons of perks for him and his family.

Morgan and Susannah Stansill moved to Spencer and were already members of the Spencer Country Club. Their son was away at college. Misty, their seventeen-year-old-daughter, was enrolled at the exclusive Spencer Day School. Shortly after the family's arrival, Isaac introduced Susannah and Bonita and suggested to Bonita she invite Susannah serve on the debutante committee. Since Isaac had been so generous and helpful with Bonita's plan, she immediately issued Susannah an invitation to serve.

Jesse, meanwhile, sent emails to thousands of porn customers from his and Bartie's database and from lists Isaac provided from his past days as a distributor of the trash plus copious lists of potential customers had been purchased.

Orders for the kiddie porn were rolling in on Bonita's computer and being processed all over the country. Isaac's company was already making several hundred thousand dollars a day.

Raven called Bonita to say her father had suffered a massive coronary and it was touch and go. She explained she wouldn't be able to come to work for full days for a while, but she would be in the next morning to take care of anything Bonita needed. Bonita was grateful Raven called. She needed her to make up the list of the committee members and to notify them of the first meeting.

Raven arrived the next morning and took care of Bonita's debutante ball business. Before she left, she told Bonita she wanted to stay at her father's side for the next few days as the doctors had explained the next seventy-two hours were critical. Bonita was completely understanding and told Raven to take all the time she needed. Raven returned to her office and collected her papers.

As she started to leave, she had an idea. *I wonder what would happen to whatever Ike is doing on Mrs. Roberts' computer if I unplugged it? I think I will. No one else here uses it. Mrs. Roberts won't know it's unplugged. Ike must be using it as some kind of mainframe. If it's unplugged, whatever is coming over the Internet will be stopped until it's plugged in again.* Raven reached behind the desk and pulled the plug on the computer and on Isaac's profitable business.

Within minutes, Jesse was on the phone to Isaac.

"Big problem down there."

"What?" Isaac asked.

"Roberts' computer is down."

"You're the man. Fix it!"

"I can't fix it. It's down."

"What do you mean down?"

"Is there a power failure there?"

"Not here, but I don't know about at Bonita's house."

"Well, find out, man. Everything has come to a screeching halt."

"What do you want me to do?"

"Call old lady Roberts and ask her if her power's down. Get in touch with her secretary. Whatever you have to do. We're losing money fast and you know how fickle these customers are. We're down and they'll find another source. Get on it, Ike."

Isaac was so rattled, he didn't bother to correct Jesse and remind him his name was Isaac now. He called Morgan and told him what Jesse had relayed.

"Let me check. He's right, Mr. Kahn. Mrs. Roberts' computer is down."

"Why?"

"I don't know. Let me get right back to you."

Isaac called Bonita.

"Hello, Bonita. This is Isaac Kahn."

"Well, hello, Isaac. It's so nice to hear your voice. What can I do for you today?"

"I was wondering if you've experienced a power failure over there. All of my lights went out a few minutes ago."

"No, everything is on here. I can't imagine why you would lose power. It's a beautiful day. There's not a cloud in the sky. You don't think someone was racing around the lake and slammed into a pole near Les Enfants, do you?"

"I don't think so. Well, okay, thanks."

"Is there anything I can do to help?"

"No, thank you, Bonita. I simply wanted to know if this is an isolated incident. By the way, is Raven working today?"

"No, she isn't. She was in earlier to help me with the list of committee members and to send out notices about the first meeting, but she's at the hospital with her father now. He suffered a massive coronary. She probably won't be back until the end of the week. Did you need to speak to her about something?"

"No. I merely wanted to ask how her father's doing."

"Not well. The doctors told her the next seventy-two hours are critical. That's why she's planning to stay with him at the hospital until the end of the week."

"When you see her, tell her I asked about her father. Talk to you later, Bonita."

"Good-bye, Isaac."

Bonita was a little disappointed. When she heard Isaac's voice, she had hoped he might be calling to invite her out to dinner or to his home for drinks or something social. At any rate, he had called her rather than someone else on the lakefront, about the power failure. That was a good sign!

Morgan called Isaac as soon as he hung up from talking to Bonita. "The power's not out. The only thing I can figure is the computer's unplugged."

"Damn it to hell. That's exactly what's happened. I'll get that little bitch!" Isaac yelled as he disconnected and called Jesse.

"She's unplugged the computer."

"Great! Get it plugged in right away."

"And how do you suggest I do that?"

"I'm not the idea man, Ike. I run my end of the operation. You run yours."

Isaac drove to the florist shop and told Travis to make him a bouquet suitable for a hospital patient while he waited. He took the flowers to Spencer Memorial and asked to see Mr. Keyes.

"I'm sorry, sir. Mr. Keyes is in Intensive Care. His only visitors are family members who are allowed in one at a time ten minutes every hour."

"Where are his family members? Can I see them?"

"Certainly. They're in the Intensive Care Waiting Room on the tenth floor. The elevator is right over there."

"Thank you."

Isaac hit the button for the tenth floor. When the elevator door opened, Isaac looked left and then right. He saw the arrow pointing to the waiting room. As he approached the waiting room, Raven entered the hall from the ladies' room.

"Raven!"

She turned and saw Isaac.

"Mr. Kahn, what are you doing here?"

"I brought some flowers for your father."

"He can't have flowers. He's in Intensive Care, but that was thoughtful of you."

"Here. Give them to your mother then."

Raven took the flowers, thanked him, and turned to go back to the family waiting room.

"Not so fast, Raven."

She stopped and turned back.

"What have you done to Bonita's computer?"

"Nothing."

"Yes, you have. Her computer is down."

"I used it this morning."

"And it was working fine?"

"Absolutely."

"It's not working fine now. Did you unplug it?"

"No. Why would I do that?"

"I have no idea, Raven, unless you thought if the computer wasn't plugged in, the Internet access wouldn't work, and perhaps you could throw a wrench into the business I'm conducting over it."

"I didn't do anything to the computer, Mr. Kahn."

"Well, you're going to have to get your tail over there and figure out what's wrong with it right away."

"How can I do that? I told Mrs. Roberts I wouldn't be back until the end of the week. My father could be dying, Mr. Roberts. My mother is a mess. I have to stay here with them. I can't go to Mrs. Roberts' house now and besides what would I tell her? How would I know there's problem with her computer when I'm here at the hospital?"

"You're smart and quick, Raven. Tell her you forgot something. I don't care. Tell her anything. Get over there *now* and get that computer up and running!" Isaac yelled.

Raven's mother came out of the waiting room.

"What's going on, Raven? What's that yelling about?"

"No, mother, there's no problem. I'll be right there. Mr. Kahn, I can't go right now. Please leave. Please have some respect for my situation. I'll go as soon as I can."

"It better be within the hour," Isaac said in a guttural tone and there was no mistaking the threat in his voice. He turned and left.

Raven visited her father for the ten minutes allowed family members in the next hour and then explained to her mother she had to leave for about an hour, but she would be back before her next scheduled visit. Raven and her mother alternated going in to see Warren Keyes. She drove to Villagio and was relieved to find Bonita was out at one of her multitudinous social functions. Raven went into her office and plugged in the computer. As she headed for the front door, Hannah came into the hallway.

"Well, hello, Miss Raven. I thought I heard that door open. I wasn't expecting you no more today."

"I know, Hannah. I didn't want to bother anyone. I forgot one of my lists."

"How's your daddy, honey?"

"About the same. He's heavily sedated. I'm not sure he knows when my mother or I go into to visit him."

"Oh, I bet he does. Jest 'cause he ain't talkin' don't mean he don't know y'alls there."

"Hannah, I need to ask a huge favor of you and I need you to promise me you won't tell anyone."

"What you need, sugar?"

"Tonight, before you go to bed, could you go into my office and unplug my computer?"

"I reckon I could, but if you needs to unplug it, why don't you jest unplug it now?"

"I can't explain that, but it would really help me if you could unplug it tonight and then sometime tomorrow, if you think of it, plug it back in."

"Law, Miss Raven, to borrow a bit from Miss Butterfly McQueen, I don't know nothin' 'bout unpluggin' no computers!"

"That's clever, Hannah. You don't need to know anything about computers to unplug it and plug it in. If it wouldn't be too much trouble, unplug it tonight, plug it back in tomorrow whenever it's convenient and then unplug it tomorrow night. I'll be back in on Friday. Please, Hannah, do this for me, and don't mention it to Mrs. Roberts, okay?"

"All right, but I sure don't understand why you wants that thing unplugged."

"I hope I'll be able to explain it sometime, but I can't right now. You trust me, don't you, Hannah?"

"'Course I do. I'll take care of it, Miss Raven, and I won't say nothin' to Miz Bonita."

"Thank you, Hannah. You're the best."

"Ain't that the truth? You give my regards to yo momma and yo daddy too when he's feelin' better."

"I will, Hannah. Thank you. I have to run now," Raven said as she gave Hannah a hug.

Once in her car, Raven called Isaac from her cell phone and advised him that the computer had been unplugged, but that it was plugged in now. She told him she didn't know how it had happened."

"See that it doesn't happen again, Raven. I'm warning you."

"I can't promise that. I'm not always there."

"Who unplugged it?"

"I don't know."

"Well this little problem cost me a great deal of money, Raven, and it better not happen again."

"I can assure you it won't happen on my watch, but I can't stay in the office at Mrs. Roberts' house twenty-four hours a day."

"Has this happened before?"

"No."

"Then for your sake, let's hope it won't again," Isaac said and Raven's phone went dead.

Raven drove to the hospital with the faintest of smiles on her face. She may not be able to stop Isaac Kahn from whatever illegal activity he was performing on Mrs. Roberts' computer, but with Hannah's help she could certainly throw a monkey wrench in it.

38

The Committee Meets

Bonita had selected her committee and was preparing for the first meeting. Those serving with her were Lydia Henley, of course. Rhetta Ricks about whom Bonita had reservations, but she had decided not to attempt to blackball anyone until she got her ball established. Others included were Candy Martin, Susannah Stansill, whom Isaac had insisted be invited to serve; KD Dodd, Precious Woodson, and Desiree Compton, who would have to serve in absentia. Marietta Ball, Marjorie Gibson, President of the Spencer Junior League; and Lucy Mapleton, President of the Spencer Garden Club, recently a first-time guest at Desiree Compton's house and a long-time social climber, filled out the list. Lucy knew there was a God when Bonita Roberts invited her to sit on the debutante committee. Serving on that prestigious committee with all the important people in Spencer was more than she had ever asked for in prayer.

The meeting was to be a luncheon at the Spencer Country Club. Bonita would open the meeting, give a talk about the charitable foundation, describe the renovated cave where the ball was to be held, open the floor for suggestions as to what the ball would be named, and ask each member to submit names of potential young ladies to be invited to debut.

Bonita was dressing for the inaugural meeting. Today, she would be all in yellow. She recalled a yellow ensemble she owned while residing at the Beverly Wiltshire. One of her gentleman callers told her she looked like an exquisite daffodil.

Bonita hoisted the fringed mid-calf skirt over her head and pulled it down to settle at what was once her waist. The upper garment had fringe along its hem and at the ends of the long sleeves. Bonita's Jimmy Choo shoes were strapped affairs with fringe at the ankles.

She was wearing a hat to the luncheon too, as she felt ladies should be thus attired when going out in the afternoon. The large picture affair resembled a bolero with fringe matching her outfit around the brim. Once Bonita arranged the yellow and the fringe on her massive frame, she closely resembled a yellow Big Bird float in the New Orleans Mardi Gras Parade.

She cast her once critical eye in the mirror and thought she looked absolutely stunning. Similar to the anorectic who peers in the mirror and sees a fat reflection Bonita gazed into her mirror and saw the gorgeous woman she had been twenty years ago when her face and figure had stopped men in their tracks.

Arriving at the club early, Bonita checked on the table arrangements for the luncheon to be served. She made sure everything was in order. Raven had come to Villagio earlier and given Bonita the lists she needed and an agenda to be provided for each attendee next to her place setting.

Bonita left her purse at the head seat of the table, which was graced with two lovely daffodil arrangements she specifically requested. She moved into the club's grand hall to await the arrival of the other committee members. Once everyone arrived, Bonita led the way into the private dining room where champagne was served as Bonita mingled and made sure everyone was introduced to each other.

Following the luncheon of cups of lobster bisque, steak Tartar, deviled eggs, sliced tomatoes and avocados, crusty French bread, Perrier, and more champagne, Bonita requested dessert be delayed until after the meeting. She banged her gold gavel, a vestige of her days as Chair of the Magnolia Ball Committee in Dorchester County, South Carolina, and called the meeting to order.

"Ladies, I wish to welcome all of you and to thank you for serving on the Selection Committee of the First (that I'm sure will become the Annual) Spencer Debutante Ball. I think this idea of ours will be a marvelous addition to our town and to our community. Mr. Harcourt Ball has established a charitable foundation to sponsor our social function. Proceeds from the ball each year will go to helping those less fortunate than we are in Van Buren County. We have plowed through dozens and dozens of worthy causes and have settled on seven to receive major donations this first year. If you will refer to the pages in front of each of you, you will see the charities listed.

"We gave a great deal of thought to where we could hold the ball and while I'm sure the club here would have been suitable with the addition of a large rented tent or perhaps we could have used one of the lakefront homes, we desired a unique location. It happens Mr. Isaac Kahn of Les Enfants, owns land outside town that includes a huge cave. He graciously and generously offered to renovate it for our annual ball. I have been to the cave and it is indeed a sight to behold. Mr. Kahn installed central heat and air conditioning, exquisite lighting, a fully equipped commercial kitchen, a stage, men's and ladies' lounges, a marquee out front and more than sufficient land has been cleared and paved for parking. We'll be the talk of society throughout Tennessee with this unusual venue for our function.

"Before we move on to the real purpose of our business today, that of submitting names of prospective Van Buren County debutantes, I would like to suggest when the invitations are sent, we advise each young lady that prior to the ball she is expected to host a social function which will include all of the other debutantes. She may include parents and escorts at the function or not. We might also offer some suggestions as to what type of functions would be appropriate.

"Additionally, I would like to hold a few sessions with the selected to make sure they are aware of proper attire and behavior and then of course, they and their escorts must attend several sessions to learn the German." (The German is a somewhat complex figure. essentially a dance, performed by the debutantes and their escorts after the presentation of the young ladies.)

Precious Woodson raised her hand.

"Yes, Precious?"

"First of all, thank you, Bonita, for this wonderful idea and all the work you've done. You are one organized lady."

"Thank you for the compliment, Precious."

"However, I'm not sure there's a need to instruct the young ladies about proper attire and behavior. Hopefully, those we invite will be up to snuff on those aspects. Also, I'm concerned we might appear snooty if we suggest such sessions."

Candy Martin agreed.

"Ladies, I have been involved with these debutante balls before and believe me, these sessions are a must."

KD Dodd asked Bonita where she had been involved and to explain some of the problems she had encountered.

"Oh, California and in New York City. We always attempted to select young ladies from the best of families with the only the purest of backgrounds. Once in a while a black sheep somehow got on a list and that proves to be an embarrassment to not only the committee, but also to the other girls debuting."

"Then we'll have to make sure we don't select any black sheep, won't we, ladies?" Precious asked.

"Perhaps we can table this suggestion for the moment, Precious. Once the young ladies have been selected and we meet all of them at the tea, we can decide whether protocol sessions are necessary or not," Bonita responded.

"I think that's an excellent idea, Bonita," Lydia chimed in. "We'll use the sessions on an as-needed basis."

"Fine," Bonita answered, but she was miffed. Bonita wanted everything to go her way. But she wasn't going to let the rest of the ladies know she wasn't happy with this decision because the most important item to her the name of the ball. She was dead set on its being called The Magnolia Ball.

"Our next order of business is to decide on a name for our ball. The floor is open for suggestions," Bonita announced.

Susannah Stansill said, "I knew the ball hadn't been named yet, so I have thought about this a great deal and I think we should name if after a flower. Two lovely flowers that grow here in Tennessee are the camellia and the azalea. I recommend we go with either The Azalea Ball or the Camellia Ball."

There was a general murmur of enthusiasm.

"As some of you recall from our initial meeting when I suggested the ball, my choice is The Magnolia Ball," Bonita was quick to inject.

Marietta piped up, "We're planning the event at Christmastime, aren't we?"

"That's correct," Bonita answered.

"Then I think it should be something to do with the season. We could name it The Poinsettia Ball or The Mistletoe Ball or The Holly Ball."

"That's an excellent thought, Marietta," Bonita piped up, "And don't we all use magnolia leaves at Christmas time?"

"We certainly do," Rhetta chimed in. "We use magnolia leaves all over RickShaw and there are dozens of magnolia trees right here in Spencer. We could use magnolia leaves as the focal point of the decoration. They look beautiful in their natural state or sprayed with gold or silver leaf. I vote for The Magnolia Ball."

"Thank you, Rhetta," Bonita smiled at her. Who would have thought Rhetta Robin Ricks would be her biggest ally?

"That is a good point, Rhetta," Susannah acknowledged.

"How do the rest of you feel about The Magnolia Ball?" Bonita asked.

"I don't think it matters what we call it, but Marietta did make a good suggestion that we use something appropriate for the time of year and magnolia leaves certainly are used profusely at Christmastime. I say we go with The Magnolia Ball too," said Candy.

"Would someone care to make a motion?" Bonita asked.

"I move that the name of the annual Spencer Debutante Ball be officially called The Magnolia Ball," Rhetta motioned.

"I second it," Candy said.

"All in favor?" Bonita asked.

It was unanimous. Bonita would once again chair and emcee The Magnolia Ball.

"And now, let's move on to the submission of names of young ladies. I hope all of you have several," Bonita continued during her adrenalin rush she was experiencing at having succeeded in having the ball so named.

Once a glass bowl Bonita produced was passed to each committee member and all the names had been dropped into it, Bonita placed the bowl on the table and drew the first name.

"The first name is Corinne Ricks. That's your and Trace's daughter, is it not, Rhetta?"

"Yes. Corinne's our older daughter. She's a lovely girl and will be debuting in Nashville in September. I think it will be so nice for her to debut here, too, because she has spent so much of her time here, practically every summer, and she considers this her second home. She knows so many of the other girls that live here, and—"

"Rhetta, you don't need to sell us on Corinne," Precious interrupted.

"We'll now vote on Corinne Ricks," Bonita announced.

Each lady again placed a slip of paper in a second glass bowl. Lydia Henley took the bowl and removed each slip of paper. All of them were blank. No black mark had been cast against Corinne Ricks. Rhetta's daughter was the first of the debutantes to be presented at the forthcoming Magnolia Ball in Spencer, Tennessee.

Other nominees included the Dodd's daughter; Misty Stansill' BD and the late Darling Huxtable's daughter; and Sarah Smithson, the daughter of Avery Smithson, senior partner in his law firm and the attorney of the late Mrs. Baines, former patient of Dr. Trace Ricks. While not residents of Spencer, Mr. and Mrs. Smithson owned a summer home in the county.

Mrs. Mapleton had placed her daughter Sherry Louisa's name in nomination and after the voting was concluded, she was among those selected. Numerous other young ladies of whom Bonita had no knowledge, but whose credentials were vouched for by the natives on the committee, were also to be invited. When the final count was completed, nineteen young permanent residents, summer residents, and residents of Van Buren County had been chosen to be the recipients of the soon-to-be-coveted, Bonita was positive, vellum envelopes containing invitations to debut at The Magnolia Ball.

Only two names hadn't made the cut. One was Cynthia Patman, daughter of the locally owned bank's president. She had been involved in some type of drug scandal heralded on the front pages of several *Spencer Spectators* the previous summer. The committee decided they wanted no scandal attached to the ball. They knew there was going to be hell to pay when Cynthia's daddy found out she hadn't been included.

The other was Lindsay Mary Bassin, daughter of a late prominent attorney in the little town, whose mother was now openly living with a Mexican construction worker. The committee decided it would not be appropriate for Lindsay Mary to be invited. *The sins of the fathers, or in this case, the mothers, and all that rot!* Plus they didn't want to entertain the possibility of the Mexican construction worker all dolled up in a rented tux presenting the daughter of one of Spencer's revered late citizens.

The late Mr. Bassin was one of Harcourt's business partners in the firm that continued to keep his name in its title. Marietta felt she should say something on Cameron Bassin's behalf, but decided to keep mum. She would take the situation up with Harcourt that evening. Her brilliant son would have a solution.

Bonita adjourned the meeting after the prerequisite motion and second and signaled to the waiter dessert could now be served. Grapefruit Alaska, a light but sensational dish when flambéed, was placed before each lady and general chatter and conversation ensued. The meeting had been a success. Bonita had triumphed in every area with the exception of her *charm sessions,* but she was sure she'd eventually be able to hold those too!

39

Rhetta's at It Again!

Rhetta couldn't wait to get home and tell Corinne she been selected to make her debut at The Magnolia Ball in Spencer. She also had been the first debutante selected. Rhetta was already making plans for Corinne's party. She'd have a formal black and gold dinner dance to be held at the Spencer Country Club. Everyone would be asked to bring gifts to Corinne wrapped in black and gold, as the lucky young lady's birthday fell on December seventeenth, eleven days before the ball was to be held.

Rhetta further decided that although Bonita had suggested each debutante have a party prior to the ball, Corinne would have several. Rhetta would call on her friends, family, and acquaintances to make sure Corinne was feted party after party. What with Trace's newfound wealth, Rhetta could offer to pay for everything if someone else hosted a function for her child.

Of course, a shopping trip to New York for her and both girls was an absolute necessity. Corinne was debuting in Nashville in three weeks and Rhetta, Corinne, and River had their gowns for that affair. Many from Spencer attended the Nashville Terpsichorean Ball and they couldn't be seen in the same gowns for the Spencer events. Several gowns would be needed for all three of them for all the parties Rhetta was planning for Corinne and then there were the little socials the other debs would be hosting. The Magnolia Ball and its attending events were going to set Trace back a bundle!

The *good* doctor was in Nashville tending to his patients. He had successfully transferred money here and there and everything had settled back to normal. His receptionist buzzed his office phone and told him his wife was on hold.

"Hello, Rhetta."

"Hi Trace. I'm just back from the first meeting of The Magnolia Ball Committee. That's what we're going to call the debutante ball. It was Bonita's suggestion, but then some of the other women made other suggestions, but I said magnolia leaves were a big decorating accessory at Christmastime, when the deb ball is going to be held, so that would be a good name. Everyone voted and it was unanimous! Then we selected the debutantes and guess who the first one selected was?"

"I don't have any idea, Rhetta."

"Corinne. Isn't that exciting, Trace?"

"Corinne is making her debut in Nashville at the end of the month, isn't she?"

"Of course, but she's also making her debut in Spencer at Christmastime. I think it'll be so good for her, Trace. It'll help build her confidence and once everyone here attends her parties, she'll definitely be the belle of the ball."

"Her parties?"

"Yes, each girl selected will have her own party prior to the ball. I'm planning for us to have Corinne's on her birthday, December seventeenth. I want to have a black and gold formal dinner dance at the club and have everyone bring presents for Corinne wrapped in black and gold to celebrate her birthday. Isn't that a super idea?"

"Do you think you can ask people to bring gifts to a deb party, Rhetta?"

"It's her birthday, Trace. We'll be shelling out thousands of dollars for the party. Her guests can bring Corinne a little trinket I should think."

"Well, you know about these things."

"That's right, darling, I do. And then several of our friends will also be entertaining for Corinne too. Are you coming down this weekend? This'll be our last one before the girls go back to school. I want to go over our schedules because the three of us will have to block out at least a week to go shopping in New York for the gowns and outfits we'll need for the goings on in Spencer. We'll plan to go after Corinne debuts in Nashville. What does your schedule look like for October, Trace?"

"Rhetta, I haven't the slightest idea. I *am* coming down this weekend and we can discuss it then, but I have patients waiting right now."

"Well, why didn't you say so? I simply wanted to tell you about Corinne and her invitation and how excited we all are."

"Then I'm happy for Corinne and for you and River too. I have to go now, dear. I'll see you Friday."

Trace made a mental note that after he finished with his last patient he must fire up his computer. He needed to check on the accounts he managed for his old ladies because it was obvious from the amount of money Rhetta was planning on spending on her newest social extravaganza, he was going to have to raid another unsuspecting old lady's life savings.

Rhetta dialed Candy Martin's number.

"Hi, Candy. Rhetta here. Good meeting, wasn't it?"

"I thought so."

"Candy, I need a favor."

"What?"

"I want you to give Corinne a deb party in December."

"I'd be happy to, Rhetta. You won't be giving her one?"

"Oh, yes. Trace and I are going to have a dinner dance at the country club for her on her birthday and invite all the debs, escorts, and their parents."

"So you want me to host an additional party for her?"

"Yes, just because Bonita suggested each girl have one party doesn't mean it's limited to one. I think it would be so fantastic if Corinne had several, don't you?"

"I suppose. What kind of party do you want me to have?"

"I haven't thought about that yet. I just wanted to make sure you wouldn't mind doing it. I'll get back to you later about a theme, and Candy, I'll be happy to pay for everything."

"Rhetta Robin Ricks, you insult me. You will not pay for one peanut. I've known that child since *before* she was a gleam in Trace's eye and if I'm giving her a party, then I'm giving her a party. I don't want any money from you."

"I was just offering, Candy, 'cause I'm asking you to host a party for her."

"I'm delighted to host a party for her and that's the last time I want to hear any mention of money, Rhetta. Money-talk is crass, you know?"

"I'm sorry, Candy. Forgive me, Candy, and thanks so much. I'll talk to you later about the details, okay?"

"That will be fine."

Next, Rhetta called two of her Nashville acquaintances with summer homes in Spencer and prevailed upon them to entertain on her daughter's behalf. She was definitely on a roll!

40

Intrigue in Tennessee

As Bonita and her committee readied the invitations to be mailed to the potential debutantes, there were many goings-on in little Spencer. Rhetta was making grandiose plans for the mother of all shopping trips to New York and had booked herself and the girls at the Plaza for a week of unprecedented spending. Isaac was spending a great deal of his time on the phone with a frantic Jesse as Bonita's computer was plugged in, unplugged, plugged in, and unplugged sporadically.

Isaac was in contact with Raven several times a day. She continued to plead her innocence and was in fact enjoying Isaac's plight immensely. She hoped she was interfering terribly with his bottom line in whatever shady deal was involved. Desiree had confided in Monique about the conversations she overheard at the salon and the two of them spent hours running and rerunning the tapes trying to figure out what was going on with Isaac, Raven, and Bonita's computer.

"I think you should call Bonita and tell her what you heard, mother," Monique said for the umpteenth time.

"How can I do that, Monique? I'd have to tell her *how* I heard the conversation. I certainly don't want all of Spencer knowing I spy on them at my Sunday get-togethers."

"This is obviously a very serious matter, mother. We're sure Isaac Kahn is involved in something illegal and he's somehow using Bonita's computer for it. I think advising your friend overrides your fear of Spencer learning you're spying. Besides, you can swear Bonita to secrecy. The information you'd be giving her should guarantee her silence."

"All right, I'll think about it, but there must be a way we can find out what's going on before I tell Bonita what little bit we think we know."

Marietta trotted right to Harcourt's office after the committee meeting and informed him Lindsay Mary Bassin would not be receiving an invitation to make her debut at the forthcoming ball.

"And why not, mother? Edward Bassin's family has been in Spencer since long before it was incorporated. His widow is a Rockford, another old Spencer family, and she was certainly left with more than comfortable means. I've never heard anything untoward about the girl. Why isn't she to be asked?"

"Because Cameron Bassin's openly living with that Mexican construction worker, Harcourt."

"Well, I'm sure Cameron won't ask the Mexican to escort Lindsay Mary at the ball. She'll get her brother or father, old man Rockford is still alive and kicking, to escort the girl. This is not acceptable, mother. Did you speak up and remind the committee who Lindsay Mary was?"

"No. I didn't want to make any waves. I came here as soon as the meeting was over because I knew you'd know what to do about this mess."

"And I do. You run on home, mother. I'll handle this. I'll call Bonita Roberts right away. I set up the foundation and am a member of the founding committee. Cameron Bassin has a lot of money invested in this firm to this day. All I need is to get a call from her about why I'm on a committee funding an event in which her only daughter is not included."

Meanwhile, auditors descended on the First National Bank of Nashville, the depository where the late Olivia Sanborne's accounts were held. The audit was an annual one and had not been brought on by any problems within the bank. In the course of checking deposits and withdrawals, one bright young auditor, Josh Knowlton, noticed a discrepancy. Moneys had been withdrawn from Olivia Sanborne's account on the Monday after she had expired on the previous Saturday. This, in itself, was not unusual, but the person who had withdrawn the money was.

A person holding another's power of attorney has access to assets only as long as the grantor of the power of attorney is alive. Once, the grantor passes away, only the executor or executrix can withdraw any money from the accounts of the deceased. Dr. Trace Ricks, using his power of attorney, had withdrawn money from Olivia Sanborne's account on Monday after her death and had deposited the same amount in her account on Tuesday, the following day.

The young auditor thought this highly unusual. He checked and the bank had not been aware of Mrs. Sanborne's death at the time of Dr. Ricks' first transaction, he wondered why seven-hundred-two-thousand-dollars would be withdrawn one day and replaced the next. Josh made a note regarding the anomaly and circled it in red ink.

That evening when the auditors and the upper management of the bank gathered for an informal discussion, young Knowlton mentioned Dr. Ricks' transaction to the bank president.

"Yes, I recall Dr. Ricks making the withdrawal," Harvey Chesterton, the bank's president, remarked. "When a sum of money that large is withdrawn, I'm notified right away. At the time, we were not aware of Mrs. Sanborne's demise and Dr. Ricks had her power of attorney, so we cut him a cashier's check.

"I was not aware that he deposited the same amount of money into Mrs. Sanborne's account the next day. We don't mind how much our customers deposit, Mr. Knowlton, so I wasn't advised of that transaction," Chesterton said with a chuckle.

"The money was replaced. There doesn't seem to be a problem, but I think this is an issue that bears some investigation."

"Oh, I agree. What do you want us to do here at the bank?"

"Nothing at the moment. We'll complete the audit and at that time, I'll take this matter up with the home office."

"Good. I hasten to assure you we had not been informed of Mrs. Sanborne's death at the time of the withdrawal."

"So noted. I'm not concerned about any wrongdoing at the bank, Mr. Chesterton."

On Friday afternoon Harvey Chesterton and his wife Lucinda and their three teen-age boys piled into their Lincoln Town Car and headed for their weekend retreat in Spencer. Lucinda had asked Harvey to leave the bank early as they were entertaining Grace and Timothy Patman at their Spencer home that evening. Timothy Patman was a long-time friend of Harvey's. They were fraternity brothers at Old Miss together in the eighties. Their friendship had continued through the years and was made even more *simpatico* because they both held the positions of bank presidents, one at a large conglomerate bank in Nashville and the other at a small privately owned family bank in Spencer.

After dinner, the two bankers retired to the wrap-around deck of the Chesterton's large cottage to smoke Cohiba cigars. After several moments of small talk, Chesterton mentioned an annual audit was taking place at his bank.

"Don't you hate those audits? We never have had any problems, but I dread the week they come. All those people are in the way, asking questions, pulling files, getting on the computers, checking every transaction, and then how about the daily *friendly* debriefs where you know they're just shot-gunning to find something amiss?"

"Yeah, I hate'em too, but so far so good. Well, I think so far so good. Do you know Trace Ricks? He's got a home here. He's a doctor in Nashville. He's married to that social butterfly, Rhetta Robin, whose daddy was Governor Shaw?"

"I know who he is. Why?"

"Several weeks ago a woman named Olivia Sanborne died in Nashville. She was a big depositor in our bank. She died on a Saturday. The following Monday, Trace Ricks, who had her power of attorney came into the bank and withdrew seven-hundred-two-thousand-dollars from her account."

"That's some serious shit, Harve."

"Not true. The bank didn't know she'd passed away, so there's really no problem there or at least I hope not. The snot-nose auditor who must be all of twenty-one picked up on it and assured me there isn't a problem anyway, because you see, the very next day, the doctor deposited exactly seven-hundred-two-thousand-dollars into Mrs. Sanborne's account."

"Who was this Mrs. Sanborne? What's the doctor doing with her power of attorney?"

"Beats me. She's was an elderly lady living at one of those assisted living complexes and had only distant relatives is all I know."

"Was Ricks her doctor?"

"I would assume so."

"Then I imagine he must have known she was dead. Was he the executor too?"

"Nope, her attorney was."

"Then Ricks knew he couldn't use the power of attorney to withdraw money."

"*If* he knew she was dead."

"He was her doctor, man, or at least it appears he was. Why else would she give him her power of attorney?"

"I don't know, but after *Snot-Nose* called this matter to my attention, I checked into a few accounts of elderly widows in assisted living facilities in Nashville who are clients of ours, and the good doctor has the power of attorney for thirteen of the old broads."

"Get out!"

"I kid you not."

"He has access to their money. You know that means he can do anything he wants to with it."

"I'm with you, Tim. I know what it means, but why are they giving them to him and what is he doing with their money?"

"Someone should be informed of this."

"Informed of what? They can give him their powers of attorney if they wish. No one can stop them."

"Maybe you should contact the late Mrs. Sanborne's attorney. What you think?"

"I may do that. I want the auditors out of there and I want to see what *Snot-Nose* does with the information. He's going to 'take the matter up with the home office.'"

"Great!"

Before Harvey could continue, the wives joined the gentlemen with a tray holding a decanter of Drambuie and four liqueur glasses. Banking talk came to a screeching halt.

The morning after the committee meeting, Bonita returned Harcourt's call. She had gone straight from the meeting to Lydia Henley's plantation for cocktails and dinner and hadn't arrived home until far too late to call him back. The attorney's secretary put her through right away.

"Bonita, I tried to reach you yesterday afternoon."

"I know, Harcourt. I had a social engagement after the meeting and didn't return until quite late last evening. I didn't think you would relish my returning your call after eleven last night."

"Well, I'm glad you've called now. We have a situation on our hands."

"What kind of situation?"

"Mother tells me the committee isn't extending an invitation to Lindsay Mary Bassin to make her debut."

"Harcourt, you must bear with me for a moment now. As you know, I'm a recent *come-here* and I don't recognize names as quickly as you natives. Who is this Lindsay Mary Bassin?"

"She's the only daughter of Edwin Bassin, one of my late law partners. If she doesn't receive an invitation, her mother Cameron Bassin is going to be all over me. In addition, I'm sure Cameron's aware I set up the sponsoring foundation for the debutante ball and am on the founding board. You can imagine the embarrassment this is going to cause me once Cameron learns Lindsay Mary is not included."

"I remember now. The problem is not with the girl. It came up at the meeting that her mother is openly living with a Mexican construction worker.

Why, Harcourt, we can't have some Mexican presenting one of the young ladies at The Magnolia Ball."

Bonita apparently suffered a temporary loss of memory because a Mexican had conjured up the whole idea of the ball, was chairing the selection committee, and was to emcee the hallowed event.

"Bonita, I have no idea what Cameron is up to at the moment. She's always been somewhat of a loose cannon, but she is a Rockford. That's old Spencer. The Bassins have been here since the monkeys climbed down the trees and met the folks coming over on the Nina, the Pinta, and the Santa Maria. If Lindsay Mary doesn't receive an invitation, the entire debutante ball will be sham."

"Harcourt, the committee has voted."

"Then they'll have to *un*-vote!"

"That's not the way these things are done."

"Bonita, let me put this to you another way. Either Lindsay Mary Bassin receives an invitation to debut at The Magnolia Ball or I resign from anything to do with the foundation, the ball, the cave, and any and all magnolia trees in Van Buren County. I'll expect to hear from you regarding this matter within a few days because if those invitations go out and Lindsay Mary doesn't receive one, there's going to be hell to pay! I'll look forward to hearing from you within the next forty-eight hours. Good day!"

Who does he think he is that he can talk to me that way? Kind, gallant, gentlemanly Harcourt Ball. But, I can't let him resign. On the other hand, I can't very well go back to the committee and ask them to change their votes. What a mess! It was so much better in Dorchester County where all these politics could be swept away because the selection committee was a secret—we had absolute power!

No, it wasn't, Bonita, or you wouldn't be living in Spencer. Let's not get caught up in reliving the glories of the past. You have a problem right here right now and you better get it resolved or you're going to lose a very esteemed, very important member of your committee and with it a great deal of your credibility. Leave it to a Mexican to cause trouble in paradise!

Bonita called Desiree and explained the situation to her and asked for advice.

"Send her an invitation, Bonita. Cameron Bassin won't let the Mexican show his face at the debutante ball. He's only twenty-six or something, for god's sake. He's Cameron's boy-toy. She's simply having a fling. You don't want to lose Harcourt on the committee. That could be disastrous!"

"Desiree, don't you see once the committee's voted, it's sealed in blood? I can't go back and ask them to change their vote."

"Bonita, don't take the committee so seriously. You simply call an emergency meeting, explain the situation to the committee, and change their minds. No one on that committee wants to see Harcourt resign, I promise you. Emergency meeting, explanation, problem solved."

"Well, all right, if that's what you think, Desiree."

"It's what I know, Bonita."

Candy Martin was making one phone call after another. Several of the girls in her Girl Scout Troop were working on a charity badge and the troop had decided to hold a rummage sale. Candy was lining up donations. Several of the mothers commented that their little darlings had outgrown their scout uniforms and asked Candy if it would be appropriate to donate those for sale.

"I don't see why not," Candy answered. "In fact, I think it's a wonderful idea. We have new scouts moving up from Brownies all the time. I'm sure a lot of their families would be delighted to be able to purchase a Girl Scout uniform at a nominal price."

After Candy called all the Brownie and Girl Scout mothers, she started on her list of fellow members at the Hunt Club. She was sure there would be donations of tack and riding habits to benefit her troop's venture.

While the wealthy and elite of Spencer were dealing with their day-to-day traumas, there were those in Van Buren County who were knocking on starvation's door. Not blessed with particularly rich soil and little or no industry, Van Buren County was not proud of the fact that it held one of the highest poverty levels in the State of Tennessee. Bonita's foundation was sure to be a boon to many of the poor there who depended on welfare, Medicaid, food stamps and Aid to Dependent Children programs.

Some, while taking advantage of all of the social programs, also resorted to other methods to make money, although many of them found ways to make a few extra dollars without actually having to find or hold a job. Some crept into the homes of those better off than they and took a few items now and then to pawn.

Others used a small portion of their mobile homes or run-down shacks to manufacture crystal meth and sell it on the streets or the back roads. A substantial number of the teen-age boys of these poor families sold pot and crack while many of the teen-age girls and some of their mothers sold their bodies.

And then there were the parents who rented or sold their children either as child prostitutes or to *star* in child pornography flicks. Those folks raked in a lot of money, but it wasn't the kind of money they declared on their income tax returns, so they continued to take advantage of the dole.

If Bonita and her committee had visited some of those targeted to receive benefits from the magnanimity of The Magnolia Ball Foundation, they would have been shocked to see the interiors of some of the tumbled-down houses and dented double-wides setting askew on their crumbling cinder blocks. The folks who sold or rented their children were *living large* with big-screen televisions, DVD and CD players, Cadillacs parked behind the huts or trailers, and ample food, high fashion clothing, and three-hundred-dollar a pair sneakers for their meal-tickets, the child pornography stars.

The children were often threatened within an inch of their lives not to tell anyone about their activities. In addition to being rented out by their *doting* parents, many of these children were also sexually abused by those same loving couples. The Van Buren Social Services Office had identified numerous sexually abused children, but thus far the social workers were completely in the dark about parents in Van Buren County renting their children to child pornography filmmakers.

Snot-Nose Knowlton was very thorough. As he continued to conduct his audit, he noted Dr. Trace Ricks was listed as the holder of the powers of attorney of thirteen of the First National Bank of Nashville's depositors. He further noted all the Grantors were elderly ladies who were well to do and all were residents of assisted living facilities.

Josh accessed the bank's computer and printed a copy of every transaction Dr. Trace Ricks had made at the First National Bank of Nashville, where coincidentally the doctor had an account. Young Knowlton was particularly interested in those transactions where money was drawn from one of the elderly's accounts and deposited into Trace's or where transfers of funds were made from old ladies' accounts to Trace's account via computer access.

Bonita decided to call each committee member and speak to her individually rather than call an emergency meeting. She realized she had to convince the members to change their votes and to issue an invitation to debut to the Bassin girl. Having had a great deal of experience with groups of women in the past, Bonita felt her chances were better and she could be more convincing if she used her powers of persuasion on a one-to-one basis. Surprisingly, as Bonita spoke to one committee member after another, she met no resistance until she called her ally who had assisted her in getting the ball named for the magnolia—Rhetta.

"No, Bonita, I certainly won't change my vote. A young lady's debut is an important moment for her. I can't see risking having the other girls' evening ruined by Cameron Bassin. What is she were to have that Mexican construction worker present Lindsay Mary?"

"I have been assured Mrs. Bassin will either ask her father, Mr. Rockford, a gentleman of great social standing here in Spencer, or her brother to present Lindsay Mary."

"By whom?"

"By Harcourt Ball. Cameron's late husband and Lindsay Mary's father was one of his law partners, as I'm sure you are aware."

"And has Harcourt spoken with Cameron? She's a wild child. You can't imagine all the crazy things she's done in the past. We all want the ball to be spectacular, Bonita, not a spectacle."

"I'm in absolute agreement with you, Rhetta, but all us committee members have one thing in common—we all want to *hold* the ball. Harcourt has told me if Lindsay Mary doesn't receive an invitation, he will resign from the foundation committee."

"Why would he do that?"

"Because Cameron Bassin has money invested in his firm and sits on the board of the firm. It is Harcourt's contention if Lindsay Mary is not invited, her mother will throw a fit and Harcourt will be placed in a most embarrassing position. After all, he drew up the papers to form the foundation and he is a member of the foundation's board."

"Bonita, Harcourt is blackmailing you and the rest of us on the committee. He's set up the foundation. Let him resign if he wants to. This debutante ball is not going to revolve around Harcourt Ball, the old fag."

"Rhetta, isn't that rather harsh?"

"I don't think so. Everyone has speculated about Harcourt being light in the loafers for years. He never dates and he still lives with mommy. He must be queer."

"His sexual preference is not what this discussion concerns, Rhetta. I, as the founder of the ball, really feel we must keep Harcourt on the foundation's board. Can't you see your way clear to change your vote? Please. As a personal favor to me?"

"I've never liked that Bassin girl. When she was little, she teased Corinne every chance she got. She's got a nasty disposition. I don't want her invited. It'll simply ruin Corinne's evening."

Bonita recalled it was Rhetta who brought up Cameron Bassin's living arrangements. She was the one at the meeting who had been the most adamant about Lindsay Mary Bassin not being included on the list. So, it really didn't have anything to do with Cameron and the Mexican. It had to do with some slight from years back.

"Rhetta, that was years ago. Surely, Lindsay Mary is not going to tease Corinne now."

"I'll have to think about it, Bonita. I'll call you back shortly. I have to run now," and Rhetta disconnected.

"Rhetta Robin Ricks, you twit," Bonita said aloud. "The only reason you're involved at all is because you nearly had a nervous breakdown when you weren't included in my initial meeting.

"I know your luau was arranged for my benefit so I would include you on the committee and now you're balking at not only a very strong suggestion I have made, but you also have to think about doing me a personal favor. Your days in Spencer society are numbered, little lady. No one bucks Bonita, baby, and the sooner you learn that little lesson, the better off you'll be."

Rhetta called Trace at his office and told his receptionist it was an emergency. The receptionist called Trace from examining a patient to speak to his wife.

"Trace, do you remember Lindsay Mary Bassin who used to tease Corinne on the tennis courts at the club?"

"Rhetta, did you tell my receptionist this was an emergency and have me leave a patient to talk about someone who teased Corinne ten years ago?"

"Well, there's more, Trace. Lindsay Mary was nominated to be a debutante, but I convinced the committee she should not be invited because Cameron, her mother, is openly living with a Mexican construction worker who's young enough to be her son. We can't have some Mexican presenting one of the debs. Now, Bonita has called me and wants me to change my vote because Edward Bassin was Harcourt Ball's law partner and Cameron Bassin sits on the board of his law firm—"

"Rhetta, that's enough! I'm running a medical practice here. I thought something had happened to you or one of the girls. *Do not call me at work* to discuss this nonsense! I have to go!"

"Wait, Trace. I only need another minute of your precious time. Do you think I should change my vote?"

"Who cares, Rhetta? For heaven's sake, this debutante ball is not the most important thing in your life, is it? How asinine of me, of course it is. Let the girl make her debut. She's not going to tease Corinne about her tennis game at the Ball."

"Is that what you really think I should do, Trace?"

"Rhetta, I have to go. Good-bye."

Rhetta made a cup of tea and sat on her deck pondering the situation. She loved her feeling of power. Bonita Roberts was asking her for a personal favor. She was firmly entrenched socially and was a member of the debutante committee. She wanted Lindsay Mary Bassin repaid for the times she made Corinne cry. Rhetta marched into her kitchen resolved to call Bonita and tell her she would not change her vote.

Glancing at the television with the sound barely audible, Rhetta was transfixed. There on the screen were Buffalo Bob and Howdy Doody. The history channel was presenting a reprise of children's shows of the fifties. Rhetta watched the screen for a few moments and burst into tears.

All the horrible memories of her childhood rushed back. She recalled the parties to which she had not been invited and had attended anyway, the embarrassment she had suffered, but pretended she hadn't, the lies she had told her parents about her popularity, her feelings of total isolation, and her fervent desire to be liked and included both then and now. Rhetta dried her eyes and called Bonita.

"I'll change my vote. Send Lindsay Mary Bassin an invitation, Bonita."

"Thank you, Rhetta. I'm in your debt."

"No, you're not, Bonita, and neither is Lindsay Mary. I'll talk to you later; the workers are finishing up for the day and I need to talk to them about some changes I'm making in the renovations. Bye, bye."

The following day, after an invitation was addressed to Miss Lindsay Mary Bassin, all of them were posted. A week later after the young ladies who were either away at boarding schools or in their first year of college received the invitations, Spencer was atwitter with talk of who *had* been and who had *not* been included.

Timothy Patman read about the foundation and the forthcoming Magnolia Ball in the *Spencer Spectator* the week prior and commented to his wife what a grand idea it was and it was sure to be a fun holiday season for Cynthia as there was no question his daughter would receive an invitation. After a few weeks passed during which time, both Grace and Tim had spoken with their daughter on the phone and she had not mentioned anything about the Ball, Grace asked her why she hadn't told them about her invitation.

"I haven't told you because I haven't received one, mother."

"Well, I know you were sent one. Perhaps it got lost in the mail. I'll make some phone calls and see what happened. Have you been reading the *Spectator* we send to you each week, darling? It sounds like it'll be loads of fun."

"It does and I'm really looking forward to it. Maybe they didn't put my room number on the envelope. Just the name of the dorm isn't enough information."

"I'll get right on it. We'll plan a shopping trip when you're here for Thanksgiving. You're going to need scads of new clothes and we'll need to discuss your private party."

"I already have an idea for that, mom. I have to go to class now. I'll call later and tell you all about it. Love you."

"Love you too, sweetheart."

Grace replaced the receiver and walked to the den where Tim was watching the evening news.

"Cynthia did not receive an invitation to make her debut at the Magnolia Ball, Tim."

"Why not?"

"I don't know. I finally asked her about it and she said she hasn't gotten one. I told her I was sure she was on the list and I'd check into it. They must have failed to put her room number on the invitation. I'll call Precious Woodson tomorrow and see what the problem is."

"Good idea."

As early as was acceptable, Grace phoned Precious and informed her Cynthia had not received an invitation to debut at The Magnolia Ball as yet and that whoever did the addressing must have omitted her room number on the envelope.

"It's been a problem ever since Cynthia went to Tulane, Precious. For some reason, the post office there won't deliver mail if the address contains only the name of the dorm. Cynthia's room number is one-two-nine. Perhaps the committee should send Cynthia another invitation as it's no telling how long it will take for the first one to be returned by the US Postal Service."

"Grace, I'm going to give you Bonita Roberts' phone number. She's the chair of the committee and her social secretary addressed the envelopes. I think perhaps you should speak with her. Her number is 555-4223. Give Bonita a call, why don't you?"

"Thank you, Precious. I'll call her right away."

They said their farewells and Precious let out a sigh. She hadn't voted to keep Cynthia Patman from making her debut and she had known it was going to cause trouble. Let Bonita handle it. After all, she was the chair. The buck stopped there.

Bonita reached for the phone. Who in the world could be calling at this ungodly hour? Raven wasn't in yet.

"Good morning," Bonita said with the emphasis on *morning.*

"Hello, Mrs. Roberts. This is Grace Patman. My husband is president of the bank here."

"Yes, Mrs. Patman."

"Grace, please. I just rang off from speaking with Precious Woodson and she suggested I call you. Our daughter Cynthia has not received an invitation to debut at The Magnolia Ball. The post office at Tulane will only deliver letters if the room number of the dormitory is included. I was calling to tell you Cynthia's room number is one-twenty-nine and perhaps it would be advisable to mail out another invitation as it sometimes takes forever for a letter to be returned by the postal service."

Oh, thank you so much, Precious, for suggesting she call me.

"Mrs. Patman, Grace, there was no mistake made on an envelope to Cynthia."

"That's odd. Then I can't imagine why her invitation hasn't been delivered.

"She wasn't sent an invitation."

"And why not?"

"Her name was placed in nomination, but she didn't receive the requisite number of votes to be included on the list. It seems there was some problem with drugs last summer that was reported all over the front page of the *Spectator* several weeks running."

"For heaven's sake, Cynthia simply got mixed up with a bad group of kids. She doesn't do drugs, I can assure you, Mrs. Roberts."

"I'm sorry, Mrs. Patman. There's nothing I can do. The committee has voted."

"Who do you think you are, Mrs. Roberts? You blew into town seven or eight months ago and now you're telling me, Grace Patman, who has lived here all my life, and whose husband Timothy is president of the bank, that *my* daughter is not to be included in your debutante ball."

"It's not *my* debutante ball, Mrs. Patman. It's sponsored by the Magnolia Foundation. I don't have a vote as the chair of the committee. I'm sure Cynthia is a lovely young lady, but there's nothing I can do once the committee votes."

"Oh, there isn't? Well, we'll see about that. I'll have you railroaded out of town on a broom, you old witch!"

Grace slammed the phone down in Bonita's ear. Ah, the fun begins. I had forgotten how horrible it was for the parents and the girls who were not invited. Poor Trudy's daughter Sandy killed herself over The Magnolia Ball in Montiac. I can't very well call the committee members again and ask them to rescind a vote after getting Lindsay Mary Bassin on the list. I wonder what Grace Patman plans to do. She's feisty, that one. Old witch indeed!

Timothy was at his desk at the bank perusing the copy of that day's *Spectator* the secretary had placed on his desk when Grace called his private line in an absolute frenzy. She told him about her phone calls to Precious and Bonita.

"Precious bowed out. She didn't have the guts to tell me Cynthia hadn't been sent an invitation, but that old bag Bonita Roberts spelled it out plain and clear. That dipshit committee is not inviting Cynthia because of the drug mess last year. Timothy, you have to do something. Cynthia will be devastated and how will it look if the bank president's daughter is not included in the first Magnolia Ball in the town where our families have lived since before the fricking flood?"

"I'm not sure what I can do, Grace."

"Well you better think of something. Exercise your authority. Call in loans. Foreclose on mortgages. Whatever it takes."

"Grace, may I remind you that the people serving on the committee don't have mortgages or gigantic loans with the bank. For the most part, they're all wealthy, I assume."

"Timothy, this is serious. Cynthia has to be included."

As Grace was speaking, Timothy realized he was looking at a paragraph on the front page of the local paper listing the members of The Magnolia Ball Committee. A name jumped off the page—Rhetta Robin Ricks.

"I'll get right on it, Grace. Calm down. I'll get this straightened out."

Tim placed a call to his friend Harvey, President of the First National Bank of Nashville.

After exchanging pleasantries, Tim said, "I was thinking about our conversation the other evening about Trace Ricks. Anything else come up about that?"

"Interesting you should ask. I just got off the phone with *Snot-Nose.* I guess this thing is going to blow wide open. Ricks has an account here and he's transferred funds from the thirteen widows' accounts into his own on numerous occasions. He's written checks on their accounts that weren't to financial institutions for stock purchases. Supposedly the reason the old ladies gave him their powers of attorney was for him to invest their money for them. Why do you ask?"

"Curiosity. There's been talk around town about the Ricks' big expenditures lately. They're doing a major renovation job on their house RickShaw here in Spencer and they recently returned from a round-the-world trip."

"That *is* interesting. I wonder if the good doctor has been skimming funds from the old ladies."

"It's beginning to sound that way, huh? What is the auditor going to do about it?"

"He hasn't said, but I imagine he's going to make a report to the FDIC. I hope this thing doesn't bring on bad publicity for the bank."

"It won't, Harve. How can it? The bank didn't do anything wrong. With those powers of attorney, Ricks could transfer money and write checks. He's the one who's done something wrong."

"Of course, you're right, but you know how people twist the facts and get everything screwed up."

"Yep, but be thankful you're in the city. You can't fart here without it being in the Local News in the *Spectator.*"

Laughing, Harve replied, "That's the truth. I'll keep you posted on what's going on with Ricks."

"Thanks, I'd appreciate it. Just idle curiosity."

"Of course. And I don't have to remind you, Tim, this has to be kept under wraps."

"No, you don't. Talk at ya later, Harve."

Tim buzzed his secretary. "Hold my calls, Martha. I have to make a phone call and I don't wish to be interrupted."

Tim reached in the bottom drawer for his Spencer Phone Directory and looked up the Ricks' number. He dialed.

"Hello," Rhetta answered.

"Mrs. Ricks?"

"Yes?"

"This is Timothy Patman of the Spencer Bank."

"Hello, Mr. Patman. I hope we're not late with our mortgage payment."

"No, at least I don't think you are. I'm not calling about bank business."

"Oh. How can I help you?"

"I read in the *Spectator* that you're on the Magnolia Ball Committee. Congratulations!"

"Why, thank you, Mr. Patman. Yes, I am."

"Then I'm sure you're aware our daughter Cynthia was not included on the list of young ladies to be invited to debut."

"I am, Mr. Patman, and let me say how sorry I am. I know Cynthia. She's friends with Corinne and River. A lovely girl."

"Why isn't she receiving an invitation?"

"I didn't have a thing to do with that, Mr. Patman. Some of the committee members brought up the unfortunate incident about Cynthia and that drug mess that was reported all over the front page of the local paper for several weeks running."

"Cynthia does not do drugs, Mrs. Ricks. She temporarily got mixed up with the wrong crowd."

"I understand completely, Mr. Patman. If I'd had my say, Cynthia would be included."

"Then you can have your say now."

"What do you mean?"

"Get the committee together and vote again."

"I'm not the chair. I can't call a committee meeting and once the committee votes, the issue is dead, Mr. Patman. I don't see how I can help you."

"Well, then I'll have to show you how you can help me, Mrs. Ricks. I'll help you first. I imagine you're aware your husband has powers of attorney for some thirteen old ladies who are in assisted living centers in Nashville. At least, he is the guardian of thirteen accounts at one bank there. Who knows how many other accounts he handles?

"It seems your husband has been transferring money from those old ladies' accounts to his personal account. He's also been writing checks on their accounts for his, and I assume your, personal use. You see, he's supposed to use those powers of attorney to make investments for the ladies. What your husband is doing, Mrs. Ricks, is called embezzlement. It's also fraud. It calls for serious jail-time. I may be able to help your husband, but I won't lift a finger until Cynthia's name is placed on that debutante list."

"Mr. Patman, I am appalled that you would threaten me. My husband has not taken money from any old ladies. He's a very successful doctor in Nashville with a booming practice. And for your information, he does NOT steal! He's as honest as the day is long!"

"He certainly seems to have a lot more money of late. Previously, when there's been work done at RickShaw, your husband's come in to take out a home equity loan. I understand extensive renovations are being made at your summer home and no one's been to my bank to borrow any money."

"There are other banks, Mr. Patman."

"You're right, but if your husband borrowed any money, he would have to list his mortgage on your home here at our bank and we would have to verify the amount. No paperwork has come in from another bank, Mrs. Ricks."

"Where did you hear this fabrication?"

"I have my sources. Bankers talk to bankers. This thing is huge, Mrs. Ricks. Your husband's activities are about to reported to a federal agency."

"Mr. Patman, I have several items on my agenda today and I'm not going to waste anymore of my time listening to your ridiculous and unfounded accusations. I was sorry Cynthia wasn't included, but if she's anything like you, a despicable liar, I'm glad she won't be making her debut. Good day!"

Rhetta hit the speed dial on her phone and called Trace. The receptionist answered and Rhetta told her it was an emergency.

"I have to speak to Trace right away."

"He's with a patient, Mrs. Ricks."

"Did you hear me? I said this was an emergency. Get him to the phone."

"Mrs. Ricks, please don't be upset with me, but Dr. Ricks has instructed me that should you call with an *emergency,* I am to notify him as soon as he's finished with his patient and he'll call you back."

"I don't believe you. My husband would never do that. Now you get your fat ass up off that chair and march yourself into whatever examining room he's in and get him to the phone now!" Rhetta was screaming.

The receptionist knocked on the examining room door where Trace was tending to a patient.

"What is it?" Trace called.

"Dr. Ricks, I'm so sorry. I know what your instructions are, but Mrs. Ricks is on the phone and she's hysterical. She says it's an emergency and she has to speak to you immediately."

"Tell her I'll call her back within five minutes and don't let her convince you otherwise, Hedda. Rhetta is always having emergencies."

Back at the phone, Hedda said, "Mrs. Ricks, I knocked on the door where Dr. Ricks is with his patient. He said to tell you he'll call you back in five minutes. I'm sorry."

"Fine. You make sure he does or it'll be one of your last official duties in my husband's office. You're history, Hedda."

True to his word, Trace returned his wife's call within the time limit.

"What is it now, Rhetta?"

"Trace, I'll skip to the chase. Timothy Patman, the bank president, called here about his daughter Cynthia not receiving an invitation to be presented—"

"Rhetta, please. I cannot believe you have once again called here screaming like a banshee about that debutante nonsense."

"Listen to me, Trace. He wants me to do something about his daughter not being invited. When I told him I couldn't help him, he said he could help me. Then he told me this long tale about how you had the powers of attorney for thirteen old ladies in Nashville who have accounts in the same bank, a bank where you also have an account. He said you were transferring money from their accounts into your own and writing personal checks on their accounts.

Isn't there something we can do to him, Trace? He's making slanderous statements about you."

"Where did he get his information?"

"I asked him. He said bankers talk to bankers and your transactions are going to be reported to a federal agency. Why would he say those things, Trace?"

"I have no idea, Rhetta. Calm down. I'll call you later. I have patients to see right now. Don't worry. I'll get to the bottom of this and I apologize, sweetie. This really is an emergency. I'll talk to you later."

"All right, Trace."

"Rhetta?"

"Yes."

"I love you."

"I love you too, Trace."

Trace's last words to her would give Rhetta something to hold onto for the next several months for after Trace hung up, he walked into the reception area and told Hedda to cancel his appointments for the remainder of the day. The doctor walked out of the front door of his office in his white jacket with his stethoscope still around his neck and…disappeared!

41

Discoveries for Ridge and Rhetta

A month after his heart attack, Mr. Keyes had recovered as well as could be expected and was home. He was to undergo several months of physical therapy to ready him for a quadruple bypass as soon as he could withstand the operation. Raven was back at work.

For the first few days after her return, she prevailed upon Hannah to continue unplugging the computer at night, but that ploy was to end soon. Isaac was tired of Raven's little tricks. When she left Bonita's one evening, he was waiting for her on the lake road. He pulled her over.

"Raven, I've had enough of your bull shit. I don't know how you're doing it, but I know what you're doing. You've gotten someone in that house to unplug that computer every night. Well, this shit is going to stop."

"I'm not unplugging the computer, Mr. Kahn. And I don't have any control over the situation if someone else is unplugging it."

"Tomorrow, you find out who's unplugging it and you make sure it doesn't happen again! Got that?"

"How am I going to find out?"

"I don't know and I don't care, but let me put this in terms you can understand, Raven. If that computer is unplugged again after tonight, your father isn't going to last long enough to have his heart bypass. Do I make myself clear?"

"Yes," Raven answered and tears began to run down her face.

"Cry all you want, but I'm through playing games with you. Make sure that computer stays on twenty-four-seven!" and he got in his car and drove away.

Raven collected herself once she stopped shaking and made a U-turn on Lake Road. She went to Villagio and told Hannah not to unplug the computer anymore. In fact, Raven explained, it was imperative the computer never be unplugged again.

"All right, Miss Raven. I 'spose you still can't tell me what this is about?"

"I can't, Hannah, but thank you for all your help," Raven said and hugged Hannah.

"You crying, chile? Whatsamatta?"

"Just feeling a little blue, Hannah. I'll be fine. Thanks again. I have to run."

Desiree and Monique watched the tape of the salon all the through again.

"Well, what shall we do, Monique?"

"If you're still not ready to talk to Bonita, I think we should speak to Ridge Dodd. He tried to get Raven to talk. It seemed to me as I watched the tape he knew something. Otherwise, why would he be so interested in Raven and what went on with Kahn? He obviously didn't know her since he introduced himself to her."

"Do you think we can trust him?"

"Trust him with what? We'll simply ask him some questions."

"Monique, you forget how we received our information. We'll have to tell him I spied on my guests."

"Mother, I think there might be something more important going on here than your spying on your guests."

"I guess you're right. Give Captain Dodd a call."

Ridge was intrigued with the level of technology in Desiree's boudoir. He also found the whole idea of Desiree watching her guests hilarious. His interest in Desiree's electronics quickly moved to a back seat however when Monique played the tape for him where he could see and hear clearly Isaac's conversation with Raven.

"There's definitely something afoot, ladies. It's obvious Raven knew Kahn before he moved to Spencer. It's also obvious he's holding something over her head. You saw how frightened she was when I asked her about their conversation. I'm glad you've called me, and believe me, Mrs. Compton, your spying secret is safe with me. I think it's brilliant. I have a little information about Mr. Kahn myself. I did the lighting for him at Les Enfants and learned a few things, but I don't want to trouble you ladies with that right now. I'm not trying to keep you in the dark, but I'd like to do a little more investigating on my own. Then I'll get back to you. Thanks for apprising me of your tape, Mrs. Compton."

"You're entirely welcome, Captain Dodd. Do you think I should warn Bonita?"

"Not yet. Let me do a little checking and see if I can get to the bottom of this. I'll call you soon and we can meet again and discuss our next course of action."

"All right. Thank you, Capt—"

"Ridge, please."

"And call me Desiree and this is Monique."

"I'm not sure I can call a countess by her first name, ma'am."

"You can when the countess insists upon it," responded Monique.

"Then Desiree and Monique, it is. I'll get back to you as soon as I come up with something."

It happened that Ridge was going to have an opportunity to go to Les Enfants sooner than he thought. That afternoon, Isaac called to inform him of an impromptu gathering he planned to have a week hence. He was not only calling to invite Ridge and KD to the party, but he wondered if Ridge might come over a day or two before and make sure everything was ready to go with the lighting since this would be the first time it would be placed on public view.

"I'd be happy to come over and check the lighting, Isaac, and I'm pretty sure KD and I will be able to attend. I'm looking at the calendar and I don't have a flight scheduled, but I'll have KD call you back as she keeps track of our social schedule. I'm not allowed to make those decisions," Ridge chuckled.

"Of course not. I remember that from my married days, Ridge. I'll look forward to hearing from you and I'll see you Wednesday or Thursday to check out the lights. You still have a key, don't you?"

"I do, but I've been wanting to get it back to you."

"I'm glad you have it. Then you can come over at your convenience. You can leave it here when you come."

"Will do. I'll call before I come anyway."

"Good. Thanks and please give my regards to KD and Jean Ann."

"I will."

Ridge decided he wouldn't call Isaac before he went to Les Enfants. He'd conveniently forget. Maybe I'll cruise by his manse a few times Wednesday and try to go in when Isaac's not at home. That way, I can snoop around a little.

On Wednesday, Isaac had scheduled a conference call with Bartie and Jesse on one line and the number one man at his kiddie porn warehouse on another. Early in the morning, Cars Internationale, where Isaac had his Corniche serviced, called to remind him of his eleven o'clock appointment. That was when he scheduled the conference call and Isaac told Chang to take the car in for servicing.

Ridge was approaching Les Enfants when he saw the Corniche pull out and head toward Spencer. He drove on past the mansion's entrance. He didn't want Isaac to see him pulling in just after he pulled out. Ridge made the circle around the lake and then drove to Isaac's home. He parked out front and used his key to open the front door.

Nothing and no one was stirring. He guessed Chang must be in the bowels of the house somewhere attending to his myriad duties. Ridge moved into the great room where he heard Isaac and other voices speaking in hushed tones. He moved closer to the library, Isaac's inner sanctum, and realized Isaac was on a conference call and he was conducting it on his speakerphone.

"The computer won't be unplugged after tonight. I can assure you of that. I made Miss Raven an offer she couldn't refuse."

"Good, because that on again, off again crap with Roberts' computer has been screwing us royally," said another voice.

"How's the order processing end going, Smiley?"

"We're on top of it, boss. *Jack and Jill* is the biggest seller this month. It's flying outta here."

"And production is keeping up?" asked Isaac.

"Absolutely. Everything's running smoothly. Your man in Brooklyn emailed the clients and explained orders couldn't be taken during certain hours because of demand. That just made business better."

"That doesn't mean the computer can be unplugged anymore, Ike," the second voice warned.

"Isaac, Jesse. How many times do I have to tell you?"

Aha, the second voice is Jesse's. So it's Isaac—I wonder why he's so averse to being called Ike?—Jesse, and then there's Smiley, who must be in charge of orders for the kiddie porn.

"Sorry, boss. Forgot."

"And I've already told you the computer situation has been remedied."

"What took so long, boss?"

"Her daddy had a heart attack. She wasn't at Roberts' house all the time, but now she's back at work. I don't know who's been unplugging the damned thing, but I assure you, it will cease starting tomorrow morning."

"Gotcha!"

"Okay. Got new films in the making, boys?" Isaac asked.

Bartie replied, "Some fantastic ones. We made a bunch of new contacts of loving parents who want to rent out their kiddies. Our next film is going to feature a Girl Scout Troop. It's the dirtiest yet. Group kiddie sex. Better than those cookies they peddle, that's for sure!"

"You're a dirty old man, Bartie," Isaac responded.

"And ain't you glad?" Bartie laughed.

"Indeed I am. Everything's good at the Internet Company. Morgan wants to hire more people to go out and sell it to the locals and I keep telling him we don't need to do that," Isaac said moving on to another topic.

"How much does he know?"

"Enough, but not everything. What he knows is he's being paid the big bucks to make sure Bonita's computer isn't identified and to keep his mouth shut about the hacking job. Other than that, he's on a need-to-know basis."

"Good. The less the fewer people know the better, but this is one slick operation and the money just keeps rolling in, hey boss?"

"It does. You're a genius, Jesse."

"Then I guess it's time to ask for a raise."

"How much more money do you want, boy?"

"Always more. I'm learning from the best."

The rest of the conversation was compliments, accolades, and how much money was being made, but Ridge had heard enough. He put it together almost immediately. Isaac and Jesse and Bartie, whoever they were, but he recalled Jesse called when he had answered Isaac's cell phone, were making child pornography films. One of them was entitled *Jack and Jill*

Bonita's computer had been hacked into, he supposed by the genius, Jesse, and Raven was in on it but wasn't a willing participant. Morgan Stansill was running Isaac's Internet Access Company. It was clear Isaac had purchased it only for the purpose of covering up the kiddie porn operation. Stansill, the CEO, didn't know everything, but he must know he was involved in illegal activity. Somewhere out there a warehouse existed where Smiley was in charge. Money was rolling in so this definitely wasn't a small-time operation.

Ridge's first reaction was to wait until Isaac finished the conference call and confront him. He waited a few more seconds and decided that wasn't the best plan. Jesse had called Isaac *Ike* and Kahn had brusquely corrected him. Ridge had the name of one of the films. He quickly headed for the front door while Isaac and the others were schmoozing and took off for his log cabin and his computer.

Ridge began a search that seemed as daunting as looking for the proverbial needle in a haystack. He began by typing *Isaac Kahn* into the search engine. Once he had pulled up information about the man Spencer knew, he further defined his search with a series of plus signs and added the name *Ike.*

He tried child pornography plus the nickname and every possible combination he could conjure. His persistence paid off and eventually, Ridge was looking at a picture strongly resembling Isaac Kahn, but the name in the cut line identified him as Ike Perl. Once Ridge got that bit of information, he pulled up reams of data about the condominium-conversion mogul.

Numerous pictures from different angles were available on the Internet of the man. Ridge found a period of years missing where nothing could be found about either Ike Perl or Isaac Kahn. Kahn had dropped out of sight. *That's when he had the facial reconstruction!*

Ridge thought long and hard before he started his next search. He was an airline captain and was extremely cautious about a number of areas of his life. Airline captains do not want speeding tickets. A DUI on an airline pilot's record is the kiss of death. They will tolerate no drug use in their homes or anywhere around them. They don't drink when they're on reserve or when they have a flight the next morning. Now, of course, there have been some exceptions, but by and large commercial pilots toe the line. They, before all the current problems airlines are experiencing, made serious money and were wont to do anything to jeopardize the big paychecks.

While Ridge's next search wouldn't jeopardize his job the way a DUI would if he at some time dribbled off a runway, one never knew these days if a hacker had gotten into a computer. Ridge was reluctant to look up the child pornography film *Jack and Jill,* but he felt he must to make sure he had his facts straight and his ducks in a row before he approached Isaac.

Ridge took a deep breath and typed in the title of the film. At first, he got lists of thousands of references to the grade school primers and sales of them on e-bay. After winnowing through the material for several hours, he hadn't come up with anything useful. He tried again. He tapped in the title and the words *child pornography*. Immediately, the screen lit up with hundreds of titles of child pornography films, he assumed. And there under the "J" was *Jack and Jill.* He tapped it and an order form appeared on the screen. Ridge hit the escape button. He wasn't about to place an order.

Several weeks before Desiree and Monique alerted Ridge to the salon tape, Candy Martin and her troop held their annual rummage sale. The troop mothers, true to their word, had donated four outgrown Girl Scout uniforms. The uniforms were snapped up immediately. Candy realized she had been right—there were mothers looking for bargains because the uniforms had become so expensive. She looked forward to welcoming at least four new members into her troop in the near future.

Gossip was rife in both Spencer and in Nashville. Dr. Trace Ricks had vanished! Rhetta was beside herself with worry, although she was determined to keep a brave front. She told Corinne and River, who were completely shattered by their father's disappearance, they were going to New York to shop for the debutante season as planned.

"Oh, mother, how can you even talk about the debutante ball? We don't know where daddy is. We don't know if he's all right. We don't even know if he's alive. I'm not going to make my debut. I can't think about something so trivial. Besides, without daddy, who would present me if I did want to go?"

"Don't you worry about that, Corinne. I have loads of friends who would be honored to present you. And you mustn't worry so about daddy. I'm sure he's fine. There must be something bothering him and he needs to get away for a while. I'm sure by the time the ball is held he'll be home safe and sound. Now, it's only two weeks before the tea at the club and we have to get our outfits for the season. We're going to New York next week and shop, shop, shop!"

"Suppose we're in New York and daddy comes home? He won't know where we are."

"Corinne, we'll leave him a note. Besides, I'll have my cell phone with me. If daddy should come home before calling us, he'll call once he's here and reads the note. I'll keep the cell on all the time. No more fussing. We're going to New York."

River and Corinne couldn't believe their mother's attitude. She seemed a little worried, but her social life seemed to take priority over everything else.

Rhetta wrote a check for the hot tub she and Trace had ordered to be installed on the deck of RickShaw the week after Trace disappeared. It bounced. When she called about one account after another, she came to the realization there was hardly any money in them plus Trace had cleaned out her household account in Nashville and their savings account there. Trace's office called her repeatedly saying there was not enough money in the office account to pay the monthly bills or to meet the payroll.

While Rhetta was indeed worried about Trace, she was angry with him too. He had left her and the girls high and dry. She had stopped the renovations on RickShaw. If she hadn't had a little of her inheritance to fall back on she and the girls would be living on the street. She didn't have a lot of her own money left, but she was going to make sure Corinne made her debut. If she didn't, the gossip about Trace would escalate even more. It was already difficult enough for Rhetta to put on a happy face and go into town. She wasn't about to undergo the humiliation of Corinne not debuting.

Rhetta hoped against hope Trace was experiencing some kind of depression and that he had not been embezzling money. So far, she had heard nothing else about the old ladies' accounts or Trace having anything to do with them after that initial call from Timothy Patman.

It did not escape her however that Trace had *disappeared* immediately after her phone call warning him of what Patman had said. She tried not to think about Trace's sudden change of heart about her spending habits and how the money flowed for several months prior to his disappearance.

He'll come home soon and there will be a logical explanation for all of this, I know. He just had to get away. I know he needed to take some money with him, but I'm furious he left us with nothing other than what little I have left from my inheritance. I'll be glad to see him and I know he loves me, but he's going to have to grovel lots and lots to make up for the embarrassment and humiliation he's caused me, not to mention what this is doing to the girls.

42

Tea for Two: Feds and Debs

The federal agents had finished their training and were monitoring the pornography business with heightened scrutiny. They employed any number of ploys including posing as customers. After purchasing films they watched them intently looking for any clues that might lead them to where a film was made or the identity of any children in it. *Cookies for Sale* was released the first week in November and agents were poring over it hour after hour.

Isaac viewed the film and was quite pleased. It was totally immoral and disgusting. He expected it to top all sales records for the year. In addition to raking in an astronomical sum of money, Isaac was heavily involved with the Magnolia Foundation since the welcoming tea for the debs, their mothers, and the committee was to be held at the Spencer Country Club on the Saturday after Thanksgiving. Bonita called Isaac two and three times a day with questions regarding the cave and emergency committee meetings of the foundation's board. She wanted everything to be absolutely perfect.

Saturday, the twenty-seventh of November arrived and the debutantes made their way to the club for the first event of the first debutante season in Spencer, Tennessee. Bonita was duly impressed with the group of young ladies assembled. Lindsay Mary Bassin was a definite stand out and Bonita concluded Harcourt had been right; it would have been mistake not to include her. Cameron Bassin, likewise, was a lovely woman. She was immaculately dressed and coiffed, was well spoken, and was obviously quite intelligent.

After socializing over the refreshments, Bonita tapped her little golden gavel on the podium and asked for the assembly's attention.

"It is my pleasure to welcome all of you here today and to congratulate you young ladies as the first debutantes to make their debut at the first Magnolia Ball. I wish to welcome your proud mothers too. I welcome the members of The Magnolia Ball Committee who have worked long and hard to make this an event all of us will remember for years to come.

"In the past few weeks, I have spoken with all of you, either the debutantes themselves or with the mothers. The committee has prepared a list, which Lydia Henley will pass out, giving the dates for the functions each of you will be giving during this year's season. I am quite pleased, as is the committee, with the proposed social events. There are dinner dances, masquerade parties, a fifties sock hop, brunches, teas, a square dance hoe-down, a Tennessee barbeque complete with all the fixings, an indoor swim party, a dinner following the rehearsal for the ball, and a breakfast after the ball among the festivities planned. We're going to have such fun!

We have compiled a second list with each debutante's name, those of her escort and her presenter along with the phone number of each debutante and parents' numbers too as most of you will be going back to school until the middle of December. Lydia will see that each of you receives a copy of that list also.

"The only other business we have to cover are the rehearsals. We're going to have two. One will be the morning of December twenty-third promptly at ten at the cave. Directions are in your packet. Please be on time. You may dress casually if you wish, but I would suggest the debs bring long skirts as you will have on gowns when you perform the figure called the German. The second rehearsal will take place the evening prior to the ball. We will begin promptly at seven o'clock, so we can finish at a reasonable time for the dinner planned by Cameron Bassin and her daughter Lindsay Mary."

Mrs. Mapleton raised her hand.

Bonita recognized her.

"Bonita, Sherry Luisa's escort won't be here until the day after Christmas. He won't be here for the first rehearsal. What are we going to do about that?"

Several others mentioned their daughters' escorts wouldn't be available until after Christmas either.

"You're right, ladies. I hadn't taken that into consideration. How would the morning of the twenty-sixth work out?"

It was determined the out-of-town escorts were arriving at different times on the twenty-sixth. After much discussion, Bonita changed the schedule so there would be only one rehearsal the day prior to the ball, but it would commence at four in the afternoon rather than at seven and it would be a real work out.

Everyone agreed. More chatting and socializing ended the affair and Lydia went home to write the press release for the first debutante function of the year. As Lydia sat down in front of her word processor, Fred, an FBI agent in Washington, D.C. called to a fellow agent, "Hank, look at this!"

He had paused the *Cookies for Sale DVD* on a shot where a young *Girl Scout* was about to remove her clothing. Fred zoomed in on the cap sleeve of her uniform. Three numbers were sewn on the sleeve. The zoom lens showed the letters clearly. Two, four, and seven!

"We've got something here, Hank. Get in touch with the Girl Scouts of America and find out where Troop 247 is located!"

"I'm on it, Fred."

Within twenty-four hours, Fred and Hank stepped off an American Airlines jet onto the tarmac at Nashville International Airport. They walked into the terminal and headed for the Hertz Rental Car Desk where they'd arranged for a car to be waiting. The two men were whisked to the Hertz lot. Within fifteen minutes they were on their way to Spencer, Tennessee, home of Girl Scout Troop 247. Candy Martin was the troop's leader.

Candy's maid informed her there were two federal agents at the door.

"Millie, you must be mistaken. Why would two federal agents be at my door?"

"I don't know, Miz Martin, but they showed me their badges. They're from the FBI."

"Then they must be at the wrong house. Show them in."

Millie ushered the men into the living room where Candy was watching a horse show on television.

"Just a moment, gentlemen, I must see who wins this steeple chase."

The two men looked at each other with amusement.

After a few seconds, Candy hit the power button on the remote control and stood, "Good afternoon. Forgive me. That was my horse and I wanted to make sure he won. Millie tells me you're from the Federal Bureau of Investigation. I'm sure you must be at the wrong house."

Fred spoke, "Are you Candace Martin?"

"Yes."

He introduced himself and his partner and flashed the FBI badge. Then he said, "And you are the leader of Girl Scout Troop 247?"

"Yes, I am.

"We're investigating child pornography, Ms. Martin, and in one of the latest trash films to hit the market, a child is removing a Girl Scout uniform. There's a number on its sleeve-247."

"That's impossible. None of my girls would be involved in child pornography. Perhaps the filmmakers happened on that number. That's possible, isn't it?"

"It's possible, but we have some pictures here we'd like to show you."

"I don't want to see child pornography pictures."

"You won't. We have shots of the number on the sleeve of the girl's uniform and a close-up of the child's face. We want to know if you can identify her."

They showed Candy the picture of the child first.

"I don't know this little girl. She's not one of my Scouts, I can assure you."

Fred handed her the close-up of the number.

"My heavens! That is our troop number and the patches look authentic. That's how the girls wear their troop numbers. You can see each number is individual and has been sewn on the sleeve, but I'm sure anyone can get the numbers any place Girl Scout uniforms are sold."

"Let's say this is an authentic uniform and these numbers are from your troop. Is there anyway someone other than a Girl Scout could have gotten a hold of that uniform?"

"I don't think so. I don't know why anyone would want to." Candy sadly shook her head and suddenly had a thought. "Oh, dear!"

"What?"

"Every year, my troop has a rummage sale. This year, for the first time, several mothers asked if they could donate their daughters' outgrown Girl Scout uniforms. I said they could because the uniforms have gotten so expensive. I was sure there must be mothers of girls getting ready to fly up from Brownies, that's what we call it, flying up from Brownies to Girl Scouts, who would love to get secondhand uniforms at a good price. Four mothers donated used Scout uniforms and they were among the first items snapped up at our sale."

"Do you know the people who bought them?"

"I knew two of them. Both mothers are parents of Brownies I know are flying up this year."

"What about the other two?"

"I don't recall who purchased them."

"Who else worked at the sale with you? Do you think any of them would remember?"

"I'm not sure. It was frantic. Our sales are so well attended. There were a crowd of people, but I could call the other ladies who helped me and ask them."

"Could you do that now, please?"

"Certainly."

Candy made the calls. "I spoke with Precious Woodson. She was one of my assistants. She said she sold one uniform to Bess Higgins. Mrs. Higgins is a married woman with no children, but she's tiny, tiny, tiny! Precious said Bess wanted it to wear to a costume party. Our sale was right before Halloween. Lydia Henley was my other helper and she said she sold the fourth and last uniform to a woman she thinks might live over in the trailer park near the county line. Lydia said she had seen the woman at previous sales. She doesn't' know her, but she thinks she's from that trailer park—Hillcrest Heights Trailer Park is the name of it."

"How do we get to Lydia Henley's place?" Fred asked.

"I'll write down the directions for you. This is so upsetting. I promise you, I don't know that little girl. None of my Scouts would be involved in anything like this."

"No ma'am. Now how do we find Lydia Henley?"

Candy gave them the directions and showed them to the door. She called Lydia and told her what was going on and said the FBI agents were on their way to see her.

Lydia greeted the two men at the door and ushered them into the living room. They glanced around at the life-sized dolls in amazement, but said nothing. "I'm not sure I can be of any more help to you than what I told Candy. I've seen the woman before. She comes to Scout sales every year. I don't know her and I don't recall why I think she lives in Hillcrest Heights—that's the name of the trailer park, but I'm almost positive she does, although I don't know why."

"Maybe you heard her mention it at the sale this year or in the past?"

"That's possible. I don't know why I feel so strongly about it."

"Could you describe the woman, Mrs. Henley?"

"She's about thirty-five, I guess. She's slender, probably about 5' 4" or 5". She has bleached blonde hair and wears a lot of make up. She wears a lot of bling bling, chain belts and fringe."

"Bling bling?" from Hank.

"Oh, sorry. That's the latest fashion terminology for jewelry."

"Real or fake?"

"I would think faux, sir, for some of the stones were quite large and would be extremely expensive. Oh, one other thing. She has very long fingernails and I think they're real, not acrylic. They're well cared for—painted bright red."

"Did she have a child with her?"

"Not that I noticed. Of course, if she did the child could have been at another area of our sale. It's a huge sale and we have a roped off area with toys, games, and stuffed animals. Often, the children head right for that section while their parents shop."

"Thank you. You've been quite helpful. This woman didn't happen to write a check, did she?"

"No. We don't take checks. It's a cash and carry operation."

"One more thing, Mrs. Henley. Can you direct us to Hillcrest Heights?"

"Certainly, you're actually quite close."

She gave the men directions and called Candy. They talked for several minutes about the troop number showing up in a child pornography film. After exhausting that subject, they moved on to the disappearance of Trace Ricks and that no one had heard a word from him yet, and lastly they discussed the forthcoming ball rapidly approaching and some of the delightful parties they were anticipating.

Ridge called Desiree and Monique and again visited Desiree's bedroom suite and passed on what his investigation had produced.

"Isaac Kahn is involved in and is more than likely the head of a child pornography business. He had someone hack into Bonita's computer and is using it as the mainframe for orders. He's threatened Raven to keep her from telling Bonita, but he needs her around in case there's a computer glitch. Raven is afraid to tell Mrs. Roberts and she's doing what Isaac tells her, I suspect, because he's threatened her with harm to herself or a member of her family. This is bad stuff, ladies."

"I'll have to tell Bonita."

"I wouldn't yet, Desiree. We want Isaac Kahn to get caught. If we tell Bonita and she confronts him, she could be in danger. We also don't want anything to happen to Raven. I think we need to talk to some authorities first. Bonita will probably be called in once everything falls into place, but we'll be able to protect her. You've got the tape. We know she isn't directly involved in this business. I'm going to call the District Attorney's office and make an appointment to speak with him. I should think he'd be quite interested in this information."

"If that's what you think is best, Ridge, but be careful. We certainly don't want Kahn to find out what we're up to or what we know."

"Then I'll call for an appointment and get back to you."

"All right. This is so frightening."

"There's nothing to be concerned about, ladies. No one knows we know anything except the three of us. We're absolutely safe."

"True," Desiree sighed.

Ridge left Desiree's and called the District Attorney's office. He was told by the receptionist who answered the earliest he could get an appointment would be the following Monday with one of the DA's assistants.

"I'd really like to meet with the District Attorney himself," Ridge explained.

"I can put you down for the first of the year if you want to meet with him."

"No, that's way too late. All right, what time should I be there Monday and who will I be meeting?"

The receptionist gave Ridge the information. As soon as there was a break in traffic, he pulled over and entered it in his palm pilot. He'd have to wait until Monday. Pulling out in traffic again, he called Desiree and reported what had occurred.

"I could give the District Attorney a call if you like, Ridge. I was instrumental in helping him get elected," Desiree said.

"That would be great, Desiree. I'd rather to talk directly to him than to an assistant, but he's not available until the first of the year."

"Let me see what I can do. Give me your cell phone number."

Ridge gave her the number and started for home.Jean Ann had a friend staying overnight so he was grilling this evening. Tomorrow night, she would be at her gymnastics class and spend the night at her friend's home. He and KD were planning a quiet evening together Wednesday.

As Ridge neared the edge of town and was about a half mile from turning onto Lake Road, he remembered KD had asked him to stop at the store and get steak sauce. He made a legal U-turn at a stop light and headed a few blocks back to the locally owned *Park-It-And Market.* Ridge picked up the steak sauce and a few other items he'd knew he'd hear about when he got home and went to stand in line to check out.

"Hello Ridge," Harcourt Ball said as he came up behind the pilot with two tomatoes and a head of lettuce.

"Hey there, Harcourt. I see Marietta has you doing the shopping. KD only wanted steak sauce, but I always see a few other things I'm sure we need."

"You're a better man than I am. I hate the grocery store. I'm in and out as quick as possible."

Ridge liked Harcourt Ball. He'd heard good things about him and knew he was an excellent attorney and an honorable one. Maybe Harcourt could give him some advice.

After he paid for his groceries, Ridge waited outside the market for the lawyer. When Harcourt came out, Ridge said, "I wonder if I might ask your advice about something, Counselor. I'm sure this happens to you all the time, but what would you recommend I do if I have material evidence that someone in Van Buren County is involved in an illegal activity?"

"Go to the police."

"That should be my first step, you think?"

"I should think so."

"The illegal activity involves a person of pretty high social standing."

"The police arrest people of high social standing too, Ridge."

"I thought maybe I should go to the DA's office first. This involves Isaac Kahn."

"I see."

"I called the DA's office and have an appointment with an assistant on Monday."

"Be sure you have your ducks in a row then. I must be going. Mother's waiting to make the dinner salad. Nice seeing you, Ridge."

"You too, Harcourt, and thanks for the advice. Send me your bill."

"There's no charge, Ridge. I don't think I was much help."

After Harcourt was home and had poured himself a drink, he excused himself and went into the library. He placed a call to Isaac Kahn, his client.

"Hello," Isaac answered.

"Isaac. Harcourt, here."

"Hello. How are you doing? All ready for the debutante fest?"

"Quite. Isaac, I ran into Ridge Dodd at the market a little while ago. He asked me for some legal advice. It was quite disturbing."

"Oh?"

"He wanted to know what he should do if he had material evidence that an illegal activity was being conducted in the county. When I told him to go to the police, he said it involved a person of rather high social standing. I said the police arrest those people too. Then he mentioned your name and said he had an appointment at the DA's office on Monday."

"What the hell is he talking about, Harcourt? I'm not involved in any legal activity. What is this alleged legal activity?"

"He didn't specify that. What's he talking about, Isaac?"

"You're asking me. I haven't the faintest idea. He did my lighting. He's flown my plane a few times. I don't have a clue what he's talking about."

"Good. Anyway, that's all he said. Just wanted to give you a heads up."

"What did you tell him about the DA?"

"Nothing really other than he should be sure of his facts. Besides, you've told me you're not involved in anything illegal, so what do you care?"

"Right. I don't. Thanks for the tip, Harcourt. I'll see you at *whatever* Bonita has us attending this weekend."

"You will. Good-bye for now, Isaac."

What was Ridge Dodd up to? He didn't know shit from Shinola. Oh, he'd seen a few of the videos and DVD's, but he didn't KNOW anything. What did he have up his sleeve? Well, whether he knew anything or not, he had to be stopped. If he went to the DA's office investigators would start snooping around and one thing would lead to another. Isaac didn't want any hint of scandal attached to his name. What day was it? Tuesday. What did he say when I had dinner there? Ridges said every Wednesday lovely little Jean Ann had her gymnastics class. She wouldn't be home tomorrow night. Good. Isaac didn't want her to be there when her parents had an unexpected caller.

Isaac called Bartie, "I need some help down here."

"What kind of help?"

"A cleaner."

"Whoa! Who you want hit?" Bartie asked.

"Ridge Dodd and his wife KD. They live in a log cabin off Lake Road. It has to be tomorrow night. They have a kid, but she won't be home then."

"That's awful short notice, boss."

"Get it done, Bartie. Everything's riding on this. The airline pilot is on to us."

"How?"

"I don't know, but he told my lawyer today he has material evidence about an illegal activity in Spencer and he mentioned my name. Fortunately of all the shysters he could have picked in Van Buren County to mention it to, he happened to pick the one I have on retainer, so my boy called me and gave me the scoop. Dodd is going to the DA on Monday," Isaac explained.

"Holy shit! Give me the directions to the cabin. I'll have a cleaner in Spencer by tomorrow afternoon. How much you willing to pay?"

"Whatever it takes and he better be here, Bartie. The job has to be done tomorrow night. Both of them taken out. And then the cleaner gets outta here."

"I'll take care of it, boss."

"Good. Copy down these directions," and Isaac terminated the call.

Enid Martin called to her daughter, "Candy, come in here right now."

"In a minute, mother."

"Not in a minute, right now, I said."

Candy appeared at the door of the study, "What is it, mother?"

"Listen to what the man's saying on the idiot box."

The announcer said, "A man found today unconscious in a car on the side of the road in rural Nebraska has been identified as Dr. Trace Ricks of Nashville, Tennessee, a prominent physician who has been missing from his home and his practice for several months. The doctor has been taken to a hospital in Omaha. His next of kin has been notified and the hospital staff is expecting Mrs. Ricks and the couple's two daughters to arrive any moment. We'll keep you posted on this breaking story."

"My heavens! What in the world was Trace doing in Nebraska and why was he unconscious in his car on the side of the road? Rhetta must be frantic."

"I should think Rhetta would be relieved. He's alive and he's been found. What the hell has he been doing since he disappeared?"

"I don't know, mother. He must have suffered some kind of break-down."

"Or done something wrong."

"Why do you say that?"

"Been around a long time, darling, and I've seen this kind of thing before. People disappear when they're guilty. Usually it's an affair or they've stolen money."

"Well in this case, I don't think it's either one."

"Mark my words, Candy. Trace Ricks has either been playing around or he's stolen money."

"I'll keep that in mind, mother. I have to call Desiree."

The telephone/*telewoman* message service began and soon everyone in Spencer who hadn't watched the news knew about Trace Ricks' having been found. The Patmans and their daughter Cynthia were among those who had seen the news program.

"See, the son-of-a-bitch is going to get his now!" Tim Patman shouted.

"A lot of good it's doing us," Grace replied.

"What are you two talking about?" asked Cynthia.

"Dr. Trace Ricks. His wife Rhetta is on the Magnolia Ball Committee."

"I wish you two would quit beating that dead horse. I couldn't care less about the Magnolia Ball or making my debut in this hick town. You said I could make my debut in Nashville in the fall, right?"

"Absolutely, baby. The fix is in," her father answered.

"What fix?"

"That's simply an expression, Cyn. I promise, you'll be invited."

"Then who cares about this stupid little ball here?"

"My sentiments exactly," echoed her mother.

"Trace Ricks is going down. He's embezzled all kinds of money from accounts at Harvey's bank."

"How do you know that, Tim?" asked Grace.

"Harvey told me. You watch, this news is going to be in every paper in the United States when the whole story comes out."

"Well, you really do reap what you sow, I guess," Grace stated.

"Believe me, Ricks is going to rue the day he ever started sowing," Tim said through his grin.

Rhetta, Corinne and River stepped out of a taxi in front of the hospital where Trace had been taken in Omaha. They were bombarded with lights. It seemed every television station west of the Mississippi had sent a news team there.

"What in the world?" Rhetta exclaimed.

Microphones were shoved in her face and reporters began firing questions.

"Were you shocked to hear your husband was found unconscious, Mrs. Ricks?"

"Have you heard from your husband since he went missing?"

"Did you know where he was?"

"Why do you think Dr. Ricks vanished?"

"Has he ever done anything like this before?"

To every question, Rhetta responded "No comment" just as Trace's attorney had instructed her.

She hustled the girls into the lobby where a hospital representative stopped the press.

An aide rushed to Rhetta's side and escorted her and her daughters to an elevator and took them to Trace's room. Trace was lying in bed staring into space.

Rhetta moved to his side, "Hello, Trace."

There was no response.

The girls rushed to their father's bedside and began embracing him and saying, "Daddy, we missed you so much. Where have you been? Are you all right?"

Trace neither responded nor looked in their direction.

Frightened, River turned to her mother, "What's wrong with him, mom?"

"I don't know, dear. You two stay here. I'm going to find a doctor."

Rhetta went to the nurses' station and asked to speak to Dr. Ricks' doctor.

"Dr. Shield's with a patient at the moment, Mrs. Ricks, but we'll send him to Dr. Ricks' room as soon as he's free."

"Thank you."

Rhetta returned to Trace's room. She asked the girls if there had been any response. Both shook their heads. "Dr. Shields will be here shortly."

Rhetta sat beside Trace's bed and took his hand. "Trace, it's Rhetta. Can you hear me?"

Nothing.

When Trace's doctor arrived, he signaled Rhetta to join him in the hallway. After introducing himself, he told Rhetta Trace was in good shape physically, but was in a mild state of catatonia and was not responding to outside stimuli. A battery of tests would start in the morning.

"Why isn't he responding, Doctor Shields?" Rhetta asked.

"We don't know, Mrs. Ricks. It could be he's reacting to a trauma or he could have received a head injury, although there's no outward evidence of that, or he could be in the throes of a complete mental breakdown. I know none of that sounds very reassuring, but we'll know more tomorrow. Now, there's no need for you to stay here tonight. Get some rest and I'll see you in the morning."

Snot-Nose had done his homework and had notified not only Mrs. Baines' attorney, but also the proper authorities. A full investigation of Trace's activities regarding other peoples' money had ensued. The investigation was kept under wraps while Trace was missing. The news of his discovery in Nebraska hit the airwaves and the tangled web of Trace's financial antics began to leak out.

Television stations and newspapers were carrying the story of how Dr. Trace Ricks was discovered unconscious on a country road in Nebraska. Details of his disappearance followed along with information about his financial affairs being investigated.

Reporters gleefully announced it had been learned Dr. Trace Ricks had the powers of attorney of over twenty elderly ladies residing at assisted living complexes in Nashville, Tennessee. There was also speculation about Dr. Ricks having used the ladies' money personally.

Trace lay in his bed fully alert. It had been difficult for him not to acknowledge Rhetta, but it had broken his heart not to speak to his daughters or to respond when they hugged him. He couldn't!

How could I have been so stupid as to drink myself into a stupor and pass out in the car? Thank god, no one thought to check my alcohol level. I have to get out of this hospital tonight. Neither the papers nor television have reported anything about my patients' bank accounts yet, so I think I'm safe so far, but I can't risk being caught at this point. If I can get out of here and stay on the lam for a few more months, I hope this whole thing will blow over. I'll return to Tennessee and rest a few weeks in a private hospital and have a miraculous recovery and proceed as usual. I know I shouldn't have started "borrowing" money from my patients, but hell, they don't need it and it made Rhetta so happy to be able to have everything her heart desired.

A nurse entered the doctor's room and attempted to give him a pill. No response.

"Okay, then, if you won't take your pill, I'll just leave this pitcher of water here for you, but I don't imagine you'll drink any of that either. Doctor, if you don't take some nourishment, we're going to have to hook you up to an IV. Don't want that, do we?"

She stared at Trace, but he didn't move a muscle. The nurse turned and left. She left the door ajar. From a distance, Trace heard a television blaring.

"And now for more breaking news coverage. Dr. Trace Ricks, prominent physician from Nashville, Tennessee, who's been missing for months, was found unconscious earlier today in an automobile on a country road in Nebraska. Our news crew has learned that Ricks is in a catatonic state and that tests will begin tomorrow to determine the nature of his condition. Mrs. Ricks, the doctor's wife and daughter of the former Governor Shaw of the State of Tennessee, and her two daughters arrived in Omaha tonight to be reunited with their husband and father.

"Now that Ricks has been located, an investigation of his financial affairs has come to light. It seems Dr. Ricks was in possession of over twenty powers of attorney from elderly ladies in assisted living facilities in Nashville. Dr. Ricks therefore had access to the ladies' bank accounts. Ostensibly, Dr. Ricks was making financial investments for these patients, however an audit at the First National Bank of Nashville has turned up some discrepancies in the ladies' accounts. More on Dr. Ricks and his finances as information becomes available."

Shit! It's begun. I should have known. You have known, Trace, ever since Rhetta called you. They're onto you. You're going to prison for a hundred years.

Trace lay still until the nurses passed out the evening meds. Slowly, televisions and radios ceased. Visitors left. All was quiet. He crept out of his bed and looked out his door, first to the left and then to the right. No one was stirring. He heard a few voices at the nurse's station. The caretakers were laughing. Someone had told a joke. Trace knew from experience most of the patients were asleep and the nurses, even though still on duty, were taking a break. In an hour or so, they would rouse themselves to go and check on the most seriously ill patients, but unless a patient hit the call button, they weren't moving.

After retrieving his watch and wallet from the wardrobe in his room, he checked the hallway once again and stepped out of his room. He sidled down the hall until he came to a utility room. He opened the door slowly and stepped into the room. The lights were on. He looked around and saw what he needed.

Hanging on a hook was a maintenance uniform complete with a baseball type cap with the name of the hospital emblazoned on it. Trace threw off the hospital gown and got into the clothes. The pants were a little short and the sleeves of the shirt reached his mid-arm. He rolled the sleeves up and looked around for something to put on his feet. There didn't seem to be any shoes about. He opened a locker and found a pair of Doc Martin boots. Apparently someone in the maintenance department was into the punk movement. Trace pulled the boots onto his feet. They were tight and uncomfortable without socks, but this was no time for him to concern himself with creature comforts.

Trace smoothed back his hair, placed the cap on low over his forehead, grabbed a mop and a bucket, pulled open the door to the utility room and strode out of the hospital.

Once outside, he disposed of the utility items and the hat and headed for the highway. By the time the nurses checked his room, he was eighty miles outside of Omaha, having hitched a ride with the second eighteen-wheeler that streaked down the four-lane highway.

In Spencer, Enid and Candy Martin were enjoying an after dinner liqueur when the evening news came on with an opening story about Trace Ricks. When the announcer reported the financial investigation, Enid gave a hearty laugh and said, "*Now*, can I say I told you so?"

43

Bad Times for Spencer

Spencer was in a feeding frenzy with the news of Trace Ricks. It's all Melanie's parents talked about when Jean Ann Dodd spent the night with her friend. After dinner, the two girls and Melanie's parents were involved in a rousing game of Scrabble when the evening news reported the latest news about Trace Ricks. All play ceased as everyone crowded around the television to catch every word. Shortly after, Jean Ann called her parents to see if they were listening to the news, but there was no answer.

"Gee, I wonder where my parents are. They didn't tell me they were going out tonight. In fact, mom said they were going to enjoy a quiet evening at home."

"Maybe they ran out of something and went to the convenience store," Melanie offered.

"Yeah, I guess," Jean Ann replied.

After several minutes of discussion about Dr. Ricks, the four resumed their game until Melanie's mother suggested it was bedtime for the girls for they had school the next day. They were day students at the Spencer School for Girls. Both were in their senior year and both were excited about their forthcoming debuts. Only one more week of school and they would be out for the Christmas holidays and the fun and parties would begin.

While the girls attended classes the next day, Bonita held the final committee meeting prior to the Ball. KD Dodd was not in attendance.

"It's strange she's not here," Lydia Henley offered, "I spoke with her yesterday afternoon. She assured me she was planning to attend. Something must have come up."

"Wouldn't she have called?" Precious asked. "This is an important meeting!"

"No matter," Bonita interrupted. "KD is on the decoration committee. She's been out to the cave. She and her committee have met with Travis on several occasions concerning the theme and what needs to be done. I'll give her a call when I return home this afternoon and apprise her of anything she needs to know about our meeting today."

Jean Ann went to gymnastics practice after school, so she wasn't ready to go home until almost five o'clock Thursday afternoon. She called her mother as soon as she finished practice and before she headed for the showers. That was the system they had worked out. By the time Jean Ann finished showering, dressed, and collected her belongings, her mother would be out front. The phone at the Dodds rang six times before the answer tape picked up.

"Mom, it's me. Guess you went to the store first and you'll be here when I finish showering. See you soon. Bye."

Jean Ann headed for the showers. A few times earlier in the school year, she had called home and the answer tape had picked up, but by the time she emerged showered and dressed her mother or father were outside waiting for her.

Twenty minutes later, Jean Ann left the gym and walked to the campus center where she expected one or both of her parents to be waiting. Neither was there. She sat down on the front steps of the building. Forty-five minutes later when no one had arrived to get her, she started to get annoyed. She crossed back to the gym and called home again. Once more, the answer machine picked up. Jean Ann returned to the campus center and sat on the steps a second time. At seven o'clock when she was still waiting, she went to the phone and tried again. Answer tape. She called Melanie's mother and asked if she would be so kind as to take her home. Her parents hadn't picked her up and they weren't answering the phone. Melanie's mother came immediately.

When they arrived at the log cabin, the lights were on and both cars were in the driveway. "I can't believe it! I think they forgot about me," Jean Ann lamented.

"I've forgotten to pick Melanie up a time or two. We parents aren't infallible, Jean Ann. Would you like for me to wait while you go inside and make sure everything is all right?"

"Oh, no ma'am. They're obviously here. You don't want to wait anyway. It's not going to be a pretty sight when I start fussing at them for forgetting me," she said with a smile. "Thank you so much and I'm sorry to have inconvenienced you."

"No problem at all, Jean Ann. I'll see you Friday at the school Christmas party."

"Okay, I'm looking forward to it and getting out of school. Then the parties can begin. Thanks again. Bye."

Jean Ann ran up to the front door and waved to her friend's mother who was already turning her car around and heading out the long drive to Lake Road. She threw her books on the table in the entrance foyer and yelled for her parents. There was no answer. She noticed a strange odor and headed for the kitchen. There was a pot on the stove burned to a crisp. The burner was on. "Mom! You've burned dinner! Where is everyone?"

Jean Ann turned off the stove, grabbed a potholder and took the pot to the sink where she ran water into it. She turned on the exhaust fan and headed down the hall to her parents' bedroom. The door was shut but light was shining under the door. Jean Ann knocked, but there was no answer. "Where are you guys? No one picked me up at school. Is it all right if I come in?"

When there was no answer, Jean Ann tried the knob and opened the door. She walked into her parents' bedroom and screamed! KD was on the floor nude covered in blood. The girl ran to her mother and knelt beside her. That's when she saw the bullet hole in her mother's temple. A blood-smeared bath towel lay next to the body. Jean Ann couldn't move. She knelt there screaming!

After several minutes, she called out to her father. Again, there was no answer. Jean Ann stumbled out of the bedroom to the den and dialed 911.

"Send someone to 826 Lake Road right away. My mother's been shot! She's dead! I don't know where my father is. Hurry, please!" She hung up and sat on the sofa in the den rocking back and forth as she cried and moaned. Suddenly, Jean Ann abruptly stopped crying. *Suppose the person who did this is still in the house! I have to get Daddy's gun.*

She tiptoed to a gun case at the end of the room and removed the key concealed on top of it. Quietly, she unlocked a drawer in the bottom of the case and removed her father's 357 Magnum. Ridge kept it loaded and had taught Jean Ann how to use it.

She slowly, so as not to make a sound, released the safety, and crept toward her parents' bedroom. Jean Ann was thinking how modest her mother was and she didn't want EMT's and policemen coming in and seeing her mother nude.

She entered the bedroom and looked around to make sure there was no one else in the room, all the while avoiding looking at her mother's body. Gingerly, she stepped over her mother to get to the bathroom where the linen closet was located. Jean Ann wanted to cover her mother with a sheet.

As she stepped into the bathroom, she saw blood on the shower curtain and on the floor beside the shower stall. Trancelike, Jean Ann opened the linen closet and removed a sheet. It was then she realized there wasn't blood anywhere else in the bathroom. This blood wasn't her mother's. Jean Ann dropped the sheet, pointed the gun, and pulled back the shower curtain. There lay her father's body.

Before the scream escaped her throat, Jean Ann fainted. When she fell, she hit her head on the edge of the shower stall. Seconds later, a thin stream of blood trickled down her cheek from her right ear. The 357 was clutched in her hand.

An ambulance and two police cars sped down the tree-lined lane to the log cabin. The police rushed to the door and gave it a cursory knock. When there was no answer, they tried the door. It was unlocked. Three Spencer policemen entered with weapons drawn and started a systematic search of the house. Upon reaching the master bedroom, Sergeant McWithy yelled out, "Got a body in here!" Officer Decatur joined him while the third policeman continued to search the house.

"Shot through the head," McWithy said he surveyed the body. He stepped over her and went into the bathroom. "Holy shit!"

Decatur moved into the bathroom behind him and saw Ridge's body and that of Jean Ann, whom they assumed was also dead. "Who called 911?" Decatur asked.

"The girl."

"What'd think she did? Killed'em, called, and then wasted herself?"

"Looks like it, but I think they've been dead a lot longer than she has. Blood's drying around the woman and on the shower curtain. Hers is fresh. Check for a pulse."

"She's alive!" Decatur said.

"Get the EMTs in here!" shouted McWithy.

The EMTs burst into the room, stepped over KD's body and hurried to Jean Ann. While they were checking her vital signs, Jean Ann regained consciousness. She looked from one face to the other and then turned and saw her father's body. She began to scream hysterically! One of the EMTs administered a sedative. Within seconds, Jean Ann was in *la-la land*. They placed her on a stretcher and headed for Spencer Memorial Hospital.

McWithy called in the station and requested the homicide squad and the county coroner.

Bonita heard sirens on the Lake Road. "What in the world do you think is going on out there, Hannah?"

"Sounds like there must have been an accident. You know how some of them kids races around that lake."

"It must have been a terrible one. That's the fourth set of sirens I've heard going one way and just now, I heard one heading towards Spencer."

The phone rang. Bonita answered and it was Precious. "What in the world is going on? Have you heard all the sirens?"

"Yes. Hannah and I were just discussing it. There must have been a terrible accident."

"I've looked out. I don't see any flashing lights anywhere on the road. I've heard several sirens go by and I just saw an ambulance whiz by on its way to Spencer. I'm going to call Candy. She lives in that direction. I'll call you back."

Precious called Candy, but she didn't know what was going on either. "Something big, though, I guess. So many sirens. I don't think Spencer can stand much more bad news or excitement after the Trace Ricks mess. I feel so sorry for Rhetta."

"I know. Listen, Candy, let me know if you hear what all these sirens are about. I'll give Isaac a call and see if he knows anything."

Precious called Les Enfants. Isaac answered on the second ring. "Isaac, this is Precious. Do you have any idea what's going on with all those sirens?"

"I was wondering the same thing myself, Precious. My guess is there's been an accident on Lake Road."

"That's what Bonita thought, but I have a pretty good view of the area and I don't see any flashing lights. It sounds like they might have been going north of your place—up near the Dodds' house."

"I couldn't tell where they were going, Precious."

"An ambulance went by here a few minutes ago heading for Spencer. Let me know if you hear anything, Isaac."

"I certainly will, Precious, and you do the same."

"By the way, Isaac, this is none of my business, and I've never mentioned it to you, but whatever happened after your meeting with Jesse and Bartie? And again, I apologize."

"Nothing to apologize about and nothing happened. They had a business deal to discuss, but I didn't want to get involved with those people."

"How did you get them to leave? They were so insistent on meeting you and were sure you'd go along with their deal."

"They're small time thugs, Precious. I have my methods. Anyway, they left happy. There were no hard feelings and there's nothing for you to worry about. I'll call you if I hear what's going on down the road."

"Thanks, Isaac. Talk to you later."

When Spencer awoke the next morning and heard on the early news about the double homicide on Lake Road, its citizens were in total shock! Ridge and KD Dodd were two of the nicest people in Spencer. Who would have wanted to harm them? The townspeople were speechless! That is, with the exception of two. Isaac Kahn, of course, wasn't surprised. Desiree Compton was indeed surprised, but when her shock subsided, she thought she knew what had happened to the ill-fated couple.

"Monique! Monique!" Desiree called at the top of her lungs.

Her daughter ran into her room rubbing the sleep from her eyes. "What is it mother? Are you all right?"

"Sit down, Monique. I couldn't sleep, so I turned on the television to watch the six o'clock news. Ridge and KD Dodd have been murdered!"

"What?"

"Their daughter Jean Ann spent Wednesday night with Melanie Harris and didn't get home until last night after seven. She found her parents murdered. Her mother's body was lying on the bedroom floor and her father's body was in the shower stall. A pot of potatoes had burned up on the stove. The burner was on. There was no sign of forced entry. According to the news report, the child said her parents never locked their doors because where they lived was so isolated and remote."

"My god!"

"We know who did this Monique."

"We do?"

"Isaac Kahn."

"Mother, you're jumping to conclusions. Why do you think Isaac Kahn did this?"

"Because Ridge was going to the DA on Monday with what he knew."

"But Isaac Kahn didn't know that."

"How do we know he didn't? You know how news travels here"

"No one else knew, mother. No one except the three of us."

"Someone did. I know Kahn did this or had it done as sure as I'm lying here."

44

The Feds Move in

Fred and Hank, the two FGI agents, parked in front of the office for the Hillcrest Heights Trailer Park and went inside. They flashed their badges to the manager, one Cyrus Dobson. "How can I be of help to you boys?" Dobson asked.

Fred placed a still shot of the child featured in *Cookies for Sale* and asked, "Ever seen this child?"

"Of course, I've seen her. That's Little Tamsy Dawn Swift. She lives here in the park with her mother."

"What's her mother's name," Hank asked.

"Tammy Dawn Swift. Cute, huh? Tammy Dawn and Tamsy Dawn. What do you want with them?"

Fred spoke, "Which trailer is theirs?"

"It's 1716 on Avenue B."

"How do we find Avenue B?" Hank asked.

"Take a right out of here. That's Street A. Go to the second right. That's Avenue B. First right is—"

"Avenue A, I bet," Fred said.

"You got it. What'd you want with'em?"

"Thanks," and the two men headed for their car.

Cyrus called Tammy Dawn. He knew the attractive single mother quite well and occasionally he paid for her favors if things were slow in the trailer office.

"Yeah?"

"Tammy Dawn, it's Cyrus."

"Not tonight, sugar, I'm bone tired."

"I ain't calling about that. Tammy Dawn, two FBI agents just left this office and they're on the way to your trailer. Get out!"

Tammy Dawn threw down the phone and yelled to her daughter to get in the car.

"Where we going, momma? Can we go to Dairy Queen and get a blizzard?"

"Get in the car!" Tammy Dawn said as she pushed the child in front of her, grabbed the keys and headed for the car. She got the child in, slammed the door, ran around to her side, fired up the engine, and started out the driveway. A black rental car pulled in and blocked her.

"Shit!"

Both agents exited their car and went to opposite sides of Tammy Dawn's. Fred signaled her to lower her window.

"Mrs. Swift?"

"Yeah?"

"Step out of the car, please."

Tammy Dawn got out of the car and Fred cuffed her as Hank read her rights. Fred said, "We're placing you under arrest for contributing to the delinquency of a minor, child molestation, and white slavery."

"Are you nuts?"

Fred walked her over to the black rental car, told her to lower her head and locked her in the back seat.

Hank assisted Tamsy Dawn out of the car. "What shall we do with her, Fred?"

"We're taking her with us, Hank. She has to be questioned too."

"Right." Hank led the child to the car, unlocked the door, and put her in the back seat next to her mother.

Fred backed out of the driveway and radioed the local sheriff's office. He told him who he was and said he and another federal agent were in Van Buren County on an undercover operation and they had made an arrest. He requested a room at the sheriff's office where they could conduct an interrogation. He further stated they would more than likely need a cell at the sheriff's office until other arrangements could be made.

Sheriff Bendleton told them to come on in and he'd see they got what they needed. *Only one year of my term left and I'll retire with thirty-four years under my belt as the Sheriff of Van Buren County. Thirty-three years with nothing more than a few drug busts, some bad checks, settling domestic squabbles and one shooting when Travis' wife offed Darling Huxtable. Hell, that didn't even take an investigation. Cut and dried. No one to prosecute 'cause Estelle whacked herself a half an hour later. My final year in office and I'm in the middle of a man-hunt for Trace Ricks, the investigation of a double homicide, and now the feds are here on an undercover operation. Sweet Jesus! What else can happen?*

The agents questioned Tammy Dawn until they were blue in the face and she denied any and all charges. She declared she had no idea what the two men were talking about. The only admission she made was she had bought a Girl Scout uniform at a rummage sale in Spencer because Tamsy Dawn wanted to join the Scouts.

"Where is the uniform now?"

"In Tamsy Dawn's closet."

The men left Tammy Dawn in the dreary examining room and took the child in another. They questioned her for hours. The child didn't speak. She either nodded or shook her head and she wouldn't look at the two men.

They asked her if her mother had taken her to make films. She shook her head.

They asked if she had been hurt, if people had touched her private parts, if she knew what she was doing was wrong, if she knew her mother was bad for letting her be in the films, and on and on. The child admitted nothing. At last, Tamsy Dawn said she was thirsty and sleepy. She asked for a drink of water.

"We'll get you a nice big drink of water or a milk shake or a soda or whatever you want, Tamsy Dawn, and we'll let you go to sleep, but you have to tell us something we want to know, okay?"

Tamsy Dawn nodded.

"Did anyone hurt you when you made that film?"

"I can't talk about it," the child responded.

"Why?"

"Because I'm not allowed. I can't."

"Who told you not to talk about it?"

"The men."

"What men?"

"The men who made the movie."

"And your mother?"

"She didn't tell me not to talk about it."

"Your mother took you there, didn't she, to make the film?"

"No."

"Who took you?"

"I can't tell. I'm so thirsty. I've answered lots of questions now. Can I please have a glass of water?"

Fred and Hank decided to give the kid a break. They took her out to the reception area of the sheriff's office and asked the deputy to get her a glass of water and to find a place for her to lie down. Fred stepped outside to smoke a cigarette while Hank poured himself a cup of the county coffee that tasted as if it had been in the pot for a century. Ten minutes later, the two men started in on Tammy Dawn again. The child's mother continued to profess her innocence.

As light was dawning, Fred finally came up with the question that would eventually break the case. "Where is Tamsy Dawn's father?"

"He lives four trailers down from us."

"And you're divorced?"

"No. We never married."

"And does he have anything to do with the child?"

"He has her every other weekend. He's a good daddy. Almost every time he has her, he takes her on a trip. He took her to New York a couple of months ago. He provides for her real good too. He gives me money for her clothes and food and some extra every month. He's always on time with the money. I'm a lot better off with him for her daddy than a lot of my friends who're divorced. The courts award them child support, but most of'em don't pay. Bennie pays every month."

"Do you think Bennie is at home now?"

"I reckon so."

"We're going to keep you here for the moment, Tammy Dawn. We can hold you for seventy-two hours without cause. I apologize, but we're going to put you in a cell. Tamsy Dawn can stay in there with you unless you have someone who can care for her until we can question Bennie. On the other hand, until we question him, we would prefer to keep her here so he cannot communicate with her.

"All right. I ain't partial to getting locked up, but I don't want nothing to happen to my baby. Has Bennie done something bad to my child?"

"That's what we going to find out, Mrs. Swift," Fred answered.

Cyrus Dobson didn't have any use for Bennie, so he didn't bother to advise him two federal agents had left the trailer park with his kid and her mother. The next morning, Cyrus wasn't surprised when he saw the agents heading down Street A again. He guessed Tammy Dawn had told them where Bennie lived. The trailer park manager watched as the black car returned from Avenue B with Bennie in the back seat.

45

Ball—Yes or No?

Bonita didn't know what to do. She wasn't sure whether to proceed with the Ball so shortly after the death of the Dodds of to postpone it. Of course, Jean Ann would no longer be debuting. Bonita spoke to Rhetta after Trace's disappearance and Rhetta assured her Corinne would be participating. Bonita had to hand it to Rhetta. She had guts. On the other hand, Bonita realized what Rhetta was doing. She was keeping up appearances. Now that the financial scandal was in the news, she wondered if Rhetta was still planning for Corinne to make her debut. Bonita picked up the phone and called RickShaw. Rhetta assured Bonita Corinne would be debuting.

"Isn't it such a tragedy about Ridge and KD Dodd, Bonita? I feel so sorry for Jean Ann. Who in the world could have done such a thing? There are all kinds of reports going around town. Some say it had to be someone they knew. Others think it was a contract job. Why would anyone put a contract on such nice people?" Rhetta talked a mile a minute.

Bonita mused about something good coming from everything. Rhetta had something to talk about and so did the rest of Spencer. Maybe they would lay off Trace Ricks for now and move on to this new topic.

After chatting with Rhetta, Bonita called the other committee members and asked their opinions. Everyone agreed the Ball should proceed with a moment of silence before the presentation in memory of Jean Ann's parents. Desiree concurred, but seemed distracted. *Oh, well, Desiree won't be at the Ball anyway, but she sounded odd.*

By Sunday following the deaths of the Dodds, all the young ladies to be presented were home from their various schools and colleges as the halls of academe were on Christmas break. On Wednesday, the first party was held. The 2004 debutante season in Spencer, Tennessee, commenced! And there was plenty to talk about if there were the slightest lull in the cocktail chatter.

Rhetta hung up the phone. There was another problem she'd been wrestling with for weeks. Corinne didn't have an escort for the Ball. The girl had never had a date. Prior to Trace's escapade, Rhetta thought of several young men from nice families that could be enlisted to escort her daughter, but now, she didn't know. It would be horrid if Corinne asked one of them and they refused her because of Trace's shenanigans.

After racking her brain, Rhetta decided that the only thing to do was to hire an escort. She could give him any name she wanted. The escort would be briefed on what was expected of him. He could stay at RickShaw in the maid's room, which wasn't being used at the time. Rhetta had very little money so she was doing her own housework these days. Good mother that she was, Rhetta was going to use her last few shekels to *pay* for her daughter's happiness.

Rhetta placed a call to an escort agency in Nashville. She questioned the receptionist at length to make sure the escorts were discreet, skilled in social mores, and that no one would know she had hired the young man to escort her daughter.

Rhetta asked the agency to email her pictures of several of the available young men. She perused them and selected the handsomest of the bunch. When she spoke with the agency again, she gave them her credit card number, told them the dates the young man was to be in Spencer, the apparel he would need to bring, and yes, she understood she had to pay for his clothing and transportation too.

Rhetta instructed the young man was to give his name as Robert Whitney Hartington, III. He was to introduce himself as the son of Rhetta's dear friend, Beverly Whitney Hartington of Savannah, Georgia and he and Corinne had been *friends* since childhood. Further, he was to say he had recently returned to the United States after serving two years in the Peace Corps in wherever, but he should do some research about the place he selected, and would be attending UCLA in the fall. Rhetta was hoping there would be no one else at the Ball remotely connected to *the land of fruits and nuts.*

Once the arrangements were made, Rhetta informed Corinne she had spoken with her dear friend Beverly from Savannah and her son Robert, recently returned from two years in the Peace Corps, would be arriving in Spencer two days hence to escort her to the season's festivities and the Ball.

River asked, "What's his name?"

"Robert."

"I've never met him," pouted Corinne.

"You surely have. The two of you used to play together before Beverly and her husband moved to Savannah. Once you see him, Corinne, I'm sure you'll remember."

"I don't think so. I don't remember anyone named Beverly. What's their last name?"

"Hartington. Surely you remember them Corinne."

"I don't. Where did they live?"

"Up the street. Beverly and Robert used to be at our house all the time. You played with Robert almost everyday before you started school."

"I don't remember him or her. Mom, do I have to do this? I don't want to make my debut. Daddy's gone again and people are lying about him taking money from old ladies. I'd want to stay home."

"Corinne, you are the granddaughter of the former Governor of the State of Tennessee. It is your social duty and your obligation to your good name, your family, and to me, to make your debut."

"I already made my debut in Nashville in September when daddy presented me. Why do I have to do it here with daddy missing and an escort I don't remember. At least in Nashville, the escorts were from the Citadel and none of the girls knew them beforehand."

River spoke, "Give it up, Corinne. You are the granddaughter, blah, blah, blah. Don't you know how important this is to mother? It doesn't matter what you want. Can't you get that through your head? The Magnolia Ball is not about you. It's about Rhetta Robin Ricks, daughter of blah, blah, blah—"

"River, go to your room. Now! And don't come out until I tell you, young lady!"

River threw down the magazine she was perusing and stomped to her room. She couldn't believe her mother was insisting poor Corinne do this. River had always thought her sister was pathetic, but she had come to realize her mother was even more so.

Marietta Ball was in the kitchen when Harcourt returned from his day at the office. "How was your day, son?"

"Fine, mother," Harcourt responded, but Marietta knew better.

She took off her apron, handed her son a Mai Tai and said, "Let's sit down in the study and enjoy a drink before dinner."

Harcourt removed his jacket, took the proffered drink, and joined his mother.

"Something's the matter, Harcourt, and don't deny it. I can always tell."

"Only the usual, mother."

"I don't think so. You haven't been yourself since you heard about the Dobbs' deaths. What's going on with you?"

"Really, mother, just the usual. I'm a little tired with all the debutante business and staying out late night after night plus I have a few sordid divorce cases coming up."

"Harcourt, I'm your mother. What is it?"

"All right, mother. Let me put it another way. I don't want to talk about it. It comes under lawyer/client privilege."

"And who am I going to tell?"

"It doesn't matter if you're going to tell anyone or not. My lips are sealed."

"Would it make you feel better if you could talk about it?"

"That's not a consideration. I can't."

"You could talk about it if you didn't name names."

"In Spencer? I think you could put two and two together."

"What's the difference? You're my son. That's a stronger bond than lawyer/client privilege. My lips will be sealed tighter than yours ever were."

"You are so persistent. Why won't you take no for an answer?"

"And aren't you glad you inherited that quality from me? That's what makes you so tenacious and unbeatable in the courtroom."

"You win, mother. Besides, I'm too tired to argue with you. I ran into Ridge Dodd at the market Tuesday afternoon. The coroner places his time of death as Wednesday evening. He mentioned that he had material evidence about an illegal activity involving Isaac Kahn."

"What illegal activity?"

"Mother, I'm telling you information I'm bound not to, but I'm not going to answer questions. As it turned out, I don't know what illegal activity, for which I am truly thankful. As soon as Ridge mentioned Isaac, I said I represented Kahn and could not discuss anything about my client with him. He tole me he had an appointment at the DA's office on Monday. He asked if I thought that was a good idea. I had suggested he go to the police. That's when he told me who the suspect was. I concurred the DA's office was the place to start since he felt he had material evidence."

"That's it?"

"That's it."

"I don't see a problem."

"I'll *ask* you a question then. Let's say you represent a client. A person runs into you at the supermarket and says he believes that client is involved in an illegal activity. You tell the person you can't discuss anything about your client with him and send him on his way. What do you think you might do next?"

"Hmmm. The lawyer/client privilege didn't extend to Ridge, did it, because he's not your client and he didn't come to see you in your office to retain you?"

"That's right."

"I imagine I would give my client a call."

"You would?"

"I think so. Did you?"

"Yes."

"I still don't see the problem."

"Suppose Isaac Kahn is involved in an illegal activity. I told him what Ridge said and he'd made an appointment at the DA's office Monday."

"What did Isaac say?"

"He assured me that there was no truth to Ridge's accusations and thanked me for calling him."

"And now you think Isaac might have had something to do with Ridge and his wife's deaths?"

"I don't know if I think that or not."

"But it's worrying you."

"Yes, it is. We don't really know anything about Isaac Kahn, do we?"

"No, we don't, but I think you're jumping to conclusions, Harcourt. The coincidence of the timing is what's bothering you. I doubt very seriously Isaac Kahn jumped in his Rolls Corniche and motored over to the Dodds' log cabin, killed them, went home, and ate dinner."

"I doubt that also, mother, but the man is absolutely loaded. You wouldn't believe the assets at his disposal. What would prohibit him from hiring someone to do the job?"

"Where would he find someone in Spencer to commit murder for hire?"

"He wouldn't have to find someone in Spencer. He owns a plane. He could have sent it for a hit man. I'm sure he has contacts all over the world. He didn't suddenly spring up from a cabbage patch in Spencer one lovely spring day."

"Harcourt, you're an attorney and a damned good one. You always look for hard evidence. You hate circumstantial cases and you don't have any circumstantial evidence here. You have coincidental musings, but no evidence."

"You're right, mother. I simply can't shake the idea that somehow my phone call to Isaac may have been the catalyst in the death of the Dodds."

"Tragic as their deaths were, you were not involved, Harcourt, and I don't believe Mr. Kahn was either."

"Then I'll yield to your intuitive instincts, mother. They've always been much better than mine."

"Good, now let's dine. I've prepared a marvelous coq au vin."

"My favorite. Thank you, mother, for getting me to talk to you about this. I do feel better and even though I shouldn't have mentioned any of this, I know you'll never breathe a word."

"You're right, darling, I won't."

46

The Rehearsal and the Chase

It took hours of questioning Bennie and Tamsy Dawn, but Fred and Hank finally broke them both. Bennie had been renting Tamsy Dawn out for pornographic films for six months. An aficionado of them himself, he had responded to an ad in one of his smut magazines announcing auditions for children to act in the films. Once he called the number, he was assured if Tamsy Dawn were selected (fat chance she'd be rejected) she wouldn't actually be touched or harmed in anyway. "All the dirty stuff is done with computer imaging these days," the voice on the other end of the line explained. Bennie was told the pay scale, how the children were protected, that he'd never get caught, and a hundred other lies.

Bennie took Tamsy Dawn to New York the next weekend to meet the *producers.* Tamsy Dawn was a pretty little thing and the trash purveyors were thrilled with her looks. They *starred* her in several films and paid Bennie handsomely.

Tamsy Dawn didn't seem to mind. When Bennie asked her about what she did and what happened at the filmings, she always said everyone was nice to her. Bennie warned his daughter not to tell her mother or anyone else about the films. "We'll keep this out secret, baby, and one day you'll be a movie star living in Hollywood in a great big house with a swimming pool and tons of money. Won't that be fun?"

"Can I take mommy with me when I move to Hollywood?" the child asked.

"'Course you can, doll. You'll be able to do whatever you want."

Tamsy Dawn smiled. She loved her daddy. She loved her mommy too and prayed every night for the day when all three of them could be together as a family. Maybe that would happen if she kept making the films and became a star. Then they could all move to Hollywood together.

Bennie gave Fred the number in the ad he had called for Tamsy Dawn's *audition.* Bennie knew only the first names of anyone where he dropped Tamsy

Dawn off for filming. The child didn't know any last names either. Bennie provided the address where the filming took place. The agents read Bennie his rights and arrested him. The Sheriff incarcerated him. Fred and Hank drove Tammy Dawn and Tamsy Dawn to Hillcrest Heights and warned them to keep mum. "If one word of this gets out, Mrs. Swift, we'll be back and lock you up so fast, it'll make your head spin," Fred cautioned as he let the two out in front of their trailer.

Fred leaned out the car window, "Mrs. Swift, would you get the Scout uniform out of the closet and bring it out here, please?"

"Yeah."

She was back in a flash, "It's not there."

"Did you ask your daughter if she knew where it was?" Fred asked.

"No. Tamsy Dawn, come out here please."

The little girl came out of the trailer door toward her mother.

"Do you know where your Scout uniform is?"

"Uh-huh."

"Where?" her mother asked.

"It's at daddy's."

"What's it doing there?"

"Daddy told me to get it. I wore it in the movie."

"Thanks, Tamsy Dawn," Fred said and put the car in reverse. The agents weren't out of the trailer park before Cyrus was on the phone to Tammy Dawn. "What the hell was that all about?"

"Nothing."

"What'd you mean nothing? You been gone two days. They came here and got Bennie yesterday. Why ain't he back?"

"It was a case of mistaken identity, Cyrus, and I don't know where Bennie is. It's not my week to watch him."

"Don't lie to me, Tammy Dawn. Those feds showed me a picture of Tamsy Dawn. It wasn't no case of mistaken identity."

"I can't talk about it, Cyrus. We're back. We're safe. Everything's okay. Don't ask me any more questions."

"Tammy Dawn, you can tell me. I thought we had a little understanding."

"The only understanding we got, Cyrus, is when you want your rocks hauled you call me and I charge you fifty-dollars. I understand you get horny and you understand I charge for my time. I have to go now," and she hung up.

Well, I'll be damned. Ain't she the high and mighty one? What the hell is this all about, I wonder? And where the dickens is Bennie? Federal agents. That's heavy-duty shit. This ain't no little misdemeanor crap!

Fred called the home office, told them what he'd found out and gave them the address and phone number he'd gotten out of Bennie. The home office said they'd send agents to the address right away, concurrently check out the phone number and get back to him as soon as they had something. Fred picked up Hank at the Sheriff's office and they headed for their motel and their first opportunity to eat or sleep in almost forty-eight hours.

The FBI agents in New York burst through the door of the address Bennie provided and were fortunate enough to witness a child pornography film in the making. Technicians and adult actors recognized the two men as cops. Filming ceased and some headed for back exits and windows. Back-up for the agents were posted outside and as those involved with the film company began making their exits stage left, stage right, downstage, and upstage, waiting agents took them into custody.

After extensive questioning, the only information gleaned was that once a film was *in the can,* the editor of the porno film fed-exed it to a post office box number in Tulsa, Oklahoma. The head office notified agents in Tulsa who went to work in an attempt to locate the post office box and its owner.

Meanwhile, in Spencer on Lake Road, Bonita's computer hummed on and orders were processed practically at the speed of light. Raven sat at the computer and tried every search she could think of to find out what was lurking in the memory banks of the computer sitting in front of her. So far, she had been unsuccessful.

Raven was surprised she was able to function at all. She was so shaken by the Dodds' death and she couldn't help but think Ike had something to do with it. She recalled that nice Captain Dodd asking her about her conversation with Ike at Desiree's salon. She hadn't told him anything, but it seemed to her he had known something about Ike. She certainly wouldn't put it past Kahn as Raven considered Ike the devil incarnate *and* he had threatened her father's life if she didn't keep the computer plugged in. More than anything, Raven wanted to confide in Bonita, but she was so afraid of Ike and what he could and would do.

People were tense in Spencer. They were edgy about the murders. Everyone was double-checking their doors to make sure they were locked. There had been a run on security systems and some of the wealthiest folks around the lake had hired security guards. Even with the citizens' concerns and fears, The Magnolia Ball continued to loom. It was only one day away. While most of Spencer was reeling from the shocking deaths, the upcoming festive event was paramount on the minds of Spencer's elite.

Robert Whitney Hartington, III, had arrived days before to escort Corinne. He was indeed a handsome young man and played his role to the hilt. He was courteous and gallant to Corinne, so much so in fact that she was beginning to *recall* their happy times together as children. Rhetta was quite pleased with him. Rhetta's cousin, son of her father's brother, Ashton Shaw, was arriving from Charlottesville, Virginia, that afternoon for the rehearsal and the Ball. He would be presenting Corinne since Trace remained among the missing.

Isaac called Bonita the morning of December 27th and asked if he might escort her to the rehearsal that afternoon.

"Thank you, Isaac, that will be delightful. I didn't know you were planning to attend the rehearsal."

"I think I should, Bonita. Poor Ridge Dodd was going to accompany me to make sure the lighting was up to snuff. We had already discussed it. I've placed a call to Home and Garden Light Design. They installed the lights in the cave. I asked them to have a technician there for the rehearsal, so if you want any changes he can make them before tomorrow night. I want the Ball to be perfect."

"Thank you so much, Isaac. I want it to be perfect too and you've done everything possible to make that a reality. Have you seen the press we've been getting in the Nashville and Knoxville newspapers? I hear Nashville is sending a television crew tomorrow evening."

"That certainly is exciting. Well, I'm happy for you, Bonita. This is a wonderful idea of yours and you've worked so hard on it. It'll be fantastic! I'll see you later this afternoon."

"I'll be waiting," Bonita cooed.

Isaac smiled. He thought his reference to Ridge Dodd had been inspired. He wanted to take advantage of every opportunity to remind anyone in his presence the two of them had been friends. Isaac's funeral spray was the largest and most lavish at the double funeral. He attended the service and sat in the pew behind Jean Ann and the relatives of the couple who had come to Spencer from near and far. Jean Ann left the day after her parents' funeral with an aunt and uncle who lived in Hilton Head, South Carolina. The log cabin was to be cleaned and put on the market once the murder investigation was concluded. Thus far, there were no suspects. And no clues.

There never are any clues with a good, clean hit. Bartie definitely hired a pro. In and out. A stranger kills two strangers. Who's to find out?

One hundred thousand dollars was a little steep, but a small price to pay to keep Mr. Blabbermouth from going to the DA. Now some would wonder why I had KD taken out too? Insurance. Who knows what Ridge told her? I bet neither of them discussed anything with their pretty little daughter. People don't like to upset their kids. But I had to figure Ridge told KD about his plan to go to the DA and why. You buy a hit, you purchase insurance same as with a house or a car. You protect your investment. And since the pilot didn't make it to the DA's office, everything's copasetic.

The Magnolia Ball's the thing! Once that ball is held and the Spencer crème de la crème sees my cave and the bucks I dropped on it to make their shindig the swishiest in the South, I'll be the man in Van Buren County and eventually in Tennessee society. Then all of the dreams of the little Jew boy from Yemen will have come true.

Bonita took the stage at the rehearsal with her gold whistle around her neck. She explained how prior to the presentation the girls would be in a small *room* of the cave adjacent to the ballroom.

There was a stool covered in lovely fabric with each debutante's name embroidered on her personal seat, gifts from The Magnolia Ball Committee. The stools would provide the young ladies with a place to rest until each name was called.

The presenters and escorts were to be in yet another adjacent room. The girls and the fathers and escorts were to go to their assigned areas following dinner. Bonita would ascend to the stage. The orchestra would play a fanfare segueing into soft music. Bonita would introduce the first young lady.

The debutante was to exit the room, meet her father and her marshal and proceed toward the stage. As the young lady and her father moved onto the stage, the marshal was to pass below the stage and wait for her presentation. After a debutante was introduced and presented, she and her father were to descend the stairs. The first young lady presented and her father was to stand to the left below the stage with her presenter. Her marshal was to move to her right side.

The second girl would proceed to the right of the stage after descending the stairs and the girls were to continue to alternate left and right. Once all had been presented, the orchestra would segue into the music for the German, the figure Bonita was about to teach the youngsters.

Bonita suggested everyone take seats at the tables and when she blew her whistle, it would signal the dinner part of the evening was over and that the girls, presenters and marshals were to head for their designated rooms.

"Of course, I won't be blowing my whistle tomorrow night. The committee has asked several handsome young Spencerians to serve as pages. They will come to each table to signal you to go to your assigned places. Now remember everyone, I'll be presenting you in alphabetical order, so make sure you're in the right spot. Girls, your stools are set up in that order, but gentlemen, you'll need to memorize your places. Committee members will be in your rooms to assist you with the order both this afternoon and tomorrow night. Be sure to know where you need to be so this will flow smoothly. Now let's all take seats at the tables and once you're settled, I'll blow my whistle."

Rehearsal continued for five hours. Everyone was exhausted and out of sorts by the time it was over with the exception of Bonita, who was having a perfectly delightful time. Once the German had been executed to her satisfaction, she released everyone so they could attend that evening's party. She reminded the girls not to stay out too late as they all wanted to look their very best for tomorrow evening.

"A television crew will be here from Nashville, ladies. We're about to put Spencer on the map! See you at six o'clock tomorrow night. Don't any of you dare be one millisecond late!"

While the rehearsal was winding down at the cave, the two FBI agents decided to get a bite to eat. As they entered the diner near their motel, Fred's cell phone rang. "Hughes."

"Fred, we found the guy who rented the mail box. He's hooked up with someone in New York. This thing's got more trails than a damned snail in heat. The boys in New York are ready to roll. I'll get back to you ASAP!"

"Right." Fred turned to Hank, "They found the guy who rented the post office box in Oklahoma. Now it's back to New York."

"Whoever set this thing up is a genius," Hank said.

"You got that right, Hank, but I think the genius might be getting ready to take a fall."

"Let's hope so because Christmas was two days ago. I like you, Fred, but I would much rather have been home Christmas Day with my family and had my wife's turkey dinner than that crap we here at this joint."

"You and me too, man. Spencer, Tennessee, and the Super Four Motel are not my idea of a place to spend the holidays."

"It's The Pines Motel, Fred."

"I was making a joke. You know, if the Super Six is bad, then the Super Four is worse. Hell, at The Pines, they don't even leave the light on for you."

"A joke?"

"Some of us FBI agents have a sense of humor, Hank."

"Good thing. Let's eat. I'm starving. I don't know how I can get so hungry sitting in that motel room watching television."

"You're not hungry, Hank, you're bored."

"Oh yeah? Tell that to my stomach."

47

The Ball at Last

Bonita spent the morning of the Ball going over final details by phone with the caterers and the decorators. She advised them she would be at the cave at two in the afternoon to make her final inspection. Work was progressing at a frenzied pace at the *Ice Palace*, the theme chosen by KD and the Decorations Committee. Travis and his floral artisans were unloading flower vans filled with fresh white flowers including orchids, magnolias and camellias flown in that morning from Hawaii along with artificial silver leaves, ferns, and eucalyptus sprigs to accent them.

Silver magnolia leaves were prominently in evidence and garlanded the cave's entrance under the canopy Isaac had installed. Huge crystal pyramids and prisms obtained from *RentaYenta* in Nashville were shipped in the day before and men were strategically placing them in the cave's huge room.

Caterers covered the tables with iridescent silver cloths and were busy placing crystal fountain centerpieces on them. Each fountain contained its own tiny battery and when switched on, water filled with tiny, plastic *ice* crystals cascaded down the prism into a pool at the bottom where one perfect magnolia lay.

Additional twinkling lights had been added to the ceiling of the cave and the bandstand was swathed in silver with a giant prism on each side. Bonita's podium was a Lucite column with simulated icicles gracefully *dripping* from it.

RentaYenta had further supplied a follow spot, complete with pink gel, to focus on each young lady from the second of her entrance throughout her presentation. The rental company technician was busy at work making sure the giant ellipsoidal was ready for action.

Plastic icicles ranging in sizes from two to six feet in length were attached to the roof of the cave. Faux snow would be arriving later in the day to be sprinkled over the floor. The effect promised to be absolutely dazzling!

In the kitchen, twenty workers prepared Shrimp Bisque, wilted lettuce with apple slices, blue cheese, and pecans to be dressed at the last minute a light teriyaki sauce.

Steamship rounds of beef marinated awaiting their trip to the commercial ovens. Yorkshire pudding pans stood at the ready to be baked a half-hour before they were served. Mountains of green beans were snapped and rinsed to be completed an hour before dinner. The beans would be boiled, removed while still crisp, tossed into giant sauté pans, and splashed with a mixture of olive oil, balsamic vinegar, and tarragon.

Hundreds ofParker House rolls lay in jellyroll pans rising and fifty crystal bowls filled with trifle made from white pound cake, blanched pears, whipped cream and silver sprinkles were under refrigeration for the dessert course when each would be delivered to a table by a tuxedoed waiter and served on site.

The theme for the Ball, arrived at after much discussion among the committee members, was a closely kept secret, therefore all preparations had to take place in one day. When the young ladies rehearsed in the cave the previous night, none of the decorations were in evidence. Bonita and her committee were the only ones, other than the hirelings, who were privy to the theme.

Always an opportunist, Bonita took advantage of her foreknowledge and planned to dress accordingly. Her gown was silver lame with an overlay of flowing iridescent silver chiffon. Crystal icicle earrings especially made for her by her New York jeweler would adorn her ears. A single diamond approaching the size of the famed Hope stone would grace her neck and she planned to add a crystal tiara, another custom-made item from Harry Winston's. Bonita had not suggested a queen for the Spencer Magnolia Ball, so she wouldn't be stealing anyone's thunder with her crown.

At two o'clock, Bonita entered the cave to inspect the preparations and it literally took her breath away. The Ice Palace was gorgeous, so lavish, but so tastefully done. Mrs. Roberts, Chair of the Spencer Magnolia Ball Committee, was gushing in her compliments. Bonita regaled Alphonso with descriptions of the cave's decorations all the way home to Villagio.

Alphonso made the appropriate sounds when Bonita stopped to take a breath. Bonita realized she was probably wasting her time telling her chauffeur about the sumptuous Ice Palace, but she was too excited to contain herself. If Bonita used a word in her description she thought Alphonso might not understand, she quickly amended it and used a simpler word for her uneducated employee.

Little did Bonita know. While he had scant formal education, Alphonso was a self-educated man. Every minute he wasn't driving Bonita or providing her with his sexual favors, Alphonso read voraciously. The chauffeur also spoke perfect English. He used the *step-and-fetch-it* speech pattern because that's what he knew Mrs. Roberts and those in her social set expected of him.

Many servants whom Alphonso knew spoke as well as their employers, but they used the wrong tenses and left the endings off words because it was considered quaint by those who signed their paychecks. Alphonso chuckled to himself when Bonita used a large word, then hesitated, and substituted a simpler one for her *simple* employee's benefit.

Another area of Alphonso's life of which Bonita had no knowledge was the vast amount of money he put away in the years he worked for her. She paid him extremely well for his chauffeuring and handyman skills, but when she approached him about his *after hours* job, the salary she gave him was more than many executives who'd graduated from the Wharton School of Business.

Alphonso, who didn't take days off, although Bonita offered them, worked twenty four/seven. He didn't need to spend any money as Mrs. Roberts provided him with lodging, meals, uniforms, a clothing allowance and a personal automobile. Alphonso didn't drink and he didn't smoke.

The library at Villagio had more books than he could ever read and Bonita had about twenty magazines arriving in the mail every month. If Alphonso mentioned a magazine to her he thought would be interesting, she ordered it immediately, so monthly he read *Popular Mechanics, Science Digest, Consumers' Report, Time, Newsweek, Ebony,* and *Gentlemen's Quarterly.*

Just about the time Bonita wound down from her excitement about the decorations for the Ball, Alphonso wheeled the Rolls into Villagio's driveway.

"I'll be ready to leave for the cave at five o'clock, Alphonso."

"Yes'm. I'll be waitin' right out front for you."

"Good. I'll see you then. I must begin my dressing routine now."

"Yes'm."

Bonita entered the house and called to Hannah to meet her in her bedroom.

"I's comin', honey. Yo clothes is all ready."

Morgan Stansill was preparing to leave the Internet Access Company building. His lovely daughter was making her debut tonight and Susannah had given him an ultimatum, he must be home no later than four to shower and dress so they could leave for the cave by quarter after five. Morgan gave his assistant some last minute instructions and started for the main entrance.

Fred and Hank were stepping out of their car in front of the building simultaneously. Early that morning, a call came in from the home office. The address agents extricated from the post office box holder in Tulsa turned out to be a warehouse for pornographic films plus hundreds of kiddie porn flicks including *Cookies for Sale*. It took a while to get an FBI computer expert to the warehouse, but once he was there it didn't take him long to trace the orders. They were coming from a computer in Spencer, Tennessee, a computer that used theVanBuren.net Internet access.

The agents spent the next few hours after the call from headquarters at the courthouse presenting their case to a district judge there. The men were now armed with two search warrants—one for VanBuren.net to go through their files to locate the computer serving as the mainframe for the illegal child pornography orders and the second for the computer's location so it could be impounded.

Morgan opened the door and was face-to-face with Fred and Hank. They introduced themselves and showed Morgan their badges. "You can put your briefcase down, Mr. Stansill, you're going to be here for a while."

They ushered Morgan into his office suite, produced the search warrant, and began to question him.

"I'll be more than happy to help you gentlemen in any way I can, but please allow me to call my wife. My daughter is making her debut tonight and I promised my wife I'd be home by four o'clock. I'm sure you fellows are married and can understand."

"Sure, we can," Fred replied, "But this is a pretty sensitive investigation we're conducting here, Mr. Stansill, so you buzz your secretary and have her call your wife. Tell her to say you've been unavoidably detained and you don't know when you'll be home. That is, unless you want to tell us what we need to know right now."

Morgan buzzed his secretary and told her to call Susannah.

"What is it you want to know?"

"There's a computer using your access that serves as the main frame for a child pornography film business. All orders funnel into it and are picked up by computers all over the country. The orders are processed and sent to a warehouse in New York, a warehouse that was shut down a few hours ago. That's where our agents found out where the mainframe computer was located."

"I'm sorry, but that's impossible. We have a relatively small operation here and we don't allow any commercial use. Your agents must be mistaken."

"Nice try, Stansill," Hank replied, "But our computer geeks don't make mistakes. If they say the computer is in Spencer and it's hooked up to your access, you can take that to the bank. Now let's start looking at your list of customers and their IP numbers, shall we?"

Stansill couldn't stop them. They had a search warrant.

So that's what Isaac is up to, child pornography. He was involved in that years back when he was Ike, but I thought it was over. He got away with it once. That's why my salary is seven figures and why he spent so much time finding me. I'm going to have to make sure the Feds don't crack this or it's jail time for me and for Isaac. And if Isaac goes to jail, I won't be safe anywhere, not even in a cell.

Morgan remained as elusive as he could. He attempted to stand by a confidentiality statement the company signed with each customer.

"This search warrant overrides your confidentiality statement, Mr. Stansill. Now let's get to the files. Maybe you aren't seeing a clear picture here—this is a bust!"

"I think I need to call the company attorney."

"Call him, but we're going to conduct a search, attorney or no attorney. When you call him, you are not to tell him we're here."

Stansill dialed Harcourt's office. "I'm sorry. Mr. Ball has left for the day. May I be of assistance to you?"

"Where can I reach him?"

"I'm not at liberty to give out that information, sir. I'll be happy to take a message."

"I need to speak to him now. This is Morgan Stansill. I have FBI agents in my office and I must speak to Harcourt right this minute!"

Fred moved into Stansill, "I told you not to say we were here."

"That's the only way I can get his girl to contact him," Stansill explained.

"That's not my problem. You better get this straight—we're calling the shots here!"

"I'm sorry. Just a minute, she's back."

"If you'll give me your number, Mr. Stansill, I'll see if I can reach Mr. Ball and have him call you."

Stansill gave her the number. Fred used the break to go outside and smoke. Hank roamed around the room glancing at pictures of Stansill's family and personal mementos.

Hank reminded Stansill, "When your lawyer returns the call, remember not a word about why we're here."

Within minutes, Stansill's phone rang. "What's going on, Morgan?"

"Get over here, Harcourt. I need you to come immediately. I've got big trouble and I need legal assistance."

"Tell me what the problem is, Morgan, and perhaps I can help you over the phone. My girl said there are FBI agents there."

"True, but that's all I can say. You have to come down here. Please, Harcourt, this is a matter of life and death."

"I'll be there in fifteen minutes."

Harcourt grabbed his jacket and told his mother he had to go out. "Harcourt, we need to leave for the Ball in an hour."

"If I'm not back, mother, go without me."

Morgan's phone rang again. "Don't answer it," Fred said. "Tell the secretary to hold all calls."

"Hold my calls, Georgia."

"It's Mrs. Stansill, sir."

"Tell her I'll call her later."

"She insists on speaking to you now."

"I can't talk now, Georgia."

Susannah was furious. *The last thing I said to him this morning was to be home by four o'clock or else .I can't believe he isn't here by now. And he has the nerve to have Georgia call me and say he doesn't know when he'll be home. Now he can't talk to me!*

Well, she'd see about that! Susannah donned a trench coat over her gown and drove to Stansill's office. Misty was in the shower so Susannah didn't bother to tell her daughter she was going out.

Misty was notorious for staying in the shower a half hour or more. Susannah knew she'd be back by then. She'd march into Morgan's office and insist he come home with her that instant. Susannah walked in the main entrance of Morgan's company and asked Georgia where her husband was.

"He's in his office with two men, Mrs. Stansill."

Susannah strode to the door and attempted to open it. The door was locked.

"Morgan, it's Susannah. Open this door."

"Susannah, please go home. Take Misty to the Ball. I'll be there as soon as I can. Something critical has come up."

"I'm not going home unless you come with me, Morgan. Nothing is as critical as this night is for Misty. Open the damned door, Morgan!"

Fred crossed to the door and flung it open. "Hello, Mrs. Stansill, I'm Fred Hughes," he said in greeting as he showed Susannah his badge. "You should have listened to your husband and gone home. Now that you're here, you're staying."

"Why does she have to stay? She's not involved in whatever you think is going on here."

"Because we don't know who else in Spencer is mixed up in this game. Your wife might tell someone what's happening, so she's staying here."

Fred hadn't closed the door after Susannah entered. Harcourt tapped on the partially open door and entered Morgan's office. "Hello, I'm Harcourt Ball, Mr. Stansill's attorney. Hello Susannah."

"Fred Hughes and this is Hank Lowery. We're with the FBI," and both produced their badges.

"What's going on, Morgan?"

"I wish I knew."

Hank shut the door and locked it. "Stansill, you can send your girl and any other employees home. Your company is shutting down for the evening and I don't mean just its doors. We're turning everything off."

"I'll tell the employees to go home, but I can't allow you to shut down the servers. We have hundreds of customers depending on us. Can they make me shut everything down, Harcourt?"

"I'm not sure yet, Morgan. You take care of your employees. Gentlemen, can you bring me up to speed here?"

Fred passed the search warrant to the attorney who looked it over and said, "Have you placed anyone under arrest? I don't see how you can hold Mrs. Stansill if you haven't arrested anyone or read them their rights."

"I don't care what the hell is going on here. Are you two men married? Do you have children? Our daughter is expected to be at The Magnolia Ball in less than an hour. She's making her debut tonight. Can't whatever this is wait? This is so important to Misty."

"I'm sorry, Mrs. Stansill, but it can't wait. I wish you hadn't come down here. I'm sorry your daughter is going to be disappointed, but I have a job to do."

"Please let me go. Whatever is going on here, I don't have a clue about it. I won't say a word. I swear it. I'll get someone else to serve as Misty's presenter. I'll tell everyone Morgan took sick. I'll even tell my daughter that. Please, Mr. Hughes."

"Unless you are going to arrest Mrs. Stansill, who as far as I can see is not involved, I believe you have to allow her to leave."

Fred looked at Hank and Hank looked away. He wasn't going to get involved in that kind of decision. Fred was the head agent.

"You swear you won't say a word?"

"On my daughter's life."

"You do and I'll follow you too the ends of the earth, Mrs. Stansill, and I'll see you're locked up with your husband."

"What are you talking about? Locking up my husband? Morgan, what's this about?"

"Susannah, this does not concern you. If Agent Hughes will let you go, go and take Misty to the Ball, but whatever you do, don't breathe a word of this. I can't stress how important it is for you to keep quiet."

"I won't say a word other than to tell anyone who asks you were suddenly taken ill."

"Okay, Mrs. Stansill. Go, but not a word! And if your husband isn't home when you return from the Ball, don't make any phone calls or come down here. We'll contact you. Got that?"

"Yes."

Hank crossed to the door and opened it. Susannah turned and looked at Morgan, shook her head at him, and headed for her car. Georgia was outside the main entrance.

"What's going on in there, Mrs. Stansill?"

"I have no idea, Georgia, but please don't mention it to anyone, all right?"

"Okay. Whatever's going on, I get to leave early. That's always a plus. Have a nice evening."

"You, too, Georgia," and Susannah got in her car and drove home. She was in tears most of the way, but got herself somewhat together before she entered her house. Misty was in the foyer.

"Mom, where have you been? I called you to help me with that Merry Widow bra thing and you weren't anywhere to be found. How come you left without telling me?"

"You were in the shower, honey, and you know how long your showers are. I thought I'd be back before you were finished. I only had to run out for a minute."

"Where's daddy?"

"He's meeting us there. Come on, honey, let's get you dressed."

Isaac was ready to leave for the Ball when he realized he'd planned to ask Bonita if he might escort her that evening. It had completely slipped his mind. He dialed and asked Hannah if Mrs. Roberts had left yet.

"No, but she's 'bout to. I'll get her, Mr. Kahn. Miz Bonita, Mr. Kahn's on the phone."

Bonita answered, "Hello, Isaac. Is anything the matter?"

"Yes. I forgot to ask you if I might escort you to the Ball this evening. So much has been happening, I think I assumed we would be going together. It was only as I started out the door on my way to Villagio that I realized I hadn't asked you."

Bonita was charmed. "Well, now, Isaac, I don't usually accept dates for a function taking place in less than two hours, but let me think about it. I suppose I'll be able to make an exception in your case. Are you on your way now?"

"As soon as I fire up your chariot."

"I'm waiting then."

Fat old bitch, simpering and cooing. How could she possibly think for one instant I or anyone else for that matter could be attracted to her? I'm using you, Bonita. I need your social acceptance until all the shit settles. I hope she doesn't get carried away and plant another smacker on my cheek. That is one ugly sight seeing that face coming at you.

Bonita picked up the house phone and called Alphonso in the servants' quarters behind the main house.

"I's on my way, Miz Bonita."

"That's not why I'm calling, Alphonso. It completely slipped my mind, but Mr. Kahn is escorting me to the Ball—I've been so distracted. As I mentioned this afternoon, I told Raven we would collect her on our way. I forgot all about Mr. Kahn—temporarily. Would you be so kind as to drive her to the Ball? Then you can pick her up at the cave around one in the morning."

"I'd be happy too, Miz Bonita. She's such a sweet chile. You have a nice time with Mr. Kahn and I hope your Ice Palace Ball is a big success!"

"Thank you, Alphonso. Bye."

Isaac called for Bonita within minutes looking dashing in his designer tux accessorized with a silver cummerbund and diamond studs. Isaac was no slouch. He knew the theme of the Ball too. "Bonita, you look positively gorgeous!" Isaac exclaimed. "I love the tiara!"

Who does she think she is-Queen of the Fat-Assed Fairies?

"Why, thank you, Isaac. You don't think it's too much, do you?"

"For the Queen of Spencer Society? Absolutely not! It's perfect!"

You're too much, Bonita! You could take two prizes at a costume ball for the most hideous and the most hilarious get-ups and here you are running the damned debutante ball. What a farce! We're cut from the same cloth though, Chubs. Both of us are living proof that enough money allows anyone to be whomever they want to be, do whatever they want to do, and wear anything they like and best of all—no one will dare to say a word!

Bonita practically swooned as her escort made sure she was comfortably arranged on the front seat of the silver Corniche—even the car matched her ensemble.

Precious was wearing silver too, but her dress was completely different from Bonita's. First off it consisted of several yards less material and secondly was a series of silver ruffles, one beneath the other, with tiny crystals attached along the edges of each one. Clusters of crystals decorated her ears and she wore a family heirloom diamond clip in her auburn hair. She created quite a sensation when she stepped from her white Jaguar onto the snow-covered entrance to the Ice Palace.

Precious' arrival was quickly eclipsed when Randolph and Lydia Henley stepped out of their chauffeured limousine. Lydia was spectacular in the palest of pink. Her diaphanous gown was gathered in a large rose below her bosom. The creation had been made in one piece so as the material pulled toward the rose, it made the hemline shorter in front than in the back. A dramatic slit in the gown's front center allowed more than a glimpse of Lydia's fantastic legs. She was ablaze in pink diamonds with a white fox fur draped over her arm. The fur skimmed the ground and dusted the faux snowflakes into a flurry as she and her husband made their grand entrance.

Bonita decided at the final committee meeting the committee should form a receiving line at the Ball, so all of the committee members were to arrive early. Precious arrived moments after Isaac and Bonita and the two women billed and cooed over each other, their gowns, and their jewels. Precious thought Bonita's tiara was a little over the top, but she certainly wasn't going to mention it because everything else about her was horrid and over the top also.

Marietta emerged from a chauffeur-driven limousine alone. She looked elegant in a rainbow striped beaded sheath that shimmered in the carefully placed lighting at the cave's entrance.

"Where's Harcourt, Marietta?" Bonita asked.

"He had to rush out at the last minute. He received a business call at home, so it must have been quite important as the Ball has been number one on his agenda for months. I'm sure he'll be here before the festivities began. He sends his apologies."

Bonita was noticeably miffed.

Didn't these people understand when the Ball was taking place, everything else had to take a backseat. Harcourt should have made some excuse to the caller. He needed to be here to receive the guests with the rest of the committee.

Mrs. Mapleton arrived in a yellow satin gown with a stand up collar, slit long sleeves, a fitted skirt, and bourgeoisie jewelry. She obviously hadn't attempted to tie her dress to the theme of the Ball but Bonita decided she looked presentable enough. Her husband was quite attractive and their debutante daughter looked pretty in a simple white column with a strand of pearls at her neck. Bonita thought the girl's ensemble was tasteful, demure, exactly what a debutante was expected to wear, and extremely boring.

But then they all look the same in a white dress when there are nineteen of them. Maybe I should pass that tidbit on to the girls next year so their mothers won't shell out thousands of dollars for gowns that are NOT going to make their baby stand out in the crowd.

Susannah Stansill brought her car to a screeching halt and jumped out almost knocking the valet over. She looked lovely, but was obviously in a distressed state, in ice blue with a spray of silver sequins down each long sleeve of her gown visible to onlookers as her floor-length white mink coat was draped over her shoulders cape fashion.

Coats weren't really necessary. It was unseasonably warm in Spencer with only a hint of chill in the air. Clear skies were studded with millions of stars as far as the eye could see. Misty stepped from the car in a cloud of white strapless chiffon. She looked like some kind of yummy confection.

"And where is your father, Misty?" Bonita asked.

"He'll be here shortly. He got held up."

"Hello, Susannah. Misty tells me Morgan will be here directly."

"Not true, Bonita. I haven't told Misty yet as I know she'll be devastated, but Morgan has come down with some strange stomach virus. He's at the doctor's office as we speak. He won't be here this evening. I need you to help me find someone to act as Misty's presenter."

"How awful and he was so looking forward to this event. Let's see. How about Mr. Kahn? He could stand in for Morgan."

"What a wonderful idea!"

Bonita took Isaac aside and told him about Morgan's sudden illness and asked if he would do Misty the honor of serving as her presenter. Isaac said he'd be delighted and excused himself for a moment. He headed for the kitchen, whipped out his cell phone, and tapped in Morgan's private number. No answer.

He immediately returned to the main room and found Susannah. "Where's Morgan? Which doctor's office?"

He saw her hesitate and realized she had lied to Bonita. "Where is he, Susannah?"

"I can't say, Mr. Kahn."

"You mean you don't know or you can't say?"

"I can't say."

"And why not?"

"Please, Mr. Kahn, I really can't talk about this," and she hurried toward the ladies' lounge.

Isaac called the main number of the Internet Access Company. No answer. Something was up. He called Chang, "Go down to the Internet building and see what's going on. Stansill isn't here at the Ball and his wife isn't talking. I need to know what's going on down there."

"Right away, boss."

Neither of the agents had thought to lock the front door so when Chang arrived, he walked right into the building. The lights were on, although there were no employees around, but it was strangely quiet.

Chang looked around and realized all of the servers were off. He heard voices coming from Mr. Stansill's office. Chang went to the door and knocked. He identified himself and Morgan told him to leave.

"I can't do that, Mr. Stansill. The boss sent me down here to see what's going on. I have to call him back with a report."

Fred opened the door. "Come in and who might your boss be?"

"Who are you?"

Fred produced the badge and Chang zipped his mouth. He refused to answer any questions. He knew all hell was going to break loose when he didn't return Mr. Kahn's call.

Isaac joined Bonita as Rhetta, her cousin Ashton Shaw, Corinne, Robert Whitney Hartington, III, River, and her date pulled under the canopy. As the group emerged, Bonita couldn't believe her eyes. Rhetta and her two daughters were all attired in the exact same gown.

What in the world is the matter with her? Only the debs wear white. That's mistake number one. River has the same dress as her sister for Corinne's big night and I can't believe my eyes, but over-the-hill Rhetta is wearing the same one as her teenaged daughters. She needs her head examined.

"Hello Bonita. Here we are—the Gabor sisters and their mother. Isn't this cute? Oscar made Corinne's dress and River and I loved it so much, we had him make one for each of us too. I bet this has never been done at any debutante ball, do you think? I'm sure the television cameras will be on the Ricks' gals tonight. Bonita, this is my cousin, Ashton Shaw. He's the Governor's nephew. His daddy and my daddy were brothers. And I believe you've met Robert Whitney Hartington, III, the son of my dear friend Beverly in Savannah, and Corinne's escort. This is River's little friend. Meet Mosby Creighton Plier from right here in Spencer. He's in his last year at Woodbury Forest and is escorting my beautiful River whom you've met before. Well, come on folks, let's find our table. Then I'll be back to join the receiving line, Bonita. My, it's so beautiful in here. You've really outdone yourself, or should I say we've outdone ourselves? Be right back, Bonita."

Bonita hadn't gotten a word in edgewise. Precious looked at Bonita and raised an eyebrow. Bonita simply shook her head. She knew things couldn't get any worse in the attire category anyway, but she hadn't counted on the next arrivals.

Candy disembarked from her car first in beige satin and matching pumps. Sensible shoes, but at least she wasn't wearing her Oxfords and the dress was stylish enough. She had swept her hair up and wore impressive topaz stones at her ears. Bonita was quite pleased.

Her mood lasted only a nanosecond, for then the valet assisted Enid from her side of the automobile. The dress was a Dior, an ancient one. It must have been the first design Christian, as a young child prodigy, had put ink to pad to draw. The uncut diamond chunks on her ears were the stuff from which legends are made and were quite stunning, but Enid had managed to get out of the house with her damned bedroom slippers encasing her bunioned feet. The nasty old fur coat she wore had giant bare spots where the skins had separated and she had a plastic rain cap over her head. As if that weren't enough, Enid carried the ubiquitous plastic see through tote bag over her crepey right arm.

Cameron Bassin, her father Winston Rockford, Lindsay Mary and her escort swept through the entrance. Cameron wore black velvet and was glamorous and the debutante was lovely in a slim column of white satin. Bonita knew she had done the right thing to call the committee members and ask them to change their votes after Harcourt's call to her.

After all the debs, their parents, presenters, escorts, were in place, those to whom the Magnolia Ball Foundation had issued invitations began arriving. Many guests had traveled from Nashville and Knoxville pleasing Bonita no end.

The television crew was set up and was filming guests as they moved through the receiving line. A heavily made-up, but otherwise pretty young news anchor, interviewed Bonita as soon as the cameras were set up.

With the exception of the missing Harcourt and Morgan Stansill, the evening was progressing nicely. Isaac seemed a little on edge, but he was probably nervous about presenting Misty. He hadn't planned on being involved in the actual debutante doings.

Isaac glanced at his watch for the fifth or sixth time. He was waiting for Chang's call and getting more annoyed with every minute that passed.

Alphonso rang the doorbell at Raven's home. "Mother, could you answer the door, please? I'm not quite ready."

Mrs. Keyes opened the door and for the first time, Alphonso saw Raven's mother at close range in good light. He started to speak and the words caught in his throat.

"Hello, Alphonso," Raven's mother said softly.

"Billie Sue?"

"Yes."

"Billie Sue Barto?"

"Yes, Alphonso."

"O my lord!"

Raven hurried down the steps. "Hi, Alphonso. I'm sorry to make you wait. I wasn't quite ready. I wanted to be here to introduce you to my mother."

Alphonso and Mrs. Keyes were staring into each other's eyes. Neither of them seemed to hear a word she said.

"Alphonso?"

Alphonso shook himself and answered, "Yes, Miss Raven? I'm sorry."

"I would like you to meet my mother, Mrs. Keyes. Mother, this is Alphonso, the wonderful Alphonso I've told you so much about."

Billie Sue Keyes extended her hand to the chauffeur. He took it and held it, "Hello, Mrs. Keyes."

Raven had never heard Alphonso speak in such dulcet tones. She realized he continued to hold her mother's hand and that her mother wasn't attempting to remove it.

"You two act like you already know each other."

"We do," her mother answered.

"I didn't realize you'd met. Did Mrs. Roberts introduce you?"

"We met years ago, Raven, when we were teenagers," Alphonso answered.

"You did? Where?"

"In South Carolina. I worked for your granddaddy, Mr. Barto."

"It's a small world, isn't it? Well, I guess we better be going, Alphonso, you know how Mrs. Roberts is and she wants me to be there on time. Is she waiting in the car?"

"No ma'am. Mr. Kahn took her to the Ball."

"Oh. Well, then, I can drive myself."

"Oh, no ma'am. Miz Bonita wants me to drive you."

Raven looked at her mother and her employer's chauffeur. The two of them were standing in the open doorway hand in hand gazing into each other's eyes.

"Alphonso!"

"Yes ma'am?"

"Don't you think we should be going?"

"Yes'm. It was wonderful to meet you, Mrs. Keyes, and to see you again after all these years. I can't tell you how many times I've thought about you."

"I've thought about you too, Alphonso."

Alphonso slowly released her hand and turned toward the Rolls. He held the door open for Raven while continuing to stare at her mother in the doorway. Alphonso shut Raven's door and waved to Billie Sue.

"Wow, isn't that amazing? You and my mother know each other. Were you good friends? I guess you're about the same age."

"We sure were. We played together as young kids and then we was good friends as teen-agers too. The last time I seen yo momma was the night before she went off to boarding school."

"Boarding school?"

"Uh-huh. She didn't tell me she was goin' or nothin'. Mrs. Barto tole me she'd gone away to school and I ain't never seen her again 'til this minute."

"I didn't know she went to boarding school. I knew she went to Michigan to live with my grandmother's sister for a year, but I've never heard about boarding school. She didn't get along well with her parents, but I guess you knew that."

"No ma'am. I don't know nothin' about that."

"I've never even met my grandparents, Alphonso. All I know is they live somewhere in South Carolina and once in a while they used to wire my mother money. They've never sent anything through the mail. I've never understood what could have happened."

"I don't know, Miss Raven."

Alphonso glanced at the stunning young woman in the back seat and a realization hit him like a bolt out of the blue. Raven bore a striking resemblance to his sister, LuWanda, who was very light-skinned.

Billie Sue didn't go to boarding school at all. She went to her aunt's house to have a baby, my baby. Raven is my daughter. That's why Billie Sue and her parents are estranged.

Alphonso had to concentrate to keep the car on the road, but he somehow managed to get Raven to the Ice Palace.

Raven emerged from the Rolls in a strapless gown of the palest lavender at the bodice graduated to the deepest purple at the hem. One rhinestone decorative strap curved under her bodice, over her left shoulder, and down her back to attach to the glamorous gown. Alphonso noted how lovely she looked. He hadn't noticed what she was wearing when he picked her up he was so bedazzled by Billie Sue.

As soon as Raven entered the cave, three television cameras pivoted in her direction. She moved through the receiving line and when she moved toward the tables to be seated, Isaac came up behind her. "What time did you leave Bonita's today?"

"Three o'clock."

"Was everything all right?"

"I guess so. I don't know what's going on with the computer or what's in it, so how would I know if everything's all right?"

"Don't get smart with me, Raven."

"I'm not, Mr. Kahn. As far as I know, everything was fine."

"Well, something's going down."

"I'm sorry?"

"Never mind. You look nice."

"Thank you, I can't tell you how much that means to me," Raven said and moved away from him as quickly as she could without creating a scene. Ike Perl, a.k.a. Isaac Kahn, made her skin crawl.

Isaac's cell rang. He looked at the caller identification. It was Jesse.

Isaac answered, "What's up?"

"You tell me."

"I don't know."

"I can't get through to the warehouse. There's no answer and it's supposed to be staffed twenty-four hours a day. And I guess your girl has unplugged the damned computer again."

"I don't know why the warehouse isn't answering, but Raven is here with me. Believe me, she hasn't unplugged the computer."

"I can't get through. Wait a minute. Here' the problem. The server's down. That's your baby, Isaac. What's going on at the access company?"

"I don't know of anything. How can the server be down?"

"It happens sometime. I'll call Morgan. Check you later," and he hung up.

Isaac was getting more and more agitated. Something was wrong but he couldn't get a handle on what. Before he could replace the cell in his pocket, it rang again.

"Things are not good, Isaac. I just got a call from Tulsa, Oklahoma. Our guy Chip out there with the post office box is in jail. He conned a guy who got out on a work pass to call and tell me he gave up the warehouse address. I think we're in the middle of some kind of shakedown. I'm disconnecting everything up here. I don't know where you are, but you better get down to the access company and see what's happening."

"I don't think so, Jesse. If something's going down there, I don't want to be involved. Besides, what's the worse that can happen? They'll get Bonita's computer and they'll arrest her, right?"

"Right. If Morgan folds, you will have to pay a fine because a kiddie porn company used your Internet access."

"I'm trembling. Close everything up, Jesse. Morgan might give up Bonita's computer, but he won't give me up. I pay him too much money."

"Okay. I'll be back in touch in a day or two."

"Right."

Jesse hung up and called to Bartie who was *on location* in a seedy apartment making yet another filthy film, "It's time to make tracks."

"What's happening?"

"Just got a call from a work release prisoner in Tulsa. Chip's in jail. The feds found him and he gave up the warehouse address. Bonita's computer is down and so are all of Isaac's servers. The warehouse doesn't answer. I think the feds have been there. Yeah, they have. That's how they traced the mainframe to Spencer. The feds are in Spencer and they've shut down the servers. The jig is up, Bartie. They'll break Morgan, impound Bonita's computer, and arrest her."

"What about Isaac?"

"He's clean. He'll have to pay a fine because the kiddie porn was using his access company, but no big deal. Now, we're going to Plan B. The next thing that's gonna happen is some smart-ass FBI computer whiz is going to break in to Bonita's computer and careful as I was, he's going to be able to decipher where the hack came from."

"I'll pack. Okay, we go to a cheapie motel tonight, pull the money out of the bank tomorrow and catch a flight, right?"

"You got it. Aren't you glad we bought that little place in Belize two months ago?

"Very glad."

"And most of the money is already down there. I'll go online and get us two Priceline tickets while you pack. My stuff is ready to go."

"You are one smart one, Jess."

"Thank you, sir. Let me get these tickets and then we can prepare to live the life of Riley."

"What about our business?"

"We need to lie low for a spell, Bartie. We can start up again if the money runs low, but we don't need Mr. Ike Perl now known as Mr. Isaac Kahn anymore—we've learned all the tricks plus we have the capital to do it on our own. Isaac's not going to get burned, so he won't be after us."

"I hope not. I hope that cleaner I sent down there took care of whoever was chewing on his butt."

"I've talked to Isaac. He seemed calm. I don't want to cross him in anyway, but I've protected him and we made our money fair and square. He's got no beef with us."

Back at the Internet Company, the feds were making progress. They had the facts and were waiting for Stansill to verify them. "I think you should cooperate, Morgan," Harcourt advised.

"The IP number is Bonita Roberts' computer. She lives out on Lake Road."

"Morgan, I'm sure you're mistaken. Bonita Roberts would not be involved with child pornography," Harcourt interjected.

"That's who owns the computer, Harcourt."

"Hank, go get it," Fred ordered. "We'll wait here."

Hank left in the rental car and headed for Villagio. Hannah was soaking her aching feet in a basin of Epsom salts when the doorbell rang.

Who in tarnation could that be? Everybody's anybody is at that Ball. Oh goodness. I hope it ain't that person what killed the Dodds. I's here all by myself.

Hannah replaced her shoes and moved cautiously toward the front door. Whoever was there rang the bell several times and began pounding on the door. Hannah looked through the peephole and saw a man in a black suit. "Yes?"

"Open up. FBI," Hank called.

"FBI?"

"That's what I said! Now open up."

"Hold your badge up to that peephole. I ain't openin' the door 'til I see some identification, mister."

Hank complied. Hannah squinted at the badge and eased the door open.

"Is this the home of Bonita Roberts?"

"You's an FBI agent and you don't know who's house you at?"

"I'm following procedure. Yes, I know who's house this is, but I have to ask that question."

"Yessir, this is the home of Bonita Roberts, but I's sure you's makin' a big mistake."

"That's what they all say. Where is Mrs. Roberts' computer?"

"In her office, but you ain't going in there."

"Yes, I am. I'm an FBI agent. I'm here to impound her computer."

"Believe me, Mr. Federal Government Agent, you ain't pounding on Mrs. Roberts' computer."

"I'm not going to pound on it. I'm going to *impound* it."

"And what exactly do that mean?"

"I'm going to unplug it and take it with me."

"I don't' think so. You got a piece of paper with you from a judge or anything? A search warrant, that's it. You got a search warrant or a p*ounding* warrant? You got anything 'cept that tin badge to get me to let you take something out of my employer's house? 'Cause if you ain't, mister, I's gonna start yelling *rape* quicker you can blink an eye."

"What is your name?"

"What's that gotta do with anything?"

"Nothing. I just need to call you something."

"My name is Hannah."

"Hannah, here is the piece of paper. This is a search warrant."

Hannah took the paper and read it. "It don't have Miz Bonita's name on it nowhere."

"Hannah, do you know Harcourt Ball?"

"Yep, he's a lawyer."

"If Harcourt Ball told you I had the authority to impound Mrs. Roberts' computer, would you believe him?"

"I reckon."

"Good. I'll call Mr. Ball and let you speak to him." He dialed Fred's number. "Put the lawyer on."

"You having trouble, Hank?"

"No, just put the lawyer on. Hello, Mr. Ball. I'm at Bonita Roberts' house and Hannah doesn't think I have the authority to impound her employer's computer. Would you be so kind as to explain the facts to her?" He handed Hannah the cell phone.

Hannah listened and when Harcourt had finished, she said, "Yessir. I understands."

She handed the agent his phone and showed him to Bonita's office. He removed the computer, CDs, back-up discs, and practically everything in and on Raven's desk.

"Thank you, Hannah. Have a nice evening."

"Well, I hadn't planned on it, Mr. Federal Agent, but if you insists." Hannah closed the door.

Miz Bonita gonna have a flamin' fit.

Hank entered Stansill's office Bonita's computer in hand. "Well now that we have it, what are we going to do with it? Neither one of us knows dick about computers."

"The Nashville office is helicoptering a geek in as we speak. He should be here in less than thirty minutes," Fred answered.

"I gotta hand it to you, Fred, you're on top of it."

"Thanks. Have a little trouble with the maid, Hank?"

"Not at all. I didn't see any reason to scare the woman and get all heavy-handed. Once she talked to Ball here, she was sweet as pie."

The guests at the Ball were ready for the main course having progressed through the soup and salad course. Bonita and Isaac were seated at the head table. Bonita was relieved her escort seemed to have calmed down considerably. Mr. Kahn was quite charming and Bonita had high hopes for their relationship.

She wouldn't mind marrying again especially to someone with the wealth Kahn possessed. Of course, there was nothing she couldn't already afford, but a merger of their assets would elevate Bonita and Isaac to the Bill Gates' financial stratosphere. They would live at Villagio, of course. It was so much nicer than Les Enfants plus it possessed the ballroom they would surely need for their large scale entertaining.

Precious asked Marietta when she was expecting Harcourt. Her question brought Bonita back to the matter at hand. She hoped the attorney would arrive soon as Harcourt was to make some opening remarks prior to the presentation of the young ladies.

By the time the tuxedoed waiters stood at their respective tables preparing to serve trifle to the guests on sterling silver dessert plates, the FBI computer genius had learned everything there was to know about Bonita's computer. Thousands of orders for filth had run through it in the past six months, orders that totaled up to several million dollars.

"I know what I'm seeing, but it's not possible. I know Bonita Roberts had nothing to do with this. Couldn't someone have hacked into her machine?" Harcourt asked.

"Maybe," the computer genius answered. "We'll find out later. Right now, I think it's time to arrest Mrs. Roberts and then you boys can get home for the last few days of the holidays."

"Sounds good to me," Fred said. "Where is she, Harcourt?"

"Outside of town in a cave."

"Hiding out?"

"Not hardly. Bonita Roberts is the founder of the Magnolia Ball Foundation and the Spencer Magnolia Debutante Ball. It's being held this evening in a cave owned by Mr. Isaac Kahn."

"Okay, let's go. Come along, Harcourt, you can show us where it is. Morgan, you're coming too. You're under arrest. Read him his rights, Hank. Your company will be fined in the hundreds of thousands of dollars for this little episode unless we find you're personally involved. Then it's three hots and a cot for you for a long, long time! You're going too, whatever your name is," Fred said as he signaled to Isaac's houseboy.

"And what are you charging Chang with may I ask?"

"I'm not charging him with anything at the moment, but I do want to take him for questioning. I'm in the middle of a bust here so he'll have to go along with us. Got a problem with that, Counselor?"

"I do, but I guess my objections don't matter at the moment."

"Good observation!" Fred answered. "Let's go!"

The five men got in the black car and headed for the Ice Palace. When they arrived, Fred told Morgan and Harcourt to go inside. "We're not dressed properly. We'll stand out like sore thumbs," Harcourt protested.

"If Mrs. Roberts is the head of this shindig, it's not going to make any difference what you're wearing, pal. The party's gonna be over shortly."

The agents hung back as Morgan and Harcourt entered the ballroom. Bonita saw them instantly.

What in the world are they doing here dressed like that?

She rose and crossed to the men and said, "Where is your evening attire?"

"No time to explain right now, Bonita."

"Well, it's time to begin the presentation, Harcourt. You were to make some remarks before we proceeded."

"Let's skip that part. Bonita, you're going to be terribly upset shortly."

"Why?" Bonita asked as one of the girl's mothers pulled her aside to ask her a pressing question.

The debs, the presenters and their escorts were leaving the dining area to report to their designated rooms awaiting the presentation. As Robert Whitney Hartington, III, passed the head table, he and Harcourt looked at each other. "Hello, Harcourt," the young man said softly.

"What are you doing here, Brandon?"

"Pardon me? My name is Robert Whitney Hartington, III, and I am escorting Miss Corinne Ricks, debutante, Harcourt.

The orchestra blared the fanfare and the lights blinked in a wave effect around the walls and ceiling. "I must go, Harcourt, that's my cue," Bonita whispered. She saw Corinne's escort standing there, "Robert, what are you doing here? Hurry back to your room and get in your place. Chop, chop!" and she headed for the stage.

"Wait, Bonita."

"Not now, Harcourt. Have a seat next to your mother. We'll talk when this is over. Robert, run along now. I mean it!"

"Yes ma'am," the young man answered, but he didn't move.

"How is it possible you're escorting Corinne Ricks? You're a male prostitute."

"Not anymore, Hardy. I changed jobs. Got a gig at a discreet escort service in Nashville. Bigger paychecks, nice parties like this, and no corn-holing by old farts like you."

"You better keep your mouth shut, Brandon!"

"Or what?" Brandon a.k.a. Robert said as he winked at Harcourt and headed for his designated room.

Harcourt collected himself and moved toward his mother who had witnessed the exchange between her son and Corinne's young man. "I hope nothing embarrassing is about to happen, Harcourt."

"Oh, something embarrassing is definitely about to happen, mother, but not to me."

Bonita grasped the microphone and began her welcoming speech. The television cameras zeroed in on her when a ruckus erupted at the main entrance. Two men in black suits, handguns drawn and badges flashing, burst through the door and identified themselves as FBI agents. Bonita looked at them indignantly. "Gentlemen, we are beginning the presentation of the debutantes of Spencer. This affair is by invitation only. Now if you would kindly leave without creating a bigger scene than that you have already caused, I, and everyone assembled, would be most grateful."

"Broad's got balls, gotta hand her that," Hank murmured to Fred as they continued moving through the crowd and onto the stage where they allowed Bonita a glimpse of their badges before producing handcuffs, reading her rights, and placing her under arrest for the illegal sale of child pornography.

"Have you lost your minds? Harcourt! Where are you? Come up here and stop this charade. Is this someone's idea of a sick joke? Isaac!"

Kahn came out of the room where he'd been waiting for his turn to present Misty Stansill. "What's going on here?"

"And who are you?" Hank asked.

"I'm Isaac Kahn, Mrs. Roberts' escort. What are you doing? Why is she handcuffed?"

"She's under arrest for selling child pornography," Fred answered.

"That's the most ridiculous thing I've ever heard! Unhand her! Harcourt, are you here?" Isaac yelled out to the crowd.

Harcourt arose and approached the stage. "There's nothing I can do, Isaac. I know the charges are ridiculous, but I've been with the agents for hours. There's evidence pointing to Mrs. Roberts."

By this time, the ballroom was in complete chaos. The girls and the men had trickled from their respective rooms and were milling about on the stage watching the spectacle of Bonita Roberts' in handcuffs. Fred and Hank escorted her out of the cave and into their waiting car. They locked her in and returned for Morgan. Susannah was hysterical.

"What are you doing here?" Bonita asked Chang when she realized she wasn't alone in the car.

"Mr. Kahn called me from here to go down toVanBuren.net to find Mr. Stansill cause he wasn't answering his phone. When I got there, the two feds were there and they wouldn't let me leave. They haven't arrested me, but they won't let me go. They're taking me in for questioning. I don't know what's happening, Mrs. Roberts, but you're in big trouble."

Bonita Roberts, the *Queen of Spencer Society* as Isaac had referred to her only hours earlier, was taken to the Spencer Jail and locked in a tiny cell with a metal cot, a mattress the thickness of a piece of paper, a filthy sink, and a rank-smelling toilet anyone could see from the hallway or other cells.

Bonita demanded all kinds of rights, but the Sheriff locked the cell and an outer door to the cellblock. No one could hear Bonita's screams or protests and if they could, they didn't pay attention to them.

Raven grabbed her coat and headed for the door. "Not so fast, Raven. Where are you going?" Isaac asked her.

"Child pornography. How could you stoop so low? I have to tell the agents Mrs. Roberts had nothing to do with the filth on her computer."

"Oh? And how would you know that? If you tell them that, you're going to have to provide them with some more information, aren't you, Raven? Information that will incriminate me and we both know how very serious and dangerous that would be, don't we?"

"You can't let her take the fall for this, Mr. Kahn!"

"I can't? And why not?"

"You are the most despicable, disgusting human being, no I won't even grant you that distinction—you're an animal, yes an animal—a pig—I have ever met."

"Thank you, my dear, and I always speak so nicely of you too. Now, Raven, get Bonita's boy to run you home, and stay away from the jail, the feds, and Bonita Roberts or all kinds of terrible things could happen at your house. A fire would be horrid, wouldn't it? Especially a fire after all the exits had been sealed. Very ugly! Run on home now. I'll be in touch."

Raven stumbled outside to the Rolls where Alphonso waited. "Thank god you're here, Alphonso. I thought you went home."

"Miss Raven, what's going on? Hannah sent me back here 'cause some men came and took Miz Bonita's computer. Then I seen them bring Miz Bonita out here in handcuffs."

"She's been arrested, Alphonso, for selling child pornography."

"That's the dumbest thing I ever heared tell of. Miz Bonita ain't sellin' no child pornography."

"I know that. Isaac Kahn is."

"What you say about Mr. Kahn?"

"Nothing, Alphonso. Please take me home. I am very upset."

"Right away, Miss Raven. What'd you think I oughta do about Miz Bonita?"

"Call her attorney."

"Mr. Ball's her attorney."

"Well, he won't help. He was in there when she was arrested. He said he couldn't do anything."

Alphonso dropped Raven at home. She entered her house in tears and her mother asked over and over what had happened, but Raven was crying too hard to explain.Once she calmed down a bit, she came downstairs in jeans and a sweater, "Mother, I can't explain right now, but I have to go out. If you need me, I'll be at Desiree Compton's house."

"At this time of night?"

"I have to go, mother. I'll explain everything to you as soon as I can."

Raven told Desiree and Monique what had occurred at the Ball.

"He's been running a child pornography business on Mrs. Roberts' computer. That's what Ridge Dodd found out and that's why he was going to the DA. I know Isaac Kahn murdered Ridge and KD or hired someone to kill them. I know it! I know it! But I can't do anything about it. I'm so afraid for my family. He's threatened my father before, but tonight he told me if I said anything, he'd burn my parents' house down after he sealed the exits. I don't know if I have the courage to go to the police or not."

"You won't need the courage, Raven. I'll tell them."

"Mother, you can't! He'll come after you."

"Call the Pinkerton Agency and hire round-the-clock security, Monique. After they're on the job, I'll call the Spencer Chief of Police and the Sheriff of Van Buren County and have them come here to me. Before I tell the cops what I know, I'll demand police protection."

"It's too dangerous, mother."

"I agree, Mrs. Compton. You don't know what kind of pig you're up against. Isaac Kahn is capable of anything."

Alphonso drove to the jail after he dropped Raven off, but he wasn't allowed to see Bonita. Once home, Alphonso told Hannah about Bonita's arrest. Hannah was fit to be tied. "They can't keep my baby in no jail. Miz Bonita need her special mattress and her down pillows. She can't be sleeping on no cot. Get the car, Alphonso. I's gotta get some clothes together and some food for that child. You's takin' me to her right now."

"It's no use, Hannah. I went to the jail after I dropped Miss Raven off and they wouldn't let me see her."

"Get the car. Whether I can see her or not, I can take some things to her."

Several days passed and Bonita remained incarcerated. She had used her single phone call to contact the attorneys retained by Roberts' Publishing Empire. Two of the country's finest attorneys checked into the Volunteer the following morning. They were working frantically to get Bonita out of stir, but the magistrate refused to set bail citing child pornography and the sale of it as one of the most heinous of crimes. The officer of the court further maintained that with her wealth, she could easily leave the country.

After Chang was questioned, he was allowed to go. A deputy sheriff drove him to his car at VanBuren.net. When Chang pulled away from the curb, he was tailed and led two undercover officers to Les Enfants. The local boys called Fred and Hank, who were back in town after their brief holiday break.

"So the little fellow's boss man is Isaac Kahn? Let's get a little information about him, shall we?" Fred asked as he alerted the home office and told them to get everything they could on Chang's employer.

Alphonso was at loose ends. He couldn't believe Billie Sue Barto was living in Spencer and had been so close to him since he arrived there almost a year ago. He knew Raven must be his daughter. That would explain her dark complexion while her parents were so fair. He hadn't heard from Billie Sue since the night of the Ball and he didn't know if he should try to speak to her again or not. He wanted so desperately to see her.

Alphonso and Hannah had worked together for years and were good friends. They discussed everything with each other except for Alphonso's extracurricular activities with their boss lady, but the chauffeur was sure Hannah was aware of the situation and simply chose not to approach it. When he felt like he couldn't stand another minute without calling Billie Sue, he asked Hannah if they could talk.

"We sure can, Alphonso. I seen you was upset. I know you miss Miz Bonita and is jest as worried about her as I is."

"You're right, Hannah, but that's not what I want to talk to you about."

"What then?"

Alphonso started his story back when he first went to work on Mr. Barto's plantation in South Carolina. He didn't leave out a detail and by the time he finished, Hannah was in tears. "And your Billie Sue is Raven's mother?"

"Yes. And, Hannah, I'm pretty sure I'm Raven's father."

"Of course. That 'splains her coloring. What you gone do, Alphonso?"

"I want to call her. I want to see her. I want to hold her. She's the only woman I've thought about my whole life and now she's so close."

"She's married to a white man and she for sure ain't never told Raven Mr. Keyes ain't her daddy."

"I know. What can I do, Hannah?"

"Take the bull by the horns, Alphonso. Call her up. Ask her to see you. Tell her what you told me. See where she stands. 'Til you done all that, you's gonna be a mess."

"What if she won't see me?"

"Then you knows your answer and you gonna have to live with it,"

"What if I can't?"

"You can. We don't never get no more burdens heaped on us than we can tolerate. Call Billie Sue."

Alphonso made the call and Mrs. Keyes answered the phone. He asked if he could see her. Hannah left the kitchen. A few minutes later, Alphonso let out a yell. Hannah hurried back, "What'd she say?"

"We're going to meet at the Lake Cemetery in half an hour. Thank you, Hannah. You always have the best advice."

"Good luck, Alphonso, now don't go getting your hopes up too high, but I'm glad she's gonna meet you."

Bonita's attorneys prevailed upon a District Court judge to hold another bail bond hearing for her. They called character witnesses who attested to their client's standing in the community and Bonita was finally released on one million dollars bail—unheard of in Spencer. Alphonso was waiting for her in front of the jail in the maroon Rolls. He helped Bonita into the car. He hardly recognized her. She wore no makeup and her hair was flattened against her head. She wore black slacks and a sweater, no jewelry, and she had lost weight. She was still colossal, but he could see she had dropped many pounds.

"Miz Bonita, I'm so sorry about all this," Alphonso began.

"I know, Alphonso. I don't feel much like talking. Just take me home, please."

"Yes'm."

Hannah hugged her when she came into the mansion and said, "I got your bath all drawn, sugar."

"Thank you, Hannah," Bonita answered as she leaned on the maid to help her up the stairs. Bonita was a broken woman.

Shortly after her arrival, the doorbell rang and the most beautiful flower arrangement Hannah had ever seen was delivered. Palm leaves, long stems covered with baby orchids, Amazon lilies, gardenias, and about six other kinds of flowers Hannah didn't recognize were creatively placed in a oversized bouquet and it was so heavy Hannah could hardly get it to the foyer table. The flowers were in an elegant etched sterling silver vase. "Miz Bonita, you got to come down here and see these here flowers."

"Bring them to me, Hannah."

"I can't. Come on down here."

"Get Alphonso to bring them up."

Alphonso carried them to her room. Bonita looked at them with no particular interest and said, "Pretty."

"You want to see the card, sugar?" Hannah asked.

"You can open it."

"They're from Mr. Kahn. The card says, 'Welcome home to the Queen of Spencer Society. We'll knock'em dead next year. Love, Isaac.'"

"Not I," Bonita said wistfully.

"'Course you will, honey, soon as this mess is straightened out."

"No, Hannah. My public life and my social life are finished. My life is over. This humiliation is far worse than anything that happened in Dorchester County. Even when my innocence is made known, everyone will remember my arrest at The Magnolia Ball for selling child pornography. It's too horrible to comprehend. Go, now, both of you. I just want to be alone."

Hannah and Alphonso went downstairs, "I ain't never seen her this bad, Alphonso. I's worried about her."

Isaac tried repeatedly to reach Jesse with no luck.

Little bastard has skipped out on me!

Isaac was due to appear in court for what he knew would be a large fine onVanBuren.net, but he had to hand it to Jesse. So far, no link had been made between the little shit and Bonita's computer and therefore no link existed to him, but Raven knew. Isaac had decided he had to get rid of her. She was a pretty thing and he hated to think of her lying dead somewhere in a ditch, but her day was rapidly approaching. He didn't want to kill her off just yet. It was too soon after the Dodds' murders, but perhaps an arranged car accident would be an acceptable way for her to go.

Billie Sue had never stopped loving Alphonso just as he had loved her every day since he'd first laid eyes on her. The two met in the cemetery every day for a week. It was as if time had stood still and they were again in their teens. Alphonso asked Billie Sue if Raven was his daughter and she confirmed his suspicions. They talked for hours on end and made the decision to tell Raven of her heritage, As soon as her husband fully recovered from the bypass surgery, Billie Sue planned to file for divorce. Alphonso was going to give Bonita notice and he and his beloved were moving to California where no one knew either of them. Their biggest concern was for Raven and how she was going to react to their confession.

The night Alphonso and Billie Sue planned to tell Raven the truth about her heritage was the very one where Isaac had set up a fatal accident for her. He planned to call her and demand she come to Les Enfants. He knew she would. While she was at his house, he'd get Chang to cut her brake lines. When she left driving on the curving Lake Road, it would be only a matter of time before Raven would total her car and be history. So tragic!

Raven thought a lot about the night of the Ball when she introduced Alphonso to her mother. She remembered their lingering glances and hand-holding. She recalled how she used to think she was adopted because she didn't look like either of her parents.

Lastly, she thought about finding her birth certificate when she was a young girl and how her father's name wasn't on it. Given all she'd been pondering, Raven was not shocked when her mother and Alphonso gently confided their love for each other to her and told her Alphonso was her father.

Raven felt closer to the chauffeur than she did to the man who had reared her. Her *daddy* was so cold. He had always seemed like a stranger to her, but Alphonso was so warm and so loving and had been kind and sweet to her from the instant they met. Through tears, Raven gave the couple her blessing. She would visit them, but she planned to remain in Spencer for a while to comfort the man she'd known as *Daddy* as long as she could remember.

After Raven left her mother and Alphonso, her father, at the cemetery and was on her way home, her cell phone rang. It was Desiree asking her to come to El Architecto right away. "The security guards are here and I've called the Chief and the Sheriff. It's now or never, Raven."

"I'm on my way."

Raven sat in Desiree's bedroom with her and Monique while the three of them told their story. As they were winding it up, Raven's cell rang. She glanced at the caller identification. "It's him."

"Who?" asked the Sheriff.

"Isaac Kahn."

"Answer it," he directed.

"Hello. Just a minute," Raven said. She hit the mute button and said to the policemen, "He wants me to come to his place."

"Tell him you'll be there directly," the Chief told her.

"I'll leave right now, Mr. Kahn."

Raven went to her car, tailed by the two top policemen in Spencer and Van Buren County. They radioed for back up. Raven went to Isaac's and knocked on the door. The police officers trained several sets of binoculars on the exterior of Les Enfants. Within a few minutes, they watched as Chang came out with wire cutters in his hand, glanced around, and proceeded to slide under Raven's car.

"I think that's all we need," the Sheriff said, as he switched on the siren and roared down the paved driveway to arrest Ike.

"You little bitch, what have you done? That's a police siren."

"I haven't done anything, Mr. Kahn."

Before he could move to do her any harm, the officers burst through the door and placed him under arrest. As his rights were read to Kahn, Raven felt she could finally take a breath after almost a year.

The Chief said, "We'll send a car for you, Raven."

"I'll drive mine."

"No, you won't. Kahn's man cut your brake lines. Mr. Kahn had an accident planned for you this evening. That's premeditated murder. You're in a deep heap of shit Kahn or Perl or whatever your name is."

"Oh, I don't think so, officers. You're making a grave error here."

"Let's see, child pornography, attempted murder on Miss Keyes here, and I think there'll be a few questions about the murders of Ridge and KD Dodd. And there's the little matter of kidnapping in Miami Beach several years back. You're going away for a long time, Mr. Perl."

Raven would always remember the look of pure unadulterated hate Ike gave her when the policeman mentioned his old identity and the kidnapping. He knew Raven had spilled her guts then.

Spencerians had more on their plates than they could digest in a year.

The Dodds' murders were still hot news.

The Magnolia Ball had been a fiasco.

Bonita Roberts was in jail for two weeks.

Her black chauffeur and Billie Sue Keyes were going to walk off into the sunset together—a highly verboten union in Spencer, Van Buren County, and the State of Tennessee.

That nice Mr. and Mrs. Stansill were involved with Isaac Kahn. It turned out Stansill had a prison record.

Isaac Kahn wasn't Isaac Kahn, but someone named Ike Perl. Not only was he in the child pornography business, but he kidnapped Raven Keyes when she was missing all those months when she was a teenager, and he was a suspect in the Dodds' murders.

Cameron Bassin eloped with the Mexican construction worker on New Year's Day. They were married in Juarez.

Enid Martin *shopped* at a new boutique in town owned by come-heres who weren't privy to the Spencer routine. They had the old lady arrested.

Desiree became quite ill and was diagnosed with double pneumonia and was in Intensive Care at Spencer Memorial not expected to live.

Robert Whitney Hartington III told several of the debs and their escorts about Harcourt Ball and his antics at bathhouses and with male prostitutes in Nashville.

Chang was unemployed.

Princess Alexandria filed for divorce from Prince Ruslan for wife beating.

Lydia and Randolph left on yet another world tour.

Mrs. Mapleton, social climber extraordinaire, was invited to join the Junior League;

Bonita lost almost forty pounds during her incarceration—a good thing.

And when the citizens of the tiny Tennessee town thought they couldn't deal with another incident, it was announced on the eleven o'clock news that the body of Dr. Trace Ricks had been discovered in a roadside motel in Biloxi, Mississippi. Ricks was the apparent victim of a self-induced drug overdose.

Within weeks, Rhetta Robin put RickShaw and the Nashville manse on the market and she and the girls left Spencer for parts unknown.

Epilogue

Hannah checked to make sure Bonita was asleep and tip toed down the stairs to the kitchen and called Izonia, her old friend in Montiac, "Izonia, it's Hannah. You ain't gonna believe what's been going on down here, chile."

"Hannah. I'm so glad you called. I do miss you so much, gal. Now fill me in on little Spencer."

Hannah talked for almost an hour and Ionia's black eyes were almost as big as saucers by the time Hannah came up for air. "My law, girlfriend. Is you all right?"

"I reckon, but I'm telling' you, Izonia. I don't think I can take much more. Alphonso's gonna be gone soon and Miz Bonita is jest a shell of herself. She don't even get out the bed most days. She' don't eat hardly nothin'. And you knows there ain't never been a time Miz Bonita didn't eat. It don't matter what I fixes her, she jest tell me to take it away. It's some kinda terrible down here, Izonia, but let me hesh up now. I wanna hear 'bout you."

"Everything's 'bout the same up here, Hannah. There ain't too much news. Miss Celestine and Mr. Jamison's on another trip. They been gallivanting' all over the place lately, so I's here with Anthony."

"Baby-sitting' again, huh?"

"Yeah, but he's right much company."

"Izonia, he's a doll."

"I knows, Hannah, but you know how Miss Celestine do carry on wif him. Perty soon, you starts to think he's real too."

"Izonia, I think I hear Miz Bonita stirring. I don't want her to catch me talkin' to you. She still don't want no contact with South Carolina. I gotta go. I loved talkin' to ya. I wish we could see each other and sit down and talk like we used to. I gotta run though, Izonia. I'll call you again soon as I can. Now don't you be telling Anthony nothin' I told you, you hear?" and Hannah laughed.

"I hear ya. Bye, gal. Call me again soon."

Izonia replaced the phone.

Poor Hannah. Things sounds real bad down there. I can't believe I knows all these goings on 'bout Spencer in Tennessee and about Miz Bonita and I can't tell a living soul.

"All right, Anthony, come over here and sit with Izonia."

She lifted him up and arranged him next to her. She had dressed Anthony earlier that morning in blue jeans, a plaid flannel shirt, cowboy boots, and a spiffy red bandana tied rakishly around his tiny neck.

Once he looked comfortable, Izonia said to him, "You want to hear all the gossip from Spencer, Tennessee? Yeah, you right, that was my friend Hannah. You does wanna hear? All right, Anthony, I's gonna tell you everythin' and Anthony, sugar, you jest ain't gonna believe all what's goin' on down there. But before I starts, you gotta remember one thing, Anthony. You can't go atellin' none of this, you hear me?"

Afterword

The final recipe

SPENCER STEW

One come-here recently from Montiac, South Carolina
Several natives of Spencer, Tennessee
One low-life Yemeni
One former Governor's daughter who spends too much money
One po' doctor
A few Brooklynites
A cave
Lots of $$$$$$ Lakefront houses
Plenty of spare time
More money than sense

Mix together and generously sprinkle with gossip, show a few dirty movies, throw in designer clothes, jewels, fancy cars, fine wines, gourmet meals, hors d'oeuvres up the wing-wang, lots of idiosyncrasies, some four-letter words here and there, and stir thoroughly. The result? **Spencer Stew**—hearty, satisfying, "hot," sticks to the stomach, causes some giggles, and hopefully leaves fun memories!

Made in United States
Orlando, FL
15 October 2023